THE GREAT DISILLUSIONMENT OF NICK AND JAY

The Great Disillusionment of Nick and Jay

RYAN DOUGLASS

HARPER
An Imprint of HarperCollinsPublishers

HarperCollins Children's Books,
a division of HarperCollins Publishers,
195 Broadway, New York, NY 10007

HarperCollins Publishers,
Macken House, 39/40 Mayor Street Upper,
Dublin 1, D01 C9W8, Ireland

The Great Disillusionment of Nick and Jay

harpercollins.com

ISBN 978-0-06-331248-7

Typography by David DeWitt
25 26 27 28 29 LBC 5 4 3 2 1

First Edition

For my sister, who taught me to love poetry

1.

TIME ALWAYS MOVED SLOWEST WHEN I WANTED something. I wanted to know why Isaiah had invited me to talk.

He didn't say what was on his mind, but I knew it was about what I did on the porch in that moment of poor judgment all those years ago. It had been the pit of my shame ever since. I knew the day would come when we'd have to talk about it. I just didn't think it would be today.

I sighed and fell back against the wooden shelves. It was nearing the end of my shift and the time showed 4:54 p.m.—only six more minutes until I was free.

Free from brushing mud out of shoelaces, polishing church shoes, and attaching straps to slingbacks.

Warm air blew through the room's window—the only breeze I had in this place. It was always hot in here, on account of Mr. Wallace's protest against air-conditioning. "The world don't need more machines," he said. "More machines means more toxins. More toxins means shorter lives, for all humankind."

Mr. Wallace was a shoe-shiner but make no mistake—he was whip-smart. I never would've connected air-conditioning to doomsday, but it made sense I guess.

I wiped sweat from my forehead as the floor creaked beyond the door. Mr. Wallace was approaching the backroom from the parlor.

I quickly closed my pocket watch to sort the remaining shoes into boxes, but then Mr. Wallace opened the door and the watch slipped from my fingers, rolling across the carpet and stopping at his shoe.

He reached one of his long arms down over his belly and picked up my clock, eyebrows tensed as he handed it back to me. "You dropped something," he said.

"Thank you, sir." I took the watch and tucked it into my shirt pocket.

My mentor looked around at the mess. "How long does it take to box a few shoes, young man?" he asked, his tone carrying a sting of judgment.

"Sorry, Mr. Wallace," I said. "I got distracted."

By all my memories with Isaiah, I didn't add. *The fact we're growing different, like a sweet gum and a black gum, each in its own swamp.*

Mr. Wallace looked at me like he knew something was wrong. "What's on your mind, son?"

What would I say? *Friendship meltdowns?*

I could talk to him about some things. More than I could talk about with Pa—that's for sure. But I knew what was between me and Isaiah was for us to work out.

Mr. Wallace sat on a stool with fatigue. He'd worked for generations. His shop was a staple of the community. It had outlasted every business that popped up and called it quits soon after.

"If it's about your father," Mr. Wallace said, "you know what I'm going to say, Nick."

Ah, there was a change of topic that felt daunting, but somehow more approachable. He'd advised me on my issues with Pa before. Like a rooster in the morning, he told me to forgive him—*forgive him!* Cock-a-doodle-doo.

"With respect, sir, I can't forgive somebody for something they ain't sorry for," I said, before he got around to saying it.

"You stay waiting on people to apologize to you, all them grudges gon' crush you like a ripe grape!" he said. "Do *you* want to win, or do you want your grudge to win?"

"I suppose I want to win," I mumbled.

He leaned back with righteousness. "So . . . ask yourself what your father's choice in denying you apprenticeship is teaching you about your own *sovereignty*. Take the lesson, leave the pain."

"Sovereignty, sir? Like power?"

"Not quite." Mr. Wallace pulled a dictionary out from a drawer under the shelves. "That would be the *A* definition. I, myself, prefer the *B* definition."

He looked like an explorer in his loose canvas pants, spouting out knowledge. *"Freedom from external control, or autonomy,"* he read from the dictionary, while looking at me over his glasses. "Your sovereignty is your choice. It's what leads you in life. If you intend to be a writer, it shall be that you become one, whether you have your father's blessing or not." He closed the dictionary and placed it back in the drawer.

"See, we don't need apprentices and masters," he went on. "It's the structure of things, not by necessity, but because each of us makes a choice to uphold this order. In reality, each of us needs only the discernment to guide ourselves."

It's funny. I knew I could do things and be someone without my father's blessing, but I so desperately wanted it. He was my blood. All I had since Mama passed and Daisy moved away.

I began sorting polish into the pockets of a wooden case. "Papa thinks I don't got enough brains to write for *The Star*," I said. "So, if I do end up writing, it would have to be for someone else."

"Did he say that?" Mr. Wallace asked. "That you don't have brains?"

"Naw, but he implied it."

"Perhaps have another talk with him and ask for his reasoning—ah, ah," Mr. Wallace said, pulling a black canister from my hands. "Careful, this shouldn't be with the polish." He placed it on a side table.

"What is that, sir?"

"*Toxic chemicals* that will *burn* your skin to the bone if you touch 'em!" Mr. Wallace crooned like a dramatic stage performer. "I should have warned you before leaving it out on the worktable." He stretched to pull a safe box down from a top shelf. "Mrs. Millie has forgotten the combination to her late husband's safe box and has asked me to crack it open."

Mrs. Millie was my neighbor. She was about seventy years old, and one of the first to buy land some twenty years ago from Mr. Gurley when he started selling plots to Negroes looking for a new start. Lots of my elders was coming from tenant farms where they worked like slaves for a tunic and some cornmeal.

Since Greenwood was new, we still acted like folks on the run. We were real secretive with our money, like storing cash in a shoe-shiner's shop secretive. If the white folks ever came to loot us, they'd go straight for the banks, never here.

Mr. Wallace screwed the top off the canister. He dipped a pipe cleaner into the soppy stuff and then rubbed it along the door of the safe. "This locked safe? Think of it like your life. You could waste it trying to find the perfect series of clicks to open the door. Or you could work smarter and not harder." He continued to delicately rub the substance in a rectangle. I could already smell burning steel from what it was doing.

"There are many ways out of a trapped situation," my mentor said calmly. "Not just one combination. My personal favorite is *sulfuric acid*, otherwise known as *grease*. This stuff is highly dangerous, son—you may want to stand back."

In seconds, the grease caused the metal door to curl and melt off the safe, sending tendrils of dark smoke into the air between us. Inside was an ocean of banded dollar bills.

"What?" I exclaimed. "That's slick!"

Mr. Wallace let out a long whistle as he pulled some money out and inspected it, seeming impressed. "Never knew Old Man Francis had it like this."

He was fascinated with the sight of money—typical for the son of Easter Wallace. His father was a reckless kleptomaniac who stole his old master's safe before escaping his farm for Greenwood. He taught his son safecracking, and though Mr. Wallace followed a more legitimate career, best believe he still knew how to crack one open.

"Say, out of curiosity, how do you make that st—" My question hadn't left my mouth before a hard object smacked me on the side of the head, landing with a *clack* at my feet. "Ow!"

The object was still rattling slightly between my brogans—a small pebble that had been hurled in from outside.

"What in the—?" Mr. Wallace limped toward the window and barked, "Who's there?"

"Sorry!" came a familiar voice. "I didn't mean to throw it that hard."

I felt a throbbing in my temple as my old friend's open hands appeared in the shop window.

"Sorry, Mr. Wallace," Isaiah repeated.

"Don't be throwing rocks through my windows, boy!" Mr. Wallace screamed.

I started laughing.

"Sorry!" Isaiah called, backing away across the grass. "Sorry!"

Mr. Wallace turned around. I stood up and ran toward the window, sprouting out of it so my upper half could be outside.

"A pebble?" I asked. "Really?"

"Just trying to toughen you up." Isaiah sauntered forward with a smile, drawing closer to me across the field. "What time do you get off? I wanna show you the Vanderbilts' estate."

Ah, the Vanderbilts. They were the rich family he'd become a groundskeeper for. Isaiah moved up in life faster than me, that's for sure.

I pulled out my watch and found the hands showing five p.m. "Right about now! But I'm supposed to be home before the sun goes down."

"Well, move back! I'll help you finish up."

I moved, and he climbed clumsily through the window and landed with a *thud*.

Mr. Wallace was stringing up a money bag with Mrs. Millie's cash. He raised an eyebrow at Isaiah. "You break something, you paying for it!" he said, then left to go back up front.

Isaiah looked judgmentally at him and then my work quarters. "What's got his buttons in a bunch?"

"He's sensitive to violence," I said. "Mr. Wallace is a gentle man."

"Is that why you work here?"

"No," I said, fitting two shoes in a box like puzzle pieces. "I work here because I don't have a choice."

I could feel Isaiah rolling his eyes. "Nick, you always have a choice in being a shoe-sniffer."

"What a terrible way of framing it! We all need a shoeshine every now and then."

"Not the point."

"Then what is the point?" I turned to face him and then caught our reflections in the wardrobe mirror. Even our fashions were more at odds lately. I wore a flat cap and loose shirt with suspenders to hold my knickerbockers up. He wore a blue suit that fit his muscled form and a matching fedora that complemented his square face. Isaiah's hair underneath was in close-cut, brushed waves. His complexion was a warm, reddish brown, like chestnut. Mine was similar, but a bit darker.

Three weeks ago, we'd finished the school term, likely our last, and now our futures were the main focus of our lives. Isaiah thought about where he was going more often than I did, and anyone could tell from our clothes that he was destined for greatness and me, for less.

"The point is," Isaiah went on. "We gon' be eighteen soon and you still letting life control you, like you some kind of tumbleweed. I ought to call you Tumbleweed Carrington."

"*Tumbleweed* is a nice name," I said, turning away to put the final pair of shoes in its box. "Maybe it would suit me better. I'm named after my grandfather, after all."

All I could do was joke in the face of Isaiah's criticism. He talked opportunity all day! Never music, family, romance—the stuff we used to discuss. Just what I should've been doing to move up.

What if I didn't wish to climb as fast as he did in the first place? The world he'd gotten into scared me—its pristine polish, its strange emptiness underneath. It was as if the main purpose of being rich was to impress people rather than to be happy.

I didn't say anything about it. I preferred not to touch a sore conversation, and to keep the remnants of our friendship intact.

I finished up my final duties and called, "Bye, Mr. Wallace!" as I grabbed my satchel off the coatrack.

I curled out the window, slid down the little gap between the bricks and grass, and fetched my bike from its post outside. Isaiah followed close behind.

We rolled into the streets, where golden sun stretched across the cobbled road. We biked through the channel of brick and wooden storefronts as the shopkeepers reversed their signs from *Open* to *Closed*. The radio operators hung their headphones on the wall and the mail trucks returned to the post office parking lot.

We were headed past the city and toward the big oil derricks at the end of town. The big, latticed triangles, shaped like Christmas tree angels, manned a strip of country road that separated Greenwood (the Colored district) from the rest of Tulsa, which was white. It was best to travel the road by car and to keep a look out for white people hunting down Negroes. I'd never travel it by myself, but with Isaiah, I could make it through without feeling scared.

The rustling of crickets and cicadas grew louder as the noise of people faded and darkness set in. Here, with no one around us, I nearly remembered that moment—the moment I messed up our friendship. But then, his voice took me out of it.

"You'll love it, Nick," Isaiah panted, slightly out of breath. "I promise."

Soon enough, a glowing streetlamp showed us to the first sign of white Tulsa. It was a little train post at the bottom of a hill. I followed Isaiah up the street that flattened out to a private property. A stern guard in black uniform stood by an iron gate protecting a grand house.

"Hi, Edward!" Isaiah sang as we approached. "I left something in the courtyard, if you don't mind."

"Of course, Isaiah." Edward gave a friendly smile and twisted a key through the gate and pushed it open.

It gave a groggy squeak, and the courtyard expanded before us. A short walk brought us to the heart of the space: a huge pool of light blue water, with palm trees forming columns beside it. These trees, which threw shade everywhere, took me to a tropical place. The house was three stories, with arched windows, a big balcony, and pillars connecting the floors.

I spied a woman at a third-floor window watching us enter, and a familiar discomfort set in my bones. The discomfort that led me to find work in Greenwood rather than Tulsa.

"It's getting so dark already," I noted, feeling anxious.

"No offense, Nick, but your pop needs to lighten up on the curfews," Isaiah said, as he sat on the edge of a fountain and crossed his legs like he owned the place.

"None taken," I replied. "Maybe he'd listen to you if you told him."

Isaiah laughed. "No way I'm listening to a lecture on the dangers of the white man. The white man pays me well here. I say if I stick it out for a year, smile, and trim hedges good, I can work my way up to a Touring."

My friend thought having a nice car would solve all his problems.

"That's no good," I said, sitting beside him. "Because then you'll leave Greenwood, and I'll have no friends."

"Well, you might have more if you put yourself out there!"

"Out where? I don't want to put myself anywhere. I want to be a turtle."

Isaiah ran off to a white veranda between the fountain and pool, perhaps to get a better look at my pathetic self. "You ought to learn to be a hare!" he said, folding his arms, leaning against the wood. "That brings me to what I wanted to talk to you about. If you're interested, I'm sure the Vanderbilts can find you a nice job that would level up your money."

I looked up at the woman in the window again. "I don't think that lady wants me here."

Isaiah looked up too. "I know Mr. Vanderbilt better than the missus, but I would hazard that staring back makes it worse."

I took my eyes off the woman, but she continued to watch me. I could feel it.

I found a wobbly version of myself in the clear water of the fountain as I pondered Isaiah's offer. Deep down I may have been tired of being such a dewdropper. "Perhaps I should get a better job," I said. "Say I leave Greenwood to write for some paper outside this town. What could Pa say about that?" I met Isaiah's eyes and felt a boldness creep into my bones. "What law is there says you have to work in the town you grew up in?"

"Not one." Isaiah shrugged. "You could potentially take the first train up North tomorrow morning. But where would you go?"

"Chicago," I answered.

He raised his eyebrows. "Not New York?"

"New York is too far," I said. "And possibly too big. And too close to the water. I'd hate to drown."

"So, you want to be somewhere better," Isaiah said, his tone softly asking for assurance.

"Yes," I admitted. "Not here, in Oklahoma, but if I could see more of the world, I think I would find my place in it. To become charming and adaptable, like you."

Isaiah laughed lightly, accepting the compliment with a muted grace.

A low noise—a hiss—came from the grass, and then sprinklers around the property turned on, spraying us with water. I looked up to the window again and the woman was gone. Had she done that?

"Probably a sign it's time to go," Isaiah said, holding up his arms to shield himself from the spraying mist.

He broke into a jog down the pathway toward the gate, and I followed.

Once home, I waited on my front porch in the dark for a moment, watching lightning bugs glow every few seconds around me. At last, the air was cool outside, but I hated this part of the day.

I unlocked and opened the door, stepping over the threshold as quietly as possible.

"Nick?" Pa called from his study, before I'd even closed the door. "That you?"

I found him in his room—a cave of the fixations that fueled his writing. His walls were covered with newspaper clippings from

The Tulsa Star. They told of politicians trying to take our rights away and the rising heroes who would save them. On his desk, a burning candle sat beside a big globe, and behind the desk, a three-dimensional sailboat jumped out of its frame.

He gave me a glance, in between clacks on his typewriter. "Where have you been out so late?" His tone was direct. But his focus? On anything but me.

"Isaiah was showing me the fancy estate he works at now," I said.

Pa paused his typing and faced me gravely. "You went to that side this late?"

"Yeah, he invited me after work. It was the only time I could go. But Isaiah got all kinds of connections over there and they all know him."

Pa crossed his arms and furrowed his brow, a mixture of disappointment and quiet anger on his face. "But they don't know *you*. They don't know you from a wild hog, and they damn sure won't treat you any better."

I knew this already. Every other day it was some dismissive lecture about how little I knew of the world. How I'd only understand things when I was older. I was sick of it!

"I don't think I should have a curfew anymore," I said. It came out almost against my will. My words drenched the room in uncomfortable silence, and I regretted them right away.

Pa looked very confused. Then he started to laugh—something he rarely did. "That's an odd statement because you've never had a strict curfew."

"I mean I don't think I should have to be home before dark. I don't think . . . well, I think I'm old enough to come home when I please."

"When you please." Pa raised an eyebrow at me. "Nick, what are you talking about? What do you have to do at seventeen, besides go to work and come home? Are you looking to be traumatized by the world?"

I couldn't quite explain to him what I wanted . . . a chance to explore life without worrying about trauma at all. The confidence to move through the world like I belonged in it. Like Isaiah. He was effortless. He didn't waver. The only way I'd get like him was by breaking free from my father's rules.

Pa looked from my eyes to my feet. "Your weight is down," he said. "There are boys far more strapping than you being taken down every day. White folks are trying to take a young man down as we speak, over a rumor he's attacked a white woman in an elevator, for which there is no evidence. Do you know what that means?"

I shrugged. I knew he'd tell me anyway.

He leaned forward in his chair. "It means a white man needs no true motivation to want to kill a Negro. Don't ever tell me you should do what you please, Nick, until you're really out there on your own. Understood?"

"Yes, Pa."

I had to resign. He exited the conversation as if it were a story he had finished printing, already forgotten in favor of his next lead, and placed his full attention back on his work.

I stormed to my own room, heart in my chest. *Maybe if I didn't have to go somewhere else for work in the first place, I'd have no reason to be out late, sir!*

I closed the door to my room and plopped down at my desk. I kept a little Chinese fan my mother had brought back from New York when she went to help Uncle Beet, Auntie Lorraine, and my cousin Daisy move seven years ago. Mama was in heaven now. A fire at her hospital took her away, but the fan helped keep her nearby. Next to it was this rolled-up map that Daisy gifted me before she left. She found this map at the train station; someone had left it behind.

In my annoyance, I unraveled the map. It showed the world in perfect detail, and it was labeled by color, which showed colonial possessions. So many places in the world were owned by people who weren't from there originally. The colonizers tried to control them but they still found joy. Their spirits were invincible!

I traced my finger over the printed image, mapping exactly where I wanted to go. French West Africa and Brazil were at the top of my list. There were Negro boys there too, fighting back against control, but the boys there had different customs of living entirely.

Perhaps their fathers didn't doubt their ability to brave the world on their own. Perhaps they were in control of their own destinies.

2.

I WAS CERTAINLY GROWN UP ENOUGH TO LEAVE the house without exchanging words with my father, but when I tried to sneak past Pa's office in the morning, he called me into the room.

"Nick, take these papers to the office," he said, without lifting his eyes from his notes.

There was a stack of papers waiting for me on the side table by the door. "Yes, sir." I read the headline on one of the sheets—"Dick Rowland: True Criminal or the White Man's Scapegoat?"

Pa's little radio crackled with a newscaster's voice. "This just in: Tensions are still rising between protestors downtown. We see white people in outrage surrounding the courthouse where they have Rowland."

"This man's safety is in danger because of the crimes they accuse him of," Pa mumbled to himself more than me. But then louder than before, he added, "We need this story on as many doorsteps as possible. You hear me? Go directly there or we risk missing the printer deadline."

"Yes, sir." There was nothing to say before I left, my bag packed to the brim with his papers. I was not allowed to write stories, but Pa always asked me for help distributing.

I was a human mule, visiting the little *Tulsa Star* office where seven writers in one spacious room typed away. My father as senior editor did not have to be there all the time. His position gave him all kinds of special benefits, like working from home. These seats were all filled by people who had impressive backgrounds and could write about sports, or politics, or current events with amazing insight. But me? I knew next to nothing except how to drop things off, according to him.

I was so fed up that I just dumped Pa's papers on the first desk I saw.

The writer, a tired woman with round glasses and her hair in a bun, snatched the papers up and read the headline. "These are from Mr. Carrington?" she asked.

"Yes."

Her eyes widened as she scanned the words. "A bit inflammatory, isn't it?"

"Don't know," I said, with a shrug. "Haven't read it!"

And I walked out the shop! I was just a boy working for a shoeshiner, right? Who cared about my opinion?

I checked my pocket watch every hour during work—what I was waiting for, I did not know. Perhaps for Isaiah to come back again and take me on some new adventure.

The shop was quiet as dusk rolled around, and I noticed Mr. Wallace didn't come in to check on me. I found him outside, standing in the road between the shop and the pawn shop across the way.

There was a commotion on the corner. A white man stormed out of the pawn shop with a gun. Usually the white tourists were respectful, but this guy . . . He was going wild, running down the street, screaming at random people, "Your kind ain't welcome in Oklahoma!"

People started shouting. And then he fired a gun at someone, who had just broken into a run.

He missed, but my heart stopped and I froze. Mr. Wallace turned quickly, grabbed at my shoulders, and screamed, "Inside!"

I followed his lead and ran back into the shop, but not before turning around and seeing the gunman get taken down by a sheriff.

Mr. Wallace was thrown off when we got inside. He turned to look through the blinds. "Let them haul him off. And then you should get home before the sun sets. Take your bike and avoid the scene. No detours, young man. I mean it."

"Okay, sir," I said. "What's going on?"

"More drama between us and them over this elevator situation. Just go, so you're safe."

I followed his orders and once the shooter was gone, I took my bike. As I rode home, I saw more sheriffs gathering out front of several businesses. They were just standing there with their sticks, and there was a tense feeling in the air—a quiet mixed with chaos.

What was that toxic flavor in the wind? I wanted to graduate from Greenwood, but not because it felt unsafe. When I was home before dark, I usually didn't fear something scary coming to hurt me. So, the tense feeling in the air took me by surprise.

I pedaled down the dirt roads and across the train tracks, where the commercial district made way for the houses, to my home. I saw mothers pulling their children inside, and a man standing on his roof, using binoculars to get a closer look downtown.

There were some horses in the stable yard whinnying more than usual. The scenes and sounds from my ride hung over me even as I crashed through my front door.

Pa was in the living room with an open shirt and a slack jaw. He was pouring himself a glass of something, but he'd stopped to look at me like a crazy man when I came through the door.

"Where *have you been*?" his voice boomed, cracking some.

"I was at work," I said. "Like always. Pa, what's going on?"

Pa went to the window and looked out, just as a lightning bolt blinked through the sky. "A storm is coming." Thunder rumbled as Pa fished a tin of breath mints out of his shirt pocket. "Maybe the only thing that saves us tonight. It's our word versus theirs on Mr. Rowland's innocence."

"I don't understand what Mr. Rowland has to do with the rest of Greenwood."

"Yes, you do, son," Pa said, impatient at my naivete. "Dick was doing well. And *we* are doing *very well.* Running businesses better than they do, leading by example. And they feel threatened, so they've targeted one of our men, falsely accusing him of assaulting a white woman. And now they have their reason to attack the rest of us. Just like that." Pa went to check the window again. "I want you to know, Nick, that you're a fantastic writer."

The words struck a funny chord in me—one that made me stare at him in confusion. I was sure I heard him wrong. Any time I showed him a piece of my writing, he said my words were overly sentimental, far too opinionated to make it in the news world.

"But I could not let you follow my path," Pa went on, looking at me. "Words are dangerous—true words are lethal. You are innocent to life, and what it means to be a man. And you are far too well-spoken for your own good."

"Pa, why are you saying this now?" I asked. Nothing else that I had seen today frightened me more than the timing of Pa's praise. "You never let me publish so much as a single story in *The Tulsa Star.*"

"There would be a target on your head the minute the press printed. You want this world to be a place where everybody's welcome to all the same fruit, and it's not that way—not yet. I can see you dream of it. I see the hope in your eyes. Your idealism is a threat to them, and anything that is a threat to them is a threat to you." Pa turned to look at the window once more, and his face dropped. He spoke his next words into the glass, "I'm sorry, Nick. I just wanted to protect you. Don't ever hold your tongue. No matter how afraid you might feel."

BANG! A gunshot snatched the silence.

Pa twisted and fell, clutching the curtain, and he lost his grip.

He stopped moving, slouched over like a folded couch cushion. He looked at me, his face like a cadaver come to life. Blood was leaking through his shirt.

I choked out a gasp. *What . . . what just happened?*

"Pa?" I whispered, running to him.

He held up his hand for me to stop, and so I did, one knee bent forward, the other poised to change direction.

"*Run*," he whispered, shaking his head with urgency. "Run!"

Run? Where?

The white man who shot my father appeared on the porch. Through the white curtains, I saw his cowboy hat and a gun forming a long angle against his arm like a crocodile's open jaw. He was coming toward the window to look in.

I ran to my bedroom, heart pounding, my brain only processing that one foot moves after the other.

Another gunshot.

The front door went crashing to the floor with a bang, drawing in the noise from outside.

A woman screaming. Gunshots gutting all hope from the afternoon air.

I fell through my bedroom doorway, catching myself on my nightstand. I grabbed my piggy bank, dropped it into a long sock, and climbed in my wardrobe to hide. I sank through my clothes, the story of my life passing through my mind like a bittersweet film reel.

Would I die?

Was I okay to die?

Had I done enough? Had I done anything?

I was silent with these thoughts, because any noise I made might bring my death on quicker. Smells of wool, wood, mints, and shoe polish melded into a toxic aroma around me, and it made me feel sick, like I'd drunk poison.

"I saw you go in there," the invader said.

And his footsteps, which approached the wardrobe at a pace quicker than I was ready for, made the reality of the moment set in—I'd either die or fight.

He ripped open the door and pulled me out by my shirt.

In the clumsy collision, I threw my weight into his body and crashed us into the wall. The gun fell from his hand and I kicked it across the floor. He pushed me off and then swung, but I ducked, landing a punch into his stomach, which caused him to keel over. More white men charged into the house as he got his bearings, and I ran to the open window. A gunshot popped behind me, whistling by my knees as I dove into the grass. And I sprinted forward.

Forward toward the bushes of the neighboring house, and then through their back lawn. Over the fence to the next one, my heart pulsing through my throat, my feet moving on instinct.

I climbed over a wooden fence and ducked low as I pressed forward. I glanced to my left and saw through the small channels between houses that horses steered by white men were galumphing through my town. The men came with other men, in sheriff's hats, who were on foot. I paused as one man kicked down a warning sign on a lawn that read *Careful: Children*, and barged into the house to start shooting.

And there it set in: We were being massacred. Not because we did anything. Just because we were us.

Run, came Pa's voice, as if he were still with me.

I climbed over another fence, still moving on impulse, as my mind was not stable. Gruesome images of the past few minutes flashed through my brain—the face of Pa's killer.

I lost balance and landed in a heap in the mud.

I was in a stable yard, belonging to one of my neighbors who lived near the forest. There was a horse confined in a wooden stall, who reared up on her hind legs and whinnied at the sight of me. She'd be my companion. On horseback, I could shift my weight to make my head harder to strike for anyone pursuing me from behind. I didn't need to see more to know that the horror of this day was only getting started.

I approached the horse's gear, which hung on the stable wall. Pa kept no horses, but my grandparents did, so I knew how to do this. I placed the saddle on the horse's back and mounted it in the shade. And then I kicked off, adjusting to my new position of power, gripping the reins and working up some momentum. When the moment was right, I pulled and we soared, over the fence and out of the yard, into the forest.

The canopy took me into its shadows. Still, through the gaps in pine, I caught glimpses of the invaders, coming toward our homes as I rushed away. There were dozens and counting, as more arrived. A mob was upon us.

I had to get to Mr. Wallace. I worried for his safety, and he was about the only person I knew who could protect me.

Deep in the forest a cross burned, and a church burned behind it, so hard that the smoke blocked my airways, even from yards away. I could've sworn I saw bodies dancing in flames. I didn't recognize their faces in that haze—all I saw were flames, as the horse galloped through the woods, trampling the underbrush with its manic gallop.

I steered the horse back toward civilization, so we could emerge from the woods and ride into downtown. There was fire here too, and more invaders, who were only partially visible in the thickening smoke as I approached Main Street.

Men shooting through the windows of a bank, more raiding the grocery store, laughing evilly and loading our food into their cars.

Our hotel had been set ablaze—all corners of the place targeted somehow. It had become a standing meteor, doomed to collapse.

Our men were trying to stop the invaders, camping out behind cars to return their gunfire. I saw a white man in a cowboy hat melting down the side of a car, bleeding from a bullet wound and thought, in a moment of triumph, *We're getting hits in too.*

But the violence hurt to see. I blinked away from it and kicked forward until I found Mr. Wallace's porch. I dismounted the horse and set her free to run off where she may—I had no time to tie her up before running for the door to escape stray gunfire.

Mr. Wallace was already pulling me in before I could knock.

"Almost gotcha self killed, Nick," he said as he closed the door. "What are you doing back out here?"

I coughed out dust and took in the cold air of the shop. The smell of chair leather was like a hug from someone familiar. A much-needed hug.

"Mr. Wallace," I muttered. My attempts at thanks came to a halt when he tucked a pistol into the back of his pants and started ripping up the floorboards to pull out hidden safes.

"Mail train runs through town at six p.m.," Mr. Wallace said as he twisted a safe open and packed a bag full of money. Then he went and pulled back the curtain on the door to gaze out the window. Beams of fire reflected in his eyes. "God is outnumbered here," he said somberly. "Greenwood will go down."

"Go down? What? What do you mean?" All I had were questions, but seeing him go back to put more money into bags made me join in to help without a second thought.

After another few minutes, we were racing toward the back room with five strung up bags. Just as we were leaving, Mr. Wallace reached up on the shelf, grabbed the tin of grease and threw it into one of the money bags. Then he went to climb out the back window.

Each of our hands weighed down by the heft of the money, we darted away from town, across open land to where the woods began in a slope about a football field away. If we were fast, we could escape into the forest and disappear into the hills, but nothing would stop a bullet from hitting us on our way there.

The day was still here, the sun just tipping beneath the horizon, as we drifted out further.

I noticed in my periphery a white man chasing us from town, raising his rifle. Looking past the barrel, I saw a familiar face. He fired suddenly and the bullet cracked just above us.

"That's him!" I screamed. "That's the man who killed Pa!"

Mr. Wallace spun in front of me, and I crashed into his body. He wrapped me into his coat and fired his gun over my shoulder. Then he released me, and I turned, shaking and stunned by the sound. My father's killer was lying still, face up to heaven, dirt twisting around his dead body like a desert wind trail.

"Come on," Mr. Wallace said as I stared at the body.

He pulled me by the wrist and toward the woods.

We forged through the underbrush and fell under a canopy, where the ground became steeper. The forest air dewed my mouth like chilly water as we left behind the fire, the screaming, the gunshots.

Where the ground leveled out, I dropped to my hands and knees, dizzied by the smell of wet soil. "Th-th-they killed—" I said, breath hitching, my eyes squeezed shut. The world was this dreary carousel around me. "*Everyone*," I panted. "They're killing everyone."

"Come on now. Get up," Mr. Wallace ordered, his voice steady.

But what motivation did I have for that? Why not just melt into the mud?

"GET UP!" Mr. Wallace screamed, giving me a great scooping, which lifted me one hundred feet into the air.

For a moment the world shrank in perspective beneath me, and I was floating above the trees, as a universe unfolded behind my eyelids. I saw my grandparents seated in the sky, wearing necklaces of stars. Mama was there too, watching to see what I'd do—if I'd press on.

"Get up!"

Mr. Wallace's voice pumped another rush of adrenaline through me. And I stood, and got to moving, like a puppet, as if someone else was controlling me.

It was strange to forge through the woods. I'd had nightmares of dying in a quiet forest for many years—Pa had always warned me about it, having my throat strung up by a Klansman where no one could hear my screams.

But now the forest was peaceful. The forest was safe.

As the trees thinned out again, a train whistled toward us. An engine groaned and a light came out, slowly at first. Then it burst through our bones with its speed, size, and strength. Big bucket cars rattled like giants were trapped inside them.

Mr. Wallace watched the train pass. He dizzily shook his head, as blood trickled down one side of his face. He'd been grazed by a bullet. He tucked his pistol away and handed me the two money bags he was carrying.

Gesturing to the train, which had come close to passing us, he said, "Go." And when I didn't move, he screamed, "I can't jump a moving train! Go!"

I couldn't go on without him though. What would I do without his wisdom to lead me?

I grabbed his forearm just before jumping up on a railing. We flew forward with the speed of the train, Mr. Wallace hanging off my arm, his body a loose limb. I stepped inside a train car and hoisted him in behind me. He clawed at the door handle until finally he found a grip to get inside.

We fell on a bed of newspaper and caught our breath. Mr. Wallace moaned like a whining hinge, rubbing his shoulder, which looked dislocated. The bone jutted forward like an awkward wing.

"I told you not to do that," he rebuked.

"I'm sorry, sir," I said.

But I couldn't leave him. I was not brave enough for the world yet. Not independent enough for adulthood. Barely sure of who I even was.

Normally, Mr. Wallace would tell me I apologized too much, but this time he accepted it. And we lay there, quietly, as the train chugged on, mechanical and uncaring.

The night crept in quickly, as if throwing a blanket over the day to hide it from memory. I scrunched in the corner with my knees to my chest. "Why would they do this?" I asked.

"They're afraid," Mr. Wallace said. "That if we rise, we'll do to them what they do to us."

White folks thought us competition. So, any time we did well, they'd take it as a threat.

"You got family in Harlem," Mr. Wallace said, half asleep. He was upright with his eyes closed, and in the sparing moonlight, the train rocked his skinny body back and forth.

The train hit a bump, and he fell over, blood from his head smearing the newspapers. But he got back up again and sat up, wincing, as his eyes closed. This was not a small graze. A piece of the bullet had embedded itself into the side of his head.

"Sir?" I started ripping open packages to find something that could save him, but all this cart had was mail. "Mr. Wallace? Please don't—" *Please don't die.*

I didn't want to be the last person he would ever see.

"Your uncle migrated that way—Beet, Lorraine, Daisy, and them," he said, opening his eyes again, looking woozy and out of it.

"Oh . . ." I balled up some paper and held it against his head.

I hadn't seen my extended family in years, not since they moved.

Mr. Wallace fell over again and didn't get back up. He fell asleep in the fetal position. I took his hand in mine—a hand that carried years of experience in the calluses.

How could I be so stupid as to complain about working with Mr. Wallace, who made his way through life with integrity and persistence? He ran a shoe shop that made people feel good and sharp about themselves. And he ran it with pride! Now here he was, and all the man had for years of struggle was a whiny brat to die beside.

Somewhere along the way, he stopped breathing. I knew it because the car started to feel lonelier.

I slid back the train door as we coasted over a lake—a stretch of trees, night and stars above us. I hung my legs out and let them swing and waited, as if God would rapture me next, as if that were the only possible turn things could take.

But nothing happened. So I tucked back inside, curled up on the newspapers, and fell asleep.

3.

WE ONCE HAD HORSES, BUT WE SOLD THEM FOR A CAR. BEFORE those days of machinery, Daisy and I would take the horses to the woods to ride.

When I was too young to steer, I rode on Grandpa's horse, facing the back of his suede leather shirt. I had no control—my one job was to take in the surroundings, the trees that rose around in the shapes of fingers and veins, the stars that sugared the night.

Then I turned six, and it was my turn to steer the horse myself. Grandpa tried to hoist me up in first position, but my boot nicked her side. She reared up, causing Grandpa and I to fall backward, and the giant horse scraped its hooves against the air in front of the sun.

I looked up at the animal, heart nearly stopping at the size of it from this angle.

Grandpa said, Get on up, *and pulled me to my feet alongside him.*

Grandma got off her horse and came to me, pulling me into her cloak. She rocked me, soothed my wincing, but only for a moment, once she realized there was no real pain.

Get back on, *she said, so I got back on.*

Her voice echoed in my ear as I opened my eyes, to the sun slipping through the train door cars. It was morning and Mr. Wallace was gone, eyes closed and at peace.

We crossed into a different town, and the train passed a sign that said, *Nigger don't let the sun go down on you.*

Wonderful. Terror coursed through my temples. *Where were we going now? Would this nightmare ever end?*

The engine stopped at a little barn surrounded by trees, and I got us off. I pulled my mentor down along with the money bags we'd brought with us. As the train left me behind, I dug a grave with my hands and laid him in it as best I could.

I hummed a song to bring life to the moment—one I'd learned from Grandma. *"Soon I will be done with the troubles of the world, troubles of the world, troubles of the world . . ."*

Once it was done, I sat in the grass for a bit beside the mound of dirt, my skin covered in sweat and body half dead, but still awake.

Get on up, said Grandpa's voice, as clear as if I were still in my dream.

I got to walking under the dry sun, looking for signs of human life. Another Negro man was hiking the railroad tracks the opposite way with a walking stick, all alone. We nodded at each other but did not speak.

My arms grew sore from carrying the loot. Should I need to kill a cow, I lacked the strength for it—my hunger took it out of me. Out where there was no one, my throat went dry, and me and death played a game of tag. I was strangely apathetic to it, because how much crueler could death be than this? A life that could swat you with grief like a switch and ask, *How will you deal with this? Who else will understand its pain but you?*

I had no answers, but my questions followed me to an inn, where a woman was smoking on a bench outside. It gave me some relief that she too was shrouded in an unpleasant stench. I could smell the odor on myself and so could the circle of flies that followed me.

The woman watched me as if I were a monkey in a freak show—in interest and humor. She went into a check-in booth as I walked up.

I emptied some dollars and coins in the slot under the glass between us. "Could you point me toward Harlem, miss?"

"This is Peoria," she said. "There's a bus to New York tomorrow morning, six a.m." And then she offered me a room the size of a walk-in closet, but I was too happy for both the bed and privacy to care.

On the cot, I lilted like a soldier in a lonely boat floating out to sea. The wallpaper swirls made me dizzy. I was hungry and hollowed out and stunned by my past as if it were a grenade actively blowing me to pieces.

But some people were still nice. The innkeeper here was kind, and it was a relief she didn't call me a *darky* at the door and send me on my way.

I walked to the bathroom and found it was nice too, with lovely pink tiling. It was shared by the guests of the inn, so I quickly took a shower before someone else came around with the same thought. Afterward, I returned to the room to read some papers.

There was one report on the massacre, saying how maybe a dozen people died. But that was not true; it was maybe a dozen per building. Or at least it felt that way.

I thought, *It's a miracle you can still read! It's a miracle you can process information with the loose strings in your brain.*

And that's because I was a human despite the invaders' efforts to make us think we were not. I was not the lesser color. That was a myth. A rumor.

This is what got me to keep moving. The awareness, or maybe the foolish hope, that this world was big and that not everyone in it would want to kill me.

I began looking around the room for a way out and found a phone book on the lower shelf of the nightstand table, but in it, I only found local names.

"My name is Nick," I said to myself, as I closed the book, folded the papers, and tucked in to sleep. "I got some family in Harlem."

The next day, I picked up the receiver at the inn's phone, located in a little booth near the lobby. After a few clicks, a woman's voice came on the line.

"Operator."

"Yes, I need to place a long-distance call to New York," I said. "Harlem. The name is Lorraine Whitley."

There was a pause—some background voices, papers shuffling.

And then she said, "I'll connect you."

A girl answered. Her vocal cadence was familiar but more

mature than when I'd last heard it. "Hello?"

I hesitated at first. "Hi, um . . . Daisy? It's Nick. Your cousin? From Greenwood?"

"Oh, Nick!" she said. "We've been trying to call your dad since the news came in! We couldn't get in touch. Please tell me everyone is okay."

I was silent. I could not form the words, *He is dead*. It would make it real, and I wasn't ready to accept that both of my parents were gone. So I didn't say anything. But somehow, she picked up on it.

Her tone turned somber when she said, "Where are you?"

"I'm in Illinois. I was wondering if I could come up and stay with you and Uncle and Auntie for a bit? I don't have anywhere else to go."

I took the train out of Illinois to Grand Central Station in New York. There was clearly a great influx of people coming into New York City. I could barely navigate my way through the crowd at the station to find the arriving bay and Daisy.

She was as cultured as she imagined herself to be as a kid, as if all her planning made her dreams come true. Her hair was short and wavy, a far cry from the braids she wore when we were kids.

This version of Daisy had lost no hope in her eyes, but young adulthood seemed to turn her rough-and-tumble energy into daintiness. Her white nail polish looked too perfect to go digging in the mud, and her day dress would not take to stains well either. Her skin was cinnamon with golden undertones and looked lighter than it used to. Perhaps the sun didn't shine up here like it did down South.

She approached with a pep in her step, but then she paused. She took me all in, her eyes treating me like something that could break if mishandled.

"Nick. My cousin!" she said, hugging me carefully but no less warmly. "It's so good to see you."

"You too," I said, forcing a smile.

She looped her arm through mine as if I were a designer bag and led me to a cab that was waiting on the street.

I didn't speak during the ride into Harlem. I felt bad for it, but Daisy didn't press. Our shared silence was an oasis of peace.

The car stopped on Amsterdam Avenue in front of a two-story, peach-colored wooden house. It was almost joined to a tall brick apartment building on its left and another on its right. The house was jam and the two buildings bread, coming to squeeze its walls in.

I followed Daisy up the porch's tiny staircase and through the front door. She didn't give me a tour of the house—just showed me straight to my room on the first floor.

She asked me how I felt. I lied and said I was fine.

I could tell Daisy didn't believe me. "I'll give you space," she said. "But let me know if you need anything."

I needed everything and nothing, so I chose silence again. And she left me about my silent business.

I curled into bed and slept for hours and hours. When I woke at night, I heard Daisy and Auntie Lorraine whispering outside my door.

"Poor thing must be in pieces," Auntie said. "His father was a heck of a man."

"We'll just give him more time?" Daisy returned.

Auntie Lorraine then knocked and opened the door to bring me my toothbrush, towels, and some of Uncle Beet's old clothes. She was tall and sturdy with a crown of springy curls half tamed beneath a colorful headscarf, and she wore an apron with faint stains on it.

All she did when she came in was say, "I brought you some things," and then she pulled me into a long hug. The hug was so long and tight it made me weightless. I forgot about gravity. In those moments, the world wasn't dragging me down.

And when she let go, I was alone in my room again, facing the mundane and unfeeling passage of time.

As the days passed, my cousin and Auntie left silent offerings at my door—sandwiches and soups, but the food didn't hit like it should've. My stomach was always hurting.

I spent my waking hours staring outside. I wrote poetry by the window, which faced a brick alley wall, where people had left their mattresses and unwanted furniture leaning. A stray autumn leaf skittered across the hem of the bricks.

I felt as lonely as that leaf. Lonely as the homeless man digging through the garbage can and the three boys who came to throw a rubber ball against the wall so hard it seemed the air inside the ball would rip out of its horsehide prison.

Pop! it said. *Pop!*

My eyes flew periodically to the money bags resting at the foot of my bed, until I mustered up the strength to assess them. I knelt beside the bed and opened the bags, pulling out the wrapped bundles—folds of bills smelling brand-new, untouched by the smoke and fire that took Greenwood.

Who did all this belong to? A bank? A crooked man? Someone who'd earned it honest?

I didn't know, and that thought made my hands sweat as I handled the bills. I felt like a bandit, wrong as I sorted through the outcome of someone else's labor. Two hundred dollars total—enough to eat for a few months and disappear again, if I needed to.

I emptied the money into the bottom drawer of the room's dresser as if it were a secret worth hiding. At the bottom of one bag—underneath the bills—I came across Mr. Wallace's tin of grease. The only trinket I had to remember the man by.

I pulled it out. Screwed the lid off. Gave it a sniff. The chemical stench sliced at my nostrils, sharp and burning, as if pulling me into a toxic trance. This stuff was deadly.

Knock knock knock.

Someone was at the door. I froze, waiting for the knocking to stop. And when I was sure I wouldn't be pressed with questions, I went to open it.

At my feet, just beyond the threshold, was a small shopping bag, the scent of laundry detergent drifting up from it.

Laundry. A harmless chore that could be an excuse to creep outside, tiptoe down the stairs, and go to the garage where the Wash 'N' Fold was, just to check things out. That's where Auntie and Uncle served the community all its laundry needs.

I packed my sweat-stained clothes into the money bags and went out back. I walked past Auntie's crop garden to get to the garage door that was left half open. I curled underneath it to get inside. There were two large laundry machines with giant cranks, and clothes folded in carts or strung up on thin wire hangers. A couple of dryers stood against the far wall, their mouths open as if waiting for me to feed them.

Auntie's washing machines looked like they belonged in a factory. I tried to figure them out, how the cranks and scary-looking spinners worked, but it was a failing task without help. So I left my laundry in the room, hoping someone would take care of it.

There was another knock the next day, and outside my door, I found a basketball. I took it outside after the sun set and bounced it some on the sidewalk in front of the house.

I walked aimlessly down the street, until I reached a wooden sign that read *Harlem Square Park*. I listened to some drummers by the trees and watched girls jump rope.

I found a watch tower that stood as tall as the trees and had an enclosure on top. I wound up the spiral staircase and sat alone against the railing, staring off at the sun as it set over the city. The world had gone so dull that even the sun shone dimmer.

And yet, hope reared its head at the center of the ache, and what it said was, *Things will get better. They have to.*

The knocks had sounded quickly and were gone just as quickly. But in their absence, I cracked open my door. I found a bag of stamps along with a note that said, *Just in case you want to send any mail! Love, Daisy.*

I was on to Daisy—she'd have none of my wallowing in my misery forever.

Seeing the stamps made me realize I might want to send a letter back to Isaiah at some point. But would he even still be alive to receive it? What happened to him when the mob came? Did he look for me?

I could write a letter asking him how he was faring. But I needed to make sure I knew where to mail it from. I slipped out of my room and opened the front door.

Three boys were waiting at the bottom of our stoop—a bit younger than me, approaching the end of secondary school, maybe. I'd seen them before, throwing the ball at the wall outside my window.

"You play wall ball?" one of them asked me.

I just shook my head.

"It ain't that hard to understand," he said. "Come play."

But I didn't want to. Doing something new like that with new people was an invitation to mess up and make a fool of myself.

"I'm set," I said, but it was like I offended the boy.

He looked at me like I was some creature. "Your hairline look like a runaway train, you know," he said, which made his friend laugh.

But it wasn't funny. I felt I'd been stabbed!

"Boy's hairline look like high tide on a slanted hill," he continued.

I had nothing to lob back. My brain had not picked up much about his appearance. He was average in his white shirt and flimsy hat, and good for him.

"Excuse me!" chirped a voice from behind them. The boys moved their bikes as Daisy pushed her way past them, bob swinging, holding two heavy garment bags. She stopped to look at both of them. "What are you two doing in front of my house?"

"Just saying how that boy needs a line up," he said, laughing.

"And you need to stop buying all your clothes from discount bins." Daisy grimaced at the bully's outfit. Then she looked at the sidekick. "And you—I could smell your breath when I was standing *behind* you. Think twice before you speak on my cousin."

Daisy walked up the stairs, pulling me along.

The bully shouted, "We ain't know he was your cousin, Daisy!"

And she spun back around. "Think twice before you speak on anybody, then, Maurice! Maybe if you spent less time running your mouth and more time figuring out why you're sixteen and still riding a tricycle around town, you wouldn't have to embarrass yourself in public. Now, shoo!"

The boys started to pedal off and I followed Daisy into the house. "Um, nice meeting y—" I said to them, but the door slammed before the words got out.

"Don't be nice to them, Nick," Daisy said dismissively, as she went to my room and put the bags on my bed. "I didn't know your sizes. But if they don't fit, we can get them tailored."

I looked in the bag and found a suit. A nice one—one that I would be the first to wear. "Thank you, Daisy. I never know what to say to boys like that. I mean, I'm not mean like they are, so . . ."

"You don't have to be mean. You just have to tell them who you are. Nick Carrington the Third, descendant of Ruth and Nick

Carrington of *Langston Herald* fame. Those boys have never done an interesting thing in their lives."

My family's history in journalism had never been something to brag about—it was just a thing. "How do I bring up something like that without sounding like a rotten egg?"

"You need no excuse here, and actually, some will support you more for coming off that way. New York is a different ball game from Greenwood. Everybody comes here for status. You have all these opportunities to be whatever you want. Once you find your fashion, it makes everything better." Daisy reached up to pick gently at the naps in my hair. "We could start with a haircut."

I wasn't opposed! I wasn't much of a looker—my teeth were buck and my frame too small to be considered handsome—but someday I might want to impress someone in Harlem.

"Okay," I said with a sigh. "I think I'm ready." If I was to find the life inside me once again, I wasn't going to discover it hidden away in this house.

Daisy smiled with a satisfaction that told me this was all according to plan—she'd gotten me out of bed. "I'll see if we can get you an appointment today," she said.

I felt like an alien among Harlem's stoops, but I was absorbed by this unique way of entering a home, and by how tall this city's buildings were—how they reached for the sky.

We took a cab to East 128th. My head was in a whirl taking it all in! New York was loud as a live-music gig at any given moment. Pedestrians ran in front of cars and forced them to adapt. Newsboys shouted at passing people about coupon vouchers to see concerts. Screaming matches would break out, then were quickly resolved, as if they never happened.

The cab stopped at our destination, and Daisy held my arm as we ran across the street to a salon called Queen of Hair. It was for ladies—that much was evident from the deep sinks and vanities, mirrors, and apparatuses for careful grooming. And then there were the ladies, sitting under domed dryers and reading magazines, their legs crossed or their feet resting in tubs of hot water.

In one of the chairs, a girl was sitting with her legs up over the side, a magazine in her face.

"Nick, this is Vivian," Daisy announced.

Vivian dropped the magazine. She had a face full of makeup—deep crimson lipstick and high-arched brows. Her posture held the confidence of someone who didn't care what you thought of her. She fluffed her big curly hair before holding out her hand. "How do you do, Nick?"

"Some boys said Nick's hairline was crooked," Daisy explained, without a care to my pride. "Do you have time to fix it?"

She spun around and opened the drawers behind her. "Um . . . I'm a bit out of practice on boys but I could see what I can do." Vivian pulled out a pair of clippers, turned them on, and almost fumbled them because of how hard they buzzed. "Oh, wow."

"Don't worry," Daisy said, winking at me. "She's a professional—I promise!"

Funny, she sure didn't look like one.

"Yeah, don't you worry," Vivian said. "I'm gonna fix you right up. It's only a dollar for a texturizer, and you'll need one."

I switched spots with her to sit, and she reared my chair back as another stylist came to work on Daisy.

"Is it going to burn?" I asked. "I've heard they fry hair."

Daisy reclined and said, "Don't worry, Nick. It'll look great with your texture."

As Daisy's stylist peppered her with questions, Vivian popped her gum, slathered white cream on my hair with a paintbrush, and looked to me to fill the void of conversation. "First day of finishing school hair, I assume?"

I met her matter-of-fact gaze in the mirror. "Oh, I don't go to school," I said.

"*Good for you*," Vivian returned with more enthusiasm than expected. "Ever since I devoted my life to the streets, I've been much happier. That's what it takes to *survive* in New York City. You get your main job and your street hustle."

I felt a strange mix of respect and fear. "When you say *street*, what do you mean, exactly?"

"She means nothing!" Daisy interrupted, her eyes darting around nervously. "But on that note, Nick, have you given some thought to what you'll be doing while you're here?"

It wasn't something I'd thought much on. I hadn't been able to think much at all.

"I feel like I'm still trying to get my thoughts in order," I said, my voice low.

"Well, if you want to study, there's this new academy, West Egg, that's accepting Negro boys." Daisy closed her eyes as her stylist tipped her chair back and washed her hair. "It's private."

"Private?"

"It means they only take the sharpest minds from the bunch, so your application's gotta be spotless. When I applied to their sister school, I made sure to mention Grandpa founding the *Langston Herald*—a Negro journalist? They ate that right up. I'm on the track for maids, which means I'll be placed in a wealthy man's house, getting a front-row seat to how the other half lives. Their food, their habits—I'll know it all. Right now, I'm working toward a full-time spot at Tom Buchanan's estate. He's big in real estate. Once you're in at West Egg, Nick, the right connections can take you anywhere!"

All of this sounded truly lovely yet empty. I'd never wanted to be rich—not really. Just comfortable. "Yeah," I said. "I mean, I guess I could try? Why not?"

"And if it doesn't work out, there are always other opportunities!" Something outside the window caught Daisy's attention. "Oh, look what the cat's drug in. Anna May! Back to throw more pennies at the poories!"

Vivian turned to look at a red-haired woman strutting down the sidewalk. She wore a plush red mink coat, her movements fluid and theatrical as she waved at merchants, her tan skin glowing under the sun, her presence demanding attention.

"Who's she?" I asked.

"Girl who got her certificate, moved uptown, and went through some changes," Vivian explained, judgment in her voice. "Found a rich husband, and now she blends right in with the white elite.

Comes down here to flaunt her wealth and support the little businesses."

I watched Anna May touch an African necklace on a street salesman's table and engage him in conversation.

"I wonder how long it takes to lift your natural tone three complexions?" Daisy said, staring at her with a mix of awe and contempt.

"Is that even possible?" I asked.

Vivian spun my chair around, tilted it back, and began to run water over my hair. "You'd be surprised the inventions Negroes are coming up with to blend nowadays."

Her words didn't surprise me. What other choice did we have in this world? Although, in New York, the pressure to move up may have been worse.

Vivian washed my hair and gelled it. She finished up the cut with the clippers, and when she put the mirror in front of my face, I hardly recognized myself. All the kinks in my hair ironed into round curls.

"I don't know what's been done to me," I said.

Daisy and Vivian both laughed. I felt more alive, just hearing people laugh at something I'd said. I could create humor! I wasn't a depressing black hole.

Daisy reached over to run her fingers through my hair. "It looks wonderful!" she chirped.

Looking different made me feel different. Like I could throw my hat in the ring with the natives of this big and strange city. I did not need to go invisible or spend my life in bed. I could go on, despite my every impulse telling me not to move.

I could see myself starting again in the big, strange city of Harlem, with all its soaring buildings that carried the promise of new possibilities. My days of lying around in my undershirt should end! The world had not ended—so why should I?

4.

EARLY THAT NIGHT, AFTER MY HAIRCUT, I LAY in bed under a strip of dusky light shining in from the window. I flipped through a pamphlet for West Egg that Daisy had given to me when we returned.

Inside were interviews with the school founder, Jay Gatsby Sr., who spoke of the school. *I decided to open West Egg after my son spent a semester in France*, he'd said. *Jay Jr. loved Paris's diversity and wanted to create that in New York. He envisioned a school with a culture of acceptance where migrants from the South could escape prejudice and access the opportunities of an elite education.*

I didn't hate the idea of an "elite education." I'd learn everything I needed to understand life.

Could I attend an integrated school? Study math and English at the same desks as whites?

Well, it would depend on what kind of whites I'd find there, and I'd never know if I didn't apply. My story could pave the way for my acceptance; surely white integrationists would love to hear about a grief-stricken Negro boy who fought his way up to New York, against all odds?

The pamphlet also highlighted various scholarships that could help cover the expenses. To get one, my application would have to be as bold, surprising, and showstopping as real life.

I sat on the floor and opened my notebook, but my hand shook on the page as I tried to write. All I could think about was how two unwavering pillars in my life—Pa and Mr. Wallace—were not here to help me. I had to discover my own way to express my purpose and what I hoped to become.

Come on, Nick. The words were somewhere at the bottom of an empty well. Pa's voice was here to guide me, but came through my brain in staticky waves, as if through a radio.

I wrote and rewrote my story until the night inched closer to midnight and the homeless had started to dig through garbage outside. While fishing for the beauty in my tragic plight, I decided that the best way to get into West Egg was to make it seem like they could give me a second chance I couldn't get anywhere else.

By morning, I was ready to seal up my letter and mail it off. All that was left to do was wait.

And check the mail.

And wait.

Checking the mail became my favorite afternoon hobby. During the day, I occupied my time at the Wash 'N' Fold out back, sorting through some abandoned clothing from clientele to find dress shirts that weren't ill-fitting. I found a shirt of virgin wool that fit like a poncho and stared at my reflection from every angle, trying to convince myself it could work for the first day of school.

Uncle Beet appeared in the mirror, and the sight of his large and portly frame behind me made me feel like I'd been caught doing something I shouldn't.

Uncle raised an eyebrow. "What's got you all excited to put nice clothes on all the sudden?"

I was nervous to say it aloud but did so anyway. "I'm hoping to get accepted into West Egg Academy."

That made both of Uncle Beet's eyebrows raise, like he'd seen a night demon. "*West Egg*. Well, that's impressive, nephew, but just how do you plan on paying for that? West Egg is one of the most expensive schools in the city."

I was surprised at Uncle Beet's reaction—it was so different from Daisy's. "Well, they say they offer scholarships to people traveling up here from down South."

"Even so, you'd have to set about thirty dollars aside for room and board," he said. "You'd need bus fees to travel across Manhattan weekly. Then there's books and supplies." Uncle started pulling clothes out of a hamper and throwing them in the washer. "East Egg's got us dried out for Daisy's education already—to be a *maid*, at that. Working for a white man—Can you believe it? I don't know what it is about these elite schools that excites your auntie so."

I stayed quiet, thinking of how to shift the focus from money. I didn't want to spend the few dollars I had stashed away. That money would be my safety net if my world fell apart again. Better to keep it close. Quiet. To myself.

"If I don't go to school, I'll sleep all day, Uncle," I said. "I don't think anybody wants that."

Uncle looked at a pillowcase with some dried drool on it. "Definitely go to school if that's the alternative," he said. "Pretty soon your slobber is gonna fuse with the fabrics."

He stopped what he was doing, looked at me, and assessed my interest. Then he chose to support it. "Matter of fact?" he said, coming to put his arm around my shoulder. "I know just what you need, nephew." He led me out of the Wash 'N' Fold and walked me to the end of the driveway, where he pointed to the shops at the end of our street. "You see what I'm pointing to?"

I squinted out, but there was a lot to see on the corner of Amsterdam and 130th. Some men passing by in tailored suits, cigars in hand. The store for haircare, and a man outside the store waving this tub of cream around.

"We have strayed so far from our *roots* that we now try to change the very *root* of our scalps!" the man shouted, as people moved around him. "*Texture* planted by a one-handed *jester* on a *quest* to run us from our home! For *shame*! Who's to blame? Boycott the relaxer, my brothers and sisters. *Refuse* to play the white man's game!"

"Um . . . a demonstrator?" I said.

"No, boy," Uncle responded. "*Behind* Megaphone Melvin."

I squinted at the haircare shop behind him, where a *Help Wanted* sign sat in the window. "Oh. That."

"There you go!" Uncle Beet let out a hearty laugh. "I got three friends I want you to meet—J, O, and B. They'll get you everywhere you need to go and further, without running my bank account into Hell!" He gave me a big slap on the back. "Good luck, nephew," he said, and turned down the driveway.

Okay, so my uncle may have had a point. To have a real shot at finishing my West Egg diploma, I'd need a job—scholarship or not.

I decided to take the train downtown and start there. It would help me practice my commute from West 131st to 124th for my travel to West Egg, in the event I got in.

I started at a corner jewelry store with a *Help Wanted* sign in the window. I straightened my cap and pushed through the door, but before I could even ask, the manager—a Negro man—was already shaking his head, eyes glancing over me with disinterest.

"We need someone who's done this work before, son," he said, his tone final.

What was he, some sort of psychic? How did he know what I'd done before? Or that I was even here to apply?

I swallowed my pride and tried the hardware store next door. The owner listened, politely enough, as I stumbled through my experience, hands fidgeting, trying to sell myself on my willingness to work.

"Sorry, young man," he said, finally, with a shrug. "I got boys out in trade school for this. You understand that, don't you?"

I nodded humbly and left the store, the rejections from my own people weighing heavy on my soul. Where would I stand a chance, if not at the Negro-owned places in Harlem?

My third try was for a restaurant, tucked into a narrow storefront, half hidden by a red awning, a cardboard *Staff Needed* sign out front. It was small inside, with a handful of tables crammed together. Lanterns created a soft glow, and tapestries of mountains and calligraphy hung on the walls. It smelled of ginger and smoke.

Through a window to the kitchen, I saw a man who looked Chinese stacking plates. At the far end of the restaurant was a young person around my age—a boy with neatly combed dark hair, dressed in an apron that was too big for his slim frame—wiping down tables.

The man looked up at me and immediately shook his head. "No," he said as if he knew what I was here for. He came through a door to the main area. "Our customers . . . they want a certain *type* of person," he explained to me. "It's not personal. You understand?"

I nodded humbly and left without a word, shoulders sagging, my confidence chipped away.

I'd only gotten a few steps down the street when I heard footsteps rushing up behind me. I looked back to see the busboy, running toward me.

"Hey!" he called, holding out a square of paper.

I hesitated, glancing from the application in his hand to his earnest face. He was doe-eyed, with long eyelashes, a natural gentleness, and a lightness to his movements.

"Don't listen to my stepfather. We could always use more help," he said quietly, with a smile, his eyes holding an apology for the man who rejected me. "Just fill it out, and I'll try to talk to my grandparents."

"Thank you," I said, taking the paper. I would not be filling it out, but I'd keep it as a reminder that there was support for me in unexpected places. I for sure knew I'd never be working there after his stepfather's reaction.

The boy ran back into the restaurant, and I went about my search, finally trying this place called *Kirby's*—a diner with a chrome exterior. The design inside was like a refurbished train car, stools lining a counter, and a column of little booths.

A sturdy man whose build was like my grandfather's was sweeping behind the counter. He stopped to look at me when I walked in.

"Hi, sir," I said, guiltily, feeling already as though I'd been rejected again. "I was wondering if there were any jobs available."

He set the broom down and wiped his hands on his apron, and then he sized me up. "Cook. Night shift. Can you do it?"

The offer caught me off guard. I couldn't believe it was real at first. "Sure," I said, trying to hide my excitement and relief.

"Follow me," said the man. "I'm Mr. Kirby. Bought this new space with my wife about a year ago."

I trailed after him through the kitchen and into an adjacent room. It was an office, the size of a cupboard, with a ceiling barely tall enough for him to stand.

Mr. Kirby sat at a cramped desk, from which he pulled a notepad and pen. "Everything before it lasted two or three months. And now, we on month twelve. Fighting allegations we'll run out of steam just like all the others. What skills do you have that would make you a good fit here?"

"I worked for a shoe-shiner," I answered, as I took a chair across from him. "He taught me a lot. And my father taught me to cook. And I can clean too!"

Mr. Kirby paused for a second, then looked up at me and burst out laughing. He found that so funny, for some reason. And it made me start laughing too.

"And that's all it is, ain't it?" Mr. Kirby said, still laughing.

There was a connection between us suddenly. I could sense the weight of Mr. Kirby's wisdom without even having to know anything about it, because it shined through his humor.

Once he finally stopped laughing, he wiped a tear from the corner of one eye and said, "Oh, I needed that. I can give you the opening for the night shift, son, if you want it. You'll learn on the job."

"I'll take it!"

Night shift. Saturday and Sunday, two p.m. to ten p.m. The other cook, Leanna, had been carrying this place on her back and approached the work with the steel-hearted resolve of a Viking. She taught me to blanch potatoes and get the temperature in their world-famous fried chicken just right.

Mr. Kirby was from Louisiana, started his business in a truck and had just moved up to a real space recently, so I couldn't mess this up. My eyeballs might fall out from how focused I was on learning the ropes.

And every night I returned from my night shift, I continued

to check the mail until I came across a letter from West Egg Academy.

I took a deep breath and opened the envelope. At the bottom was a signature from the founder, Jay Gatsby Sr., himself.

Dear Mr. Carrington,

Congratulations! We are pleased to inform you that after careful consideration of your personal character and potential for growth, you have been selected as a recipient of the West Egg Academy Tuition Scholarship for the upcoming academic year. This scholarship, awarded to a select few, will cover the full cost of your tuition fees should you choose to study with us.

At West Egg, we pride ourselves on preparing young men to excel in their studies and their contributions to society. We are confident that you will uphold the values of discipline, respect, and integration that form the foundation of this institution.

We ask that you confirm your acceptance of this scholarship within two weeks of receiving this letter to allow us to finalize arrangements for your arrival in the fall. Once again, congratulations, Mr. Carrington. We look forward to welcoming you to West Egg Academy.

Yours Sincerely,
Jay Gatsby, Founder

West Egg Academy
for Boys

The door to the house flew open with a force that scared me, even though I was the one who'd opened it!

I burst down the hallway, screaming, "I got in!" I held the letter up in the air like a beacon of hope, joy rattling through my body. "Auntie! Uncle! Daisy!"

Auntie came out from her room and found me first, her smile even wider than mine. "They accepted you?" she asked, and then hugged me and screamed, "Nick, this is wonderful! I knew you'd get it!"

Uncle Beet came casually to the kitchen next and patted me on the back, laughing with pride and joy. "Way to go, young man. You got more than enough to keep you busy now, that's for sure."

Daisy flew down the stairs screaming with joy, already knowing what the energy was about. "AHHHHHHH! NICK, YES!" Her joy matched my energy and caused Uncle Beet to plug his ears and wince. "Cake!" Daisy screamed, running to snatch up the phone. "We'll need to order a cake!"

So commenced a celebration in the kitchen for me. Everyone was happy that I'd finally got up and was going to do something. The walls of my new home felt like a refuge, full of care and support. My family took me in when my world shattered, and now they surrounded me, making sure my future would not fall through the cracks!

Thank you, Mr. Wallace, for pointing me here! Thank you!

After the party, I stayed up in my room, rereading my acceptance letter. I wanted to fully feel my joy, but some part of my brain turned toward the dark side of things. Like, the fact I'd never get to tell Pa about this positive turn in my life.

These thoughts kept me up well into the night. And when it was so late that the house had gone silent, I heard someone sneak past my room and quietly leave the house. I looked out through the crack in my door to find Daisy's silhouette slipping out of the front door and closing it gently behind her.

I rushed to my window facing the front of the house and peeked through the blinds. Daisy carried a bag down the stairs out front—a bag nearly as big as she was. She tossed it into the trunk of a car—not a cab—that was waiting for her to get inside.

What was Daisy up to? I had to know.

I opened the window as the car pulled off and crunched my body to step out onto the sill. Precariously perched on the little bricks between the pane and empty air, I swung my leg over the ledge and closed the window, leaving it cracked enough so I could push it open later.

Uncle Beet's bicycle sat by the side of the garage collecting dust. I mounted it and pedaled into the streets, just in time to see the car turning up ahead. I'd be hidden from its rearview as long as I kept my distance, but I'd have to move fast to catch up.

I raced under telephone cables and over sewer tunnels, fear cinching my breath. I watched the ground carefully as I traveled to be sure I didn't hurt myself. What untold horrors might this city carry at night? I kept hearing my pa's voice, telling me to stay in after dark. Harlem's tiny mazes were a great place to fall down a grate or get kidnapped, and how would I come back from that?

Finally, the car took Daisy through an alleyway. There were two dumpsters and two doors into seedy businesses. The alley opened to a freight yard, bordered by a calm river. I hid behind a wall, crouching beside a lost fruit vendor's wagon to watch Daisy load duffel bags into a separate car.

This was a business deal that could only be done at night—that much had become clear. There were big freight cars here, so it had to be a trade hub. But those cars were also great cover for criminals to do shady deals.

"Excuse me," said a voice. "Are you working the show?"

I spun around and found standing behind me a boy whose picture I had just seen weeks ago in the West Egg pamphlet—Jay Gatsby Jr.

I was starstruck and embarrassed by the current of nerves running through my chest. I hadn't heard of him until recently and yet I felt I was meeting a celebrity.

What reason did he have to be *here* at this hour of night?

Jay's question had gone unanswered long enough for him to turn and point to an electric sign on the alleyway wall that read *The Green Light*. The establishment was right next to where I was standing, and I'd only just noticed the muffled jazz coming from behind the door.

"Oh, I don't work here," I said. "I was just spying on my cousin."

"What?"

I wanted to shove the words back into my mouth because only after seeing his twisted expression did I realize how odd they were. "I mean, she's been going somewhere late at night, and I wanted to know where. I shouldn't be sticking my nose where it doesn't belong though."

"Interesting." Jay looked at me sideways.

I couldn't look away from his bold eyebrows, which framed a pair of soulful brown eyes. His strong nose gave him an air of confidence, while his hair—curling in velvety waves—caught the light like polished walnut. His lips were full and plum-colored. He held an allure that photographs of him could not capture.

A car door slammed behind me, reminding me of my original purpose. I turned back to see Daisy getting in the car, and then it spun around to come back toward the alleyway—Daisy and her driver were moments away from catching me if I lingered.

"Excuse me!" I slipped around Jay and banged on the establishment door, hoping with everything that someone would let me in, lest I be caught spying.

"You can just open it," Jay said, twisting the knob and pushing it ajar.

The moment it opened, I sighed with relief and slipped inside, drenching myself in the cool atmosphere of the joint, where music and distant voices vibrated from deeper inside.

The wheels of the car whooshed by outside. A chill crept into my bones as I wondered where my cousin might be going next, if it would get her into trouble.

Jay was standing across from me in the narrow entrance, his mindset somewhere else entirely. "You're breathing rather heavily," he said. "Are you okay?"

"Yes, just fine," I replied.

He closed the door behind us and tilted his head for me to follow him inside, down the brick entryway. "Any interest?" he said.

"I should probably—"

"Get home?" he said, cutting me off. "Why? What's there?"

Good question. *Safety* was my first thought for an answer. But Jay's curious and adventurous gaze made me forget about that for a moment. I'd also lost Daisy's trail already; there was nothing to be done but wait for her to return home.

And then, there was something about Jay's presence that relieved my fear of doing something unexpected. It magically convinced me to allow the night to take on a character of its own. Together, we slunk down the hallway, which was bathed in a green light, until we reached the lounge area—a big room where lamplight kissed the leather of booths, like moonlight on the river at night. The clientele was mixed between Colored and white, mostly keeping to themselves, but also mingling, in friendly, distant ways.

Jay walked me to a counter where waiters were serving patrons and waved down a man pouring beverages. "The usual!" he called. "Two?"

I sat on a stool, my eyes scanning the dimly lit room. Jazz drifted from the corner stage, where a performer, dazzling in a sequined dress, captivated the crowd. Their movements were exaggerated, grandiose, as though every sway and twirl was meant to defy the laws of gravity. The crowd roared with applause and laughter, their voices swelling with the rhythm of the performance.

"There is . . . a man dressed as a woman?" I said, my voice

hushed, in awe, as I watched the performer glide across the stage, their heels clicking against the black wood.

Jay laughed—a soft, musical sound. With a smooth spin, he turned his stool to face me, his eyes glowing with curiosity. "Have you never heard of a female impersonator before?"

I shook my head. "I don't think I have."

Jay raised an eyebrow in disbelief. "Where are you from?"

"Oklahoma."

He snickered, like it was amusing. "Well, that explains it."

Strange as it was, I liked that he laughed. There was something comforting in it—like my past could be as light as a joke.

The performer onstage continued their dance, their long, frilly gown shimmering like starlight. Their eyelids glittered with powder; their lips were painted red.

"So, this is normal in New York?" I asked, my voice softer now. "For men to dress as ladies?"

Jay's eyes didn't leave the stage. "Not everywhere, but here it is. The Green Light has drag shows every Thursday. It's where the men dress up as women, and vice versa. I guess you could say it invites people of the queer variety."

"*Queer* as in strange?" I asked, trying to make sense of it.

Jay nodded toward a booth at the far end of the room, where two men sat across from each other. They were speaking quietly, their hands grazing on the table. They were intimate—too intimate to be just friends. I could hardly fathom the sight, yet it made my stomach churn with both fascination and discomfort. No one seemed to mind. Everyone else went on with their drinks and laughter, as if the sight was normal.

"Yes, strange indeed," Jay said. "It's become attractive to artists and vaudevillians of all sorts. People like the places that let them be free and loose. It's why my father gives donations to the owner every year."

I glanced around again, taking it all in—the expensive chairs, the ornate wooden bar where people in fine suits sat with people in dresses, the plush curtains that separated different parts of the room. The air was thick with freedom and rebellion.

The waiter appeared with our drinks in hand—two delicate, triangular glasses.

Jay slid one toward me with a smile.

"For me?" I sniffed the glass, and a sharp, chemical scent hit me—something faintly like nail polish. "What is it?"

"Gin and soda," Jay said, casually.

"Gin?" I gasped. "That's . . . that's *alcoholic*! They serve alcohol here?"

"Shh!" Jay whispered, leaning in a little closer, his smile playful. "Yes."

"Isn't that . . . *illegal*?" My words were hushed, like saying it too loud would get us caught.

"This is why we don't scream about it. We just drink it in private." He took a swig of his own drink, his face twisting a little at the sharp taste. "What do you know about mixology?"

I shook my head, the word unfamiliar. "Is that some sort of science? I never made it past tech."

Jay grinned, waiting for the waiter to turn his back before

he quickly reached over the counter and pulled out two glass bottles—one clear, the other dark. He left the bar, vanishing behind a long burgundy curtain, and motioned for me to follow.

I met him where he was. He poured something and then handed me a glass.

"Try it," he said, his voice lowered now, like he was letting me in on some secret. "I find a little juice gives it some added sweetness."

I eyed the drink skeptically. "Surely, I can't try this."

"Why's that?" Jay asked.

"Liquor makes people stupid!" I whispered. "*And* you stole it!"

Jay laughed at my reaction. This posh boy with his perfectly pressed shirt, his charming smile . . . a drink thief? What was this? I had no idea what was real anymore.

"I couldn't possibly have stolen it," Jay said. "Did you miss the part about this juice joint thriving by the power of my father's money? And who says liquor makes people stupid? I drink it and I'm quite smart."

"My grandmother," I said, and realized a moment later how it sounded. Who brings up their grandmother at a juice joint?

Jay took a sip of the drink and shook his head with pleasure. "More sweetness for me!"

Okay, he was out of his mind, so my weirdness blended in, in a way. Half of me liked it, and half of me was afraid I'd get myself killed by being with him any longer.

"I hate to run off," I said. "But I should be finding my cousin."

"Of course. That is what you came to do—my apologies for disturbing your stalking mission."

Stalking? I believe I said *spying.*

"What's your name by the way?" Jay asked, before I could retort.

"It's Nick."

"I'm Jay." He held out his hand.

"Of course." I shook it, my fingers bunching together in his grip. "Nice to meet you, Jay, and to see this place. Who knew there was such a population of proud cross-dressers in New York?"

"It's only the beginning of what you'll find here, friend."

The word *friend* . . . well, that struck something in me. It was as if a string in my heart had been out of tune and the sound of that word made everything musical again.

Jay noticed the pause it gave me. He seemed pleased by it. Again, excitement beat through my chest. I wanted to stay. But I couldn't.

I still didn't know what Daisy was doing—where did she go? Since she'd taken such good care of me upon my arrival in Harlem, I needed to keep an eye out for her to make sure she wasn't getting into real danger. It's the least I could do. And that responsibility couldn't live side by side with becoming a patron of a juice joint, of all places!

I averted my eyes from Jay, gave a slight wave, and turned to go on about my night.

5.

THE MEMORY OF THAT NIGHT LINGERED LONG after I returned home. The image of Daisy moving goods from car to car played like a silent film, raising questions about the secret life she led. But when her bedroom door stayed shut the following nights, I got calmer, thinking her nighttime jaunt was a onetime deal and there was nothing to worry about.

I didn't have time to go chasing after shadows, anyway. I had my own affairs to focus on! I was about to step into something I'd wanted but also feared—a fresh start at a new school.

Come Monday, I took a cab to West Egg Academy, armed with a satchel of notebooks and pens, and a suitcase with enough clothing and toiletries to be situated for my first week.

The school rested on the cusp of Harlem and the Upper East Side, in this no-man's-land between the poor and the upscale, where tons of empty lots were just waiting for builders to lay new foundations. One of these foundations was this school.

The cab let me out on a quiet road framed by towering maple

trees, their leaves ablaze in yellows and reds. I lugged my suitcase from the back of the trunk and looked up at the entrance. An iron sign arched elegantly between two weathered stone pillars, the words *West Egg Academy* etched in old cursive within it. Beneath the arch, a brick walkway flecked with leaves stretched toward the grounds.

Campus was as clean and regal as I'd ever seen a school, with a manicured field encircled by four massive brick buildings that seemed to belong to a bygone era. Bordering the field were outdoor hallways, with open sides supported by stone columns, which featured signs that read *Afternoon Welcome Events This Way.*

I followed the signs to a main office, where four other Negro boys were waiting in the hallway. They looked up at me and then back down without speaking. We were all new and kept to ourselves. I took a fifth chair, folded my hands over my bag, and waited for the principal, Mr. Dennis.

When Mr. Dennis came out, I was relieved to see a tall and dignified Negro man. He wore an oversize suit and was holding a stack of papers.

"This way," he said, in the aloof manner of someone who'd been doing this far too long. He led us all to a classroom, nodding to some of the teachers that passed on our way there.

Once we were seated, he passed each of us an IQ test, explaining that we'd be sorted into the "Blue House" or the "White House" and this distinction would chart our destiny at the school.

I was last to finish the test. Alone in the room, I pondered an algebraic equation that felt especially useless. When I finally finished, Mr. Dennis assessed my results on the spot and escorted me into the hallway.

"You'll be on the Blue House track," he said. "Here at West Egg, we sort our pupils into trades of manual labor or intellectual."

I took this to mean that depending on your aptitude, you'd end up washing the fine porcelain of New York's elites or eating off it yourself.

"You'll train to be an elevator operator," Mr. Dennis said as he walked me from the beautiful main office to an old, gray-walled dorm behind the other buildings. "Don't worry—it's not nearly as bad as it sounds, and there will be many opportunities to move up should your performance reflect discipline and hard work."

Elevator operators closed doors and pushed buttons for a living. Your common alley cat could do it with the right intonations of *meow*.

I had to say something. "I'm sorry but how did the quiz determine I'd be an elevator operator, sir? I don't believe that's right for me. I've never even been inside of an elevator."

Mr. Dennis frowned sympathetically. "What you study here is not about what you want to do, but what you'd be good at."

"Only thing is I'm a writer, sir. My pa was a writer, and his pa before that. Everyone in my family's been writers for generations. It's what I was supposed to do before I had to flee home."

"A writer?" Mr. Dennis looked confused and then laughed. "Aren't we all?" He jingled the keys around a massive ring. "Don't let anyone shame you about being an elevator man, Mr. Carrington. Now, where did I put that . . . ah, Room 17! There you are!"

He handed me my key and I reluctantly took it.

When I arrived at Room 17, I discovered a grunting door, and behind it, a dusty little cell of a place. Ashy dead bugs cluttered the windowsill and there were more bugs in the wardrobe. Thankfully, the two beds pressed against the opposite sides of the walls appeared clean, even if the frames were squeaky.

I laid down to sleep early because there was nothing else to do. But before fully dozing off, I heard in the dark someone else come in and settle into the bed across from me.

I didn't budge. A pianist with a soulful voice from somewhere else in the building lulled me into a restful state. I soon heard my roommate snoring, and I joined him, in hopes of better days ahead.

Vinny and I met on our second day as roommates. He was lying on his bed when I came in from meeting with my guidance counselor, his hair picked out and a pair of loose overalls hanging from his shoulders, his outfit showing he cared little about blending in with New York fashion. I liked that about him already.

"Hey," I said, as I went to sit on my own bed.

"Hey," he returned. "Vinny. Calvin, but they call me Vinny."

"Nick."

"So, what brought you here?"

I paused, not sure how much to say. A part of me wanted to tell him everything, but then I felt my throat tighten up, as I tried to find the words. "Just moved up here for better work opportunities," I managed.

"Got you," he said, his tone understanding. "The Klan got my uncle and my cousin. Mom was scared they'd get me too, so she sent me up here to boarding school."

"Oh." I didn't have a good answer. Didn't have the courage to tell him what I'd seen myself. How my father's body seized up, the way the bullet shattered our window and my life with it.

Vinny's story hit too close, and in his honesty, I found myself clinging to the words he hadn't said, wondering if he'd felt the same loss, the same fear.

He pressed on, unafraid of silence. "Never been to a white school before," he admitted.

"Me neither." I tried to smile. "Are you doing elevator training too?"

"Sure am," he said.

"We'll see each other tomorrow then," I said softly.

After the small talk, there was more silence, but it was a warmer one. Someone was in this with me, at the bottom of the West Egg ranking system. And that made me feel less alone, less miserable about being so disrespected by this place. As a bonus, Vinny knew what it was to carry wounds like mine. Perhaps he'd be able to help me shoulder them.

I held on to this thought until the next morning, when I walked among other students crossing the big yard between the dorms and dining hall. The sound of the marching band playing West Egg's patriotic theme song underscored our third day. In the main yard, the mascot—a walking eagle—did a hip-thrusting dance and sang into a cone:

We are the next wave, bold and free!
Rising high for all to see!
Hand in hand, we take our stand,
Side by side, we shape this land!

The song had no soul, but I appreciated its sentiment.

I was surprised to find, however, that for all the chanting about justice, the white boys and Negroes sure divided themselves in the cafeteria.

I walked past tables while flipping through the Bill of Fare in the West Egg pamphlet—it provided a list of meals, which were served the same way each week. Today's options sat in four silver tins—split pea soup, brown beans, corned beef hash, and white bread.

As I moved down the line, my shoe slipped in something wet, and I caught myself on the tray line, elbow bent awkwardly toward the person behind me.

"Careful!" said the white boy, who had wavy red hair and a pointy nose. "Try not to bite the dust." He smiled as I recovered. Then he held out a bowl to a server behind the counter. The server returned to him a ladleful of soup. He looked at it and then recoiled. "This looks like a cat threw it up. Is there something else?"

"We got the pea soup and the corned beef hash," said the server.

"Of course," the boy said, placing the bowl on my tray. "Here—you have it. Clearly the campus-sponsored cuisine is more suited to an . . . erm . . . *outdoor worker's* palate. That's polite, isn't it?" He looked back at a friend who was with him—a dark-skinned boy with a similar pompous air.

"Sounds fine to me!" said the other boy, his voice strong and silly.

What? So I could eat the odd food, but he couldn't? An anger rose in me, but I pushed it down, assuming I must have been missing something. West Egg Academy couldn't be this unfair, could it? Unfair enough to turn Negroes against the interests of other Negroes to blend in?

"I don't know why Gatsby won't just hire better caterers," the white boy said. "We spend a thousand per month on this ridiculous food—can't we get it cooked, at least? Tell you what, Cannon—we'll get catering. Wouldn't want to get tuberculosis in our first week." He moved to walk around me and then paused as if remembering I was there. "Oh! *Bon appétit.* What's your name again?"

"N-Nick," I said.

"Charlie Buchanan. Pleasure."

Charlie Buchanan. In the hallway after breakfast, I flipped through the student directory and learned that Charlie's father was the other owner of West Egg.

Yes, I remembered now. Tom Buchanan—West Egg's cofounder—had also released a statement for the pamphlet, in the opening write-up. *"Jay Gatsby's got the right idea," says Tom Buchanan, West Egg's cofounder. "We've got empty land in New York—why not use it to bring all sorts of people in. New York is at its strongest when it works for everyone."*

No wonder Charlie treated the cafeteria like he owned it. He had parents who could afford tuition. He probably ate pineapple upside-down cakes and pimento-stuffed celery for meals. He never worried about taking loans from lenders or working to make ends meet.

I couldn't relate, and it became clear quite quickly that West Egg was no haven of equality, at least not yet. Perhaps my expectations had been a bit too high.

My weekly schedule was about as standard as they come—six hours of mathematics, twelve of practical machine-tool training, and eighteen hours of field training, manning elevators in the Upper East Side.

Field training started at the end of my core classes. A bus would take us into the city for the last quarter of the workday. To get there, I'd have to cross the main quad, where my new friends, Charlie and Cannon, were hanging around by a table of donuts and coffee. It was clear these were the champions of campus. They were inspecting every new Negro boy who walked by, pointing and laughing—*Who reeked of poor confidence? Who'd make a good target?*

They would jeer at the fear in my eyes—I knew it. But despite every bone in my body wanting to slump, I continued looking up and trekking across the grass. When Charlie noticed me, he gave his auburn waves a pompous shake, tapped his friend, and pointed me out.

Cannon picked up a megaphone, smiled with glee, and said, "Steer clear of the falling balls, Clumsy Nick."

Charlie placed a golf ball on a tee and pulled a club out of a bag I didn't see. He hit it so it flew at my head at fast speed, with torque.

I ducked and my books spilled across the grass, which made them laugh.

I quickly packed them back in and stood up, but a moment after I was on my feet, something else smacked me in the forehead. There it was on the grass—a Boston cream donut leaking a sad spot of goo.

Cannon reared his arm to throw another donut, but someone emerged from between the two menaces and grabbed his arm to stop him.

Jay.

He began to bicker with Charlie and Cannon over the bullying, but I couldn't hear the words. Still, I couldn't look away. He had the strong stature of the bullies. He wore their white T-shirts and cable sweaters, but his compassion made him look out of place with them. Like a dandelion in between two thorns.

He caught my gaze. Thank the stars he was ambling through West Egg's courtyard just in time to save me further embarrassment.

Does he remember that night? It was not that long ago, yet felt like it happened in another universe.

I nodded at Jay, worrying my expression was too blank to show how truly grateful I was that he'd stopped the antics. *Is there something more to say?* I wanted to ask.

I determined that there wasn't, so I went about my way.

The menaces made me even later to field training than I was

in the first place, and I caught the bus once everyone else was already on. Mr. Dennis admonished my lateness, and I offered an apology and shuffled to find a seat as people chuckled at me. I found an open spot next to Vinny and he glared at me when I sat down.

"You got cream on your face," he said, and turned toward the window as the bus took off.

His tone was tense and unexpected. We'd just shared pieces of ourselves the other night and I thought we could be friends. But I couldn't shake the feeling, from his behavior now, that I'd misread that entirely.

I put in my hours at the Francophone Hotel, closing the elevator gates and saying, "What floor?"

I'd make four dollars a day for this work. It almost made wearing the tight green vest with the gold *W.E.* pin worth it. Almost.

I repeatedly checked my pocket watch for the day to end, and when it did finally, I took my last trip down to the main floor with a great sigh of relief.

Vinny was in the lobby when I arrived. I saw him on the other side of the sea of students, chatting to some of his other friends I didn't know. I waved, and he didn't wave back.

Did he not see me? I was sure he did and pretended I wasn't there. That hurt like a bat to the chest. Vinny was the only person I might be able to make a friend out of at school.

On the bus, I took my seat beside him, and he pretended not to see me again. "I was trying to get your attention before," I told him.

"Oh," he said, turning to the window with disinterest. "Didn't realize."

What is wrong with me? I wondered, all through the ride. I sat there, feeling the awkwardness around us. Had I done something? Said too much?

The silence stretched between us through the ride. Each time I looked over, he seemed even farther away. I had this gut feeling I'd lost him already.

By the time we made it back to the dorm, the tension was a knot I couldn't undo. Vinny went straight to his bed, barely looking at me as he set his things down.

He started up a jig piano record on the gramophone he'd brought from home. The upbeat tune filled the room as he moved back and forth between the bathroom and the bedroom, humming to himself, picking out his hair.

The piano music bounced off the walls, but it didn't break the tension. I lay back, staring at the ceiling as he got ready for bed. And when he finally returned for good and was pulling back the top sheet of his bed, I turned and asked, "Did I do something?"

He stopped and looked at me. "What are you talking about?"

"You ignored me today at the hotel," I said.

"I ain't *ignore* you. You showed up late to class with sperm on your face."

My mouth dropped open. "It was *donut cream*," I corrected him, with haste, as I sat up in bed. "And I couldn't stop it! Charlie and Cannon targeted me the moment they saw me."

Vinny looked unimpressed with my excuse. "You could've

wiped it off before getting on the bus. Ever think of that?"

"I would have had I known it was there. There's barely enough time in my schedule to pause for a snack much less care about what's on my face."

"You ought to care," Vinny said, and from his expression, I knew to take him seriously. "Have you seen this place? These folks got enough against us already, making us work elevators all day and calling it an education. You got to do better, man."

Heat rose from my chest to my face as I considered the implications of not being "presentable." *Would I be kicked out of here?* I reached up and felt my artificially softened hair, thinking about the hoops I had to jump through already. There were too many!

Vinny reached into his dresser drawer, pulled out a black piece of cloth and tossed it to me. "Here," he said. "When you do that to your hair you got to wear a scarf to protect it at night."

"Oh," I said, draping it over my head. "Thank you."

Vinny chuckled as he watched me. "Nick, just out of curiosity, where do you go other than class and here?"

I shrugged. "I got two jobs now and six hours of classes per day. What *can* I do?"

Vinny wrapped a scarf around his own head, pushing his afro down. "There's a coed dance next month. You might as well come," he said, giving the invitation like a peace offering.

"What's coed?"

He tucked into bed. "It means West Egg boys and East Egg girls all come together for a night of fun, hoping to get lucky by the end of the night. Best not to show up by yourself. You need a date."

"Okay, so how do I find one?"

"Learn a line. Find a girl you like, strike up a conversation, and then make it seem like you don't even need her." Vinny smiled proudly to himself as if he were the king of pitching woo. "I guarantee it'll make her come to you."

He clicked off his lights and the room plunged into darkness.

I tossed and turned with anxiety through the night. Could I make a girl come to me? I *could* afford to work out more. If my frame filled out my clothes, I'd have more opportunities with girls. But how to join a gym?

I still didn't know if I was cut out for the concept of a coed dance. I respected Vinny's challenge for me to put myself out there more, but what the hell was a *line*?

On Sunday morning, I practiced my *lines* in the bathroom mirror.

"Hey, you look cute in that dress, li'l mama," I crooned to my reflection, and my reflection stared back with embarrassment. "That was horrible." I let out a sigh—my effort felt so forced I embarrassed myself in my own company.

In the shower, I decided that pickup lines were not my forte, as they all felt unlike anything I would naturally say. After getting dressed, I found a piece of paper sticking out of the pants I'd left on the floor. A letter?

It read:

Dear Nick,

I hope you won't mind that I prefer to communicate in writing. I don't mingle often as I only have a few hours of class per day. I am part-time at West Egg and studying the liberal arts.

I just wanted to say I hope the school is working out for you on your side of things. And to apologize on behalf of my housemates. I've known Charlie and Cannon forever, but I wouldn't call them devoted friends. They still invite me to parties, but I don't have much use for their silly games.

It feels like I'm hanging on to my old friends while craving new ones. I notice you're alone a lot too. Forgive me if my approach is too direct.

Yours,
Jay

My skin tingled after reading the signature. I think it was from the feeling of being noticed. It made me both furrow my brows with confusion and smile as questions passed through my mind.

Why had Jay written this to me? When did he deliver it, and how did I miss it?

I didn't know.

I only knew I didn't mind it.

6.

Dear Jay,

Your approach is not too direct, and no need to apologize for those guys, even if you were friends with them.

I'm studying elevator operation here. It's not what I was hoping for, but I've learned to make do wherever I am. My parents are both gone, so I don't have much guidance.

I haven't found many friends yet myself, but I get along okay with my roommate. I know the feeling of not being too secure with your friends. I try to see the best in everyone, just to get along.

Thanks for writing to me.

Yours,
Nick

THE FOLLOWING NIGHT, AS I SAT AT MY DESK, signing my letter back to Jay, there was a loud *bang* on our door. "Open up!" screamed a voice.

I turned to look at Vinny who'd been practicing quiet notes on his tuba but was now frozen in confusion. Neither of us knew what this was about.

I got up from my desk and opened the door to find Charlie Buchanan in a West Egg athletic T-shirt and gray shorts.

"Get dressed, little girls," he said, banging on the door frame with a sinister smile. "It's time for *midnight football.*"

He walked off and I poked my head out into the hallway. The other boys of the White House were flooding our dorm, knocking on doors. Some were going into rooms and flipping over mattresses. This was unsettling for me, and all the barking was unnecessary for a football game. The Blue House boys groggily exited their rooms, rubbing sleep off their eyes.

"Ugh!" Vinny groaned. "*This* old tradition."

I ran back inside and grabbed my letter. I couldn't have Vinny reading it if he got back to the room before me. "What old tradition?" I asked.

Before Vinny could answer, another white boy in the hallway screamed, "Speed it up, princesses! Impromptu midnight games are tradition!"

I went outside and saw them butt-slapping my dorm mates all the way to the locker room, at the bottom of West Egg's recreation building.

Once we were inside again, the white boys started taking off their shirts and admiring themselves in the room's many mirrors. Oh, how buff they were. Vinny and I were so puny as to be invisible.

I glared at the macho chaos under the light of the room, still in disbelief I was on my two feet and not snug in bed as I slipped into my shorts.

My eyes scanned the room and landed on Jay. *What was he doing here so late?*

He turned and saw me looking. I pulled up my shorts and debated whether to wave or not.

Jay gave a quick nod and left his locker slightly ajar as he hurried off to the bathroom stall. I pulled my letter out of my pajama pants, which were resting in my locker, and folded it a second time in preparation to leave it in there while he was gone.

My heart thumped with a scandalous thrill as I approached the locker. I glanced left, then right, as if crossing the road. No one was looking, so I left the little note through the gap.

As Jay came back, I noted that his modest walk set him apart from his former friends. Charlie and Cannon walked chest-forward, like they'd bulldoze anything in their way.

Jay was beautiful like them, but he walked not like he meant to conquer the earth but like the earth had conquered him. Sadness radiated like sunbeams from his chest, ordering his limbs into a languid orbit.

Someone with so much money could not be as sad as he appeared to be!

When Jay reached his locker, he looked at the folded letter and glanced back to me. All I could do was stand there like a dog waiting to be fed.

Move, Nick.

I closed my locker as Jay slipped out of his pants, the muscles in his legs flexing as he stepped into his shorts.

I followed the boys filing out of the locker room until we reached the sports field, down some stairs off the main campus.

Charlie's entourage did knee rises and stretched their arms out to prepare for the game.

It became very clear that it would be the Blue House versus the White House, by the way the white boys separated themselves from us for conditioning. I kept looking at the big guys from my dorm, like James—he was a future machine worker, and the strongest and most confident we had.

James began corralling us into a huddle, asking questions, and assigning roles. He'd be quarterback, and the rest of us would have roles that supported his throws, in the form of defense or running.

"Vinny, you running wide," he said. "And Nick"—he pointed at me—"you gon' catch. Keep your eyes on me, but run like hell."

I swallowed with anxiety but nodded—he was right to assign me that role. If I tried to defend anything, I'd be crushed like a beetle, so I'd run to catch the pass and rely on my housemates for the rest.

We lined up in the middle of the field for the start of the game, each team facing the other. And then James said, "Signal! Hike!"

The boys clashed midfield, tackling and dragging each other through the grass. I circled the action and went long, getting further than the others on our team. James spotted me and passed the ball. It soared above the stadium light, disappearing and landing again in my hands.

I held the leather to my chest and ran across the field, dodging one boy and then another. A skip here, a fake-out step there. Even Jay reached out to stop me, but I spun around him too and scored a touchdown.

Catching my breath, I turned and looked back on the people watching me, and knew immediately my athleticism had earned me some standing with the guys of both houses. It made me want to get back out there and go again.

Yeah! Not so clumsy now, huh?

Six touchdowns in, the Blue House won the game. We had an edge in athletics, at least! And we all gravitated together to give these manly half hugs once all was said and done.

But white boys didn't like to lose. That became clear when we got back to the locker room and Cannon Cleary screamed, "Didn't know you could run like that, Nick! You've got such a *girlish* figure."

There were laughs here and there. I chose silence. I didn't want to be mean in return. But my God, did I secretly wish to be stronger and bigger like they were so that they could never say a thing. Even though I was fast, I was still being chumped for not looking the part.

Jay was walking out of the showers and going to his locker—the way he stomped around the crowd made me think he was angrier at the slight than I was. "Do you ever leave people alone, Cannon? I swear it's like you spend all your time focused on someone else. Focus on *you*."

There were some *oohs* as people took sides on the back and

forth. They both looked the part. Cannon's muscles ripped smoothly through his defined, lean build. Jay was shorter, but with broad shoulders and a powerful chest—his entire torso was robust and balanced with strength.

"Says the guy who's inserting himself into something that wasn't about him," Cannon spat back.

"It is about me," Jay said. "I see you bullying someone, I'm going to say something."

"Oh, brother." Cannon rolled his eyes. "So fake righteous—isn't your father a *conman*?"

The room went watchfully silent.

Gatsby? I thought. A *conman*? What did that mean? Well, Jay did say his father gave "donations" to that juice joint we went to. And they sold alcohol there. But that wasn't exactly conning.

Jay wasn't fazed by the comment and continued packing his gym bag. "You're benefiting from my father's junior cop program," he said, plainly.

"That's beside the point," Cannon said. "I know a spin when I see one and no one makes millions through charity. He built this school to make it *look like* he isn't a crook."

A crook? The West Egg pamphlet said Gatsby Sr. built wealth through *peer-to-peer investing*. Whatever that meant, it sounded legit! But perhaps not very moneymaking.

"You know nothing about him," Jay said, his voice quieter now.

"Of course not—he makes sure to stay out of sight, doesn't he?" Cannon stepped up to Jay. "We all know that's *not for no reason*."

The room held its breath, watching as Jay didn't back down. He looked angry, and for a second, I thought he might swing at Cannon.

But he didn't. He held his ground, and when he spoke, his voice cut through the silence with a cold peace. "Anyone who talks so loudly on things they don't know about is a fool."

He left Cannon with a final glare before slamming his locker shut and striding out of the locker room.

Cannon just snickered, his smugness not faltering.

And I stood there, trying to place the emotion I had for Jay, which had sprung up unexpectedly while watching the encounter. Admiration? Loyalty? It all started because he stood up for me. He didn't know me well, and yet he'd been there immediately as if to fulfill some preexisting duty to me.

As everyone else filed out of the locker room, the usual chatter carried on. I ran forward after standing in disbelief for what felt like a lifetime of pondering.

I couldn't catch up to him in time. The last I saw of him that night was from the back. He shrank in the distance beyond West Egg's main field, his silhouette collapsing down the front steps and out of sight.

Was there a shift between us? Was I imagining it?

West Egg may have felt more like a battleground than a haven, but at least in this battle, I had an ally.

Another surprise midnight football game came around a few days later, as the White House boys were challenging us to a rematch to avenge their honor. On the night of our next game, I found a letter in my locker.

I pulled it out, making sure no one could see me, wondering if it occurred to Jay how intimate this method of communication was?

Dear Nick,

Thanks for writing back. I'm very sorry to hear your parents are no longer with us. I can't imagine what that must be like.

My mother lives in London. My parents both went to university there, and Father wanted to move to New York after I was born, but Mother couldn't stand the trouble that Americans give interracial couples.

Father is drawn to places he can help make better, but Mother just wants to be comfortable. I don't know who I agree with more, but I am technically closer to Mother, though our communication is mostly through letters. Father travels often so I'm distant from him as well.

I feel like I'm drifting, not sure where I fit. I don't know if that's something you can relate to.

Yours,
Jay

I read over his words twice, the vulnerability standing out against the rough edges of most boys around here.

Despite Cannon's accusations, I was quick to believe Jay's own view of his father, even if their relationship is distant. But still . . .

I almost flipped the letter over and used its blank side to write my response inside my locker. But there were too many witnesses, so I didn't. My one question for him would be, *What is your father's true occupation?*

Was that too blunt? It was the first thing that popped into my head. A man who earned his wealth honestly would want to help others follow the same path, right? But his school's programs didn't seem to reflect that idea. They only gave a few of us the chance to learn skills that could lead to wealth. Maybe that was a flaw on his part.

Before I could question myself further, a figure emerged from the steam near the showers, calling out, "Okay, who here's a virgin?"

It was Vinny, choosing to be confident suddenly, perhaps due to the pressures that came with being surrounded by a bunch of shirtless guys.

They all broke into laughter, and I quickly balled up the letter.

"Nick, for sure," Charlie chimed in, grinning at me. "It's the reason he and Jay are passing notes back and forth like a couple of schoolgirls." A ripple of laughter went through the room.

My face burned, but I pretended the comment didn't matter. Being the center of attention stung though. I hated it.

"That is what's going on, isn't it?" Charlie asked, his cold green eyes piercing through mine.

I tucked the balled-up paper into my bag. I'd give his words nothing and let them pass by. I didn't know Charlie well enough to let him capsize me.

Jay, on the other hand, was visibly affected by it. He walked right up to Charlie and barked, "What did you say?" as if he still hadn't calmed down from the other night.

Charlie didn't back down. They stood chest to chest, chin to chin, in a ridiculous contest of who was tougher. "I said your little friend is a virgin," Charlie pronounced. "Am I wrong?"

A crowd of eyes corralled them into an energy spotlight.

"Charlie," Jay said, shaking his head. "The only reason you'd be concerned with that is if you wanted him yourself."

Everyone *ooh*ed at that one, but Charlie rolled his eyes.

"Come on, people. That was *weak*!" He stepped toward Jay, staring him dead in the eye, and then their bodies were almost close enough to touch. "I don't want your boyfriend," Charlie said. "But I'm glad you're finally making the *kinds of friends* you've always wanted, Jay."

"Meaning what?" I said, making Charlie face me. Others turned to face me too, the room quieting as everyone remembered I was there. "What kinds of friends?" I asked.

He couldn't answer right away. He laughed quietly and then looked at Jay. "Like father like son is what it means."

"I'm not arguing anymore," Jay said, and he slunk around bodies to leave the locker room.

I followed him. This situation would push him away before we really had a chance to become friends, and I was really enjoying getting to know him! More than I could say for most people.

"That's right," Charlie called after us. "Go and smooch each other in private!"

Jay stormed away from the ensuing laughter, going for the outdoor corridor that led to West Egg's main lawn. He fell against a stone pillar as if he needed it to steady him. He pulled a tiny silver tray from his pocket and from that wrenched a shaking cigarette.

I stood and watched him try to light it. Eventually he gave up, as if he didn't even want it. I wanted to approach, but I wasn't sure if he'd tell me to leave him to his tragic thinking.

"If it makes you feel better, I'm a virgin too," he announced. Jay held up the lighter and finally turned to faced me. "No fluid," he said, shaking the lighter. "Hey, I'm not in the best mood. Wouldn't want it to rub off on you. I'll see you." And then he walked away.

I watched him go, right across the dark yard, back in the direction of the street. Didn't he want to commemorate how we'd just survived a locker room bloodbath? Why did it seem he was always escaping, and just out of reach?

"Wow, two virgins," said a voice behind me. *"How unfortunate."*

I spun around to find Artie Botts studying his face in a handheld mirror, his sleek girlish hair shining in the campus's orange lamps. He was ladylike in all ways, but so confident in it that the bullies mostly left him alone.

"Please don't tell people about that?" I asked.

Artie closed his mirror and shook his hair from out of his face. "Don't take it personally if I do. Talk is what I do."

Artie was the *West Egg Chronicle*'s first Negro writer. His essay was featured in the West Egg pamphlet, and in it he talked about how proud he was to have impressed the paper's faculty supervisor with his easy voice and punchy humor. Now he ran a column in the *Chronicle*, where he published tabloid-style journalism about popular students.

Artie's presence was at times loud and at others quiet—he'd go unnoticed as he moved like a shadow through the locker room, observing conversations and storing details away to write about later. He seemed to know each student's story before they'd told it to him.

"Late night showdown between the founding boys?" Artie continued. "You best believe I'm on it. And you . . ." He tilted his head and sized me up, in a way that made me feel small, despite Artie being inches shorter. "You really, really like Jay, don't you?" He laughed smugly and wiped lip balm off the corner of his mouth. "Another fan taking the *kind humanitarian* act a little too personally, I see."

I was not in the mood for any fighting. "Can't you focus on something else?" I asked, voice bleeding with exhaustion. "All I do is mind my own business around here—I don't bother anyone."

"Unfortunately no, Nicholas, I can't. Because *this* is my favorite subject. You know why? Because nothing is more interesting than the truth underneath a disguise." He began to advance on me, his eyes severe. "Your dear Jay, for example—charitable, oh-so-charming on the outside, but what's underneath? Anything real? His personality is *all for show*—just like this school!"

Artie wasn't technically wrong, about the school anyway.

White boys came here to look good on paper but wanted little to do with us in reality.

Artie gave me a fake smile, probably because he saw my face fall.

"I'd tell you to be careful, but it seems like you're in the full swing of things already, so good luck!" He waved with his fingers insincerely and spun away.

The next day I returned to the bathroom several times in the afternoon; something about nerves made my bladder inconsistent. I kept throwing gel into my hair and splashing water on my face.

When I caught myself in the mirror, I realized how nervous I was. I didn't think my burgeoning friendship with Jay would get attention. Now there were unwanted visitors with me when I was inside the small corners of my mind, feeling my emotions.

I liked that Jay continued to stick up for me. But I wasn't a chump—I wanted to be someone who could stick up for himself.

When I got back to the room, Vinny was sprawled on his bed, skimming through his homework. He glanced up, caught the look on my face, and raised an eyebrow. "So, how's the note passing going with Jay?"

"Ugh," I groaned, collapsing onto my bed, face-first into the lumpy mattress. I turned my head to speak, but didn't bother moving the rest of me. "It's actually fine. Like, I've got myself a pen pal now."

Vinny snorted, not looking up from his notebook. "A pen pal?

Man, we're not in grade school. You know you can just talk to him, right? In person?"

"What if it wasn't my idea to write in the first place?" I muttered. "Ever think of that?"

Vinny shrugged. "Sure, but if you're gonna write him back, that's your thing. Don't act like it's some big secret. You could talk to him anytime. Seems like you like the safety of writing, though."

I shot him a glance, suddenly self-conscious. He wasn't wrong.

Vinny caught my eye with a knowing smirk. "What's the deal? What're you holding back?"

I felt I was in the hot seat. But before I could respond, a loud voice called from outside, "Come on, baby! Give us a smile!" Someone was catcalling outside the window, and it ripped me out of the conversation just in time.

I looked outside and found some boys gathered in front of the building, barking at someone. A little further out, where the walkway toward the front of campus began, a girl in a headwrap and sunglasses was talking to a boy. When she gave him a *shoo* motion and he ran back toward the building, I realized that it was Daisy! She must have sent the boy back for me.

I raced down to meet her—I was excited she'd come to visit me here!

She'd nearly made her way to the street when I got downstairs. I caught up to her at the front of campus, where she'd gone to lean back on a roofless car, one of her heels propped up on its body. A skirt umbrellaed in black and white polka dots from her waist to her knees.

"Daisy?" I called, shuffling down the front steps and squinting.

"Hi, cousin!" she replied, waving when I reached the gravel road, her voice bright.

"What are you doing here? Whose . . . car is this?" I asked, gesturing to the sleek black automobile behind her, which gleamed like polished onyx.

"Oh, it's my boss's," she said, casting a quick look at the car. "Well, one of his cars. He let me borrow it." She glanced down at her wristwatch, a glimmer of silver and diamonds flashing. "I'm being stonewalled by Jay Gatsby. He hasn't been returning my calls, but I figure if I just show up here during school hours, he can't run away from me." She gave a small laugh at herself.

"Jay Gatsby, the founder?" I asked, disbelief in my voice.

"No," she said, rolling her eyes with affectionate exasperation. "Jay Gatsby, the son." Her voice lingered on the word, her expression becoming thoughtful, and then she smiled at me again, her fingers tightening around her watch. I couldn't quite put my finger on it, but there was something there—some secret connection to Jay she wasn't naming.

When Daisy waved to someone behind me, I turned to find Jay coming down the brick stairs. Little gold accents on his green school vest caught pieces of the sun like bicycle blinders.

"Hello, Daisy," Jay said, his eyes lighting up slightly as he walked up to us. When he turned to me, he swallowed, as if monitoring himself. "Nick?"

"Hi," I mumbled, suddenly hyperaware of my appearance, from my untidy hair down to my dusty shoes—everything felt uncomfortably visible under his sharp gaze and the sunlight.

I looked away, the sense of being an outsider among them taunting me. I was new, and they seemed like they'd known each other for a while.

"You two," Jay said, swinging an index finger between us. "You're related, aren't you?"

Daisy didn't answer in the affirmative right away. Instead, she said, "Why do you ask?" as if she wanted to draw him into a game.

Jay looked at Daisy and then me. But his eyes lingered on me as he said, "I see a resemblance. A softness in the face."

Daisy looked at me, as if she expected me to say something. When I didn't, she didn't either. It was as if there was some secret agreement between us that we should hide the true nature of our relationship, just in case. In case of what, I was not clear.

"Don't try to distract me, Jay." Daisy gave him an expression that was half annoyed, half affectionate, as she latched on to his arm. "I've been calling you for days. You never pick up the phone!" Her tone was chiding, but the cadence told me this was their usual dance.

Jay smiled, amused. "I got busy. You know how it gets." His casual shrug seemed to say it all, as if she should understand his world already.

"Okay, well, we need to talk." Daisy opened the passenger door, then skipped around to the other side to hop into the driver's seat. "Nick, do you want to go for a spin?" she called out.

"Oh, I have after-school things . . ."

Jay threw his bag over the top of the car and vaulted over the side, landing easily in the passenger's seat. "Come with us!" he called, his tone relaxed, but I caught a small challenge in it. "We love the farmer's market downtown. The bell's rung, and who wants to spend more time here than they need to?"

They both looked at me, and I felt drawn to their connection. The pull left me with no choice. I joined the magnetic pair in the car, intrigued about their relationship.

We took off, into the noisy streets, and drove until the roads went from wide and empty to crowded with people the further we went into the city proper. Here was the part of town where the people wore suits and hats as a necessity. They were the advertisers and the bankers, all about their business. There were more white people here, but it was still mixed. The streets were adorned with statues—memorials, stroked by trimmed clusters of trees.

"You coming to UNIA on Thursday?" Daisy asked Jay as we drew closer to the market.

"Won't have time," Jay said, looking back at me briefly to see if I was listening. "Other stuff to attend to."

We parked in an alley by a colorful fair of fruits and vegetables. Part of the road had been closed off to make room for it, sheriffs on horses blocking the cars.

Daisy hopped out first. "No one will hijack the car if we leave it here, will they?" she asked Jay, as if he were the tour guide of New York himself.

"If they do, Buchanan's got more where this came from,

right?" Jay smiled ironically and swung himself into the pedestrian traffic of the fair.

Daisy followed him and I trailed after her, taking in the produce carts little by little, the labels on watermelon bins that said *locally sourced*, the giant bags of peanuts and popcorn—

"Dragon fruit alert!" Jay screamed very suddenly. And he drifted off to grab the last of a pink fruit from a bin.

"How do you know him?" I asked Daisy in a subtle way, because it felt easier to do when Jay was distracted.

"We met in Garvey's group—the UNIA," she answered. "It's empowerment. We do book clubs, art shows, cabarets. All in the community who believe in true liberation from the powers that be are welcome!"

"Ah yes, Garvey," I said. "I'm familiar. Pa used to get his papers sent to us." Marcus Garvey was a speaker who'd attracted good and bad attention for his theory that living separate from white people would help Negroes more than living among them. "So, have you met Garvey too?" I asked her as we sauntered through the market.

"In passing," Daisy said. "I mostly go to UNIA because it's nice to be part of something that feels bigger than myself. And bigger than high school trifles, you know?" She looked at Jay as if he were the trifle. He was busy inspecting a stall of exotic fruits.

"How long have you known him?" I asked. "Jay, I mean."

Daisy glanced back at me. Her eyes were somewhat evasive. "A while. Why?"

"You seem close," I said. "I mean, you two fit together."

"*Fit* together?" Daisy's expression turned briefly pensive before slipping back into its usual light air. "Jay and I both have big ambitions and he's useful to know—that's all."

Her words only deepened my curiosity. *What ambitions?*

She laughed softly as she saw my mind turning, and she rubbed my back with a supportive hand. "You think so much, Nick! I have to go and ask Jay something now, but look around. Enjoy the sights! Enjoy the market!"

I stayed back as she scurried off, pretending to admire the produce, but my eyes lingered on the two of them. They shared something—a history, a purpose.

Daisy's hand almost brushed his arm as she whispered something to him, and Jay leaned in to catch her words, his expression turning serious. What was the perfect pair talking about, and why did they need to leave me out of it?

Who was Daisy beyond the playful surface—and what kind of life did the charming Jay Jr. lead when he wasn't playing schoolboy adventures?

Jay eventually wandered off, disappearing into a crowd clustered around a cart of imported chocolates. "I used to love these as a kid!" he called out, leaving Daisy standing amid the bustle of the market.

She wandered back to me, her smile dimming some as she studied my expression. "What's on your mind, Nick?"

I hesitated, unsure where to start. "I've just been wondering . . . is everything okay with you?"

Her brow furrowed, just slightly, but she didn't laugh off the question. "Of course. Why wouldn't it be?"

"I don't know," I said, but my mind circled back to the night she snuck out. My night ended with Jay in the juice joint, but hers carried on, beyond the freight yard, and who knows what happened next? "It's just . . . you've done a lot to help me get settled here and if there's any way I can return the favor, I'd love to." I gestured vaguely to the market, the people and their quiet transactions, around us. "This is all lovely, by the way."

"I thought you'd like it." She reached out to tenderly adjust the lapel of my jacket. She looked at me with a sweet smile, and for a moment I saw the Daisy I remembered from years ago—the one who used to bake cakes with me in Grandma's kitchen, laughing as we tasted batter when no one was looking. "I appreciate the support, Nick. But I'm fine. Honest."

"I only worry about you. After midnight, when you're by yourself, things can turn. I've seen it happen."

Daisy's eyes widened for a moment but then returned to normal just as quick. "Don't you worry about a thing, Nick." She squeezed my arm. "I'm usually tucked into bed before trouble can find me."

Daisy then looked off toward where Jay was talking playfully to a merchant, a clear dismissal. Whatever happened that night, whatever bond she and Jay shared, neither was meant for me to understand—not yet.

But one thing was for sure—in New York, staying small wasn't an option. This rumble in my belly told my bones I was meant for far more than what I had. Daisy and Jay moved through the world like two birds of prey, flying over a whole tundra that was theirs for the taking!

And me? I was still sprouting my wings. I'd been raised to be so humble because staying small was safer back home. Humble and quiet kept me alive! A boy like me couldn't be reckless—not in Greenwood, where the Klan lurked like phantoms in the woods. Where their fires watched us like the devil's eyes, waiting for a reason to strike.

But maybe I was due for a change. Maybe I was done keeping my head so low and pretending I didn't want to be someone—someone bigger than I'd ever dared to dream of.

7.

JAY GATSBY JR. NEVER STAYED IN JUST ONE world.

Most days I spotted him alone, wandering campus like a lonely tourist. But sometimes he jumped from clique to clique with a fluid social grace that was hard not to envy.

I didn't see him often—once a day, usually—in conversation with faculty or someone at an activities table, putting on a personable voice. He made the most of being handsome. He knew what he was and didn't pretend otherwise, but he didn't brag about it either. I think that's why everyone liked talking to him.

Even if Jay had somewhere to be, he'd always smile and wave when he noticed me. We'd exchanged further letters even following Charlie's taunting. Jay shared his fascination with carpentry and told me about how he was working on little animal pieces for fun—birds, tigers, and owls. How he liked working with his hands more than sitting in classrooms tossing around theories all day. I shared my love for poetry with him. How I often scribbled lines in my notebook when I needed to get emotions out, but had trouble finishing things.

Our letters created a secret world between us, one I kept hidden in my room. There, I yearned to share the depths of myself with a stranger, but always pulled back, unsure of how much to reveal.

I'd just left my dorm after tucking away Jay's latest letter. I was passing through the outdoor corridor when I saw him approaching me from the field. He raised his hand for a wave, but someone cut in front of him shouting, "Hey, Nick!"

It was Charlie. He blocked me from viewing Jay, so my first instinct was to look around him, but he was so tall and present that I couldn't.

He was passing me a flyer. "I'd like to invite you to a meeting in the *West Egg Chronicle* office. I am the new editor in chief and I'm looking to publish more interest stories about Negroes. Since you're always writing things down anyway, it might make a good use of your time."

This was surely a joke. "Is that so?" I asked, taking the flyer, looking at him sideways.

"Follow me quickly, will you?"

I turned to look at Jay and found he'd paused, appearing confused as to why I was talking to Charlie. I was too—for now. I gave him a wave, and he waved back with a slight but disappointed smile. His eyes followed me as I walked with Charlie into a classroom building.

I was pulled by the sudden switch in Charlie's demeanor. He

was being . . . *nice* to me now, in a way that felt like a trap but piqued my curiosity.

We reached his office at the *West Egg Chronicle* by way of a room full of white writers—and Artie. Charlie's office featured a window that looked into the writers' room. I reckon so he could watch his factory as it produced.

Charlie sat down in a swivel chair behind his desk. "I think we started off on the wrong foot," he said, with a performed smile.

"Yes," I sat quietly in the chair across from him, ready to perform in return. "I would agree." This felt strange, but Charlie was a curious person in general. He had a sense of humor that threw me off the scent of his terrible spirit.

"Don't mind the locker room humor," he said. "It's time to talk business. Jay mentioned you got into West Egg because you're gifted in writing. So, if you have something to offer to the *Chronicle*, you should write me something, as a trial run."

"I don't know what I would write," I said.

"Whatever's newsworthy to you," Charlie said. "Keeping with the mission of West Egg, we want to make sure the Blue boys are represented in the paper, and God knows good writers among you are one in a million." He laughed at himself.

Ah, *there* was the race bait I'd come to expect. Charlie was hateful, but I did want to do something at West Egg other than man the elevators. And writing was what I genuinely wanted to do before the mob came to Greenwood.

"I guess I could write something," I said, small ideas already rattling in my brain.

"Deadline's Friday." Charlie leaned back. His eyes gleamed as if he was already picturing the headlines. "Give me something that'll make people *need* to read it. Something that'll get the *Chronicle* buzzing. If you can pull that off, we might let you publish again."

I nodded with acceptance and then left Charlie's office feeling excited and uneasy. He was mean, but the opportunity to write felt like a gem under a lot of dirt. And it gave me the stirrings of purpose.

The halls were quiet as I walked back to my dorm. Students were either going back to their rooms or milling around common areas.

When I stepped into my room, silence greeted me, as Vinny was off somewhere else. I took a seat at my desk and opened my notebook.

Here was a chance to show something real to the students who read the *Chronicle*.

What could capture people's attention? Something that spoke to the Blue boys like me, who were still trying to figure out where we fit into the school.

I came up with the story in real time as I penned my thoughts straight from the heart.

DOES WEST EGG DELIVER ON ITS PROMISE?

By Nick Carrington

West Egg. What to say about West Egg?

When I first got here, it felt like a chance—like

this was a place where Colored boys like me could get the same opportunities as white boys, where we'd have a fair shot at building our futures. But now that I'm here, I'm starting to wonder: Has West Egg kept that promise? Are they really giving us the same space to grow and succeed?

It's hard to buy into the "elite education" thing when, for a lot of us, the only jobs we're being prepped for are the ones they think are good enough for us—like manning elevators or waiting tables. What good is all this education if we're only ever going to be stuck doing jobs that don't let us reach our full potential?

Look at my roommate, Vinny. The guy can play the tuba like nobody's business, but how's he ever going to make a career out of it when he's stuck pushing buttons all day? Our talents, our ambitions—they're bigger than this!

If West Egg really cares about equality, then we should all have access to the same classes, the same opportunities. They talk about integration, but I see segregation, just in a different way. If West Egg is serious about giving us a fair chance, it needs to open the doors wider.

We should be able to learn more than just what's "acceptable" for us. If West Egg wants to

help us, it can't just want us to be useful—it's got to let us be whole.

After finishing my piece, I had to take a walk to weigh the consequences of showing it to Charlie. He wouldn't want to publish something that worked in opposition to his elitist attitude. And yet, I could only write what came from the heart, so I was hopeless to change it.

Pa's words before he died thrummed through my head like a shooting ache: *Don't ever hold your tongue, no matter how afraid you might feel.*

I walked through campus until I landed inside the recreation building, where tall ceilings and tiled floors made the whole place feel like a hospital. I spied through a window a vast room with a pool, its walls pure white, Greek-like. So I went inside just to see it and take in some beauty.

When I opened the door, I was blasted with the faint scent of chlorine. A window on the ceiling above the water shone light onto the pool's glassy blue surface. One person was swimming, making ripples as they cut through the water with powerful yet peaceful strokes.

He slowed as he reached the shallow end, where he pushed himself up out of the water. He climbed the little brass ladder, big arms and back flexing with his motions. He wiped himself haphazardly with a towel and then turned, pausing when he noticed me.

Jay. Again.

He waved and gave a reserved smile.

I waved back, barely breathing and hoping he couldn't tell. The universe must have been doing this to us on purpose.

"Didn't think I'd see you here," he called, his voice echoing as he walked over.

Water trickled down his chest, and through the gridlocks of his stomach.

"Yeah . . . I was . . . just needed a break," I stammered.

Jay ran the towel through his hair. "You know, I was thinking that we don't have to keep passing notes. It was fun, but not anymore now that people know about it."

"I agree." I shifted my weight some, tightening my grip on my bag, feeling self-conscious.

"We can just talk to each other," he added.

"Sure," I said. "Hi."

"Hi," he echoed, with a jovial smile. I remembered the trial piece I'd been carrying around—it would form the perfect conversation pivot. Jay was a good writer and familiar with Charlie, so he might help me with my confidence.

I reached in my bag, pulled it out, and handed it to him. "Could I get your opinion on this? You don't have to read the whole thing, but since you're friends with Charlie—well, former friends—do you think he'd ever publish this in the paper?"

Jay took the paper, scanning it in silence, which gave me some time to watch him. *What had he told Charlie about me, besides that I'm a good writer?* I wondered. And why did my brain abandon that thought to focus instead on the drops of water dappling his skin?

He looked up, meeting my eyes. "Are you going to the dance?" he asked, abruptly.

"What?" I blinked, taking a moment to process that this question was not related to my essay. "I . . . don't know," I answered boringly.

He nodded and went back to reading. Finally, when he was finished, he said, "It's honest." And handed it back to me with an encouraging smile. "This place could use a little more of that, whether Charlie wants to publish it or not."

It gave me a sense of relief. "Thank you," I said, trying to keep my tone even.

Jay smiled. "Anytime, Nick. We're all in this together. I agree."

"Yeah. You're a good swimmer." My eyes widened instinctively at my clumsy turn of topic, but Jay just laughed.

"I do like it," he said. "Cools me off after exercise." He stretched his shoulders back and tapped on his chest with moxie, making a few drops of water splash into the space between us. "Maybe we could do it together sometime?"

"Do . . . it?" I echoed.

"Yes," Jay said, matter-of-factly. "Swim."

"Swim! Of course." I laughed it off. "Together. I never learned how—not really—but I could. I could do that. Sure. I have to go now."

I awkwardly turned to leave, but he didn't let me get far.

"Hey," he called, and I was forced to turn around, as if commanded by a sire. "If you do show up at the dance, I'll see you there."

This statement was delivered like an invitation. His persistence made me sure that he cared about my presence at this dance. But why? He'd be absorbing the attention of a dozen beautiful girls there. What did it matter if he saw me?

"Okay," I said, like some sort of wet automaton. Water from his chest had splashed me in the face, and now my parts were malfunctioning. "I'll let you know what I decide. See you."

I turned and left the pool room, legs a little wobbly as I caught my breath. Outside I waved the paper through the air to dry off the droplets Jay had left on it. Would there ever come a time when being in his presence didn't feel like swallowing a kaleidoscope of butterflies?

Jay Gatsby Jr. was confident. He was, dare I say, sexy? His energy, whatever it was, put the power of a god in me each time we had an exchange. And so I marched proudly into the *West Egg Chronicle* office the next day to deliver my article to Charlie.

"This is a fine piece," Charlie said, apathetically, after reading it. "Very sincere, and I appreciate your challenge to Gatsby's reputation as an altruist."

His reaction was a bit flat, but not unexpected.

"It was more about the entire structure of the school than Gatsby's reputation," I said.

"Sure, of course." Charlie's tone was dismissive. "You want better access for Colored boys. I appreciate the sentiment, but we can't change the whole structure of the academy. Obviously."

"Who says?"

"Um, *the structure*?" Charlie made a silly face at me, like I was dumb. "It's there for a reason. Anything else you could cover besides how much you hate it here?"

I thought for a second. "Uh . . . perhaps the political movements happening in Harlem? I think it's important for students to stay connected to politics. I know some people here go to Garvey's meetings."

Charlie grimaced. "Any article about Garvey and his followers ought to mention how his rhetoric leads to violence. If you ask me, Marcus Garvey is nothing but trouble."

"Who says?" I shot back.

"My father," Charlie said. "He says Garvey is a troublemaker, stoking violence. He even tells his followers we should hang white people the way they hang Negroes."

"He's not saying we should be violent," I snapped, growing frustrated. "Garvey is just about self-defense, about empowering us, not attacking people. My father would call him a genius."

"Your father's gone, isn't he?" Charlie retorted, watching me for my reaction.

I stared back blankly, though the comment sucked the oxygen right out of my chest.

"So sorry to hear that," Charlie continued flatly and went about his business, sorting some papers in his desk.

He left me in silence, wondering if that was truly insulting or if I was just sensitive. I thought it was insulting, but I decided to press forward. If this really was about business, my emotions wouldn't serve me well here.

"Garvey's growing in popularity because his theories are making a difference," I said.

"Ah yes, harping on about how he's going to build a big boat and take you all back to Africa is bound to be very appealing." Charlie waved his hand around like the theory was a nuisance. "If that's possible, why haven't you all gone back there? Nobody keeps you here."

"It takes resources to do that, you know. The Black Star Line is like a trade system with Africa," I explained, trying to recapture my father's language from when he told me about it. "We don't build a big boat. We start by sending resources from the United States back to the motherland until we can eventually return and leave America if we choose. That's the idea."

"Sounds fraudulent," Charlie said smugly. "And like it will not last."

"Who says?"

A look of annoyance rose in Charlie's eyes, his expression screaming, *This is a waste of my time.*

"Look, the revolution story lacks a striking angle, Nick. Nobody would care about that. Just focus on a lighter push for better curriculum access and leave it there."

"Maybe my stories belong to a separate paper," I said, stonily.

Charlie swallowed, his face hardening. "Unfortunately, West Egg only has the *Chronicle.*"

"And that may be the problem," I said. "Everyone's interests can't be represented by a single paper."

"It's not about everyone's interests," Charlie retorted. "It's about a unifying front." He flicked his hand at me in dismissal. "That's enough."

I left the office with my article still clenched in my hand, my face burning with anger. Charlie's words sat wrong with me—not just what he said about my father, but the way he looked at me, like I was already set up to fail. Like he was daring me to prove him wrong. He didn't expect much from Blue House boys. None of them did. Unless you were Artie—the one they let through to say they had.

I should've believed the first version of Charlie I met—the one who threw golf balls at my head.

On my way back to the dorm, I passed other Blue House students, their shoulders low, their eyes avoiding mine. They moved through the day the way we were expected to: quiet, small, like we were just lucky to be here.

Charlie's paper wasn't the avenue to be heard. And I didn't need his approval to make a difference.

8.

IN MY FREE TIME, I ISOLATED MYSELF IN THE library and worked on flyers to advertise a new student paper. *The Sovereign*—that would be its name! It was bold, rebellious, just like Pa's paper. This one would be mine. Something I could own!

I slipped a few flyers into my bag, a thrill rushing through me as I thought of taking charge of the narrative. As I prepared to leave, my eyes landed on a familiar person sitting at a table, absorbed in a book. It was the boy from the Chinese restaurant I'd almost applied to.

Imagine my surprise at finding him here, wearing a long-pleated skirt that fell just over his knees and heeled boots—two choices that clearly rejected the dress code and made him look almost like a schoolgirl. He wore the fashion well, even with the pressure of being the only one here who was neither Negro nor white.

He looked up as if he'd felt me staring and then gave me a happy wave of recognition.

I made my way over, one flyer still in my hand. "Hi," I said with a smile.

"Hey," he returned, leaning forward and closing the book. "Funny seeing you here."

"Likewise—I didn't know you went to this school."

"Just started," he said, holding up what he was reading, which I realized then was the West Egg pamphlet. "Zihan."

"Nick." We shook hands.

I felt this heaviness as I glanced down at the flyer in my hand. *Should I share it?* But then I thought there was no point in having an idea just to keep it hidden, and with great hesitation, I gave him a flyer.

He skimmed it, then looked back at me. "*The Sovereign*?"

"I'm starting a paper," I said, the words avalanching out of my mouth. "The school-funded one is very one-sided, so I think the Blue House boys need a way to have our own say here."

I braced for a dismissal, but Zihan nodded thoughtfully and then shrugged with approval. "I support it. I haven't been here long, but they put me in restaurant training, just because I have been doing that my whole life. But the point of coming here was to do something new, you know? They think they know you already, just from looking at you."

"Exactly," I said, sliding into a chair at the table. "And they don't—in the slightest. That's why I'm doing the paper, so we have a space to write out our own stories. You could write something if you want—share your take on it all."

He tilted his head, considering it, and then he nodded. "Maybe.

Do you live in the Blue House? I'm still living back home."

"Room 17," I confirmed.

"Neat. What are you up to now?"

We left the library at the same time. The late afternoon sun stretched across the outdoor hallway, and a breeze stirred loose leaves along the ground.

"Have you found anything to like about it here, so far?" I asked.

Zihan said, "I like the look," and gestured to the polychrome brickwork of the White Hall classroom building beyond the hallway. The complex masonry glowed in the light. "It reminds me of Great Britain. You?"

"I'm finding things to like," I said honestly. "It still feels big to me."

He looked at me, his expression open and thoughtful. "It feels big for me too. But it is still early."

We walked to the Blue House, where the common area was buzzing with noise—my dormmates joking and tossing cards at a table, someone throwing a rubber ball against a wall. Zihan hesitated at the door, then stepped in with me behind him.

He raised the flyer and waved it in the air. "Hey, just want to make sure everyone has seen this?"

My face instantly started burning up when the chatter quieted, and a few heads turned our way. One of the boys, a wiry kid with glasses named Jerome, took the flyer from Zihan's hand and squinted at it. "*The Sovereign*?"

"It's Nick's idea," Zihan said, looking back at me. "A paper for the Blue House."

I stood there frozen and embarrassed from the attention . . . but there were murmurs of agreement. Jerome handed the flyer to the boy beside him—James. One by one, the others passed it around, curiosity alighting in their eyes.

"You need writers?" Jerome asked.

"Yeah," I said, feeling a rush of confidence.

"I could do sports," James offered.

"That's good," I said. "We need different sections."

Zihan turned to me, smiling with satisfaction, and I realized in that moment—I liked the new kid! Zihan saw the bigger picture! He'd show up for what mattered! Maybe I could call him a friend.

I caught Zihan's eye, and he nodded. I nodded back, cozy in the comfort that I wasn't figuring this out on my own.

With my dormmates behind me, my defiance toward Charlie only began to blaze brighter. New ideas for how to take matters into my own hands kept running through my head, wherever I went.

As I cooked at Kirby's that weekend, I thought of how I'd need to find a way to print and distribute the paper—how much would that cost?

I'd also need to make sure no one could stop it from getting around. And that it didn't become *too* popular. *What if the White House boys reacted to it the way they did in Greenwood? What if they killed me?*

If only I could live without the constant fear of meeting death just around the corner.

Throughout my shift, when Mr. Kirby spoke to me, it took me seconds to speak back. I was so wrapped up in my paper, and the risk involved with printing it, that I was barely there. When my shift ended, I went outside to flag down a cab, and a scream exploded through the night, "Help!"

It came from a nearby alleyway.

Normally, I wouldn't get involved. But something pulled me toward that scream. I turned into the shadows, my heart drumming as I moved closer, until I saw them—a man was grappling with a woman over a bag, and she was desperate to hold on to it. I was about to call out when I recognized her: Vivian, the hairstylist!

I ran toward them, my pulse racing, but before I'd come up with my next move, the man turned, his eyes dark and cold as he aimed a pistol at my chest. "Back up," he said, his voice like ice.

"Oh, for God's sake, he's a child!" Vivian's voice was laced with fear, but it only made me more determined.

I wouldn't back down! My hands went up slowly to show him I wasn't a threat. As he turned his focus back to Vivian, just for a moment, I seized my chance.

I lunged forward, grabbing his wrist and twisting hard. The gun went off in a deafening blast, the bullet disappearing into the sky. My mind flashed back to that day with my father's killer, along with the anger, the determination to survive. I'd won that fight, and I'd win this one!

I shoved the man backward, sending him stumbling down the alley. In the chaos, Vivian had somehow grabbed his pistol.

She shoved the bag into my hands. We stood there, catching our breath as the man scrambled away, disappearing into the night.

Vivian looked at me with amazement that made me realize—maybe I wasn't a kid anymore?

She broke into a smile, shaking her head as if she'd just witnessed the impossible.

"Thank you, Nick!" she cried, wrapping me in a hug. "You saved me! These streets are dangerous. Come, let's get out of here. Don't want him returning with friends!"

Vivian pulled me down the alleyway, heels clacking at the uneven terrain. She was wearing only a leotard and fishnet stockings. Toothsome curls jumped around her head, and one half of a fake eyelash was dangling off her eye.

"Vivian? Where are we going, exactly?" I followed because I was scared, but I couldn't help but smile about the dark adventure I'd stumbled into.

"It's about time you knew," Vivian replied. "Your cousin keeps saying she wants to keep you out of trouble. But living in the big city? *Trouble finds you anyway.*"

So, Daisy *was* in danger. I knew it!

It got darker as we went, and an increasing amount of trash appeared on the sidewalks that we were traversing. In the streets behind the businesses and tenements were brick buildings that were unassuming on the outside—you'd never know what they were for. They were a grid of rentable suites, up for grabs, but with boarded up windows and rats scurrying along the curbs.

Vivian took me past a squeaky gate, through a lot, and then through a green door. There was a hallway behind it, dimly lit, filled with many doors. We walked straight through it until it opened to a small empty speakeasy, where red leather booths sat behind a counter.

At the back of the bar, nearly hidden in the shadows, a narrow staircase spiraled downward. We descended into the basement, stepping into a warehouse packed with trolleys, crates, and carts. A faint, toxic tang lingered in the air as we weaved through the maze of supplies.

My eyes darted around, searching for Daisy—something told me she had been here before.

Finally, we stopped in a room that looked like a kitchen—or a science lab. There were several counters, with liquid flowing through glass jars and tubing.

A big woman in a black tailored suit was sitting in a throne-like chair at the far end of the room. Her face was round and assertive, and a cigar smoked from between her fingertips. Her hair was long, half natural and half braided down. Another woman stood by her side braiding the rest of her hair. They both looked at us.

"Who's this?" the sitting woman asked, raising an eyebrow.

I swallowed as I took in her commanding presence. My eyes surveyed the room until I saw someone familiar pouring liquor into a bottle. I had to squint some, but I knew that face. "Daisy!"

Daisy looked up and her eyes widened. "Nick?" She dropped the bottle.

"Jordan!" the sitting woman shouted as the bottle exploded, spilling glass and pungent fluid all over the floor.

Daisy jumped away from the spill. "Oh, goodness."

The throne woman sighed and dragged a hand over her face. "Daisy—I love you, but that's *six dollars*."

"I'm sorry," Daisy said, seeming flustered. "I'll clean it up. This is my cousin, Nick. Nick . . . Jordan."

"Ahhh," Jordan purred. "Li'l cousin. How's your melancholia doing?"

"Hello," I offered with a wave, but the scene before me was unsettling. I did not know this person who clearly knew some of me.

"Sorry," Daisy said, hurrying toward me. "Could I have a moment?"

Daisy pulled me off to a small hallway, and through a door that led to a bathroom. The tub was full of clear liquid and the toilet was surrounded by a chaos of wires. "Are you following me again?" she asked.

"Huh? I wasn't!" I protested.

"You weren't?" She squinted at me. *"Really?"*

"No! It was Vivian. She was fighting with some guy in an alleyway, and I had to step in. She was the one who brought us here."

Daisy put both hands on her forehead in annoyance. "I told her I didn't want to get you in trouble."

"Funny, Vivian said the same thing. But what *trouble* are we talking about, Daisy?"

She looked at me. "First things first—what you see here can't leave here. You can't tell my parents."

"I would have to know the *what* of it all first!"

"Keep your voice down and I'll tell you," Daisy whispered to me, though it was clear she would scream if she could. Once it was clear that I was holding my tongue, she continued somberly, "You know how the mob just up and killed your people? Well, in New York, their mindsets are no better, but they're craftier in their attacks. They do it while pretending to be our friends. Jordan learned that the hard way.

"She was a housekeeper to a wealthy man—lonely, kind at first. When he passed away, she thought she'd earned his trust and a share in his business, but one of his associates, a bootlegger, betrayed her, and stole her money, framing her for his crimes. That left her to fend for herself. From then on, she swore she'd never trust another man with her livelihood."

So that's why the man was accosting Vivian—for the liquor in her bag.

I almost wanted to laugh in disbelief. "You're not serious?" Auntie Lorraine and Uncle Beet would be beside themselves if they knew!

"Keep your lips sealed," Daisy said, grabbing my arms in an appeal for trust, her eyes desperately searching mine. "Tom Buchanan is trying to take over the Wash 'N' Fold. He keeps making the rent more expensive in the area, hoping everyone will give up and leave. And with school tuition already paid, and no refunds, I can't just drop out, even if I want to. Our family's barely holding on. If I don't bring in money for us, we might be next to pack up and run."

"I . . . won't tell a soul," I said. "I don't talk to anyone anyway. I'm only surprised! I'd never believe you were running liquor in your free time."

Daisy didn't look too proud of it. "It's the only way to make enough money to support the family. Seems like you've been surrounding yourself with the wrong crowd too, because the Gatsbys? They're also bootleggers." Daisy laughed without any joy and waved a languid hand. "They sell their liquor to clients in Harlem who have no money and drink to kill the pain."

"So, the rumors of Gatsby Sr. being a criminal are true?" I asked, stunned.

"Of course they're true! That's the only reason I talk to Jay. Jordan knows the right people to bring his father more business in this part of New York. Gatsby's got connections, but mostly with rich men who get their liquor elsewhere—so he's looking for a new deal."

So, Gatsby made a school that helped people succeed in life but also played a role in flooding Harlem with liquor? No wonder Jay treated drinking like it was nothing at The Green Light.

"Now come, we can't keep Jordan waiting. Always be respectful to her," Daisy said in warning, as she pushed me back to the kitchen. And then she whispered, "She has something of a temper. And do not mention Jay Gatsby or—"

"What are you two talking about over there?" Jordan called from across the kitchen.

It was too late for Daisy to finish her instructions. Instead, she announced to the room, "Just giving him the rundown," and went to start unloading gallon glass bottles from a bag.

Vivian came and grabbed my arm to present me before Jordan. "Nick saved my life! You should've seen him! I had no idea he had so much man in him!"

"Thanks?" I said.

"So, Nick," Jordan said. "I can see that Daisy thinks very fondly of you. You saved Vivian, so I like you too. I won't ask you to replace the spilled liquor, even though it was your presence that sent Daisy halfway to heaven and caused it to spill in the first place. But I do have a question. What is it that you do?"

"Well, they've got me operating elevators at West Egg," I said with a shrug.

"Elevators?" She shook her head. "Nah, you're way too smart for that." Jordan snapped and her attendant brought me a picture of Tom Buchanan. "You ever seen this money-hungry slug before?"

I looked at Daisy, who was still distracted, or at least pretending to be so.

"In photos, I have . . . yes," I finally said.

"This man sold his shopping center to Jay Gatsby Sr. so he could build West Egg Academy. They're business partners, but that's a problem—Mr. Buchanan's a man of poor integrity, which puts Mr. Gatsby's character into question too. And now Gatsby's son has been showing up at UNIA meetings, leaving everyone to wonder what he's after."

"Shouldn't he attend the meetings?" I asked. "He is Colored."

"If you call that Colored," Jordan snorted.

"Do you have to be purely Colored to attend UNIA?"

"Not the point. The point is the father has been in contact with me. He thinks his bootlegging business could be doing better here in Central Harlem, and I agree. Our business is too small to meet all the demand, but if Gatsby handles production and we handle distribution, then everyone gets rich."

Jordan snapped again and the attendant brought me another piece of paper. This one was a flyer, which said,

NOTICE!

IF YOU ARE INTERESTED IN THE DEVELOPMENT OF YOUR RACE, YOU WILL ATTEND:

THE UNIVERSAL NEGRO IMPROVEMENT ASSOCIATION MEETING IN CENTRAL HARLEM

6 TO 9 P.M.

LIVE ART! PERFORMANCE THEATER! AN ADDRESS FROM GARVEY AND MORE!

"They say the enemy never shows you both hands," Jordan went on. "I'm not sure I can trust this . . . Mr. Gatsby. Especially not with Jay Jr. popping up at the very meetings that run counter to his papa's missions. The son could be a spy for his father—invading my territory and stealing it without us noticing. I tell you what, Nick. I'm looking for someone to push a service cart at the next UNIA meeting to earn me some patrons. Find Gatsby at the event, watch him, report back to me what he does, and I'll give you a hefty reward?"

Jordan snapped again, and this time the picture that landed in my hands was one of Jay, a few years younger. He was sitting in a chair, deadpanning the camera. His father stood behind him, smiling. The photo was so staged and stale that it made me uncomfortable.

"What kind of reward?" I asked.

The attendant pulled a briefcase off the counter and cracked it open. Inside was a blanket of dollar bills.

"How's three hundred dollars?" Jordan said.

Three hundred dollars. My first association with three hundred dollars was that I could use it to fund my own paper. I hadn't touched the money we pulled from those safes under Mr. Wallace's floor, and I didn't want to. It came with ghosts. But Jordan's money? It wouldn't haunt me. It would be mine.

Jordan leaned forward and squinted at me. "No more buying out the blocks we work from. The public ain't ready for Harlem! Harlem is our turf. If Gatsby wants to do business here, he does it our way—and no way else. What do you say?"

I looked over at Daisy. She was busy with unscrewing the lid off a bottle and pouring the contents into a gallon jug, but I could tell her ear was tilted toward us. She'd already accepted her own invitation into this seedy operation, and that made this mobster life seem less scary and more approachable.

"You want me to spy on Jay Gatsby Jr.?" I asked Jordan.

"Correct. Daisy's trying her best, but it's difficult. Jay Jr. is easy enough to find but hard to get close to. You go to school with him; you could get unique intelligence."

I didn't want this. I didn't want to spy on a new friend—one of the only true friends I'd made in Harlem. How could I?

"I don't think I can do this," I said. "Jay seems like a good person."

"*Seems like*," Jordan echoed as she lifted a cigar to her lips, took a puff, and blew out smoke. "There are plenty of people with fake faces with cracks you can only see up close."

"I think that's enough." Daisy finished her duties and came to grab me by my arm, getting in the middle of the conversation before I could respond. "We should get home before it's too dark."

"Yes, we've had enough drama for one night," Jordan said, looking pointedly at me. "But take some time to think it over. The offer stays open until the next meeting."

New York—you're way too fast-paced for me! I was expected to process twists and turns faster than I could figure out what my purpose was here.

I folded the picture of Jay into my pocket, and we turned to leave.

Daisy stomped and ranted on our walk home. "I cannot believe Vivian led you to the gang! I specifically told her not to."

"What does it matter?" I asked. "Is there a *right way* to tell me you were gangsters? I can't believe Vivian was serious about that whole *street life* conversation."

"Gangsters?" Daisy stopped walking in the middle of the street, exasperated, and threw her hands up. "Well, when you put it that way, Nick! Jesus." She slumped, looking more defeated than defiant.

"Not at all!" I pulled her to the sidewalk just as a reckless car sped by. "Actually, I was thinking as risky as it sounds, bootlegging might pay better than any normal job. Three hundred dollars a task? That's a fortune."

Daisy sighed and kept walking. "It's good money, yes. I've been sneaking some of my earnings into the Wash 'N' Fold's register to chip in at home." She turned to me, serious. "But I can't let my parents know. They've got enough to worry about with Buchanan pressing us to sell our house for his apartment complex. He makes it impossible to keep what's ours. I'd die if I had to work under him forever."

Daisy's eyes darkened when she spoke of him. There was a depth of frustration there. And perhaps the respect she carried for Jordan came from the fact that she gave her the power to stand up to men like him. I could see why Daisy would admire her business acumen and get involved with something like this. Jordan seemed ruthless and strong—important survival qualities anyone would need to fight for their family's legacy.

"I get it. Pushing elevator buttons isn't exactly thrilling for me either," I admitted. "But it's safe. And clean, I guess."

Daisy turned to me. "You know, I'd hate to see you get tangled up in something dangerous, but if you ever *really* needed money, just know you have options."

"Isn't bootlegging like delivering milk, but illegal?" I asked, trying to lighten the mood.

Daisy laughed, amused. "If you want to see it that way, I suppose you could."

So, her double life came with secrets, danger, and money—that added context to her late nights and expensive-looking clothes.

It was tempting to be a part of, because work felt meaningless sometimes and the few coins Mr. Kirby handed over weren't nearly enough to pay for anything important. Could a side job really hurt?

Even as I asked myself and wavered on my decision to pass on the job, I remembered Jordan was the kind of person who paid people well but demanded loyalty.

And I had been raised to think alcohol was an enemy. Grandma had made sure of that. But Jay didn't think it was so bad. Daisy didn't either. Perhaps the rules changed as people aged.

I glanced at Daisy, wondering how she balanced it. How did she deal with the weight of protecting her family and putting herself at risk? And Vivian—she was a good friend to Daisy, loyal and willing to take risks alongside her. She must have been pulled in for the same reasons: the need to survive, the lure of something bigger than the daily grind. They were partners, allies, both trying their best to navigate a world they couldn't fully trust.

"Nick, don't do it just because it seems like the easy way," Daisy said, reading my expression and pulling me out of my thoughts. She looked at me with a mix of worry and care, as if she didn't want to set the wrong example.

But it was more than it being easy. I couldn't really say it how I wanted to, but West Egg felt like it was pushing me out more each day. If it had been someone other than Jay, I may have taken Jordan up on her offer. I wanted something more out of this world. And I was willing to take a risk for it, but I wasn't willing to risk Jay.

The train horn and locomotive relaxed me as I worked my next shift at Kirby's. I had to keep moving—mopping, washing dishes, and cooking—because I couldn't believe my very own cousin was involved in organized crime. And mere nights ago, I was brushing elbows with liquor runners in some underground lair? What had this life become?

After a few weeks of working the diner, I'd gotten mostly used to the patrons. They were older folk who'd known Kirby for a long time. I thought that was all I should expect, until Jay walked through the door.

I instantly went to hide in the kitchen, but I turned and saw him looking for a booth before slipping through the door. I thought of him too much as of late, and my decision to protect our friendship over Jordan's proposal to become her spy. He'd see it all over my face. The pride in my choice to save us.

Get it together, Nick.

I'd never had this problem before. But the thought of his face, and his body, made my chest lift like a helium balloon.

I tightened the strings on my apron so they hitched over my butt and shook out my hands. *Why so much tension? Why?*

Finally, I went to get his order and he said, "Hello, Nick" as if he was fully aware he'd find me here. He folded his arms on the table. "I'll have wheat toast, eggs, and country potatoes, please."

Was he toying with me? Trying to keep the dynamic strictly professional after nearly asking me to a dance? What was his end game?

I could play along too. I wrote words on a pad while he watched the cars whoosh by the windows. "Coming right up," I said, and turned to take the order to the kitchen.

Through the kitchen window, I occasionally watched him writing in a notebook. When the cook left his food waiting on the counter, I took the breakfast plate to his table, and he whispered a thank-you.

But as I whisked away with various duties about the restaurant, I could not escape Jay.

He called me over once for salt. And then again for red chili flakes. A third time for garlic aioli. I started to become suspicious as I chopped it together, squirting mayo into the cloves, adding a sprinkle of thyme. He kept looking for reasons to call me over.

Jay stayed until the patrons left, and it was just him wrapped in his solitude and perfect concentration.

I'd gotten to wiping down the table just across from his when a man barged into the diner, nearly knocking the doorbell loose, shouting, "I see Tom Buchanan ain't bought you out yet, Mr. Kirby!"

"I wish Mr. Tom the besta luck wrenchin' this mop out my Black-ass hands!" Mr. Kirby, who was sweeping behind the counter, screamed out. And then both men started laughing.

After what Daisy had said about Tom Buchanan, I started to notice signs of his plans to buy out family-run stores to build more flashy apartments all over Harlem. I'd seen his face on posters around town—he was the man you called for all your real estate needs. He wasn't above calling on you either, which was clear enough with his pursuit of the Wash 'N' Fold. The integrated school was only a trifling project compared to his many enterprises.

"Good to know someone in this city still has integrity," Jay said, looking at me to see if I'd respond. I didn't know what to make of his comment.

He gave an awkward shrug at my silence.

"Yeah, Mr. Kirby's a good man," I offered, finally. And then, it just slipped out. "Why did you come here?"

Jay looked shocked. "What? Why not?"

"I mean, here of all places? A little diner in Central Harlem?"

Then, his face relaxed, as he accepted the challenge. "Why did you come to the pool when I was doing my laps?"

I plopped into the booth. "I had no idea you would even be in there."

"Okay. Likewise. I'm here because I wanted country potatoes." He stared at me for a few seconds. I tried to discern if it was a lie but couldn't. His face carried this immovable calm, a preparation for anything. I looked at him and wondered, *Where did you come from?*

"Didn't think I'd see you here," Jay added, breaking the silence.

I shrugged. "I work the late shift on weekends."

"Ah. I thought for sure you'd be tucked into bed at this hour."

His tone made my chest burn—was he calling me a baby? "What are you getting at?"

Jay chuckled and then straightened his face. "It's just you seemed rather . . . *cautious* the night we met."

"I wouldn't say that. It was a chance encounter. I was taken off guard."

"Of course. And you've joined me in the booth because you're looking for a second chance to prove yourself," Jay said, point blank.

The suddenness of that made me hesitate. I finally answered, "That night was cut rather short, but I wouldn't say *looking*."

"Ha!" Jay blurted, and then gave a satisfied smile. "You admitted it. You wanted more."

Why was this so satisfying for him? "I only wanted to make sure it wasn't some strange dream, as soon after it happened you treated me like we'd never spoken in person before."

"I really just prefer to write letters in the beginning," Jay said plainly.

But you're so personable in real life, I wanted to say. I held my tongue.

Was I in a state of endless wanting for something to revive my enthusiasm for life? Had he picked up on it before me?

"Anyway, this conversation settles it," Jay said, with a shrug. "I will see you at the dance."

I smiled against my will and stood up to mind some other business. I couldn't allow him to see me turning red, to see how much his invitation to escape the confining pens of work and school truly meant to me.

I started my cleaning again and began folding the chairs up on the freestanding tables. All I said to Jay was, "I suppose I have no choice but to be there."

And he looked more satisfied than he had all night.

Most of the lights went off, leaving his face half in shadow.

Mr. Kirby came from the back and looked at Jay. "It's closing time, brother."

Jay stood and gave us both a formal nod, but his eyes lingered on me. "If you would like to do something sooner, there's a UNIA meeting later this week." Jay pulled a flyer from his jacket and handed it to me.

This forced me to think back to Jordan's offer—something I still felt guilty for considering, if only briefly. "Okay, sure."

Jay was too nice for me to play games with him for money. All I really wanted was to understand him and discover why he seemed to carry weight on his shoulders, though he made it look effortless. Going to the meeting would be a way to get to know him better, and *that* was more fascinating to me than the offer of quick cash.

9.

FOR DAYS AFTERWARD, I WAS BUZZING WITH something foreign and light. But when I got back to Room 17 on Thursday afternoon, I instantly knew something was wrong.

The door was slightly open as if someone had been there. It looked like it was left that way on purpose. And as I stepped in, I saw the wreckage—drawers pulled open, clothes scattered across the floor.

My heart beat harder as I took in the mess and searched around to make sure my stuff was here. Most of it was . . . but the rest of the flyers I'd made for my paper . . . gone. Some rough drafts and notes I had for the content were also missing, and with them, my plans to shed light on the problems at school no one else dared to talk about.

I picked up one of my notebooks lying open on the floor. Its pages had been rifled through. Whoever did this wanted to put an end to my paper, and I already had a good idea who that person might be.

Charlie. He was one of the only people outside the Blue House who even knew about my intentions with this, who had both the power and the reason to shut me down. He'd mocked me ever since I arrived and was ready to ruin anything he saw as a threat to his world here.

I sank down onto the bed and looked at the floor.

Now what? I needed funds to print my paper—no way I'd be able to use the *Chronicle*'s mimeograph if they were this against me. I'd nearly run through the spare money I made working for Kirby. Was there anyone else I could ask?

Well, there was one, but just thinking about it felt like betrayal.

What was spying, really? Was going out with someone, picking up on information, and telling someone else about it all I had to do? That was merely gossip, wasn't it? Everyone did it.

Three hundred dollars for just a few pieces of information.

But what if . . . what if Jordan *did* something to Jay? Jay had been there for me. He'd understood me.

His invitation to the dance was something to mull over when I felt lonely, something to look forward to. We were building something, though I was not sure what just yet. If I gave that up for a quick buck, what kind of person would I be? A traitor—that's what!

But I also couldn't let Charlie win.

Tonight's UNIA meeting would be a chance to learn from people who'd fought back against people bigger than Charlie—and won. If there was one place to find inspiration, it was there. The robber could wait.

Right now, I needed to see what strength looked like in real life.

The UNIA church was on 135th at 40 West. It was a big stone fixture with three floors and a big steeple that supported its Roman Catholic design.

When I arrived, a crowd of people out front was making their way in, but Jay was arguing with a guard. She stood even taller than him, like a pillar in front of the door, burly arms crossed.

He noticed me and instantly told the guard, "See, this is my friend! We go to school together."

The woman raised an eyebrow at him. "I didn't ask who you go to school with. I asked for a name."

"It's . . . it's um . . ." He looked up as if he'd find his name in the sky.

"Jay Jr.," I offered.

"That's it," Jay said. "Silly me. Forgetting my own name."

Was I not supposed to reveal that? I thought with a tremor of horror at possibly having blown his cover.

"What is your business with the UNIA?" the guard asked. "Our focus here is on increasing the wealth of Colored people. And according to every other issue of *The Saturday Evening Post*, your family is already rich."

"Well, I wouldn't say rich."

"You wouldn't? You live with your white father in a mansion that could house a good part of this city's population."

"The mansion isn't ours," Jay said. "We only rent it."

"The point stands," said the guard. "It's suspect that you show interest in our movement at all, as someone who comes from wealth. Now run along."

"He's a friend to me," I said, stepping forward. "And as the son of West Egg's founder, his perspective is from right inside the heart of the integration movement. He could use the education he'll find here to help his father make our school better. Could he stay, please?"

The guard squinted at me, and then her expression softened as she finally resigned. "Fine," she said, standing aside. "You make a good case . . . but if he does something that harms the group, it's on you."

"He won't," I said. "I promise."

"Thank you, miss," Jay said as we entered. And then he whispered to me, "Is that all it took?"

I shrugged. "Sometimes I'll need your help gaining entry to places, and sometimes you'll need mine."

People who were lounging in the entryway looked at him when we walked in, but Jay seemed used to the stares and ignored them. He was comfortable beyond the doors, unbothered to be recognized as a person of status, or by the fact that he was lighter than most in the room.

An article about West Egg was the front-page story on a news rack—"Can Negroes Enter into Upper Echelon Society? A Deep Dive into the West Egg Experiment." I wished I could have set my own papers on the rack beneath it. That way, organizers would know about what was really happening in Harlem's so-called "integrated" schooling.

We continued walking and entered the nave, where wine-colored pews led to an open altar.

"We ought to be careful," Jay said, as we scanned the crowd, full of people in suits, feathered hats, and berets. "The federal government's waging a war against the speaker of the event as we speak."

"Of course," I said. "Garvey is a truth-teller, so why wouldn't they?"

"*And* he combines the two things America hates most," Jay said. "Colored people and Communism."

"So, you're telling me we should be prepared to run?" I asked.

Before Jay could answer, the lights went down on the crowd and up on a stage. We found our seats beside each other as the event began. First was a comedy sketch about buffoon police patrols in New York chasing down a thief. And next, there were some Swanee Bottom dancers, and then Mr. Garvey took the stage.

He wore a suit of fine wool and stood tall and powerful, with a posture that screamed leadership. Everyone cheered so loudly when he took the podium that he had to raise both hands and wait for the crowd to be silent. He smiled, and then his expression grew serious as the people quieted.

"May it please your Highness the Potentate, Right Honorable Members of the Executive Council, Deputies and Delegates to the Second International Convention of Negroes of the World, Ladies and Gentlemen," he announced. "I desire to give you a message; one that you will, I hope, take home and propagate among the scattered millions of Africa's sons and daughters."

He talked about his world travels and how wherever he went, he realized that Colored people's conditions were decrepit. Everywhere, Colored people were thought to be at the bottom of an imaginary scale. As free Negroes in America, it was our job to change that reality.

Listening to him made me feel free. Larger than life! Like I could do more, be more, regardless of how small West Egg taught me to be.

BANG!

The sound made me jump and turn to Jay.

BANG! BANG!

Someone was at the church doors. Garvey stopped and the noise continued. The guards at the door looked as though they didn't know what to do.

"Police!" the banging people outside screamed. "Open up!"

The guards blocked the doors, until the cops finally gave up. There was a period of silence. And—*BOOM!*

It was the thunderous sound of a battering ram, slamming the doors open. People instantly began to flee in various directions as the cops barged through the splintered wood and dust, screaming and swinging their night sticks to threaten us into dispersing.

"Okay, okay," Garvey said from the stage, trying to calm people down, but everybody fled anyway.

Jay grabbed me by the arm and took me away from the pews, deeper into the church. I looked over my shoulder and recognized a face among the older cops—a junior cop.

Cannon Cleary, dressed in a hat too tall for him, was smacking a nightstick against his hand. "Show's over, Commies!" he screamed, just as he made eye contact with me.

Jay pulled me through a door behind the church stage. Back here was a corridor of old brick, hidden in shadows.

Cannon weaved around the running crowd to pursue us. I followed Jay down the corridor, wondering how he knew this structure so intimately. This passageway seemed to have been half discovered by the builders of the place. It felt like it was indoors, but it was also open to the sky. It was a secret exit, which connected the church to the building next door.

We stopped at a ladder embedded into the wall of the neighboring building. Jay jumped on it and began to climb. I followed behind him, but when I was halfway up, I looked down and saw Cannon climbing up after me, the megaphone hanging from around his neck.

"You're under arrest, Clumsy Nick!" he screamed, as if this were all a joke.

The rungs were slippery, but I climbed as fast as I could, as wind swept through the channel and threatened to throw me off.

Jay reached the roof and turned to pull me up. I was on my feet on solid ground seconds later, and we ran across this roof, dodging the various pipes and chimneys sticking up from it.

Harlem extended before us like an industrial obstacle course. Roofs of varying heights and powerlines, like jungle vines, invited us to swing. Jay jumped between two buildings, rolled to standing, and sprung to his feet as if an audience should give him a round of applause.

"Jump, Nick!" he screamed.

I hesitated and assessed how much damage I'd take if I fell. There was definitely a chance I'd suffer a spinal fracture.

"Freeze, Clumsy Nick!" Cannon screamed.

"Jump!" Jay shouted.

I took a few steps back, said a little prayer to Jesus—we were friends in moments like these—and I jumped! For a moment, the slick alley dangled underneath me, and my arms were level with the telephone wire. Suspended in air, I thought of everything I'd ever done, everything I wanted to do!

And then I landed on the next roof across, my toes brushing the edge of the building.

Jay reached forward and pulled me closer to the center, his manner intimate, as if we'd been friends for much longer. Cannon jumped too, but he didn't make it. He was half hanging on the side of the building when I turned around, and Jay pretended not to see it.

"Do we help him?" I asked, stopping.

"Not at all," Jay said calmly. "Cannon's joining the police force. He should have the training to help himself! Isn't that right?"

As we watched Cannon claw and slip on the roof, I wondered if letting him fall to his doom was really worth it. And I decided it would make me miserable, even if I didn't like him.

I moved to turn back to help, but just then he finally made it and rolled over on his back. I sighed with relief as I watched him, thanking the stars he was still alive.

"Dear God," he said, eyes closed, breath heavy. "I know in my loyal heart that you'll punish these ridiculous radicals for almost *killing me*! I *release* it to you!"

Jay cupped his hands around his mouth and screamed, "You're a bootlicker, Cannon!" He snickered and pulled me by the arm, toward the edge of the building.

"One day you and your conman father will pay for your crimes!" Cannon screamed after us, his voice fading.

Jay swung onto the fire escape, his shoes clanging against metal as he vaulted over the railing and slid down the ladder. I scrambled after him, my pulse hammering, hands gripping cold iron. The wind rushed past us as we leapt onto a narrow platform, then barreled down two flights of steep stairs, the whole structure rattling under our weight.

At the bottom, a ten-foot gap stretched before us. No time to think. Jay hurled himself forward, landing hard on a trash can lid. I followed, crashing down, the impact jolting through my bones as we tumbled onto the alley pavement in a tangle of limbs and breathless laughter.

"Wow!" I screamed as I stood up. My heart was going to explode—I couldn't catch my breath! I stretched my arms to the sky before a backdrop of shops that were closing up. The Harlem air tasted so fresh! "I can't believe I made that jump. Are you insane, Jay? We could've died!"

Jay stood up and pondered it. "But we *didn't* die. Which is fantastic news, and the fun of it all!" He waved down a cab. "What do you say we get somewhere safe?"

I simply followed, sliding inside the back seat and rolling down the windows. The night melted around us. The wind raced through my ears, as the city passed us by in shades of red, blue, and orange.

"Come with me to my home tonight," Jay said.

I straightened my neck a bit. Surely the wind eclipsed his words, and I heard wrong. "What?"

"I insist," he said, with a smile, which made me certain he was serious.

"That's . . . unexpected. All the way to Long Island proper? *The* Long Island," I said. "Is it an actual island? Like Coney Island?"

"I live on a lake, so it looks like an island, but you can get to it by car."

"Okay. Why not?" I went along with it because I lacked motivation to decide what to do next. Plus, the first part of the evening was fun!

I liked Jay, but as much as I yearned for his friendship, part of my brain couldn't trust him fully. It whispered that all the mysteries I wished for Jay to reveal about himself could also hide untold dangers, the very dangers that made Jordan so wary of the Gatsbys. The only way to know if that part of my brain was irrational was to spend more time with him.

The plot that his home was built on must have been two hundred acres. In fact, you could build four different houses in the space that was occupied by long, trimmed hedges and walkways.

A gate opened to a long driveway where ground lights led us

down a gravel path. A roundabout circled a fountain, where a statue was also illuminated by tiny lights. I tried to subdue my wonder to act like I'd been somewhere similar before. The closest I'd come was the Vanderbilt estate where Isaiah worked, but that home did not have quite as much space on the property, nor did it have as many windows or a long staircase leading up to where the house really was.

Questions popped into my mind as we left the vehicle, like, *Who waters the plants and the flowers? And does the fountain never stop? Who could manage all this space?*

"So . . . you live here," I said, unable to hold my awe in as I looked up at the double-door entryway, the ivy which crept up the cream-colored limestone walls.

He shrugged and jammed his hands into his pockets. "For now, yeah. We've got too much space, if you ask me."

Jay's house seemed even bigger inside—so big I couldn't imagine it only belonged to one family. But it did. In the lobby, a long staircase led to an upstairs balcony that could be seen from the front door. The entire house was like a breath of fresh air.

"Must be nice to have the whole place to yourself," I said as I followed him up the stairs.

"Is it nice if all you hear day in and day out are empty echoes? My father is off purchasing land in Canada, so he's not here much lately. I spend most of my time alone, listening to the fountains and playing with my little cat, Meowy."

Once we reached upstairs, said little cat appeared from around the corner and nuzzled up to his leg. Jay gave Meowy an affectionate pat on the head and started speaking in a baby voice. His humor made me smile, though what he was saying was impossible to understand.

The upstairs was a vast expanse, so open that several rooms came into view at once—the entryway and two lavish rooms on opposite sides of the hall. The hallway stretched like a regal boulevard, its polished marble floor and intricate moldings seeming allergic to dirt.

Mid-hallway, nestled into the wall like a secret alcove, was a narrow passage leading to a miniature hallway—a curious space that added depth to the otherwise airy place.

We paused near a sliding ladder, perched at the edge of a mahogany bookshelf that stretched up to five levels. At the foot of the ladder stood a table. Small magazines lay atop it, alongside classics of literature, political theory, and a literary magazine.

I picked up the magazine, impressed by the array of genres found here, and began reading a poem. *"I bathed in the Euphrates when dawns were young—"*

"I built my hut near the Congo and it lulled me to sleep," Jay finished, focusing on me. "That's a beautiful poem you were mumbling."

"Langston Hughes."

"Promising new talent. He lives here in New York. I try to read as many Negro writers as I can. Not out of any guiding principle but because . . . what else is there to do?"

That was true—what else was there to do? Life was boring.

"I'm surprised," I said. "I just thought you'd study the likes of Edgar Rice Burroughs and Sigmund Freud." *White writers* was the postscript I didn't add. *Not the Negro poets.*

"I understand why you'd make that assumption." He looked at me with concealed offense, but tensely added, "It must be hard for you to come from the South and trust anyone with white in their blood." Jay left the study and guided us to his bedroom as he spoke. "I do care though, about Negro culture and politics. It's why I convinced Father to start West Egg in the first place."

Jay's bedroom was softened with a Persian rug. He had a grand four-poster bed with a carved wooden frame, a red sofa, and a desk cluttered with papers, an inkwell, and a few sketches. I spotted a hand plane, chisels, and measuring tapes stored in a leather tool roll. There was a big unfinished wooden sculpture—like a canoe—in the corner. It looked like a hobby project.

I waited at the entrance as Jay opened the doors to a connected balcony, which overlooked the back lawn and a lake.

"Come outside!" he called.

So I joined him there. On the other side of the water was an enormous white mansion whose splendor took my breath away!

"Who lives there?" I asked.

"Tom Buchanan—Charlie's father, as you know." Jay tilted his head at the view. "But so different from my father that I find it strange they work together. My father respects him, so I guess I have to as well, but Tom's got this cold way about him. I think he's trying to take over Harlem and make sure regular people can't afford to live there anymore."

I silently nodded without surprise. Buchanan seemed awful by the way Daisy reacted to his name.

"My father does it differently," Jay said, a little spark in his eyes. "He's buying up more properties to rent to Colored folks because he believes we should all be able to share this city. But, sometimes you have to work with people you don't exactly like to get things done."

"Is that so?" I squinted at him. "Couldn't your dad find someone else to work with besides the guy who doesn't want Negroes living in Harlem?"

Jay refused eye contact with me. "I can't answer for him," he said quietly. "He does things the way he wants to do them. But it's important to note the Gatsbys laid the groundwork."

"*Hello*?" called a voice from downstairs, which made me jump.

Jay barely acknowledged it. He seemed to need a moment to release tension from his system. Then he called, "Coming!" in response to the voice.

He walked back down the hallway, and to the balcony that overlooked the entry way. Standing on the plush rug was a tall, strapping white man in a vest, observing himself in a mirror.

"Mr. Buchanan!" Jay said with fake enthusiasm. "Nice to see you."

The man turned to smile, and his presence made me shrink back even from so far up. His hair was dark and his eyes piercing blue. His sharp jaw framed a face that could charm anyone, despite the person behind it.

"Good evening, Jay," Tom said. "I was hoping your father might be back by now. The property investment group delivered his letter to my place by mistake."

"He returns on Wednesday," Jay said. "But if you leave it on the table, I'll be sure he gets it."

Buchanan looked at me suddenly like my presence had fished him out of the conversation.

"Oh, this is my friend, Nick Carrington," Jay said.

"How do you do, Nick?" Buchanan said, stiffly. He gave me a look that made me shiver, though it was not technically friendly or hostile. It was as if he was observing a creature in the wild.

"Fine, thank you."

He walked farther into the entryway, as if he were used to being here, his polished shoes clicking on the marble floor. A golden pocket watch chain hung from his vest, a testament to his wealth.

"Does your father know you have boys over when he's away?" he asked Jay, voice low and disciplinary, with a subtle accent from somewhere in New York.

There was an uncomfortable silence, as Buchanan watched Jay with suspicion, as if he'd been appointed as a nanny in his father's absence.

"My father lets me make my own choices," Jay said in a guarded way.

Buchanan raised his eyebrows. "He takes an interesting approach to fathering. We never could get on the same page with that, could we?"

Jay didn't say anything, but I could tell he wanted to. The man had thrown him off-kilter.

And Buchanan seemed satisfied by his shakiness, and it made

him smile wider. "Good evening to you, Jay," he said abruptly and left without looking at me.

When Buchanan disappeared from view, Jay snapped back from his temporary haze and smiled gently at me. "Shall we?" And he nodded back to his room.

I followed him and asked quietly, "Does your father allow anyone to walk in like that?" Buchanan was not here, but his presence lingered.

"Oh, we're very familiar," Jay said, still looking disturbed. "Buchanan has lived across the lake ever since we've lived in New York, although I've never much liked him."

The niceties of the rich felt very fraudulent, but I didn't want to insult Jay's father to his face.

"I never felt like I got to say thank you to you," I said, in an effort to lighten the mood. "Most white boys—I mean, White House boys—wouldn't even make an attempt to stand up for a Blue boy getting bullied."

"You said white," Jay said, looking at me intensely. "Do you see me as white?"

What do the white people see? I almost asked—that's what mattered most. I knew he was a Negro. If it weren't for his mild brown skin tone, I'd spot the giveaway in his full lips, or his hair, obviously thicker than a white person's. And because of those features, I didn't feel the need to be on my toes with him.

Still, I could see how they might not know. In the right suit, with gelled hair, in a club with low lights, he could pass for Italian. Especially with the way he stood—straight-backed—and given his speech patterns, which were clean and polished. He had no Southern drawl, no slouch in his vowels. He spoke like the radio announcers and politicians.

I wasn't sure how he'd take my observations, so I kept them to myself. "I can tell that you're not white," I said, measuredly.

Jay looked away, his mouth hardening some, a muscle jumping in his cheek. "People see what they want. One look at a Mulatto makes people on both sides want to start a war, and there's nothing I can do about it."

"Of course. You represent where this country is going, if we can put down the pitchforks."

"Do you think they ever will?" he asked, a tinge of optimism in his voice.

I shrugged. "One can only hope."

"The divide is everywhere. In my friendships and my family. My parents divorcing."

I could tell just the thought of that bothered him, but I didn't want to pry. And I didn't want to talk about my own parents either lest I start crying in the middle of a regular conversation.

I uncovered another piece of Jay. But I didn't know his father, not truly. If my relationship with my own father was any indication, sons and fathers could see things very differently.

How independent was Jay? Did he deserve my full trust?

Greenwood's fate had taught me that anything horrible could come along and shock me at any given moment. But I knew that for the moment at least, his presence was a gift that made New York a worthwhile destination to start my life anew.

10.

I WAS ON MY WAY TO PRACTICAL MECHANICS when I noticed people looking at me strangely in the hallway. I thought there might be something on my face—*donut cream?*—and made a note to check myself in the mirror before class. But there was nothing there.

Someone I didn't know from the Blue House—a boy who mostly focused on where he was going—came up to me, looking suspicious.

"You and Jay?" the person said. "Y'all seem close."

My body froze with terror. "What?"

"The letters." He pointed to a newspaper clipping taped to the wall above the water fountain across the hall.

I ran over, pulled it down, and scanned it. It seemed someone had reprinted Jay's letters to me and written commentary in the margins.

"Are Nick Carrington and Jay Gatsby Lovers?" said the headline. "Read The Daily Dish for More!"

Artie . . . His column in the paper—the Daily Dish. He was dissecting every sentence of the letters and questioning what it meant about our feelings for each other.

My palms were sweating, my whole body hot, like a piece of ham on burning asphalt.

Everybody—not just this kid—was looking at me. There were three crowds of people around—where did they come from? Some tilted their heads, others laughed.

The boy who'd spoken seemed both amused and sympathetic. "Don't be so rattled. If it makes you feel better, I think people had already noticed."

I fled from the conversation, down hallways and back to my dorm. Scrambling to lift my cot—where I had hidden my letters from Jay—I knew they'd be gone.

The mess of my ransacked things made it impossible to tell when they had been taken. We had stopped writing to each other a while ago, now that we were talking face-to-face. Had they disappeared with the flyers and notes about my paper?

What a stroke of luck for the thief! To have not only found my writings but the letters as well—it was all they would need to ruin my life at West Egg!

Jay . . . I had to find Jay.

I ran toward the quad, shoes scraping the stone ground heavily, and scanned the yard, all the disc-throwing boys and overachievers passing out flyers from their extracurricular tables. I spotted Jay there at one of the tables—this one for the hiking club, it looked like.

I weaved through the small crowd and sidled up to him. "I don't know how best to say this, but there's an emergency happening."

"What?" Jay said, looking at me, his relaxed expression dissolving into concern. "What emergency?"

I lowered my tone so only he could hear. "Someone broke into my room and stole your letters and now they're apparently published in the *Chronicle*."

Jay looked alarmed, his eyes darting around with quick thoughts. And then, his face relaxed. "Let's get somewhere private."

My stomach churned as Jay led us to an abandoned classroom, clearly in need of repairs.

"Haven't you read it?" I asked as I closed the door behind us.

"No, read what?" he returned, as he sat halfway on the teacher's desk. "I went to man the table for hiking club first thing today."

"I'm sorry for what you're about to see then." I set my bag on a desk and fished the paper out. "I don't know if writing letters was the best way to communicate in the first place."

"Just show me," Jay said.

I gave him the column Artie wrote, and his face tensed with concern as he read it.

"So, now they know." He tore it up and threw it in the trash, with seeming indifference.

"You . . . don't care?" I asked.

"What's the point of caring?" he asked, voice low, as if he was speaking to himself, "My father being who he is naturally makes me into a spectacle, so people talk about me all the time. Who do you think it was that broke into your room? Was it Artie?"

"Charlie," I answered. "I was going to start this paper that pushed back against the *Chronicle*, what it allows us to say. I don't think Charlie liked that a Negro was challenging the agenda of his paper. So he raided my room and took what I'd been working on. Your letters, I think, were a happy accident, taken to keep the joke going about us."

Jay entertained the idea but seemed to doubt it as well. "Sounds like something he'd think to do. But the thought of him setting one foot into the Blue House is a bit of a stretch. It could have been anyone, really! This idea of *sexual inversion* is such a topic of fascination to people nowadays."

"Oh." His philosophical speech was grand on the ears. "What's sexual inversion?"

"It's the theory that some boys are attracted to boys, and some girls are attracted to other girls," Jay said. "Their attraction is flipped from what's considered *normal*, as it were. It's very scientific—well studied, in fact, and a popular topic in sensationalist press."

"So, it just could have been anyone who thought we were . . ."

He looked at me, as if ready to catch my next word like an apple fallen from a tree.

"Fruits," I finished, making Jay snicker with amusement. "And wanting to have a laugh."

"Precisely," Jay said. "Which is why you shouldn't worry. The *Chronicle* offers fifteen dollars weekly for inside scoops *and* people are desperate for an in with Charlie. They were looking for my letters and got lucky with your paper."

Though I still felt uneasy in my stomach, his words were

calming me. No need to make this gossip a bigger storm in my mind than it was.

"I'm not used to being in the spotlight," I said.

"Well, clearly the spotlight loves you," Jay replied, gesturing to the paper on the desk. "But either way, we can't have Charlie thinking he's won by pandering to West Egg's gossips."

How would I fight back? The thought of it drained me. There were moments I felt like fighting everyone who wanted to harm me, and moments when I just wanted to give up.

Something behind me stole Jay's attention, and when I turned, I saw someone passing by in the hallway behind us.

"Ah, Zihan!" Jay called, running out into the hallway.

He went out and stopped Zihan, to put his arm around him to bring him into the room. "Nick, this here is Zihan. He's studying restaurant work, *but* he wants to be a stuntman, like his father."

Why would Jay decide to pull him into our conversation? Things were embarrassing enough without an audience.

"We know each other," I finally told him, and Zihan's and my hands naturally raised for a high five.

"Oh, great!" Jay said, looking back and forth between us. "Zihan, I've called you over here because I've seen Charlie giving you the business too, over your fashions and heritage. I say we put our heads together and get back at him."

"I don't want to get back at him," I protested.

Jay turned to me. "Wrongdoing should be faced with accountability, Nick. It's the only way to keep the balance of nature."

"I read your letters," Zihan said, looking slightly concerned.

"You should carry something like a weapon, just in case people get the wrong idea. My uncle carries a cane for his bad leg, but he's used it like a bat when he's needed to."

"I'm here for an education, not a fight!" I said.

"But you must learn to fight to defend yourself!" Jay countered. He approached me in a fighting stance and started to throw jabs, forcing me to back away from him, my hands held up.

"Okay, what are you doing?" I demanded.

"Teaching you how to fight!"

"All my life I've had to fight!" I said, swatting his hand away. "Stop!"

"Boohoo—life is rough!" Jay took off his sweater vest and threw it on the desk, then unbuttoned some of the shirt underneath. "Zihan!" he said, pivoting to face him. "Hit me!"

But instead of a hit, Zihan instantly threw a kick into Jay's shoulder.

"Ow!" Jay screamed, rubbing his shoulder.

"You asked for it," Zihan said, with a shrug and a soft laugh.

"I said *hit*, but very well." Jay nodded, impressed. "See!" he said, turning to me. "Zihan can walk around in girls' clothes because he knows how to do *that*."

"What if I don't want to know how to do that?" I said. "I'm not fighting anybody, Jay. I don't need a reason to be thrown out of West Egg."

"But it does matter," Jay retorted. "Say my letters get out beyond school, and someone jumps us? Then what?"

"We get jumped, I guess."

"Ugh!" Jay groaned and rolled his eyes. "Don't you get tired of being so nonchalant?"

My reaction in this moment mattered to him—he wanted it to be as chaotic as his. And, as neutral as I was to a rumor as silly as this one, I couldn't call the question inappropriate. I *did* get tired of being so nonchalant.

I crouched into a fighting stance, and the sight of it made him smile. I threw a jab at the front of his shoulder. In response, he tackled me into the chalkboard, knocking the wind out of me. In the cloud of chalk dust that burst around us, he grabbed my wrist, rendering me half powerless.

"Nice try," he whispered, our faces so close I could smell the florals of his shampoo.

Close enough to feel the force of his inner chaos, I decided that some wrestling around was okay.

We didn't want that day to end! Each of us wanted to spend more time together. All the attention at West Egg was suffocating, but off campus grounds we could breathe again, free from the petty gossip.

After school, we shelled out five cents for a trip to Coney Island. There was a carnival on the beach—the last of the year—that stretched off Southwest Brooklyn, near to where Jay lived but so far from Harlem and school.

The day melted away as we wandered toward the coast and weaved through a wonderland of lights, carousels, and roller-coasters. Zihan got some cotton candy from a man spinning it in a machine. I got a funnel cake and then found Jay sitting on a table with his feet on the adjoining bench. He'd somehow secured a plastic cup full of gin and lemonade. I don't know how he found it, but he offered me some, and I sipped it awkwardly, careful not to touch my lips to his lip print. He watched me though, to see if my lips would touch the ghost of his.

"I don't normally do this," I said. "But I have to admit, thinking of how much worse today will make my life at West Egg makes me want to lose at least half of my mind."

"There's a great place we can do just that," Jay said, still watching my lips. "The juice joint. The queer one, where we met."

"Did someone say queer?" Zihan said, popping up between us.

"The two of you are mad, you know!" I told them. "Going back there at a time like this?"

"Why wouldn't we?" Jay said. "They're going to say we're lovers no matter what we do, so why don't we just—" He paused and watched me as if I'd finish the sentence.

Why don't we just what? I could only shrug. Like Jay, I had a desire to rebel and break expectations, to dare the world to snipe me for living my truth. But that truth was so muddied, so unclear to me, that I didn't even know where to begin sharing it.

"There are several we could try around 139th," Zihan said. "Let's go, just to see what it's like tonight."

I had fun at The Green Light when we went before but not enough. I was on board because I was not one to stop a chain of fun. Besides, the sunset and the thought of the upcoming dance brought the hope I'd find romance in the summer, not with a stranger but with someone I knew.

"Okay, let's go to The Green Light," I said, and Jay instantly looked satisfied I'd accepted his rebellious energy again. "What else is there for a bunch of outcasts to do?"

And so, we continued our night at the speakeasy in that alley by the water. Its walls were all awash in green light, giving the environment a feel that was much older than we were.

This time I did not sit on the sidelines. I danced with Zihan some, and then I turned back to Jay. A girl was throwing herself into his lap near the serving counter. I understood her choice—Jay was one of the most handsome men in Harlem. Muscular without being intimidating. Big in a pretty way.

They leaned in close, voices dropping to whispers. Only I caught the subtle doubt in Jay's expression—the crease in his eyebrows, the way his eyes darted away every few seconds as if he was worried she'd see something she wasn't meant to. He was carefully plotting with her, his smiles and winks hiding sheer terror. I'd begun to uncover the story underneath, but still there was so much more to find. If only I didn't have to share him with the rest of the world.

"Do you like him truly?" a voice said behind me. It was Zihan, his eyes safe and curious.

"No." I shook my head. "Yes, I mean—he's nice. Of course."

"He is a swell guy. Always very nice. But you share more with each other; I can tell."

I simply didn't know what to say.

"Come," Zihan said, with a tender smile. He took me by the

wrist, and we escaped behind the stage curtain to a dressing room with theater mirrors.

"Are we supposed to be in here?" I asked.

Some female impersonators sat on stools, their feet on the vanities. Others danced to music or stretched. Their fingernails gleamed, and their painted mouths hummed along with the tunes. There was a regal woman with a big old blue wig, fixing herself up in a mirror. The floor was covered with glitter and sequins.

"You know what you need?" Zihan said and picked up some green nail polish from an unmanned vanity, shaking it up.

"Green?"

"It would work for you."

I shook my head. "It's hard enough for me in school. Someone sees me in that, they'll kill me."

"Okay!" he said, putting down the polish and pulling a little skirt down from a clothes rack. "Start smaller."

"Why?" I asked. "What's the purpose of this?"

"Becoming more comfortable with yourself will allow you to become comfortable telling Jay how you feel."

I'd first have to tell myself how I felt. About all of this—people knowing that I had been secretly forming a bond with Jay. This idea of *owning the narrative* of my queerness held no power for me. It asked more than I was willing to offer, demanded a spotlight I had no desire to stand beneath.

But everyone here was doing girls' clothing too. That made me feel both under- and overdressed in my cotton pants, as if it would be more natural to experiment here than to hold on to my comfortable ways.

I went behind a dressing screen and tried the skirt. I didn't know why I was doing it. I only felt half in control of my actions. But to my surprise, it provided an odd but comforting breeze on my legs. Something about it was freeing. It felt like I'd shed a layer of expectation.

I wouldn't step out from behind the screen, but Zihan came around to look at me.

"You look like a princess!" he said, with a big smile—not one of ridicule but one of celebration. "Phenomenal!"

I laughed quietly and ran my fingers along the hem of the skirt, feeling its fabric against my skin, and for a moment, I wanted to see myself. But the thought of facing that reflection was scary. Could I even bear to see myself like this? Back in Oklahoma, something like this would have been impossible! I would've never dared! People would've crushed me, cast me out!

Zihan watched me, seeming to read my mind. "You're not back there anymore, Nick," he said, his voice gentle. "This is New York. You don't have to hide."

I received his words in silence. "It's just . . . I don't recognize this way of living," I said, finally.

"Well, you're not supposed to be the same person forever. That's what this"—he gestured around us, as if to the world—"is all about. In New York, you get to define yourself. You don't have to be what anyone says you are. You can be anything. You just have to believe it for yourself."

I knew he was right. Here, in this city of strangers, I didn't have to fear what everyone else thought of me.

The skirt felt foreign against my skin, but comforting. Like not everything had to make perfect sense. I could feel unsteady, unsure, but also deeply alive! Perhaps the skirt was more than a piece of clothing—perhaps it was a door to stop hiding altogether.

I slipped back into my pants and followed Zihan out to the main room, feeling a growing sense of unease about how often Jay had been crossing my mind. He was distant—lost in a game of entertaining strangers again.

We didn't speak until the night winded down; Jay found me alone just outside the entrance. People were exiting the place, slowly. The music faded in the background of the cars whooshing through the night.

The Green Light's sign bathed the wide alleyway in an otherworldly glow.

Jay stood leaning in the door, like he didn't quite know how to approach but couldn't stay away. "Nick," he said, his voice intimate. "Are you okay?"

I nodded. "Yes, of course I'm okay. Why wouldn't I be?" *I thought we'd spend the night together and you betrayed me.*

I swallowed my thoughts and felt my face contort with confusion, as if in shock at the current of rage passing from my heart to my head.

In the moment that hung between us, it was like Jay could sense my thoughts, and he seemed amused by them. A smile played at his lips that he was having trouble straightening. And

I was ready to scream and give him the real punch he'd been asking for earlier, but instead, I put my hands into my pockets to restrain myself.

"They're closing soon, right?" I said.

He nodded. "Oh, yeah. I'll see you back to school."

"Won't need it," I said with a tight smile, and Jay flinched like I'd really hit him.

Zihan approached and slipped by Jay to exit the place, pulling Jay along with him. "Taxi's going off duty in five minutes! Let's move, boys."

Zihan grabbed my arm too and created a three-part link as we walked down the alleyway.

I was grateful to have him between us as I sorted through my emotions. Emotions I was not comfortable with. I couldn't walk away from what Zihan had pointed out about Jay and my feelings for him. I knew there was something there.

I glanced over and took note of Jay's shoulders, tense and straight, like he was bracing for a blow. I couldn't shake the feeling that tonight, something had slipped through our fingers.

11.

THERE WAS MORE TO BE DONE IN THAT ABANDONED classroom—our sanctuary, where Jay, Zihan, and I had formed our trio.

No more wallowing! With the help of my friends, I'd hatch a plan to fight back against Charlie's hatred and Artie's gossip column. But first, we had to shape our hideaway into something that was ours.

Jay and I worked together on it, mostly. I couldn't stay mad at him for long when I witnessed his desire to help me in my plight. He was determined to make our secret room more comfortable, so when we found a torn-up leather loveseat by the dumpster out back of the White House dorm, we hauled it inside. The cushions sagged and the fabric had seen better days, but it made the place ours!

Jay wiped his hands on his pants and took a step back to inspect our furniture. "Better than sitting at a desk, right?"

He took it upon himself to smuggle snacks for us too. A bag

of donuts made its way from the White House all the way to our hideaway. He'd also grabbed a couple of dumbbells from the recreation center gym.

He said, "Now we've got somewhere to relax, and we can get strong!"

I glanced around the room, feeling a new surge of peace. I'd started reading more about stories of people who didn't fit in and their strange lives. My last visit to the Schomburg Library had introduced me to *The Autobiography of an Ex-Colored Man* and *Tarzan of the Apes*. I found comfort in knowing Jay and I weren't the first to feel out of place.

We spent hours hashing out ideas for our first issue of *The Sovereign*, scribbling furiously and talking about all the things the *West Egg Chronicle* would never dare to print: the shabby housing, the way some boys got all the privileges in class while others barely scraped by, and the divide between the ones who had it all and those of us left to make do with what we could.

Jay followed the Gatsby tradition of philanthropy and donated to the cause, which allowed us to expand. I made more flyers with Zihan's help and late one night we tacked them onto bulletin boards around campus. They made the rounds!

A week into what I'd dubbed *The Sovereign Scheme*, I was the last to arrive to our hideaway after school, holding a folder with four sheets of paper. They were submissions, which had been slipped under my door as per the flyer's instructions.

I laid them out on a table before Jay and Zihan. "We got some poetry, a story about the football team defeating East Shore, and an opinion piece on how the cafeteria should stop serving us food that still moves."

Jay hopped off the couch and picked up the opinion piece to read a few lines. "This is headline material!" he sang.

"We're doing it," I said quietly, allowing myself to feel the comfort of support. "We're really doing it!"

Jay examined me closely, and his eyes were soft and searching, as if he wanted to meet the depth of my excitement, to know where it came from. Whether he found what he was looking for or not, Jay was inspired. Two weeks into *The Sovereign Scheme*, he snatched the building keys from his father's study to help me print my first issue in the *Chronicle* office after school, when the room was empty. With him by my side, the problem of having money to fund the paper magically faded away.

I printed ten copies, which I'd distributed around school when the storm cooled down and it was finally time to retaliate.

As we packed up to head back before dark, Jay asked me, "So, the coed dance is a definite yes?"

The question closed a fist around my chest. I did not want to be on a rollercoaster of meaning with him. I wanted to always know how much he cared about our friendship, so I did not feel tugged here and there by the moments he wanted my attention and the ones he shut me out.

I shrugged, trying to look like I didn't care. "I don't know still."

Jay locked the office door and gave me a sideways look. "Why not? Afraid of a dance? Or are you upset with me about the other night?"

"Not afraid," I mumbled, though I kind of was. "Not upset, either." Though I definitely was. "Why would I be? I just don't see the point in a dance."

"The point is to have fun!" He clapped me on the shoulder and guided me back to the hallway. "Think of it as research. You've got to experience the school fully to write about it, right?"

"I reckon I do." I tried to fight off a smile but failed. "I'll consider it."

"Good," he said, smiling back. "Don't leave me to fend off Charlie and Cannon by myself."

I watched him, admiring his effortless way of taking on the world. Quietly, I hoped that a little bit of that energy could rub off on me.

The coed dance came around that weekend, and I couldn't find myself a date. Thankfully, Daisy didn't have one either, so we agreed to go together.

I got ready in the guest room of Daisy's house where I used to live, fumbling with my tie, my hands clumsy with nerves. This was the place that nursed me back to life when I felt like a hollow shell, and here I was, undoing the dust of my past, buttoning things up, thinking on trivial things like what I might talk to Jay about later, what his behavior might be like.

"*Young lady, what is that?*" I heard Uncle say from upstairs.

I went to the door and stuck my head outside to listen in.

"You can't wear that," Uncle Beet continued. "Nuh uh. No way! Nope."

"Dad, you are not serious!" Daisy returned.

"No way, no way, little girl!"

"It's all I have!" Daisy protested, throwing a fit. "I've been planning this outfit for weeks. Mom!"

"Okay, okay," Auntie Lorraine said to keep the peace. "She'll wear a shawl. And that should do it."

Daisy won her mother over. She could be very persuasive, more persuasive than I ever was.

I heard her coming downstairs so I tried to pull together the rest of my outfit from the contents of my closet. She knocked on my open door and I spied what had made Uncle so mad. She was a vision in a sleeveless emerald dress! It hugged her form and stopped just above the knee. She wore matching gloves up to her elbows and a pixie wig that made her look a few years older.

Daisy did a twirl in the hallway when she saw me staring. She loved the attention but in a good-humored way. "Ready?" she said, scanning me. "No pants is a choice, but I support it!"

"Oh," I said, looking down at myself. I'd only managed to put jockey shorts and socks on the lower half so far.

"I suppose you can't decide how much you want the world to see until you try showing it," Daisy said, still treating my bare legs as a fashion statement.

"I've only stressed about what to wear for the past three hours," I said, going to the bed to sort through the suits lying there.

"That one," Daisy said, pointing at a black and white pinstriped number. "It complements me, and it's bolder than what you usually wear. Hurry now—we'll have to walk down to a taxi and the dance is starting in ten."

So I dressed, and we rushed down the street to find a yellow cab. We entered our car on either side, and as it pulled off, Daisy asked, "How are things going with Jay? I've noticed you been out more. Is it with him? Are you spying?"

Her question felt like being called on in class when I didn't have the answer.

"Not spying—no. We've struck up a friendship," I said quietly, as I looked out the window. The sidewalks were full of pedestrians—mostly young couples out for the night. I studied their outfits endlessly and hoped I'd blend in without going invisible. "I went to a UNIA meeting with him—not for Jordan. Just for fun. I find him easy to trust, but it's only been a few months."

"Did he say or do anything suspicious in the meeting?" Daisy asked.

"Not at all. I think Jay loves Harlem too much to hurt it. I've never met his father though."

All I knew was something about Jay made me want to share my life with him, including things that I wouldn't share with others.

"I've met Gatsby," Daisy said. "He's nice, in a rehearsed way. Hard to get a read on. I find that Jay has this desire to please his dad and a competing desire to be his own man."

I'd gotten a sense of that too.

The car slowed to a gradual stop. I turned to find Daisy watching me, as if she was curious about my thoughts. Meeting Jay had changed me already—perhaps she saw it.

She reached forward to hand a tip to the driver and then said, "Well! Here we are!"

I slid out of the car and Daisy came around to loop her arm through mine. In front of us glowed a big Apollo Hotel sign—a long rectangle whose letters flashed with little bulbs. A marquee shone brightly beneath it, reading *Welcome West and East Egg Students*.

We walked inside and entered the ballroom down a set of wide stairs, our presence making people look. Perhaps they were impressed that a simpleton like myself was attached to such a lovely lady. The confident bounce in Daisy's walk started to rub off on me in the best way possible; this front could last for just a little while.

Chandeliers glittered over a large dance floor where Charlie was doing the Charleston, all by himself. Daisy observed him, arms folded. "He's an atrocious dancer, isn't he?"

"Quite bad," I said.

"I'm so glad I said no to his invitation for a date," Daisy said before noticing someone approaching her. "Betty!"

They hugged and began chatting girl business, so I migrated to the table to leave them to their conversation. I devoured some crackers and cheese and then downed a cup of punch.

Vinny was in attendance in a loose-fitting suit with his hair in braids now. He was holding his tuba and standing near a line of girls in chairs, who swayed lightly to the music. He was hoping, it seemed, that a girl would talk to him, but they were only talking to each other.

He approached me when he saw me. "You look very smart, Nick. Glad you made it."

"Thank you, Vinny. You too." I'd have complimented him in return but all I could think is how strange it was that he'd brought his tuba with him to a dance.

Lately, Vinny and I had fallen into a natural rhythm with separate social circles, but we were still friends, and I appreciated his presence here.

That is, until I spotted Jay skulking in the corner behind some balloons. His placement in the room struck me as odd. Handsome guys didn't usually sulk in corners.

He was spinning his fedora around his fist instead of wearing it—it was the only sign he was having any fun. He looked at me because he must have felt me staring. He smiled but didn't wave. We just watched each other.

"I'm gonna walk around," I told Vinny and went to approach Jay tentatively.

"You came alone," he said.

"I haven't met a single girl at East Egg except for Daisy," I returned.

"Ah. Did you know I liked her in grade school? My father always said Daisy was a fine young lady. But I'd always gotten the impression she was too focused on other things for a relationship, which is why I never courted her."

Now, Jay, why would you say this to me? I felt physical pain from his words, like he'd whacked me in the stomach with a paddle. But that was my responsibility, wasn't it? We were only friends.

The trips to Coney Island, The Green Light, his very own residence—all of that was just a way to show that rumors had no power to stop our friendship. The stir that I felt deep in my soul when he was around—that was something that I felt alone.

"I don't think she's too focused on other things," I said. "You could try your hand at providing gifts."

Jay raised an eyebrow. "You make your cousin sound so . . . materialistic." His eyes drifted to watch Daisy dance with a boy. "But I catch your drift. People like knowing you thought of them."

"Precisely," I said.

He looked back at me, squinting his eyes some. "Out of curiosity . . . what made you finally decide to come tonight?"

I shrugged. "I wanted to show I could be social and fun too, I think. But I'm quickly learning that places like this are not right for me."

"Well, I do think your energy would go further if it was aimed toward some other goal than showing people things." Jay took off his jacket and tucked his pinstriped shirt into his pants. "The design of this dance is beautiful, but the refreshments leave something to be desired." He checked his watch for the time. "I'll have to find a drink instead. But first? A dance!"

Jay jitterbugged his way to the dance floor in a comical way. Had he ever been clumsy? Had he doubted his comfort with his own body? Did he get sweaty and ugly when he danced?

I joined him on the floor. I twisted my feet a little, trying to lose myself in the music, but my dance was forced and the snaps too rehearsed. We drifted toward each other, our snaps finding common rhythm. Jay gave my hip a little bump, and I lost balance only for him to catch me by the back of my waist.

Jay grabbed my hand and tried to spin me around, but I did not spin. We would be ridiculed for getting close like this and I wasn't sure how much more I could take.

Why would you want me to do that? I asked with my eyes. He merely frowned in response. I don't think he understood.

I ran off the dance floor and into the hotel lobby, avoiding eye contact with my peers. Jay followed as if it were his duty, but he didn't say anything even as I continued through the lobby. I stopped in the hallway of first floor rooms, where it was quiet.

"So, you're following me," I said, without turning around.

"Well, yes," Jay said. "We were dancing, and you ran off. What's the matter?"

"Why did you . . . why would you do that in front of all those people?" I asked.

"Because I was dancing," Jay said, snapping his fingers and kicking his foot, lightly. "You know, dancing? Having fun? Try it sometime."

"You made me look like a ballerina! A bisque doll!"

"Your head is made of bone and flesh—not porcelain—so it never gave the people that."

I sighed. "I wasn't supposed to be dancing anyway. If I may ask, please don't touch me like that in public again."

He looked at me as if to say, *What's the big deal?* His look made me wonder if it even happened, if he really tried to turn me like a girl in front of a crowded room.

What was I to do with my hands under his stare? Jay made me feel out of place in my body and I wanted him to leave.

"Aren't you supposed to be finding a drink somewhere?" I asked. My voice came out more hostile than I meant it to.

His face fidgeted between amusement and offense. "I guess so?" he said. "Especially if you're trying to get rid of me."

"No, I just—"

"Jay!" shouted a voice, and an East Egg girl in a white dress came running down the hallway. "I've been looking for you everywhere!"

This girl, who I'd never seen before, grabbed him by the arm and pulled him away. "Join me for a dance?"

He smiled back at her as if she were far more interesting than me. It hadn't even dawned on me that he could've come with a date. But there he was, paddling me again. Reminding me I was just another person craving his time, who he'd have to fit in when he could.

Jay nodded and smiled at me, as if we had only just met. "See you around, friend."

Friend? Really? How awful of him to walk away with someone else's hand in the middle of our conversation! *He* invited *me* here, not the other way around!

I walked back to the ballroom, careful not to focus on Jay and his temporary girlfriend. But seeing him walk away with someone else's hand left pinpricks in my stomach.

I barely knew anyone else here I could feel comfortable talking to, other than Vinny, who was focused on picking up a girl. So, what was the point of staying?

Daisy was being photographed at the photo station, and I informed her I'd be taking off.

"By yourself?" she asked, breaking her pose briefly.

"Yeah," I told her. "I just need some time and air."

So, she let me go and off I went into Harlem to find someone other than Jay to occupy my time. Then we'd be even. The city was only a scary place to travel alone if you didn't know where you were going. I settled on patronizing The Green Light by myself—why shouldn't I? I'd gone with Jay more than once now.

I arrived by cab to the alley with our speakeasy, which stretched out more than you could see upon entry. And, with no one else here with me, I was able to explore its many rooms with reckless abandon. Deep in the recesses of the place was a pool table, lit only by a light that hung from the ceiling.

A boy caught my gaze before I even knew I was looking. I recognized him from my neighborhood. He was always boarding the bus alone.

Tonight, he was playing billiards, one leg hiked up on the table, shirt open just enough to show off his chest. He carried himself with such ease that it made me feel intrigued.

He held my gaze for a moment, sizing me up. That look made me feel something I hadn't expected. There was a seduction in his glance, as if he were inviting me over without words.

"What you all dressed up for?" he asked as I wandered closer.

"A dance," I said, barely meeting his eyes. "But it was no fun, so now I'm here."

"Solids or stripes?" he asked, nodding to the billiards table, like it would remove my stress.

"Stripes." I took a stick, twisting the chalk over the top, trying to calm the strange buzz of energy in my chest.

He stood up straight, looking me over. "Sure thing, cutie," he said, casually.

Cutie. The word sounded foreign, awkward, like it didn't belong to me. It stirred a little something—was it excitement? Discomfort? I wanted to think I could be someone people found attractive. But with the way Jay looked at me—sometimes his was the only attention I truly wanted.

"Alex," he said, offering his hand. "I don't think we ever met for real."

"Nick." I shook it, feeling his fingers linger a bit longer than necessary.

We played, each aiming and shooting, and I tried to concentrate on the game. But my mind wandered. Alex was charming, sure, and there was a freedom to him. He seemed unconcerned with school or work, like he'd been born for this pool hall, and I envied that sense of relationship with my immediate surroundings.

In the middle of the game, he came up and placed his hand gently on my chest, just below my collarbone, and leaned in closer. The noise of the juice joint faded, and for a second, I thought I could want this. I could let him kiss me, lose myself for a night, just to prove that I was capable of feeling something for someone else, like Jay could. But the more he leaned in, the more I felt the emptiness of it.

Even with this beautiful person's hand against my chest, my mind was elsewhere—back to Jay, to the way he saw me. This touch felt surface-deep in comparison. Jay's was down to the bones.

"Wait," I said, placing a hand between us, as if jumping out of a trance. "I don't want this."

And even if I did, I couldn't do this with people around. I wasn't a confident kisser—I'd never been given one—and with a guy who was basically a stranger? No way.

"Oh, sorry," he said, backing away. "Thought you were giving me signals."

"Sorry. Thank you. I enjoyed the game." I left the room and then the joint in an anxious frenzy, feeling embarrassed for the both of us.

I spilled into the alleyway and walked back to the sidewalk to catch a car. There were very few lonely walkers out tonight, especially not on this side. The establishment signs had gone dark, the cars were all parked and unmanned, and only the orange glow from the streetlamps offset the blue of the evening.

Did Alex and Jay and Daisy have moments of loneliness? They seemed so fantastic at socializing, but I was beginning to realize how common it was in life to find one thing on the surface and something totally different underneath.

I'd see to it that one day I had someone to see me home after a night on the town. We could discuss all these things! All my questions. Tonight, I'd make peace with my singular note, forming a tune of its own.

12.

DAISY WAS WAITING BY MY DOOR BAREFOOT AND still in her dress when I arrived home. "Just wanted to make sure you'd made it back," she said, with concern. "I thought you might have taken off with Jay when you left, but then I realized he was still there."

"What is Jay's deal, anyway?" I asked, as I walked through the door into my room. "It's like he's in some sort of relationship with every person who comes up and asks him for his time." I undid my tie and unbuttoned my sleeves.

"Jay is very popular," Daisy said, leaning against the doorway and studying my emotions. "That's how it goes."

"He seems to have a crush on even you. Was there some history between you?"

"Not at all," she said. "Did he say something?"

"Only that he wanted to pursue you back in the day to prove something to his father."

"Well, if he was only interested in me to please his father, it's good it never happened," she said with a laugh. "I don't even remember him from back then. How young do you think we were?"

I had to stop myself from taking my tension out on Daisy. I should have been upset with myself and my emotions. I felt like I may lose Jay now that people thought we were hot for each other. It was all fun and games at one point, but what if the whispers got too serious and Jay had to drop me completely to make a girl his permanent fixation?

With my shirt loose now, I picked up a notebook and sat on my bed. "People saw Jay and I dancing together. It stresses me to know that people are giving us so much attention. They were already bullying me before."

"Jay will protect you from it," Daisy said. "He likes you."

"Does he? It doesn't seem that way," I mumble. "What do you see?"

"Hmm, I see he takes every excuse to look at you, and you're the only one who doesn't quite notice it because you're never looking at him when he does—that's the point."

"Do you think he might be . . . you know?" I ventured, hesitating as new sentences formed in my mind.

Daisy didn't seem to follow. "What?"

"There are people who like people of their same gender," I said, my voice quiet.

That gave her pause. "I don't get that impression of Jay, but who knows? I've almost loved girls the way I've loved boys."

"You have?"

"Take Anna May," she said, staring dreamily off into the

hallway, fingers teasing her heel straps. "We were friends as kids. She'd make me her Valentine every year. She didn't want to have to worry about courting someone just to eat chocolates. We carried the tradition through junior high and it gave me something to look forward to year after year because it wasn't this mad dash to find love. Just an excuse to love ourselves."

I could not describe what I had with Jay so poetically. And what we had was less sweet, more rough around the edges. I didn't think Daisy quite understood what I was getting at.

What I had with Jay was not as easily described, but if I were to be fully honest, I didn't know how she'd react. How would anyone react, if they knew what I was really thinking, about him, and us, and what our friendship meant to me? It might put me on course for a lonely little life.

"I think I may be broken," I said. "Like a plate somebody dropped, just trying to piece myself together and failing miserably."

"We're all failing miserably, Nick. The key is pretending that you have it all together," Daisy said, with a sympathetic smile and a gentle parting squeeze on my arm. "Good night."

She turned to leave, and I fell back on my bed, wondering if Gatsby, the father, knew about Jay's letters being published. Did he know about the school drama? Would he care?

Whenever Jay spoke on his father, he seemed confused, less bold, less in the moment. I couldn't shake the feeling that Gatsby Sr. may have been a nuisance to me, not for the reasons Jordan didn't like him, but for new ones entirely.

Though I'd admit it to no one, I thought about Jay after the dance. Shouldn't the night have lent itself to more?

I couldn't sleep much or think of anything but my dissatisfaction.

By Monday morning, it had turned into a sharp need to channel the storm. I found myself skipping classes and staring at a blank page that would become something for *The Sovereign*.

It would make me feel better to shatter the facade of the school. To lay waste to the image—everything West Egg pretended to be but wasn't! To expose the hypocrisy of this place. The lies of its appearance.

If I just kept writing, it would give me something to do other than stew in my thoughts.

DOES WEST EGG PROTECT ITS STUDENTS?

By Nick Carrington

Let me give it to you straight, Reader: Ever since my letters from Jay Gatsby Jr. made their way through the halls, there's nothing left for me to do but dive headfirst into this storm and try to capture it from where I stand.

So, here's my question for you: What changed when you found out that a boy from the White House and a boy from the Blue House were talking to each other? And why, if the *West Egg Chronicle* can print stories that expose the private lives of its students, can't we get published when we write about real issues? Why was the editor in chief of the *Chronicle* so quick to publish something that could embarrass its students, but so hesitant to put out work that could make change?

I'll tell you, Reader: West Egg wants you to believe it's progressive, but in reality, it's doing everything in its power to prove otherwise. Negroes are treated like window dressing—just there to make the place look diverse while we're kept on the sidelines.

The papers will tell you this experiment is doing us a favor, but if you look closely, Negroes aren't even allowed to tell our own stories. If you're only inviting us to sit at your table so you can treat us like servants or a punchline, what's the point of this so-called experiment?

I've got one last question, and it's for Mr. Tom Buchanan and Mr. Jay Gatsby Sr.: If no one's willing to protect us here, then what good is an integrated school? If no one will publish us or listen to us, then I'm afraid this experiment isn't working.

That final line would hit like a hammer! This was the new front-page story.

I didn't need Jay for what came next—no telling how he'd react to his father getting dragged through the mud, and I could handle the reprint on my own anyway.

Students from Blue House often had special jobs, like delivering papers and supplies to the *Chronicle*'s office at the end of the day. I waited by the utility closet until the janitor left, then grabbed a trolley and loaded boxes onto it.

Once Charlie stepped away from his desk, I pushed the trolley through the writers' room, pretending to drop off supplies. Most of the writers were too absorbed in their work to notice, except for Artie, who watched me as I walked into Charlie's office.

I slipped my paper into the mimeograph behind the desk and began making copies.

Artie appeared in the doorway. "Excuse me? You aren't supposed to be in here."

"Tell on me, why don't you?" I replied as I rotated the knob to make the papers print. "It wouldn't be the worst you've done."

Artie pushed his permed hair from out of his face and squinted at me, pursing his lips and folding his arms. "What are you doing, anyway?"

"What everybody else is afraid to do," I said. "Telling the truth."

"You know whatever you're printing is going to be pulled instantly if it's not approved by Charlie."

"So be it. I don't need Charlie's approval or the *Chronicle* to print my papers. I just need his mimeograph. And that should do it."

I picked up the stack of papers, pushed past Artie, and left the writers' room just in time to see Charlie returning. "What you got there?" he asked.

"Nothing," I answered, without turning around.

But when I was out of sight, I spread my papers around the hallways with the reckless abandon of a dog marking its territory. I pinned them near lockers and water fountains, slid them under doors. I felt defiance and a thrill of freedom! Each paper I placed felt like a tiny trinket of rebellion against a system that wanted me to stay in my place.

By the time I ran out of papers, I was breathless and my hands were stained black with ink.

I'd called out Buchanan and Gatsby Sr.—those untouchable men whose names were etched into the Academy pamphlet like founding fathers. Their presence was a looming force, silently guarding outdated traditions and doing nothing to stop bullying in the walls of their school. I dared to criticize their legacy and call their inclusion performative. And it was liberating!

I lingered in the shadows of the stairwell, watching as students picked up the papers, reading with expressions that ranged from shocked to intrigued. Some White House boys looked around after tearing the papers from the walls as if afraid to be caught with them, but the Blue House students glanced at each other knowingly. *The Sovereign* meant something to them—it validated what they already knew but hadn't dared to say aloud, and that was all that mattered.

I noticed in the next few days that I got more attention. The paper was the talk of the Blue House, with many of my housemates coming up to joke that I should "be careful being so bold," but I was not worried! Or at least I didn't let on that I was.

My worry only set in when I was on my way to and from field training and I caught cold stares from the White House boys who once ignored me. It was typical intimidation.

Tension lingered all over campus like a storm gathering on the horizon because I'd decided to say the quiet part out loud. It was empowering! But I also felt dread, like something was coming for me. Couldn't shake it.

A week after my papers swept the school, I tucked into bed late and tried to fall asleep, my mind busy with thoughts of what my family would think if my papers got me kicked out of West Egg. I had to admit I'd grown slightly worried. It was thrilling, though, to think of how much I could shake the table!

I nodded off with excitement and anxiety warring in my chest, but I was woken up soon after by my door slamming. I was ready to assume Vinny had left the room until I saw a blinding orange glow flaring near the door. My heart stalled as I took it in—a fire in the corner of my room, flickering and flying like a growing demon.

And there laid Vinny sleeping in the bed beside mine, not yet aware of the smoke that filled our room.

"Vinny!" I shouted, thrashing up in bed. "Vinny, there's a fire!"

Vinny opened his eyes and leapt into action. He was not paralyzed by the sight of the flames like I was. He started fanning the flames with a shirt, only raising the temperature on the heat.

"Stop!" I ran over to grab his arm and pulled him back from the flames. "You'll make it worse."

The alarm blared as we evacuated the room and ran into a smoky hallway. The Blue boys flooded out of their rooms, coughing.

More than one fire had been started and they were eating the whole building! It was not a coincidence but an act of arson.

We ran to the staircases on either side of the building and rushed down until we were outside. Several people, including Artie—the RA on duty—raced to the telephone booth at the front of campus to alert the fire department. The rest of us were left standing outside, most of us in our pajamas. We were without our belongings except for the small things we'd each chosen to grab before we left. For me, it was my notebook.

Vinny was losing his marbles about his stuff and wanted to go back inside. James had to hold him from running in and pulled him back screaming, "It's over!"

I felt sort of numb thinking about the outfits and supplies in my room. I had more where that came from and had lost it all once before. I already didn't miss the mildewy bathrooms of the Blue House. But what about the boys who were here because they had nowhere else to go?

Usually, when the fire alarm went off accidentally, we would wait outside until the firefighters came to stop it. Within ten minutes, I would walk tiredly back to bed.

That was not the case tonight. In the event of an actual fire, no one came.

The flames left a black cloud rising into the air, its smog so thick it traveled over to the manicured side of campus—the side you saw in the pamphlet.

Our dorm building was made of something so flimsy and flammable I couldn't believe it supported us in the first place. But I'd met fire before. I'd met it head on.

I went back to that place as I watched the flames . . .

This boy from my neighborhood, Ronald, came banging on the door so hard one night that it startled Pa. He opened the door just to hear "There's a fire at the hospital!"

We sped downtown in the car, both of us in silence, and arrived to find the fire had eaten the exterior of the hospital, and where solid walls had once been, the bricks had crumbled away, exposing structural beams and metal. That was the hospital where my mother, her face bright and her steps light, once lifted me onto a doctor's table—the same place she turned to for work after leaving her job as a teacher. She spent long nights there, making sure birthing mothers received the care they needed.

I ran inside to find her, and Pa called after me to stop me, but I got past the flames and started screaming, "Mama!"

By the time I realized it was a lost cause, the smoke had blocked the exits and my airways. Pa came in to save me and scooped me up, but he couldn't find my mother. He was stuck with only me. And the way he only said a few words to me in the years after, unless they were for discipline, proved he wished he could've saved her instead.

A fire had taken my mother. A bullet had taken my father. And one fire had come for me. How had I escaped these fates?

I could hardly feel a thing in the days that followed, but my head thumped with this anxious thought I couldn't get rid of—*Where were the firefighters?*

I hadn't been protected a day in my term at that school. It made me wonder why I even tried. If excelling would put a target on my head, what reason did that give me to excel?

It was like Mr. Wallace said on his final day, *They're afraid. That if we rise, we'll do to them what they do to us.* But I didn't want to rise in violence! I only wanted to rise in truth!

I found three different headlines on a newsstand at the corner café, just down from Auntie and Uncle's, and brought them home. Coverage on the fire flooded the Harlem presses, but it seemed there was barely any investigation into who'd done it. No one even cared who the culprit was. Headlines read:

INTEGRATED SCHOOLING EFFORT GOES UP IN FLAMES

WHERE WILL THE BLUE BOYS OF WEST EGG GO?

ARSONIST TARGETS ELITE WEST EGG ACADEMY

I couldn't think straight until I knew more.

The timing, the suddenness—it ate at me. My paper hadn't sat well with everyone. I'd torn the veil, exposed the truth! Discomfort was inevitable. But then the fire, right after it hit the halls . . .

Had my words done this? Was this my fault?

The thought made me sick—the thought that something I wrote could've driven someone to try to kill me. But wasn't this what happened to writers? Wasn't this why Pa had warned me away from it? Keep your head down, or risk flames licking at your door.

This wasn't some accident. I was a target. And the same hand that fed me at this school—it could just as easily choke me dead.

Days later, I sat frozen in my room at Daisy's house, trapped in my thoughts. When she came home, she invited herself through my open door and dropped a stack of poster board and cardboard onto the bed.

"The UNIA and the NAACP are organizing protests," she said. "They think it was a hate crime. The UNIA's even making space for some of the boys to sleep—for now, at least."

There was no time to waste before joining them, and we immediately started to paint signs in the driveway of the house.

Daisy had been wanting to protest for some time now. New York liked to pretend it was different, but it still shut doors in our faces. Lots of stores were denying Colored girls access in Manhattan, so there was a bar for fashion that Daisy wanted to reach but the city was denying her.

"Nobody better buy my jacket before we break their windows," Daisy said as she painted an *A* into the cardboard sign. Her sign was going to say *Free Education*.

"Nobody's breaking any windows," Auntie Lorraine said firmly.

She'd spent the whole weekend in overalls. The Wash 'N' Fold would be closed for the protest, because Auntie had other work to do. She was busy loading up a wagon with coats and socks for the boys who'd lost everything in the fire.

I was sitting beside Daisy, pressing the button on my pocket watch and clicking it closed. Despite everything that happened, Mr. Wallace would be proud I was taking charge of my own sovereignty. In spite of everything, Pa would be proud I didn't let fear stop me from saying what I felt!

"I told Jordan it was happening," Daisy whispered, careful to lower her voice in case Auntie was listening in. "In case we need muscle."

"How bad do you think it can get?" I asked.

"Depends on our numbers. The more people that show, the more cops show. And if they're able to get the word out, people will come from East Egg too. It's the same way there, you know. The white girls are on track to become teachers and nurses. And the Colored girls . . ." She sighed deeply as she painted another letter on the sign. "We become maids."

"We can print flyers," I said. "I could ask Jay, and he could use the mimeograph at school."

"Tom's got one," Daisy said, offhandedly. "I'll use it at work."

"Won't he be suspicious as to why you're making flyers for a radical protest at his house?"

Daisy laughed with sudden amusement, as if the irony hadn't occurred to her. "I suppose it would be suspicious, but I don't intend for him to find out. Tom acts nicely but he doesn't seem interested in me, unless it's time to boss me around or throw his virtuous ideas at someone. He notices me when he needs me. Otherwise, I have free rein of the house."

"And if you attend the protest . . . aren't you afraid it might get you fired?" I asked.

Daisy looked amused again as she painted. "I'm not tied to one job. I'll find another rich man to work for if I lose it, but enough about that. We need to make a scene for the protest. I say we take the *Whites Only* signs down from every business in Manhattan."

"Nick?" Auntie called, dropping two lumpy burlap bags beside me. "Can you give these to your friends who need them when you see them next?"

"Yes, ma'am," I answered, half distracted. Late autumn was here, with winter soon approaching, and the Colored boys of West Egg were waiting in lines at shelters or spending their last dollars on bus tickets back down South. I was fortunate enough to have relatives here. Not everyone was so lucky.

I still couldn't shake the feeling of being watched and targeted. It took a lot to make it through the days, but somehow, I was doing it, with the help of frequent escapes to gather my thoughts in private.

I was picking up the bags to walk around to the front of the house when I found Jay standing at the bottom of the stoop.

I dropped the bags to my side. I hadn't seen him since he'd disappeared into the crowd at the dance. It felt like a lifetime ago. But here he was in a wool coat, breath misting in the air, the cold paling his chiseled features.

"Nick . . . thank goodness," he exhaled, relief washing over him when he saw me. "Oh, thank goodness."

"Thank goodness what?" I questioned, not knowing what to make of this visit.

"Well . . ." Jay pulled out a crumpled piece of newspaper from his coat pocket and began reading off a statement, his voice stiff.

"The Blue House reconstruction will be postponed through the spring semester with hopes to have new lodging by the start of the next school year." He looked up at me. "I wasn't sure if you were still here—in the city, I mean. But then I snuck your address from the admission records."

I couldn't process Jay's relief at my presence with the rest of his news.

Next school year? That wasn't good enough. "Really?" I muttered. "That's what they're giving them? It's getting colder. People need homes *now.*"

"I asked my father if there could be space made in the White House, and he just said no," Jay said, shaking his head. His frustration was raw. "I hate him sometimes."

I wanted to say something about his troubles with his father, but I couldn't comfort him—not when I knew Gatsby had the power to change things but chose not to.

"There's a protest coming up," I said, to avoid the impending silence. "Do you want to come?"

Jay's eyes sparked with rebellion. "I've never done that before," he admitted sheepishly. "But yeah, I would go. This fire's worth screaming about."

He'd stand against his father, and that meant something to me. Jay wasn't just a puppet. I hadn't realized how much I needed to know that until now.

In that moment, the awkwardness of our dance became less important than the fact that we could fight side-by-side when it truly mattered.

"I also . . ." Jay hesitated, words seeming foggy to him. "I didn't mean to make you uncomfortable at the dance. Sorry if I did."

I stood there blinking, somewhat taken off guard by his sincerity. "Oh, it's fine," I said. "You didn't—I mean, I'm the one that ran off, after all. I'm the odd one."

"Okay," he said, nodding, with a quiet laugh. "Okay."

"Okay." I smiled in return.

We stood for a moment, our energy warming the air. What was this? Two friends sorting through a misstep or something else? It was better—whatever it was—now that we had said something about it.

Days passed and people across Harlem came together by word of mouth about the horrific fire that had nearly killed our top students. I didn't even realize so many people knew about the school! But all of Harlem had been quietly rooting for the West Egg crew. Rooting for us keen-minded folk to make it to the big leagues.

At work, I barely had time to grab my apron before Mr. Kirby bounced out of his office.

"How many people you think comin' to the protest?" he asked.

I did the math on the spot. "Well, there were about sixty boys in the Blue House. Almost all of them lived at school, but about half went home. If the girls of East Egg join in, that could make close to ninety—assuming their numbers match ours. Then you've got relatives, word spreading through the press . . . maybe 150 total?"

Mr. Kirby nodded, thoughtful. "I'll double the number to be safe." He pulled out loaves of fresh bread, set them on the counter, and started slicing. Then he stopped, looking me over with something like pride. "I like the courage on you, young man. You a plucky little nigga. Stand up for what you believe—that's how you get it done."

He made peanut butter and jelly sandwiches, tucking each one into a bag and stacking them in the fridge.

A plucky little nigga. Mr. Kirby was plainspoken, and hard-knuckled, and even if he didn't say it a lot, he wanted to see me make something of myself! Just like Grandpa. They both knew that when times got rough, we had to press forward together or not at all.

Grandpa was the first Nick Carrington. He met my Grandma Ruth by the Red River in Shreveport, Louisiana, when she was singing to the ducks. Ruth was the daughter of a slave owned by a man named Mr. Morgan, and Nick the son of a Native mother and a Mulatto man. His complexion allowed him more movement in the world—he didn't have to work the tenant farms like Ruth. Instead, he traded fur up and down the river, always restless and seeking.

He spotted Ruth while delivering pelts to Morgan's estate and he knew the moment he saw her he'd risk everything for her love.

"Excuse me, miss," he said, bold as anything. "You've got the most beautiful voice I've ever heard. This might sound strange, but can I have you as my wife?"

Ruth laughed. "That all it takes?"

"That, and a beautiful soul."

"I don't want to marry you, stranger."

"I'll give you anything you want."

At first, she thought it was a trick—a test of her loyalty to Morgan. But Ruth had plans to get off her plantation. If she was ever going to run, she'd need a distraction.

"My freedom," she said at last. "Give me my freedom."

So, one evening, Nick dined with Mr. Morgan in the parlor room of the estate—a large space with velvet curtains and a pianist playing softly by the fire. The meal, prepared earlier that afternoon by Ruth and her mother, was served by one of Morgan's houseboys.

Three bites in, Morgan began pacing, agitated. "Why is this chicken not seasoned?" he barked toward the kitchen.

Nick leaned back, calm. "Ruth's likely gone to bed. Might want to wash it down."

Morgan grunted and waved toward the pianist. "Play that piano concerto—it calms me down."

As the melody rose, Nick slipped a pinch of bromide salt into Morgan's wine. One long sip, and the man started coughing—then slumped unconscious in his chair.

The pianist looked away, hands still gliding over the keys as Grandpa Nick dragged Morgan by the ankles and tucked him behind a chaise, like a stagehand hiding a prop.

Mrs. Morgan, exhausted from the day, slept soundly. If she noticed an unfamiliar cadence of footsteps crossing the floorboards that night, she took it as a dream sound, not a robber.

Nick took the safe and the keys to the stables. Out in the dark, Ruth was waiting. Together, they freed eight sharecroppers—my great-aunts, cousins, even the pianist—and fled to Langston City, Oklahoma.

Through their shared rebellion, Grandpa Nick and Grandma Ruth built a life. They bought a house. They started a paper. They had my father and Auntie. Except for Auntie Lorraine, those souls were long gone from this world. But I could feel them pumping through me now, driving me forward. Their struggles would not be in vain.

It was cold the morning we gathered to march. The air was crisp after days of rain, as if the skies themselves had wept over this dark turn in West Egg's story.

But the protest flyers on the streetlamps didn't wash off. Even the fall winds couldn't blow them away.

We bunched together and formed a crowd of moving heat. People from all over the city came. Jay, Zihan, Daisy, Auntie, and I were side by side with some folks I didn't recognize—organizers who kept track of the city's injustices.

The streets were wet with rainwater—slick and dangerous to walk on—but we walked on them anyway. As we moved through Harlem, heading south, business owners held out whatever they could offer from their eateries.

Meat cooked on grills, sending smoky aromas into the sky. There were open-air cookouts, a family passing out pieces of catfish on plates, hush puppies in tiny cups.

Mr. Kirby had his door propped open, and he was dancing like a youth behind his grill, which he rarely took control of. Today was free sandwich day! The afternoon workers ran out trays of his world-famous fried chicken, along with sandwiches, and they offered cola bottles for a single penny. Even if every business in Harlem shut down, we'd fill ourselves up!

Vinny came ready to march, in a three-piece suit and a clean hat, like a musician at a swank Black-and-tan! He brought a new tuba with him, and as we took off, he played "The Memphis Blues." The park drummers banged along to his tune. I'd never seen him as happy as he was with backup supporting his music and a crowd to jive along to it.

The tune formed an upbeat backing track to our advancement out of our neighborhood. Imagine my surprise when we found non-Colored immigrants coming out on their apartment balconies, screaming along with us, and clapping to the music!

One woman waved a flag with bold red, white, and blue stripes, marked with a single red star in a triangle. Another flag caught my attention—red, green, and white—and yet another, green with a gold harp symbol. These non-American flags fluttered above us like kites, dancing between our heads and the open sky, reminding me that this march was bigger than the Blue House, bigger than West Egg. What we were really fighting for was the idea that everyone—not just Negroes—deserved a fair chance.

We entered the business district, and all through the big city, cars honked, some with approval and some with frustration that we were blocking the roads.

The rowdier Blue boys veered into the sidewalks to do their

own thing, to make more noise, to be louder than the machines.

"Make way!" they screamed, and one boy started to bat down a *Whites Only* sign. Some shop owners stopped what they were doing to come out and see what was happening to their neighbors' business. If they had intolerant signs up, they went to take them down.

We'd only just gotten started when cops approached on horses in the distance. Two police cars blinked their lights, and together with the horses, they blocked the street up ahead, forming a menacing shadow against the skyline.

They began to advance. We pressed forward anyway as uncertain conversations broke out among us, everybody growing nervous of what could come next. The sound of hooves hitting the pavement grew louder, a thundering beat of impending doom that echoed the panic in my chest.

Then, a chant sprung out from the crowd, louder than anything. A one-man song.

"Stop the hate!" the man screamed, making everyone turn to look. "End the fear! Everyone is welcome here!"

I'd seen that man before—Megaphone Melvin! That's what Uncle called him! His only job seemed to be standing by the corner of our house in his striped shirt and beret, performing poetry. But Megaphone Melvin, even without his megaphone, had the strongest voice among our troop. Today, he was a force to be reckoned with.

The crowd repeated his song, all together. *"Stop the hate! End the fear! Everyone is welcome here!"*

The police grew more urgent at the sounds. They parked their horses and dismounted, hands going to their waists, where they removed their sticks. As they walked toward us, I shrank back, wanting to retreat. But no one else was doing that, so I couldn't either.

"Equal rights, every race!" Melvin screamed. *"Abolish hate, put love in place!"*

And I screamed it out in unison with everyone else, my voice adding a low register to a cry that swept the city like an ocean breeze.

As everyone continued forward, I shuffled through the crowd to find Daisy and Auntie Lorraine. So many people had joined us by then that I'd been separated from who I started with, and pretty soon, things could get bad.

Jay was still nearby. He called my name—"Nick!"—as I drifted away because I'd spotted Auntie Lorraine through the moving drapes of people passing by.

The cops ran into our crowd before I could reach her. The violence started instantly when one man snatched the sign out of my auntie's hand and grabbed her with force by the wrist.

"No!" The sight shocked my system, paralyzing me right in the middle of foot traffic. Someone bumped into me, throwing my body into the chest of a cop.

This cop was so offended by our collision he grabbed me by the arms and threw me to the cobble. My chin smashed the curb.

"Don't move!" he commanded.

The mist of the street's fire hydrants seemed to rush through my eyes, causing tears to burst through my vision. The man put his knee in my back. My back arched up, forming cushion around the man's knee, but my bones against the ground still felt like they'd snap at any minute.

"Get off him!" Jay screamed, and the pressure released.

The world was blurry as I gained my bearings. I turned over to find Jay pulling the policeman backward until the cop gained the advantage and threw Jay into the side of a car.

I used the curb to find my way up, not believing my eyes. Another cop swung his baton into the back of Jay's head. The hit made his eyes rotate in their sockets.

"No!" I clambered for Jay as he fell sideways and hit the pavement.

The first cop intercepted me before I could reach him. He spun me around and pushed me to the side of the road. There, he slammed me on my stomach, harder this time.

The front of my mouth caught a draft. Where I landed, my limbs almost spilled into a sewer drain built into the curb. Arms pinned behind me and my collarbones on the pavement, I took a breath in.

Ah, the sickly stench of the world beneath Harlem! The melting trash and toilet water and rotten food salting the underground streets, where the rats and raccoons lived.

What's that world like? Do they fight each other there too? I started to laugh at the visual of a congressional board of pests.

I surrender to the bottom of the earth! It might comfort me to roll into the underground, salt the earth with a root system—a root system that never stopped growing before calling it quits!

My head was against the ground, but I could get enough leverage in the cop's grip to crane my neck around and look back at the street.

Goodbye, beautiful city! The next moment may find me crunched into the fetal position and chucked into the sewer. All I could see was Jay, through a twisted, sideways angle. He had found a standing position, and the sun framed his perfect form. He still looked dizzy, unable to process his emotions, desperation red like a fever on his face as the fighting in the background waged on.

A police officer snapped handcuffs on his wrists, treating him like just another citizen, not rich, nor important. Our eyes held each other, even as my face was smashed into the cobblestone. Muffled in my ears were the rushing feet of New York's best fighters.

I felt close enough to Jay now to almost hear his thoughts. I knew he was thinking, *How did I end up here?*

Because you met me, I sent back, through our mental connection—I was convinced he could hear my thoughts too.

The cop pulled Jay through the streets, until they disappeared behind the chaos, and a thought passed through our brains at the same time.

What now?

13.

THE POLICE THREW ME IN THE BACK OF A CAR where Jay was waiting already, eyes downtrodden, his posture slumped, surely pondering his fall from grace.

I'd have touched his arm to make sure he was all right, but my hands were pinned behind my back. So I shuffled over and laid my head on his chest.

Jay didn't resist it. The policeman, as he took off, noticed it in the mirror. He kept noticing it until we arrived at the precinct, in fact, but there was no comment on the touching—only constant glancing.

The police station was a nasty place of cold white tunnels and iron bars that made you wonder why humans treated humans like animals. Once they let us out of the handcuffs and pushed us into a cell, Jay's first move was to wipe something off the bottom of my chin, but he resigned to stop wiping it when nothing came off.

He went to the little sink on the wall and washed his hands.

We were still bleeding some from our mouths when they closed the cell door behind us.

Jay looked absolutely panicked as he paced the room. "Do you know what this will look like on our records?"

"The sky isn't falling, Jay. Our faces are so dirty they may not even realize who you are."

"I'm Jay Gatsby," he said. "Of course they know who I am."

That caused me to laugh—how pompous of him to think random police officers knew who he was—but Jay wasn't laughing. He took himself very seriously.

He charged up to the cell bars and grabbed them and called to the hallway, "Hello? I need my phone call!"

Much to my surprise, a guard came and opened the cell, but he didn't even look at me. It was as if I was not entitled to a phone call.

Jay turned back to me and said, "I'll call my father," before disappearing down the hallway.

I waited for five minutes, knowing Jay would come back.

Then another five minutes passed, and he was still out there, laughing with the police as I lay on the sheetless mattress, staring up at the stone ceiling.

I felt so lonely and abandoned. Jay preferred to be out there talking to them than in here with me. I was sure the guard let him out because his skin was lighter than mine. I also knew that if I had physically fought a police officer today, I might be dead.

Jay could have been using his charisma to get something across to them about what we were fighting for and why they shouldn't stop it next time. But that's not what it sounded like.

Jay laughed again, louder this time, and I wished they would stop.

Can I trust you? I wondered as I rotted for an hour in the grime of a cage from which Jay had been freed.

His father arrived later but did not walk into the precinct. I only knew we were leaving when Jay came racing back with the keys calling, "Nick!"

I almost rolled my eyes as he unlocked the cell. He may as well have been running the place now.

Gatsby Sr. was waiting for us in a sleek four-passenger car, facing forward like the main subject of a stoic painting. Jay got into the front and I got into the back.

"Hello there," Gatsby said in a low tone, but he didn't turn around, so I could only assume he was talking to me.

"Hi," I returned.

"Can Nick come home with us?" Jay asked his pa as the car took off.

"It's okay," I intercepted. "My family will be expecting me at home."

"You need to clean up," Jay said, turning to look at me. "Somewhere better than the cell."

Does he think I don't have a shower at home? I thought, in horror. *How dare he?*

This was what I got for messing with the rich—silent judgment.

Jay's father was as white as white could be. He was not approachable. Status oozed off him like an overdose of maple syrup and it showed from the jewelry he wore. One of his hands rested on the gearshift knob as he drove, as if it were waiting for something more important to do than aid in the steering of the wheel. On just that hand were three gemstones—one blue, one green, and one a combination of both colors, all with gold bands. Did he think himself a superhero?

I was quiet on the drive. So were the two Jays, save for a quick exchange about if Jay had taken care of the washing of some linens. It was as if they had nothing substantial to talk about.

Once we were back in Gatsby's home, he told Jay to wait in his room and asked me to follow him to his study.

"Forgive the mess, if you will," he said as we arrived, but there was no mess at all. The room was cozy and inviting, filled with bookshelves and small lamps. Maps, guns, and birds adorned the walls in a striking mosaic, complementing the chevron-patterned rug beneath our feet.

Gatsby sat in a chair and motioned for me to sit on the sofa across from him. I did so, hesitant to get too comfortable. Between us was a table, and on the table, a teapot and two mugs.

"If I had a servant, I'd ask her to warm us up some tea," Mr. Gatsby said, gesturing to the teapot. "But I don't believe in that." He watched me for a response, and I didn't give him one. "My son has told me a lot about you," he went on.

"He has?" I asked. "What did he say?"

"That you are one of West Egg's brightest pupils," he replied with a smile. "That you came here from Oklahoma, as I understand it, to flee terror, and you found your way into our academy."

I thought he'd want to talk about the protest or us getting arrested, but it was like he'd invited me over for a tea party instead. In this moment, Gatsby shifted, much like a chameleon, and *almost* seemed to be a friendly man. When I looked at him head on, I saw his son's mouth and the same inquisitive spirit emerge in his eyes.

"Somehow I did," I said. "I'm thankful to you for the acceptance at West Egg." I wanted to be gracious. Despite his calm, I knew there must have been anger he was holding in under the mask.

"And yet this protest," Gatsby said, changing his tone. "It was spurred on by dissatisfaction with the school, if I'm not mistaken."

"Someone tried to kill us in our sleep," I said. "That's what started it."

"Are you sure it wasn't an accident?" he asked.

That gave me pause. "There was more than one fire," I reminded him. "It was arson."

It seemed this was the first he'd heard of it. Even so, he was strangely peaceful about the burning of his very own school.

"I understand your anger about the attack at West Egg," he said. "And what happened in Greenwood was an unconscionable attempt at mass murder—going through it twice must be highly traumatic. But you understand people are different in New York than they are there. There's a place for your passion, and it's in the debates over where this country is headed, rather than the streets."

I couldn't help but scoff. "The country ought to head in a place where students don't have to worry about their school burning down. But we do."

"I'm sorry we couldn't keep things safer on campus," Gatsby said, with no emotion.

"Speaking of campus," I said. "I couldn't help but notice the houses were segregated."

Gatsby laughed with discomfort. "Well, the sorting system is based on aptitude, rather than race. We give an IQ test on par with the model set by schools across the state of New York."

"But an IQ test doesn't really capture everything, does it? People from the North and South—it feels like we're from different worlds. I don't think your test gave me much room to show what I'm actually good at."

The man swallowed his first reaction and then said, "I can assure you that is merely coincidental. There are several nuances to account for when transitioning Southern boys to the Northern system."

"I know," I said dismissively. "Lots of people think we are naturally more stupid."

"Well, we don't—*I* don't. You've got a friend in me, Nick. But if you want to be taken seriously, I do believe you cheapen your own cause by using noise to solve your problem."

My problem, sir? Clearly, it's the problem of everybody in New York! I bit my words. I wasn't violent. It was the police that were violent.

"The protest was peaceful," I said. "The police brought the violence."

"Well, as I understand it, some of the boys were destroying property."

"Those were *signs*, not people," I told him, my tone becoming more hostile.

"You must have been a boy when W. E. B. Du Bois organized his silent march to protest lynchings," Gatsby said, his voice quieter now. "It was a powerful sight that started a national conversation about finding a peaceful solution to tough problems."

"I respect Du Bois very much," I said. "And so did my father. But Du Bois's march—did it bring any of the victims back? Or are the victims still dead?"

Gatsby went silent, and I nearly bit my lip.

Pa's words roared through my mind. *Peaceful protest comes from the right question but the wrong solution. The white man's insistence on peaceful protest is a silencing ploy. He should know better than anyone that when you want something, you must take it.*

Gatsby would tune me out if I spoke with the blazing energy of my father, so I said nothing else. But I did stand up, to show how ready I was to walk out. I watched Mr. Gatsby in silent annoyance, waiting for him to speak again.

"Nick, I have a Colored son," he said, gently.

Do you want a trophy?

"I've seen the way they've raised the bar for him," he went on. "And for you, it must be worse—I can't imagine—but you must be strategic about the way you get your message across."

"I arrived in this city with nothing but a sack of change," I said. "So I know about the bar; I've seen so much of it at West Egg, oddly. You should know about prejudice, sir. Your wife left the U.S. because of it."

His face froze like an older Colored man's would, if you'd disrespected him. "What do you know about my wife?" he hissed.

"I . . . I've been spending time with your son, sir. He's a friend to me. One of the only friends I've made at West Egg."

"And he's told you details about our family. What else has he told you?" He seemed nervous, like he had something to hide.

I'd revealed too much about my relationship with his son. All I could do was keep going and stand on my own side. "Not very much, but we understand each other. I'd never want to do anything that would put him in danger."

"I don't want you to put him in danger, either," Mr. Gatsby said. "An arrest is a bad look for our family and a bad look for his future. I don't blame you for this, Nick. I can let it go this once, but our family doesn't do things like this. With my son, I would advise you to tread carefully."

I knew then that I'd blown my chances of being a good person in his eyes. Gatsby believed that tolerance could turn bad people good and even deter them from being bad. But that to me sounded like being good and silent and waiting for justice to fall in my lap. We did not see eye to eye.

In that drawing room, under the gilded domed ceiling, I realized that all of this was beautiful—and owned by a man with a forgiving mindset for oppression.

He wanted me to stay away from Jay, but there was no way I would do that. And what Jay's father didn't know wouldn't hurt him.

The conversation with Gatsby had left me feeling like I was running out of air. I didn't like the way he delivered his message, with that polite tone as if he were above anger.

When I stepped out of his study, Jay was waiting in the hallway to guide me to his bathroom to clean up, where we walked in silence.

"Everything go okay in there?" he asked.

I hesitated, stopping to stare at the estate, which stretched from Jay's open balcony doors to Long Island Sound, with its calm, glistening waters dappled by lights on the horizon. "Yeah," I said finally, choosing to keep my true thoughts in. "Of course."

Jay nodded. "I'm sorry if he was stiff," he said quietly. "He can be like that."

"No, it's all right," I lied, eyes diving to the ground. "Truly."

I was willing to entertain, for Jay's sake, that maybe Mr. Gatsby was right about needing to be more careful, at the very least.

We reached the bathroom, and I lingered at the threshold for a moment. Jay opened his mouth, like he was going to say something, but then he stopped himself when I didn't turn to look at him.

I was grateful for the bath. But more than anything, I wished I were home. Some thoughts could only be unraveled in the comfort of the familiar—the soft bickering of my cousin and uncle, the smell of Auntie's soup on the stove. These days, it was the only place I longed to be when the world made me feel out of place.

14.

AFTER THE PROTEST, HARLEM WAS WEIGHED down by a heavy police presence. They patrolled the corners, waiting for another eruption, questioning late-night drifters once the sun went down.

But none seemed concerned with who started the fire that sparked the unrest—only with the reaction to it, and that was a problem. It meant no one would be looking for the arsonist.

I tried to let it go, but the more I tried the more it disturbed me. I was staying at Daisy's house again, back in the downstairs room that was mine before West Egg. It was probably for the best, but it left me to wonder, as I sat stiffly on the floor, if I'd ever be safe anywhere else.

Gatsby Sr. barely even cared his precious West Egg had burned down. If he didn't care, the police surely wouldn't. Besides, they only wanted to keep Harlem quiet and calm, even if that meant giving hate a free pass.

I couldn't let it go! Someone had set my room on fire, ruined everything—almost taken me down with it. If the police weren't going to find out who did it, I would.

The first person I'd confront for information was Artie. He'd been the RA on duty when the fire started and was part of Charlie's staff at the *Chronicle*.

I'd been convinced Charlie was my room robber until Jay suggested otherwise. Still, I couldn't shake the sense that Charlie was involved. If he had a hand in this, Artie would likely be in the loop. And if someone needed to handle the dirty work, who better than Charlie's favorite gossipmonger—conveniently living in the Blue House?

Lately, Artie had been loafing around outside 267 West 136th Street, where a group of well-known writers had gathered to live and work. Artie didn't get himself a spot there, but he was always outside hoping to be seen with someone noteworthy. He lived for proximity to fame.

I dressed carefully, pulling on a collared coat that hid most of my face and a cabbie hat that hung low over my forehead. I had to blend in and find Artie without attracting attention.

I found him wandering outside the brownstone as usual, waiting for a chance to pounce on some famous writer.

I seized my own chance, sneaking up behind him and pulling him into a nearby alley.

"Hey!" Artie yelped. "What the—Nick?"

"Did Charlie put you up to something?" I demanded.

"Nick!" Artie looked at me with horror. "What happened to *hello*? When did you become such a rabble-rouser?"

"Just answer the question."

"You're assuming I know what you're talking about."

"No one will do anything to find the arsonist at West Egg if I don't. Pretty soon everyone will forget it ever happened. So, again, did Charlie ever have you do anything for him inside the Blue House?"

"Fine, yes," Artie relented with a dramatic sigh. "But nothing to do with the fire. Charlie asked me to look through your things, see if I could dig up anything . . . *incriminating*. And RAs have a master key so it was an easy favor. I found your writings, your flyers, all your random scribblings—*boring*, if you ask me. I struck gold with your letters from Jay. And *you're welcome*. Those were a *great* press opportunity."

His words made my head spin. "So, you just wanted to ruin my reputation? What did you even get out of it?"

"Opportunity, Nick! Of course." He grinned shamelessly. "But I'm not some maniac—I didn't start that fire. Who would even go that far for a prank? I did Charlie one favor—and now he owes me."

Strangely, I almost believed him. Artie was an opportunist, but he would never go as far as to be violent himself. Still, there was something shifty in his energy.

"I don't believe that's the end of it," I said. "You know more. What is it?"

Artie hesitated, glancing around like he might be overheard. I could tell he wanted to talk just to talk, as if any opportunity to turn anyone in brought him a rush he couldn't find anywhere else. Or maybe he just wanted to be rid of me.

"There's a name," he whispered. "Pierre. Mr. Buchanan came to see Charlie while we were working one day. I overheard him telling Charlie to use me the same way he uses Pierre."

"Who's Pierre?"

"Some guy Buchanan uses to . . . I don't know, clean up his messes? The *mess* being *you*, and your *break-the-system* agenda. Now, if you don't mind, I just saw Aaron Douglas walk out of that door!" Artie glanced over his shoulder at someone across the street. "Mr. Douglas!" he called, suddenly animating. "Hi! I'm your biggest fan! Can I ask you a few questions?"

He scurried off, leaving me alone with what he said. *Use Artie like Buchanan uses Pierre . . .*

Charlie had used Artie to dig through my things, rob me of my work, unearth my private life. That meant this Pierre person is doing something similar for Buchanan—silencing people.

Buchanan would pay whatever it took to spin a story that kept them safe. If Pierre was the best money could buy, then maybe whoever set the fire hired him—or someone just like him—to do it.

Taking Charlie's petty vendetta out of the picture made everything clearer. This was never solely about me. It was about the Blue House. And it stank of corruption. Whoever did it had deep enough pockets to get away with it. Maybe Pierre was a dead end—just another hired hand in a city full of them—but his was the only name I had.

Whether it led somewhere or not, I had to follow it.

15.

PARANOIA RATTLED THROUGH MY NERVES—made me jumpy with fear at the noise in the city. I had a feeling someone wanted to kill me. Like they were watching me, waiting for the chance to finish what they started.

It wasn't the first time I'd felt this way, but now I couldn't shake it. I'd escaped death, and it felt as though it was impatient with my outrunning it. It was on my back closer than ever.

In the late afternoon, the doors at 40 West 135th still swung open. A place that had once seen the strength of the UNIA was now a quiet sanctuary. Loners drifted in, seeking peace from a world that seemed to want nothing but to cause harm.

I pushed through the heavy doors, slipping inside. The hush of the nearly empty church was only broken by the shuffle of occasional footsteps.

I knelt at the altar, staring up at Jesus, who looked down from the stained glass, nails in his hand and feet. The sight of him, and the mood of the church, brought to mind everyone I'd known who simply was not here anymore.

"This is all too much, God," I whispered. "Why didn't you take me with them?"

I waited for an answer, but nothing came—just the creak of wood and the flickering light from some candles in my periphery.

Someone cleared their throat behind me though, making me jump. I turned and found none other than Jordan, sitting in a pew two rows back, watching me with a faint smile from under a dramatic church hat.

"Funny seeing you here," she said wryly.

"Oh, hi," I replied, trying to steady my voice at the sight of her. "I . . . um . . . didn't know you were a churchgoer."

"I don't put too much stock in what was forced on us," she said, folding her gloved hands in her lap. "But faith is different. You can feel it, use it, without the books or the rules. And I feel it in this place."

Jordan's words made me feel closer to her, in a way. We all tried to hold onto some belief to get us through the rough times.

I went and sat in the pew beside her, and Jordan seemed satisfied by it, giving me a smirk and a slow nod.

"I hear you've been spending more time with young Jay," she said. "You like the boy?"

"I—I don't—"

"Ah, stuttering." She gave a knowing smile. "There's my answer. I asked you to keep an eye on him, and now you're falling for him."

"I'm not falling," I stammered. "Jay's just a friend."

Jordan's eyes carried skepticism. "So, he's not like his father? Not another rich boy looking to rip Harlem to shreds?"

"Not at all. Jay has his contradictions, sure. But he's not like his father. He doesn't dream of power and business. He cares."

"So, you know the father?" Jordan asked, eyebrows raising.

"No," I said, feeling like I'd revealed too much. "Well, we met one time."

"So he's power hungry." She pursed her lips. "I knew it. I'm wary of anyone close with someone who dreams of power, even if the kid himself is harmless. Power's a family business. I got the feeling Old Gatsby's the type to change the game on me when it suits him."

"Maybe, but Jay can't help what he came from." My gaze drifted around the church and then landed on a few worshippers sitting with their heads bowed, hands clasped, desperate for a miracle to solve things. "Anyway, I've got bigger things to worry about than Jay. Like why the man setting fires around Harlem is still on the loose."

"Because they ain't looking for the guy." Jordan glanced around and then lowered her voice as she leaned toward me. "One of my girls with cop ties says a rookie—*Cannon Cleary*—is on the case."

"Cannon Cleary?" I echoed, feeling a jolt of surprise. "I don't trust him to care a thing about this. His life's mission is to be accepted by the white man."

Jordan shrugged. "Cops are giving him an award at a Buchanan banquet this week. Saw flyers in Manhattan. Might be a good place to dig."

So, Cannon was my next lead. No one at the police department seemed to care about the case, and maybe that was because Cannon was in charge of it. The thought of him running the show caught me off guard. Who was he, really? What was he up to?

And how did Jordan know all this, anyway? It was like she had one foot in the shadows, and the other in some all-seeing realm.

"Odd question," I said. "Might you happen to know about anyone by the name of Pierre?"

"Pierre?" she repeated, familiarity flashing in her eye. "Oh yeah, I know a Pierre. Gambler at the Aphrodite Casino." She chuckled at the thought, shaking her head. "Used to buy from us because we let him haggle the price. What can I say? I felt sorry for the guy! He'd lose all this money and then do anything to gain it back. Guys like that—they'd do anything for a buck. Why you asking after that poor sucker?"

"He might be connected to the Buchanans," I said. "Helping them cover up their messes. If I can track him down, I might be able to find out more about the fire."

Jordan's smile widened at my knowledge, pride in her eye. "Sounds like a plan. Just be careful. That casino's Italian turf—no place for a Negro to play detective." She paused, then added, "If you are planning on going there, stop by the warehouse first. I've got something that might help. But after that, you can consider us square for giving me what I needed on the Gatsbys. The son's morals are better than the father's—that's good information. I can work with that."

That night, at the diner, I was wiping the counter when the bell over the door jingled, drawing my attention.

Jay stepped inside, and my pulse picked up, but I forced my face into a neutral expression, like I hadn't just been talking about him.

He slid into his usual booth with only a glance in my direction. I wiped my hands on my apron, took a breath, and headed over, sliding into the seat across from him, studying his face.

The energy between us felt different—more restrained. He looked tired, his gaze burdened by something.

"You okay?" I asked.

He let out a breath that was almost a laugh. "Sure. My father has me running around in circles trying to fix his problems and no matter what I do, it's never enough, but sure! I'm fine."

"Oh." His words were barbed, and I'd seen him annoyed before, but this was heavier than that. "That seems like a lot to carry."

"It is, but if I don't carry it, who will? That's what the Gatsbys do, right? Keep up appearances and pray no one sees the cracks." He looked sadly at the table, his voice lowering. "Sometimes I think about just leaving. Taking a car and driving until I run out of road."

"So, you don't like it here in New York?"

"Not always, no."

The thought of Jay, who mostly seemed like he could navigate any environment, wanting to just run away from everything made me see more in him. It was a restlessness I could relate to.

"What is it that you'd be running away from, exactly?" I asked him. "What problems of his does your father have you fixing?"

Jay's face was steely as his eyes fixed on mine. It was like he was waiting for me to provide a guess.

"Are you working with Daisy to keep your father's business running?" I asked, flat out. "I'm not talking about the school. I mean the underground business."

He shook his head. "I'm not sure what you mean," he replied, though his tone suggested he knew exactly what I was getting at.

"Your father has been talking to pushers in Harlem, for his second business. He wants to get clients from areas he'd rather not go to himself. The poorer neighborhoods. Is that right?"

He paused, weighing my words. "Did Daisy tell you that?"

"Not exactly," I said. "But it wasn't hard to figure out."

"Then there's no point in hiding it from you anymore." Jay gave a slow nod, leaning forward to keep his voice low. "My father is a bootlegger, yes. *But* he has plans to leave it behind. He wants to build housing projects for Southerners coming up North. Only problem is, lots of people aren't keen on integrated communities, and sometimes having too many morals makes you lose in real estate. And his properties are affordable, so we barely have enough to keep the mansion. That leaves me to do the bootlegging and keep us afloat."

"Your father's awfully critical of street life for a man who profits from it," I said.

Jay's lips curled slightly together. "The whole point of organized crime is to keep it quiet. The protest wasn't exactly quiet.

It brought attention to all of us."

"It was necessary attention," I countered, my voice firmer than I intended.

Our conversation paused when Leanna stopped by to refill our water glasses. Jay and I both murmured our thanks, but our eyes stayed locked, each of us holding something.

"Another question," I said. "Does your father hate me?"

Jay hesitated. "It's not hate. He just . . . doesn't understand you. And anyway, I don't care what he thinks."

I leaned back, absorbing it. "I spoke from the heart."

"And that's all you can do," Jay replied, a faint warmth in his voice. "I like you, and he'll have to deal with that."

"I like you too."

Jay's eyebrows lifted. "In what way?"

I wasn't sure how to say it. Putting words to whatever we felt had always been risky. Instead of answering, I looked outside the window, letting silence fill the space. My gaze fell on a lone man sitting slumped on a bench, hat pulled low over his eyes, cigarette smoke curling up over his face.

"The normal way," I said, shrugging it off. "You know, there are times when I want to run away too. And I might when I have the means. But this fire situation nags on me in a way I can't let go of. I have to get into this . . . Aphrodite Casino. I hear there's someone there who might have information."

Jay's expression turned serious. "Trying to play vigilante, are you?" But there was a hint of attraction in his voice. "You can't get into that place alone. If you're going, you should take me—and

Zihan too. He might be helpful. You remember his father was a stuntman?"

I hadn't thought about involving Zihan, but Jay was right. "So, you're willing to be hands-on with this too?" I asked. "Even though your father—"

"*Blast* my father!" Jay interrupted. "*And* his school and all his high-and-mighty ways!" Jay clapped his hands over his mouth, eyes wide as if he didn't mean to say it out loud.

It was as if a dam of tension broke in me just hearing him say it. I laughed like a hyena in that diner and covered my mouth too. And then we were both laughing—we were through with it all!

"Okay, so we're in this together," I said. "But we're going to need more than Zihan to take on that side of town. We'll need the equipment to keep ourselves safe should things go as badly as they did with the protest."

"Okay!" Jay gave an earnest nod. "I'm in."

Visiting Jordan with Jay made me uneasy, but I wanted to trust him. Jordan had told me to stop by her warehouse, hinting at something but keeping some cards close.

Jay and I made our way through the quiet streets to gather Zihan from the restaurant. He agreed without hesitation. He was tired after his shift, and tired of working so much. He'd been restless, caught between loyalty to his family's restaurant and a desire for something more daring.

Together, the three of us set off toward Jordan's warehouse, a sense of purpose settling over me, which replaced the hesitation.

Leading them to such a secret location may have been a bad idea, but she asked me to stop by and hadn't said I couldn't bring visitors. I had to build allies in this fight.

As we weaved through the housing projects in Jordan's part of town, Jay put his hands in his pockets and looked around at the trash on the streets. "So . . . you can't tell me where we're going?" he asked.

"You just have to see it," I said. "Like I did."

We paused at the door, and I knocked.

Vivian answered in seconds, sticking one half of her face out of the door. "Nick." And then she looked at Jay and gasped, polished nails flying over her mouth.

"Trust me, please?" I said. "I'm trying to figure out who started the West Egg fire and we need their help."

"Oh?" Vivian didn't open the door. Instead, she gave Jay a smile and stuck one ritzy leg, wrapped in a fishnet stocking out of the door, as if to caress the wood. "How do you do, Mr. Gatsby?" she said, in a sultry voice.

I rolled my eyes. "Oh, brother."

She smiled at him like she'd seen a celebrity, but then frowned at me. "Nick, you do realize Jordan will *hang* you when she sees him, right?"

"Jay's father is the bane of his existence!" I screamed, and then looked at Jay, who was wincing. "Sorry."

"Tell everybody my business, why don't you?" Jay replied, voice slightly cracking.

"You don't understand—it's crucial information," I told him.

"I'm tired of everybody having an opinion on you and all of them being wrong!"

Vivian licked her lips, fluffed her hair and looked Jay up and down. "Yeah . . . I got a few *opinions*, all right."

I could not be jealous of her advances in a moment when Vivian's interest in Jay might get us through the damn door once and for all.

She looked at Zihan. "And who are you?"

"Hello," Zihan said, with a wide smile. "Zihan. Just here for the dramatics."

"They're my friends," I said. "Please let us through. I promise nobody's gonna snitch."

Finally, Vivian resigned and opened the door wider. "Fine! But you'll be explaining this to Jordan on your own. I vouched for you, but I can't do it for your friends."

I walked them through the hideout, and to the kitchen, where the counters were crowded with tubes and tanks, glass bottles of spirit, pitchers of syrup and packages of mint julep.

Daisy was at the stove dunking droppers into a boiling pot. She turned her head, and her eyes widened as she blinked at us. "Um, Nick? Are you aware there's a Jay Gatsby standing next to you?"

"Oh, hi, Daisy," Jay said, looking up at the ceiling. "So, *this* is your hideout."

Jordan entered the kitchen as if on cue and squinted at Jay and then Zihan. She looked around at the empty air, as if searching for an answer. "Now how in the hell?" she said.

"Don't worry!" I told her. "They can be trusted—I promise."

"Nick," Jordan said, putting her head in her hand. "I told *you* to come to the warehouse. I didn't say bring your friends."

"Jordan, nice to see you again," Jay interrupted, his tone deep and measured. "I understand why you're upset. And if I'd known where Nick was taking me, I might have cautioned him to handle this more delicately. He's focused on his investigation—maybe too focused to think through every angle." He cast me a glance before turning back to her. "But you and I are in business together now, which means your needs are my needs. Whatever you need—a favor, a shipment, a connection—I can get it for you. My father knows *so* many people!"

Jordan crossed her arms, eyes narrowing at him. "Oh, I see. So, you think you can just . . . *smooth* this over with your talk about your elite connections?"

"We're here now, aren't we?" Jay said. "We can't afford to work at odds. Imagine we come out of this with new information on a crime that all of Harlem cares to see solved. You can use it to gain influence over the clientele you work with."

Jordan exhaled, mulling it over. Finally, she pointed at me. "You're lucky your man's good with words, Nick."

"My . . . *man*?"

"And I do like seeing this side of you," Jordan continued, over my words. "Showing focus and intention for once. Don't let me regret this." She turned back to Jay. "We do this? We do it my way. There are a few things you'll need before you go sniffing around Aphrodite."

"Thank you, Jordan," Jay said, his tone full of charm.

"Don't thank me yet," she growled, heading for the door. "If this goes bad, I'm not saving your asses. Now, you're going to need a few things to successfully pull this off."

Jordan led us to a part of the warehouse where punching bags hung from the ceiling and target boards were arranged on the floor. The soaring ceilings and large rooms provided ample space to train, and some of her crew, dressed in black masks, were out here laying combos into the swinging bags.

Jordan disappeared into a storage room and brought out a big black bag.

"Cops are cracking down on runners and ruffians," she said. "We have to be prepared for anything we find in the streets. And when my people are on jobs, you have to be ready for the heat to come down. No getting beat by the cops this time."

Jordan pulled out a long gun, staring at Jay the whole time, as if she wanted to make sure he saw the strength of her firepower. "So, you put the doohickeys in the whodunnits," she said, loading a dart into a vessel in the gun. "And you strap it over your shoulder, like this." She raised the musket, closing one eye, and aimed at the target.

"Some street inventors rigged my gun, so it shoots darts now. Harmless and built for training." Jordan fired the musket and out shot a dart, which hit the bullseye on the target across the room. "But in the field, we use the real thing. The guy you want—Pierre—I asked around, and you're right, Nick, he protects his clients from getting blasted in the press. If there's anyone who knows who started the fire, there's a good chance that Pierre is the one to give 'em hush money to keep 'em silent. You find Pierre, you might find the truth."

Jordan took more suitcases out from storage and opened one hard suitcase featuring another assortment of weapons and tools. "This is dangerous. You must be strategic." She turned to Jay and Zihan. "I still got half a mind to kick both of you out, so show me what you got. I want to feel comfortable sending you out with my things. Daisy's used to stuff like this, so it's probably smart for her to go too."

Daisy, who'd followed us to the training area, nodded in dutiful agreement as Jordan pointed at Zihan.

"Let's start with you," she said.

Zihan walked to the center of the room and picked up a tiny steel tube, the size of a battery. He pressed a button on the side and the tube lengthened to a staff. "Aha!" he said with a smile. "I thought that's what this was. Ba used to use this on set to train before his accident." He began to punch at the air with it. "You punch with the stick. It doesn't do much damage, but it's good to fight off crowds if there is a lot of people. The power is in the speed." Zihan tossed me the staff.

I caught it and then I stepped forward as if I was next up in a talent show. Zihan moved to the end of the line. I repeated his movements, amazed at the lightness of the stick, and how fast it could swing.

"Nice." I chose a baseball bat from Jordan's assortment of weapons. "I'm old school, I think," I said, and looked at the underside of the bat handle. "I would probably use this end if I had to defend myself, so I don't break any bones in their face."

"Mm-mm," Jordan said. Her arms were crossed as she shook her head. "You gotta get more comfortable breaking bones, Nick. That cop didn't give one snot about you when he had you pinned on the ground."

"You know about that?" I asked.

"Of course I do," Jordan said. "It's called keeping your ear to the streets."

"Not my best moment," I said, holding the bat out to Daisy.

She took it from me and immediately placed it down again, stepping up to pick a little knife with a black handle. "Tom Buchanan has a lovely kitchen, but in between mealtimes, it gets boring around the house. What else is a girl to do but learn to throw knives?" She threw a knife, and it hit the target, causing me to flinch. "But you should never throw a knife unless you have another weapon to go with it." Daisy fished a tiny revolver out of the suitcase and aimed it at Jay.

"Whoa!" Jay said, putting his hands up. "Daisy, I know we haven't always seen eye to eye, but—"

"Relax," Daisy said, opening the chamber to show him it was empty. She smiled at Jay, who was next up. "Your turn."

Jay stepped forward and took the gun from Daisy. "Never learned to use one of these," he said, setting it down gently in the suitcase. Then he took a coin out of his pocket. "Have you all heard of the disappearing coin trick?" He held a coin between two fingers, and then with a wave of his hand, it disappeared.

I was quite impressed, but Jordan wasn't.

"Really, Gatsby?" she said, raising a disapproving eyebrow. "A magic trick?"

Jay sheepishly pulled the coin out of thin air again and stuffed it in his pocket. "It's the best I've got."

"How fast are you?" Jordan asked.

"I once broke the record for the 100 meters," Jay said, pulling down the waist of his pants slightly to reveal the track shorts underneath. "But that was long before West Egg was even dreamed of!"

"Good grief." Jordan rolled her eyes. "I didn't say take your pants off. Definitely keep those on . . ." She went back to the storage closet, this time bringing out a bag full of black masks. She took out the masks one by one and tossed them to us.

I caught one and examined the thin black fabric with small silver rhinestones.

"Once you put on this mask, you become a ruffian," she said. "A trouble-starter. An outlaw. You are no longer you, but someone else entirely. You might have been working a boring office job, or as an undercover cop, or a student from an elite school. But all anyone knows when you're wearing these is that no one knows who you are."

"This isn't going to give me hives is it?" Jay said, laughing as he tried his mask on.

"What?" Jordan said with a straight face. "Don't try to be funny, Gatsby—I don't know you like that yet and I find it alarming." She gestured for us to follow her into the storage room.

Once inside, she pulled a map from one of the cases on the shelves. She laid it on a wooden table in the middle of the cramped space and motioned for us to gather around it. "You're going onto foreign turf. Can't guarantee there won't be some problems. Act like you're selling liquor—it's your easiest way inside. On entry, the password is *Lepanto. This* lets them know you're rolling with the hard stuff. Keep your masks handy. If things go wrong, find the nearest exit. But do not be seen."

She pointed to three corners of the map. "There are three exits to escape from. One on the east side of the building, one on the front floor north side, and one in the basement. The basement leads to where the car will be waiting to take you out of there. This is on loan, so I'll hold your feet to fire if it's not returned."

Jordan clapped her hands, drawing our attention back to her. "All right, enough talk. Everybody out of my spot before I change my mind. And don't forget the masks—ruffians, remember?"

Jay said, "Jordan, whatever we do out there, we'll return what's yours. I know it's hard to trust new people with your assets, but I'll make it worth your while."

Jordan's eyes narrowed at him, her suspicion still sharp as a blade, but she finally relented. "Don't slip now," she hissed. "Or I'll hold it against you forever."

We left the warehouse for streets that were mostly deserted.

Jay slid his hands into his pockets. "Nick?" he said, his voice carrying a high-pitched lilt. "Next time you've got a wild plan, do me a favor and run it by me first? I might be able to keep you from getting yourself killed by the scary mob boss."

I chuckled a bit. "Jordan is more misunderstood than scary. Daisy, what do you think?"

Daisy, who had been walking just behind us with Zihan and asking him questions, widened her eyes some. "Misunderstood as in . . . *ruthless*? Sure! But she certainly gets things done."

Zihan chimed in with a laugh. "For a moment, I thought she might kick me out."

Daisy put a reassuring grip on his arm. "We're friendly to our neighbors who mean no harm."

"Thank you," Zihan said. "I have never been part of something like this before. But it's good. I can be myself. You all make me feel safe."

A smile formed on Daisy's lips. "Very good! We've all got secrets. Well, *had* secrets. You're in good company."

Jay turned to face all of us, and as he walked backward, his eyes moving between Daisy and me, something clicked in his mind. "Okay so . . . you two *are* cousins?"

"Yes," we both said.

Jay let out an energetic laugh. "I was right! This explains so much—the way you two talk, the way you trust each other! Why you look similar!"

"Very smart of you, Jay," I said, feeling light as a breeze.

"No more secrets," Jay said. "You're full of surprises, Nick Carrington!" His voice exploded like a firework through the night.

I quickly looked away and tamed my smile. No one had ever said that about me before, and for some reason it felt like I needed a private room to respond to it properly.

Daisy stepped up beside me. "Look at us," she said, her voice carrying sarcasm and whimsy. "A bunch of oddballs with nothing to lose!"

Ahead of us lay a dangerous mission at the Aphrodite Casino. It was a place none of us were prepared for, but would be far easier to take on as a team.

16.

I ENTERED THE APHRODITE THROUGH THE WINE cellar above the joint, gave the guard the password—*Lepanto*—and slipped past. A narrow staircase led me down, the air getting warmer with each step. At the bottom, red curtains parted to reveal the cellar-turned-casino.

The space unfolded in tiers, a multilevel room draped in deep carpets. Though I could see its full layout from where I stood, it still felt deep enough to disappear in. Poker tables, gilded slot machines, and game setups crowded the floor in a riot of color and movement, filling every inch of the place.

Women in rompers sat at bars smoking from sticks, some swinging their hips to the ragtime blues that blasted through the Aphrodite. Men in suits and hats came to flirt with them. Smoke blurred all their faces, so they appeared and then dissipated.

Everyone is Italian, I realized, careful not to let my nerves throw me off my mission.

Some people looked at me funny as I entered the room because a well-dressed Negro was a remarkable sight. I was wearing a white shirt from Arrow, slacks from Dickies, and a gold chain from Bailey, Banks, and Biddle. They were anything but cheap, altogether or separate.

I settled on a stool by an empty poker table, where I could people watch in obscurity. Daisy arrived from a different entrance, a vision in shimmering gold and green, sideways bangs curling out of a black hat. She barely looked at the men who watched her walk in—she headed straight for the bar while absorbing their attention.

A voice erupted behind me. "You some kinda pusher?" A drunk Italian with a big round head was leaning off his chair, holding out his empty glass.

Already? I pulled a flask filled with Daisy's stash of liquor from my jacket, filled his glass to the top, and told him, "15 cents."

The man slapped some coins in my hand. "My brotha! Keep the change!"

Well, at least there's money to be made here!

I tucked away my flask and teased my suspenders at the bottom to adjust them. They were too tight and then too loose! My clothes did not fit as well as the older people's did.

Jay entered the casino from where I came, in a glittering black shirt and white slacks, and walked over to a row of slot machines. He put a nickel in a slot and pulled the handle. I watched as his eyes lit up at the patterns in the window.

Now we had all made it inside, while Zihan waited outside for us. He'd offered to be our lookout and getaway driver.

I approached Jay as he pressed the glowing buttons. I could tell he was hoping for a line of matching symbols to appear.

I took a padded stool beside him. "Any luck yet?"

"It's been thirty seconds," he said. "The chances we find Pierre that quickly are slim to none. Any one of these guys could be him."

"I meant with the machine."

"Oh. Ha! Not yet. I'm looking for a line of cherries."

I surveyed the room until my eyes landed on a rolling catering cabinet. Its attendant was working something out on the back of the machine, and it gave me a mischievous idea.

"Watch this," I said.

I crouched down and slipped through the doors of the cabinet. I reached out and carefully unhooked a key from his waist and then returned to the slot machine and used it to pop the plating off it. I pulled the lever that would release the back door and lifted the back panel upward, finding the stack of nickels that controlled everything. Then I pumped the lever to dispense the coins into my hand.

"Nick!" Jay exclaimed, in a loud whisper. "You can't do it that way."

"Why not?" I said, laughing. "You get the money faster."

"It's not about the money." He tried to reattach the back of the machine. "It's about the fun of playing, hoping you get a match. You take the fun out when you up and steal all the goods! Now reattach that thing and return the key before they catch us."

I dumped the nickels in my pocket and reapplied the backing.

"Okay." Jay returned to the front of the machine. He pulled

that lever, hoping for the best, and then yelled, "Dammit!" when the symbols didn't line up.

"See—it's all a waste of time!"

"Well, what else is there to do?" He dropped his hands and looked at me.

I pulled him away from his game and weaved through the people until I saw the sign for a bathroom. I had to be somewhere private with him, only for a moment, so I pulled him into the bathroom and closed the door behind us. We stood chest to chest between the narrow walls.

I grabbed the chain glinting around his neck. "What is this? Silver?"

"Nickel-plated." Jay unbuttoned his shirt some to reveal a locket with a picture of his mom inside. "Why did you drag me in here?"

I struggled to stay focused on his eyes, but it was hard. He was doing this on purpose—I was sure of it.

"Because I don't like Italian casinos," I said. "We're the only Negroes—haven't you noticed? There's weird energy from these people. Who knows if we'll even find the guy, or what he even looks like? A lot of those Italians got pistols hanging off their waists tonight too. If we're found out, we're goners."

"You brought that staff, didn't you?"

I had. Even though it was retractable, I could feel the cold rod in my sock.

"You have trouble having fun, Nick," Jay said. "Why don't you relax a bit?"

"I don't have trouble with anything. Back off, Jay." But I thought about what he said. Was I someone who struggled to relax? Perhaps I was. He was getting to know me quite well.

We were inches apart now. I caught the scent from his neck, and it smelled like a bar of eucalyptus soap.

"Let's go back to the slots." Jay took my hand as if shaking it backward and pulled me from the bathroom.

Once we were outside, he instantly let go. Of course he did. He started playing the slots again, and I left him there to go up to the balcony, where I could survey the room for Pierre.

Was he that man with the bulbous nose who laughed loudly every two minutes? Or was he someone quieter and more discreet?

From afar, I saw Daisy lean over a casino roulette wheel, whispering things to a smiling tan man she'd just met. Was that Pierre? If we were ever going to locate the guy, she'd be first to find him what with her magnetic personality and captivating beauty.

A security man came up to me, blocking my view. "Hey, big guy. Who's your boss?"

"Um . . . Mister . . ." I scanned the room, landing on a blinking concessions sign, offering snacks. "Mr. Pretzel . . . ton?" I said. "Mr. Pretzelton?"

"Who the hell's Mr. Pretzelton?"

"He's my boss," I said, as if it should be obvious.

The man held out a meaty hand. "Where's your ticket? Ain't no such thing as a Mr. Pretzelton. You ain't part of Uptown Crew."

"Ticket? My boss is friendly with those guys, sir. See, it's all about camaraderie."

"Ticket?"

"And friendship!" *How long could I bull my way through this encounter?*

I looked at Jay to signal that it was time to find Pierre *now*, but he was focused on the machine. Daisy unwrapped her arm from around a man and saw from my eyes that we were in trouble.

"I'll have to ask my friend there," I told the big guy.

When I tried to walk past him, he grabbed my elbow. "Not so fast."

Clapping my hands around my mouth, I screamed, "Pierre!"

That was the loudest I'd ever been!

Then I surveyed the room. Most people were looking to see who had screamed, but one man's eyes stayed on me—in confusion and then concern. A man in a leather jacket with a greyhound at his side.

I slipped out of the man's grip and ran while Daisy rushed to grab Pierre. Jay looked around like he was lost. I pulled a mask from under my shirt over my face and jumped over the balcony, landing on the edge of a table. It flipped, and cards and chips flew everywhere.

I was on the floor with an ache in my back, a collection of chips on my lap. The lights of the ceiling created a glare around the people whose poker game I'd bombed, but I could tell from the chaos around me that they were not happy.

Some of the people fled, but one man brought a cane down on me to whack me in the head. A shoe flew out of nowhere, catching the stick in the crook of its high heel.

It was Daisy—she'd dived through the crowd to stop the swing before hitting me. With only half a second to pull the retractable staff from my boot and extend it, I swung upward, smashing it into the man's arm, so Daisy could recover.

She reached through the slit of her dress to pull out her knife, but a man trained a pistol at her. I couldn't get up fast enough to stop him should he shoot her! All I could do was pull a coin from the pocket of my shirt and flip it into the air to distract the gunman. By some miracle, the man was so stupid, so money-obsessed, that he let his eyes follow the coin through its upward tumbles.

As he watched the quarter flip between Lady Liberty and the bald eagle, I sprung forward, tucked backward into his body, and clock-hand spun him in a different direction. His finger jerked against the trigger, but the bullet went into the shoulder of one of his own boys.

The shot man screamed and tipped over in his chair. Before I could even process that, Daisy used the tipped table like a launch-pad and moved with a speed and precision I'd never imagined she possessed. Using the table for leverage, she jumped the shooter and wrapped her legs around his neck. I spun away from him, and she twist-flipped him into a face plant.

Another table was overturned by the man's feet, flinging a shot glass into a pillar. Glass rained over the both of us as Daisy recovered to one knee, knife still in hand. She wrenched the gun from his hand and then aimed it in a circle at the goons, who'd begun to close in.

"Back up," she demanded, causing all the men to back away with their hands up.

I caught sight of Jay chasing Pierre and his dog from the venue—they both escaped through the emergency exit in the alley. And then, the room burst into even more chaos as cops flooded in. Our luck would have it that tonight was the night that they decided to bust Aphrodite's for both the drinking and the gambling.

Pandemonium broke out between the cops and the remaining patrons. As dancers ran screaming from the violence, Daisy and I ducked away.

Someone had bolted the emergency exit to stop the cops from coming in, but there was one more—wasn't there?

"Nick, get down," Daisy said, pulling me to the floor as a gunshot popped off from somewhere.

We started to crawl, navigating around the busy feet, the broken stools, the stomped dice.

"Uh, when did you learn that move?" I asked.

"Oh, that?" Daisy said, glancing over her shoulder. "They teach it to you in finishing school. Right after tea etiquette. *How to throw a man over your shoulder.*"

When we stood up again, it was at a free door—the second exit. We ran outside and up the sloped alley into the streets slick with puddles.

Across the road, we found the roofless black car where Zihan was waiting, beckoning for us to hurry up. Once Daisy got in the front and I in the back, he pushed the gas and the car sped down the street.

Jay had been chasing Pierre, but he must've gotten a cramp in his foot because where we picked him up, he was hopping on one foot and screaming in pain.

The car screeched to a halt, and Zihan grabbed him by the collar, pulling him right off the sidewalk and throwing him into the back with one hand.

"Ow!" Jay screamed as he fell backward against me.

Zihan pressed the gas and veered into the street. An oncoming car in the other lane honked as he swerved to follow Pierre down into an alley. The car ran over puddles and dips of damaged pavement as he grabbed a trash can and then threw it at the car—its nasty, slippery fruit peels and food wrappers raining all over us.

Then Pierre mounted a motorcycle—his dog tucked into the sidecar—and took off, back onto the main street. We turned out of the alley so fast the car almost tipped over, and I had to hold on to Jay to stay steady. This car was speeding like a runaway train about to fly straight off the rails.

Ours was the most reckless engine on the road until we turned to see that Pierre had dumped his motorcycle to make for a fire escape. We stopped the car, and I jumped out to chase him.

I managed to grab him and threw him against a dumpster. "Not so fast!" I punched him in the face.

I became a raving mad loon hellbent on revenge! I didn't mind it. Maybe I'd been holding this inside for too long—the way I barely got out of Greenwood, the way I'd been made to feel grateful for West Egg like it was a grand act of charity instead of a means to tame us. But we weren't boys in need of taming! We weren't strays to be thrown scraps! Students were failing at life because we were being treated like kindling. Why not punch a guy?

"Who started the fire?" I screamed, punching him again, breaking the skin on my knuckles.

"That's enough, Nick," Daisy said, pulling me away.

It was not enough though! *How dare he help someone who'd burn us alive?*

Jay and Zihan were watching me like I was a maniac. I resolved to stop punching and catch my breath. I couldn't yell at the man incomprehensibly and expect answers.

Pierre, frazzled and skinny-necked, looked even weaker with three punches in his face. "Who are you people?" he whinnied. "What do you want from me?"

"Official business, as far as you're concerned," I said, steady. "Word is, you've got a knack for coverups. What's your latest one about?"

"Whoever mentioned my name is a *liar,*" Pierre said.

"Was it the West Egg fire?" I demanded.

"I don't know shit about that! Look, I've covered up a lot of bad things, but I didn't do no cover-up for a school fire—this I know for sure."

He was giving me nothing, so I punched him again. He started laughing and shouting, "Lay it on me! Let's go again," until another punch knocked him out.

Daisy walked over to me and looked down at the unconscious body at my feet. "Well, Nick, what do we do now?"

"Leave him," I answered. "We have what we need."

Daisy raised an eyebrow, and I pointed to the motorcycle Pierre had abandoned, still sitting down the block, where the mutt was sniffing around for his owner. The tag of the dog's collar—sure to have Pierre's address engraved on it—almost gleamed in the spotlight of the streetlamp.

"Trust me," I told her.

I had a plan for this now. Sometimes just asking wasn't enough.

Daisy had work in the morning at six o'clock sharp. Jay said he was exhausted, so he was heading home. I explained that I needed some time to myself to think. Just so they wouldn't worry, I added that I would be home shortly. When they left—Jay promising to hail a cab and escort Daisy home—I asked Zihan if he'd break into Pierre's apartment with me.

"I figured you were lying to them," he said, his tone knowing. "But I'm in. Lead the way. I'll follow."

His quick acceptance only made the weight of my decision easier to carry. There was comfort in knowing that Zihan was game for whatever came next.

I never had gone to such extreme measures to get answers before. But we had to find justice on our own now that no institution was supporting us.

We left Pierre where he had fallen, leaning against the dumpster, after searching his jacket for his house keys.

I took a knife to both his motorcycle tires to get a head start, while Zihan grabbed the leash of Pierre's dog and put him in the car. Once I read the dog's tag, Zihan drove us inconspicuously to Pierre's tenement.

Pierre lived in an opulent penthouse that showed a view of Union Square—a park surrounded by office buildings. There was a filing cabinet behind his desk. I opened it to find stacks of folders and binders.

Soon I was caught up in the bizarre contents of Pierre's records. I found a stack of newspapers that showed investigative reports of several crimes, but nothing damning.

I sat on the floor and sifted through the file cabinet. I pulled out more newspaper clippings and stumbled on something unexpected.

FOR IMMEDIATE RELEASE IN SELECT PUBLICATIONS

NEW GOVERNMENT BUREAU AIMS TO TARGET RADICALS IN HARLEM

Washington, D.C.—Attorney General A. Mitchell Palmer has intensified efforts to safeguard American ideals by ordering sweeping raids on radical organizations, including the Universal Negro Improvement Association. To further these aims, his office is establishing a special bureau to investigate and monitor suspected agitators, compiling records of their activities and associations.

> Among those supporting the initiative is prominent real estate investor Tom Buchanan, who has contributed large funds to aid the bureau's work. Buchanan has expressed concerns about maintaining the character of neighborhoods such as Harlem, which he describes as increasingly affected by the unchecked migration of Negroes from the South.
>
> Thus far, Palmer's campaign has resulted in five major raids, over 400 arrests, and the deportation of 54 foreign-born radicals. Authorities insist that their efforts are necessary to rid the nation of subversive influences. Harlem, rapidly becoming a hub of Negro commerce and culture, has drawn scrutiny, with officials vowing to curb the moral and social disruption brought by the invasion of Southern migrants.

I read it, and then reread it. Tom was funding the arrest of undesirables and sweeping in to rebuild over their bones? No wonder he was buying everything Negroes owned—he wanted to get rid of us. A man who moved like this required partners to help him cover up his image. Pierre was one—a corrupt guy who wanted crumbs from Buchanan's wealth.

And Gatsby was another. He did business with Buchanan, a man who was supporting people who hated migrants. He sure as hell didn't care about West Egg's mission.

I grabbed a notebook from Pierre's desk and jotted down notes from the papers. I was connecting the dots. I arrived here looking for anything I could find on the Blue House, but I was coming away with a full chart of evidence for why Buchanan needed to be stopped. He was coming for our community in Harlem.

With his hatred for migrants clear, could he have conspired to burn the Blue House down as just one more piece in his plot? One step closer to reshaping Harlem as a neighborhood and wiping away our presence?

Buchanan must have been thrilled to see his crime push Negroes into protest, to twist our anger into proof that we didn't belong here.

"I just found what I needed," I told Zihan, my voice shivering with tension as I turned to him. "Let's get out of here."

This was bigger than just one attack. Buchanan wasn't just after real estate—he was waging war on our entire existence in Harlem. This wasn't just about justice for the Blue House. It was about saving Harlem, my community, from being entirely snuffed out.

17.

THE NEXT EVENING, I WAS TOO RESTLESS TO BE alone, and I ended up sitting on the bench at the end of Daisy's bed, telling her everything I'd found in Pierre's place.

"You were right—the guys up here are the same as the ones down South," I said. "They're just smarter about it. On the surface, what Buchanan's doing is not illegal, so he'll get away with ridding Harlem of Negroes just because no one will care enough to stop him."

Daisy pulled her knees to her chest, looking uncharacteristically exhausted without any makeup on. "You really think this means Tom had something to do with the fire?"

"Why else would Pierre—Buchanan's man—be keeping an unpublished article about his funding of this Negro-hating bureau? Buchanan doesn't want us around, but he can't have everyone knowing that. So, he works with Gatsby on West Egg, even though he hates what West Egg stands for, and sabotages it from the inside. Whoever did the fire knew how to get into the building, how to stay hidden . . . It had to be someone he hired and gave access to."

She nodded in agreement, and I could tell she was upset beneath her thoughtful composure. "Couldn't it have been Charlie?"

"No, these Buchanans . . . They don't get their hands dirty. They have people like Pierre and Artie for that."

"You're right," she said. "This might have been about someone in this city or at West Egg doing something crazy to get ahead. Which is what everything in this world seems to be about these days. I mean, what happened to morals?"

The weight of that thought pressed heavy on her the way it did me. She was frustrated, but also deeply weary of a world where the most violent people came out on top.

Buchanan's friends could control what people read and thought. It was hopeless to think of lies drowning out the truth!

"I can't tell you how tired I already am of just waiting for justice," said Daisy. "Sometimes I want to just rob the rich! You know, like Robin Hood."

Her words sparked something in me. "Wait, in a real way?"

"Could you imagine?" She laughed. "I can't say I haven't thought up my own revenge against Tom, stuck for hours in that kitchen of his. I like to think I've cooked up a fairly decent plan: You may not know this, but Jay's father used to host these grand parties. He hasn't had one in ages, but if he threw one, the whole city would come—all of the elites, Tom included. And while everyone's there, drinking and flaunting, I would search his place and steal all his money."

I snickered as I processed her words—what she was suggesting was a joke, but it was also thrilling. "You'd have access to most areas of the home because you work for him. And if you added me into your plans, I could open the safes. Together we could get a real look at his fortune and find proof he's behind the violence at West Egg—and Harlem—at the same time."

"And we could bring in Jay to help!" Daisy said excitedly as she perked up, thrilled by her own brilliance. "Stage a proposal for Jay Jr. and me, which would make Gatsby giddy to throw an engagement party. Buchanan would show up to support us, since he works with Gatsby and I work for him—there would be no question about it. That would give us time to search."

I felt some doubt as this plan started to feel more real. "I don't know if Jay would agree to something like this," I said.

Was this really all for laughs? It sure gave us a way forward that didn't leave us waiting on someone else's approval. This was something we could take into our own hands!

"What do you think Jay would *really* say . . . if you asked?" Daisy said.

"I don't know," I admitted. "You've known him longer."

"Yes, but you could ask him," she said, her tone sharpening some into seriousness.

"Why?" I asked. "I mean, why me?"

"He's never had much passion for anything but you."

I brushed it off. "He switches his affection between me and other people."

Daisy rolled her eyes. "This again. You can't see how dapper you are, but it doesn't change the truth. What he has for you is more genuine than what he has for them."

I was slightly embarrassed but charmed more than that. "I could run it by him, I suppose? It might be a tall order to get him to entertain it—he has love for his father. It's risky to ask him to lie!"

"Riskier than waiting forever for this horrible world to change?" Daisy implored.

Silence followed between us. It was the quiet of possibilities. And I realized how serious she was about bringing justice to the elites, who'd built their wealth in shady ways.

"What might happen if we stopped waiting for permission?" she went on.

"Well, we'd get what we wanted," I said. "And probably go to jail."

"And what if we fled before they could catch us?"

Daisy raised her eyebrows at me. It seemed she had considered this already and I was only just getting invited to the discussion.

"You've thought about this," I said, meeting her eyes.

She shrugged. "Maybe a bit. Only because I know Tom is corrupt and has a lot of money."

How much money? I wondered. *More than the Gatsbys?*

"I do think a lot . . ." Daisy went on. "Maybe too much, about how wrong it is that Tom is rich in the first place. His family owned slaves before the war. They made a fortune off the backs of our people. The money in his house? It only *scrapes the surface* of all that he has, written in the wills of his father and the fathers before, and yet he tips the scales more in his favor every day.

"Not because he *needs* it—just because he wants it." Daisy locked eyes with me. "All I'm saying is . . . Tom is indestructible. But we're not. And he knows it. So, he gets this sick satisfaction, watching me work around the house. Clarence handles all his odd jobs and he bosses the man around like he owns him. Funding the Egg only because he knows it will create more servants. And just as easily, he burns it all down when it strikes his fancy."

My mind opened up as she spoke, to the horrible reality of Buchanan's manipulation.

She'd made a good point. If he really was as rich as Daisy said, what harm would it do, really, if he lost some of it? An amount that could change our lives?

The Blue House was the worst of what Gatsby had inherited from Buchanan's property—a crumbling piece of architecture they turned into a dorm. Not a place for students—just a building desperate to disintegrate from the weight of the seasons, where Negroes could be corralled, locked away in case someone wanted to kill a bunch of us at once. It felt like the home I'd fled, its constant memory shooting through my brain, reminding me of how quickly we could be destroyed, forgotten.

I was queasy at the images that pulsed through my mind, of Buchanan watching from a distance as we all fell for the trap and found our demise. That didn't explain why it was so easy for everyone to get out though. If someone really wanted to harm us, wouldn't they have bolted the exits?

Well, maybe it was because it wasn't death that they wanted

but the power to control us through fear. And that required us to be alive.

"Jay is in the middle," Daisy went on, her voice soothing me out of my thoughts, some. "Rich, but he hates it. Maybe it's time we use him to help us level the playing field. You might be surprised what he would do for you."

Part of me believed her. My bond with Jay was strong, despite our ups and downs. I couldn't imagine Jay taking it so far that he'd actually steal from Buchanan. I'd have to talk to him.

What else could I do? What other option did we have? We tried for fairness through protest and it got us brutalized. Buchanan and his kind never had to feel their faces pushed to the concrete, and they did so much worse. We were running out of ways to take back our power.

Daisy and I sat in a silence that became increasingly thoughtful, holding on to this dangerous, desperate plan as if it were the only hope we had left. And perhaps it was.

I thought and worried about convincing Jay to do a major job in the coming days. Aphrodite was one thing, but actually targeting Tom Buchanan? The big guy? Stealing? I wasn't sure.

My time with Jay already had to be more private now that I was on Mr. Gatsby's list of bad apples. But Jay insisted I visit his home on Long Island again when his father was out of town, as if he wanted to break the rules.

It was an unusually warm spring day and he'd gone for a swim. He wanted to play Marco Polo, but I wanted to sit in my white speed suit, with its elastic rib, and just enjoy the warm wind. He matched me with a white pair of cotton trunks, with a navy trim. We didn't plan it. It happened naturally.

"What would it take to convince you to say . . . rob a rich person?" I asked, as I sat on the edge of his pool, teasing my legs through the water.

Jay popped out of the pool water, threw his hands backward over his hair. "What?"

"What would it take to make you rob a rich man?" I asked.

He pushed himself up on the side of the pool, his body raining like a heavy storm. "You're not serious."

"I am! What would it take?"

"A complete plan, for one," he said, still brushing it off. "Like, who would we rob?"

"Okay, how about Tom Buchanan," I said. "Hypothetically."

Jay sat beside me, raising an eyebrow. "Really?"

"Daisy could scout the safes in his place, and I could break them open. You could have a party at your place and entertain the guests long enough for us to finish the job."

"Sure, because I love talking with all my father's lovely friends," Jay said. "If we were to do that, what would we do when Buchanan notices his cash is missing?"

"Take air," I said. "You said you want to get out of here, didn't you?"

The way he paused showed me that he'd really meant it when he said it. "Where do we go after New York?"

"Chicago might be nice. I hear all the G-men are corrupt and the city breaks into total mayhem a couple times a year."

"Lovely." Jay scoffed and looked off to the side. "Don't you crave safety?"

"Controlled chaos makes me feel safe, in a way now. It means there's some awareness that the world is a bad place."

"And when the police catch us on the road with a bunch of jewels in the car?"

"Please." I knew his question was not serious. Weeks ago, he almost let Cannon Cleary fall off a building. "You're not afraid of the police."

"I sort of am." Jay winced and massaged the meat of his knee. "I think I got a cramp."

I removed his hand, replacing it with mine, to dig into the sore spot for him. "We'll put the money into things and make it look like it was earned, or you could dump it into one of your father's banks and say he earned it."

"My father's banks? How?" Jay talked about his father like he was a long-lost stranger who'd spent his entire life at this mansion.

I noticed that Jay seemed freer when he was left to himself. I think his father thought every negative emotion brought a negative outcome, so there'd be no use for the feelings like anger and rage—the ones he couldn't tie into a neat bow.

"I don't know," I said. "Shouldn't you know? You're a bootlegger."

"I don't," he said, flatly.

I looked at Buchanan's house—that white palace of excess and perfection, with long balconies and windows blocked by black portieres. The clouds behind it were like swan wings sprung in flight, spraying pinks and whites in front of the sun.

"I have reason to believe Buchanan's corruption runs deeper than a lot of people realize," I said. "Without money, he'd be forced to face the true person that he is."

"True, he would." Jay looked around, seeming eager to change the subject. "I do hope karma comes around for him eventually. Say, do you want to go to Coney Island next Sunday?"

I forgot I was turning eighteen next week, maybe because going even deeper into adulthood filled me with dread. Spending the day with Jay was the best gift I could give myself. "Sure," I said.

I didn't question the things he wanted to do with me. I accepted every perk.

"Or we could do an orchestra outing at the Lafayette," he said.

"Sure," I repeated.

Jay reached over for his watch on top of his pile of clothes. "My father will be back soon." He looked back at his house with worry. "You may want to get going."

As I stood and gathered my things, the weight of the plan hung in the air between us. I'd gotten no answer. But that also meant I hadn't gotten a no. I could feel something in him that was unsatisfied—the same way I was, though it may have been about something different.

Jay fixed his gaze on the horizon, lost in whatever thoughts were brewing in his head. I almost thought we'd work through this in a sudden moment of clarity, but then he turned around halfway and gave me a strangely formal nod.

"Stay safe," he said softly.

Oh, that made me heated! "You're not going to walk me out?" I asked, bass in my voice.

"Oh." Jay jumped up, his expression like a dog's who'd been caught peeing on a rug. "You're right. Apologies."

I tried to hide the rolling of my eyes as we walked through the yard and into the house. Everything was quiet. Then he sent me off, watching from the doorway as I went, alone into the world of my plans.

Later, I sat on the stoop, and Daisy walked the rows of Auntie's crop garden, searching for ripe tomatoes. We'd decided that we'd attend the gala at the Buchanan mansion, during which Cannon would receive an award. Daisy would go, just to support her boss's event, and I'd go as her escort.

I hadn't forgotten what Jordan had said about Cannon. It was easy to speculate now that Buchanan was the one paying him off and stalling out the investigation, but I wanted to *know*.

The gala would be flush with cops, and we'd be there to overhear their conversations, as their lips were loosened by the very alcohol they spent their days sweeping the city to confiscate.

Every now and then, the breeze lifted Daisy's skirt, and she didn't fix it, only lilted in the wind like an apple, almost fallen.

Uncle Beet opened the door behind us. "Nick, your auntie said she wants to give you this suit for the gala."

Daisy filled a basket and took it into the house. Meanwhile, I left to find Auntie in the washroom slipping a hanger through a blazer for a three-piece forest-green suit. "This used to be your uncle's, but I think it will look great on you too. See if it fits."

I checked it out in the mirror. I liked the Norfolk jacket—it looked good on me, but the sleeves were a bit too big. Auntie attached a West Egg pin to the lapel because she still loved the coveted ribbon of status, even though hate had taken it down.

"There'll be a good bit of journalists at this gala, won't there?" Auntie asked. "Get your foot in where you can."

Ah, making connections. I hated the idea. But each time I thought of disappointing her or Uncle Beet it felt like betraying my own parents. I was planning to break a few safes before the spring arrived. Life insisted I do this, and I was going full speed ahead. I couldn't crank the brakes.

"It's hard to get a real job as a writer without my certificate," I told Auntie, almost as a coded apology for my plans. "The school burned down before I could get it."

"All the more reason to make a good impression. Good luck tonight," she said with a smile. "I know you'll do great."

Auntie, I've taken to the streets, and they've taken me, I wanted to say. Isaiah was right—so much of growing up was simply taking charge of your life without explaining a thing.

I went back into the house and found Daisy in her room, trying on a top in front of the mirror.

I studied a necklace sitting on her table. "What's this?" I asked as I entered the room. It burned dark blue like the night ocean waves.

"It's sapphire," Daisy said after she saw me looking. "Nick, why don't you wear it tonight?"

I examined the gem and the tag. "Buchanan's Jewelers? Did *he* . . . give you this?"

"Charlie did, back when he was trying to pursue me. He's generous with his father's things," Daisy returned with a shrug.

When she was finished dressing, she pulled a giant piece of rolled-up parchment from inside the closet.

"Come here, I want to show you what I've been working on." She unfolded a sketch, beckoning me to hover over it. "I've been marking on the map where I've seen safes in Buchanan's house. Tom revealed at least two of the locations to me while drunk, but I think the more important ones are in the vents—one in the library, in the space under the mounted elk, and the other is hidden somewhere in his bedroom. I've never seen it, so we may not be able to reach that one. And we still need to figure out how to open them."

"Easy," I said. "Grease."

"Grease?"

"It's a chemical you can use that makes a concoction that burns safes. My mentor taught me how to crack them in a manner of ways, but that one is the easiest. I still have his tin of it."

"Okay, Nick." Daisy looked impressed. "So I'll leave that up to you. If you can get away tonight, try to scope out all the places I've marked so you can know exactly where they are later."

It was happening. And tonight, at Buchanan's mansion, we'd lay the groundwork necessary to pull it off, whether Jay chose to help us out or not.

In Buchanan's driveway later, I got out of the car first to help Daisy out, and we set out to navigate through the maze of Harlem's most esteemed. People and activity filled the round lot; policemen and politicians spilling out of limos.

I spotted Mr. Cleary, Cannon's father, holding open the door for his wife and their perfect Cannon. I'd understand his motives by the end of the night. *Why was he leading an investigation into the fire? Was this a cover-up for a sinister deed? Had he ever been on the victims' side?*

Daisy and I spotted Jay at the same time by the lion fixture at the front steps. "There he is," Daisy said, walking forward to greet him.

I got the sudden urge to squeeze a thorny stem on a rose. Instead, I retied my cummerbund and hoped no one would come and talk to me.

"Oh, Nick!" And of course someone was coming to talk to me—Cannon.

"I meant to give you this," he said, fishing a small pamphlet from his jacket pocket. "The Harlem police department is hiring. I know you must be looking for a place to live now that the Blue House has met its tragic fate. There's still time for you to get off the streets and become something more."

I took the flyer and examined the image on the glossy paper—Cannon himself dramatically lunging and pointing a gun. "Only problem is I'm a writer—not a cop." I crumpled the pamphlet in my hand and gave it back to him. "Thank you, though."

Cannon sneered as he took it, holding it like a wet rag. "If you insist on ruining your future, be my guest."

"My future will be fine, thanks."

"Hmm." He straightened his posture and the pamphlet.

"Congratulations on the promotion," I said. "It must be tiring doing the Buchanans' dirty work."

I watched to see if he'd flinch, but he was stone-faced. "I work for what I have—*legally*. Unlike some people." And he spun away from me.

Damn. Left alone once more, I spotted Daisy and Jay walking up the stairs and into the home of Tom Buchanan. I decided to follow after them. I'd attended as Daisy's escort after all, and I'd have to stay close to her, so it seemed like I had a reason to be here.

Inside, wide marble steps led down to an expansive room lit by crystal chandeliers. The beveled ceiling helped give the room its dimensions as an event space. Linen-draped tables sat to the side of an open dance floor and temporary stage. The white faces and blue stares caused my stomach to nearly erupt like a sleeping volcano. My kind was hardly welcomed.

How could I move through this room unnoticed? All eyes would be on me, no matter what I did. There'd be no poking around without intense scrutiny. In the far-off corner was a Negro band who I'd feel more comfortable in proximity to.

"Did you hear about the haul Davis's squad got last week?" someone in front of me said. A loud conversation was happening between two cops in uniform. "Found a whole stash of giggle water on West 14th . . . but the boss? Nowhere to be found!"

Another conversation from a taller man moving very slowly in front of me, blocking my way. He told the person next to him, "Glad we could get the kid promoted. It should work out well for us overall."

"Excuse me, sir," I said to the tall man, trying to move past him to get to the Negro band.

He turned around, and I realized at once I was facing the cold eyes of Tom Buchanan.

"Hi there," he said, smiling tensely. "I take it you're one of my staffers. You got any of that bathtub gin?"

"Selling liquor is illegal, sir," I told him, my voice cracking slightly.

"I was testing you." Buchanan laughed and winked. "I'd recognize you if you were staff. You do look familiar, however."

So, he hadn't even remembered our meeting, which happened weeks ago—typical.

Buchanan's wife, Myrtle, stood with her arm linked through his, but she was busy watching Daisy and Jay pass. With the movement of the party crowd, they didn't even notice I'd stopped.

Charlie was standing beside Buchanan too, digging food out of a side tooth.

He looked bored, glancing around the room and eventually landing on me. "I didn't realize you'd be attending. Happy to see you're staying social."

"Charlie," Tom said. "You haven't introduced me to your friend."

"Oh, of course, Father—it's Nick Carrington. The boy I wanted to write for the *Chronicle*. That is, *before* I read his writing." Charlie laughed at himself and then said, "Sorry."

"Oh, yes!" Buchanan crooned. "I was very impressed with your draft for the *West Egg Chronicle*. It's a shame it wasn't published. You had wonderful things to say."

"Oh." I was a bit surprised he would say that. "Thank you."

"I'm thinking of opening a new press for the youth in Harlem," Buchanan said, looking off into the distance as if imagining it. "It'd be wonderful if you would come and sit with us for lunch to discuss a potential opportunity. Channel all that rebellious energy into something positive."

Lunch at the Buchanan house? Well, one reason to want that was to get into Buchanan's home again when fewer people were around and scout things out. "Yeah," I said quietly. "Sure—I guess I could."

"Good evening, Mr. Buchanan," Jay cut in, arriving at my side.

Buchanan did not respond and instead made it a point to ignore Jay in favor of focusing on me. "Expect me to be in touch then. Jay will let me know how to reach you." He gave Jay a quick look, which felt like a warning, and then waltzed off, his son and wife behind him.

Jay turned to me, his eyes suspicious. "What was that?"

"He just started talking to me and then invited me to lunch," I said with a shrug.

"There you go! Now you can break bread with them. You'll either learn that the Buchanans are the worst monsters alive or decide your plan is actually ridiculous."

So, the plan had not left his mind. That meant he'd been kicking it around, giving it power. And I'd secured another invitation to Buchanan's house? How easy was that? It was my turn to play nice.

"Look at all these cops in here," Jay whispered, surveying the crowd as they shared gossip and discussed their successes. No one was truly focused on themselves—they wanted to know what everyone else was doing. "Wouldn't it be great to see you hit a black bottom? Bring some fun into their serious lives."

"Not a chance I would do that here," I said. "And this is the wrong song for that dance, anyway."

"You should get on the dance floor, anyway. Shake it! Show 'em what you got!"

"Jay—do you, by chance, want me to get *killed*? The lower I lie in here, the better."

A clinking noise cut through his response. Someone was tapping a glass with a fork. I turned to find a man in uniform weaving through the crowd and getting everyone's attention. "Good evening, everyone—we're ready to get started out back."

He took us to rows of white chairs in the backyard and stood in front of the crowd as he handed out awards for entrepreneurs and officers-in-training. Cannon was offered a spot as an officer at an Upper East Side precinct prior to completion of his training at West Egg, just because he showed promise in the program. He accepted the offer with a show of fake tears as the sergeant draped a ribbon over his shoulder.

Oh, brother. I was ready to go already—everything else be damned.

As the awards dragged on, I almost fell asleep. But then applause broke out, the crowd rose from their chairs, and the party filed back into the mansion.

I spotted Mr. Gatsby making his way through the crowd on our way back inside. I could've sworn Gatsby took special care not to look at me. He still wasn't over our disagreement, but thankfully, he had made sure our night in jail was kept out of public attention. I'd never be able to walk around here if he hadn't.

Back inside, a piano player tinkered through the notes to make everyone lively. Myrtle Buchanan did a little dance with her fists. This was the first time I'd seen the ginger-haired woman break a smile all night. Even the servers got their feet stomping.

Jay drifted to the dance floor and started doing his own dance in the middle of two couples. Flutes flustered the wind like locomotive air whistles, like a train was about to come through this place. Everybody let loose, and the only ones who had the time to judge were the ones who should've never come in the first place.

Jay's gaze beckoned me to the floor. I shook my head and mouthed the words, "I can't."

He mouthed the words, "You can."

Dancing in front of old white strangers? The stakes were higher here.

Still, the bass plucked some tension free from my shoulders. The cello thrummed a rickety jig through my pelvis, moving it against my will.

The singer's eyes shone on Jay. *"Do me a favor when the beat falls, young man."* He tapped his fingers away on the mic stand, voice carrying through the room. *"Show the pretty people of this lovely gala how Colored folks get down."*

Jay danced like this house ought to be The Green Light. The music set free all his worries and doubts he had of being judged, and in turn, mine.

I laughed as Jay dropped the suspenders, so they formed an upside-down *M* around his waist. A saxophone squawked like a toucan, and like a toucan, Jay did a jump and flew what seemed like nine feet off the ground. When he came down, he realized the energy in the room had shifted. People slowed their dances and muttered to themselves about him. It was awkward. Jay watched them, lips opened in concern as he pulled back. He'd gone too far and shown too much.

He ran off the dance floor, weaving through the people, and when he reached me, he only said, "I need some air," and went past me.

I followed him, but getting around people became difficult, and he was moving so fast. When I got outside, Jay was storming down the steps and off into the driveway as though he meant to disappear entirely.

I was not the only one following him out of the mansion.

Bursting through the doors came Artie Botts, the gossip queen, who had somehow found his way to the gala.

"Out of the way!" he screamed.

His entourage had grown since I last saw him. A new person

carried his camera, and a zealous fan carried his notepad.

Artie noticed me and paused, his mouth dropping open dramatically. He reached for his camera and snapped a photo of me, burning a flash into my eyeballs.

I blinked the light away. "You just . . . scorched my eyeballs. Why?"

"For my *records*," Artie said, pursing his lips.

When my vision cleared, I sauntered toward him. "What *records*?"

He looked up at me with contempt, standing his ground as I approached. "Wouldn't you like to know, Nick Carrington the *Third* . . . resident rabble-rouser, and—" He looked back at the mansion, his mouth dropping open in a theatrical show of surprise. "A *guest* for a Buchanan event? Who would've thought? The papers are dying to know," he said, turning back to me. "Is it true that Mr. Gatsby is a rum runner who smuggles liquor from Canada to New York?"

I advanced on them further, causing the whole trio to take tiny steps back. "Don't you have something better to do than follow me?"

His entourage cooed and gasped, but Artie just rolled his neck. "*Excuse me.* You should be happy a boneless country wing like yourself is getting coverage anywhere. *Gatsby* is the real cover star, honey. Don't *flatter* yourself."

I snatched his camera off his neck, causing him to trip and fall over. The violence just came over me—I couldn't stop it if I wanted to!

"Wait!" he screamed, face full of horror, grabbing at the strap.

It was too late. I smashed it, lens first on the driveway like a plate at a Greek party. It went boom like a firecracker—glass everywhere!

"There!" I screamed. "That's what it's like being Jay Gatsby's mistress! You should try it someday! Destroy all your possessions! Anything else?"

Artie was horrified. He must have spent a lot of money on that beautiful piece of junk, to snap it in people's faces until they went nuts.

Let the gossip grow grander now. I was no longer worried about being liked.

Cannon walked out the doors of the house, stepped over the camera, and said, "Uh-oh! Looks like we need some tidying up!" And then, with a giggle, he ducked into a limousine that had just pulled up to the circular lot.

Suspicious . . . why was he skipping out without his parents?

The safes would have to wait.

I darted into the lot and couldn't find a sign of Jay anywhere. I'd lost him, but there was still time to follow Cannon. I knocked on the windows of one of the idle cabs, shocking the driver into a spastic dance. I slid into the car, slammed the door, and thrust a random amount of bills and coins at the dashboard. "Please, follow that limo, sir."

Where are you going, you sicko?

"Almost gave me a heart attack, boy." The driver adjusted his wide-billed hat and started the car, taking the limo down the dark streets and toward the south of the city.

I wasn't going to be nice about this. Cannon could easily be a pawn for the Buchanans' evil deeds. He'd been chummy with Charlie from day one.

The limo moved through the city like a smooth bullet. I leaned between the two seats to watch the car from the windshield until the limo let Cannon out by two buildings, close to the place I found Daisy a few months ago. The Green Light was in an alley not too far down this road.

"Stop here," I told the driver.

I watched from the windows, slinking down in my seat to hide my face from the streetlight. Cannon tucked his hands into his long coat and took a meditative walk. He didn't seem to be doing anything suspicious.

"Okay, but you gotta get out," said the driver.

"Oh, sorry." I stepped out of the car.

I was left waiting on the pavement, looking for clues in the sway of Cannon's walk. We were the only ones here.

He stopped suddenly and turned around, grimacing at my presence. I had no choice but to approach him then in the middle of the boardwalk. *What was one to do when walking a long distance toward someone you hate?*

"Nick Carrington. If you're looking for a date, I'm not interested."

"Actually, not at all. Since the police seem to be doing nothing,

I'm looking for who started the fire at West Egg."

Cannon raised an eyebrow. "And you're asking me? How would I know?"

"You're investigating it for the police."

He rolled his eyes. "*You got me,* Clumsy Nick. We have no leads so far, okay?"

"No offense, but I worry that if you're in charge, things won't be solved."

Cannon took offense to that, and he tilted his head at me, eyes squinting. "I'm flattered you thought to come following me just to share that opinion."

I looked around us, taking in the ground slick with grime and rainwater. The air was salty with shipping yard seawater and the sour stench of coal smoke reaching us from the distance.

"What are you doing out here, anyway?" I asked.

"Can't a guy enjoy a walk?" Cannon said, holding up his hands. "I didn't think I'd have a shadow."

"Sorry," I offered. "Perhaps this was strange of me."

"Strange, indeed. You should be somewhere off with Jay *frolicking with glee* instead. Go home, Nick," Cannon said. "Let the detectives handle the case. If New York City has taught me anything, it's that poking your nose where it doesn't belong will always guarantee you an *un*happy ending. Have a wonderful night."

With that, he turned, long coat swaying as he disappeared into the misty haze of the streetlamps. I watched him go, a retort stuck in my throat as the silence swallowed me, save for the noise of his footsteps and the distant hum of the city.

I stood there until his silhouette disappeared, inhaling the harbor air, as his words echoed in my head. *Unhappy ending.* Maybe. But I wasn't done quite yet.

18.

A FRIGID WIND TORE THROUGH THE CITY THE morning of my lunch with Tom Buchanan, biting through my vest as I stepped outside. New York's lingering cold still had teeth.

I layered up in a plaid vest over a white sweater, baggy golf pants, and two-tone sports shoes—respectable enough for a wealthy man's table. After slicking my hair down until not even the wind could ruffle it, I caught the train to Long Island, bracing for whatever the afternoon had in store.

I confirmed my identity for the guard out in front of Buchanan's estate and a carriage took me down the driveway, where four fancy cars were parked behind the glass wall of the garage.

Which one will we take with us? I thought.

I smiled to myself and then stopped when I saw Buchanan standing on the porch, hand in his navy-blue waistcoat, waiting. "How wonderful to see you," he said as I folded out of the carriage.

His cold eyes betrayed the sentiment. He was performing, but so was I.

I walked up the steps, trying my best to act naturally, and shook his hand. "Likewise."

His grip was firm, the eye contact too long, but finally I looked away.

He turned and led me through the house, and the set of doors, to the patio. A dining table sat in the middle of the terrace, with coal braziers set at either end for warmth. From the terrace extended a plot of grass. The lake was beyond it, and off the lake, the tiny beach led up to Jay's house.

Myrtle was sitting at the table, and Charlie was straightening the silverware and plates. The food was abundant—roast chicken, salad, bread, olives, and carrots.

I took a seat next to Charlie, across from Myrtle.

"I always wanted to have you for a meal, Nick!" Charlie said with enthusiasm. "What's mine is yours. So go ahead! Indulge yourself."

"That's nice, Charlie. Thank you." *Why are you always switching back and forth?*

It was odd how the rich kept their fronts for social benefits, no matter how tense things got underneath it all.

Buchanan was staring at Gatsby's house for a while, mulling something over. Then he came to sit at the head of the table. "I noticed some faulty lights at the Gatsby residence," he said. "I'll have to tell Gatsby whenever he's back from his trip." Buchanan raised his water glass at me. "A toast to you, Nick, and your timely arrival."

Timely arrival? Was that a subtle dig at Colored folks being late? I had to wonder.

"Thank you," I said anyway, and sipped on water. I really wanted the flask of gin in my pocket, but no way was I losing my wits at the table with these men.

"What made you apply to West Egg?" Buchanan asked.

"I needed something to do," I said.

Buchanan and Charlie both laughed, and even Myrtle raised her napkin to her lips to suppress a chuckle. It wasn't a joke, but I was strangely satisfied they found me funny.

"As I mentioned, I've read some of your work." Buchanan leaned back in his chair and sized me up. "It seemed like you didn't quite like everything about West Egg."

I didn't know how I should respond, so I just said, "Yeah."

"I especially appreciated your sample piece for the *Chronicle*," Buchanan said. "Did you know I mentioned to Gatsby that there ought to be an arts program? This was long before the classrooms were built."

"I think the arts are good for any school," I said. "Music especially unites people. You can come from anywhere and be anyone and still connect that way."

"That's very romantic." Buchanan took a sip. "Are you a Communist?"

"What's that?" I took a sip of water, directing my eyes to Jay's house across the lake. *Save me, please.*

I wondered what he was doing. Reading? Watching me? Jay seemed frazzled when he ran out of the gala, and I never got the chance to check on him after that.

A butler ran from the kitchen to refill the water pitcher. His nametag read Clarence. He didn't get involved with any of the conversation—just silently did his work.

"Don't be shy," Buchanan said. "I'm a normal man! Ignore the chatter about how the Buchanans are trying to take over the city."

"Haven't heard that," I said quickly. "But there are talks in Harlem that you plan to buy out Kirby's. I was wondering what you hope to put in its place?"

"It wouldn't matter much, would it? The health score would rise no matter what." He laughed hard at his own joke, and I had to wait for him to stop.

"Kirby's never got a health violation, sir," I said, in a measured way. "Not that I'm aware."

"Oh! Are you a frequenter of the diner?"

"I work there."

"You *work* there."

"Oh," Myrtle said. It was a reflexive sound, like a sigh or a gasp.

"And you've never been mugged?" Buchanan squinted and smiled. "The area is a hotbed of gang activity."

"Harlem used to be a Dutch city," Myrtle said, her voice polite, operatic, and longing with nostalgia. "But it's been quite friendly to Negroes lately. It seems like everybody wants to settle there! Which is fine, but it crowds things."

Buchanan threw down his napkin and leaned back in his chair even further. "What say you, Nick, about the theory that in the next hundred years the Negro will overtake the white race as the dominant group in America?" He rested his hand on his knee and flipped his dark hair.

I looked at his plate, half full of food, which he'd picked at but now seemed finished with. "I don't think the goal of Negroes has ever been to overtake anything," I said.

Buchanan laughed, lightly now, and licked his teeth. He snapped for Clarence to pour him more water because he didn't even like the glass half empty.

"Have you met Jay Gatsby Sr.?" Buchanan asked. "He treats his Colored son like a trophy."

"We have met," I said.

Buchanan puckered his lips and then squinted as if he were recognizing me for the first time. "Was that you there in the house when I arrived to deliver his mail? It *was*, wasn't it? So, you know him well, then. I must ask you: Where is the Colored wife? Did she leave him? There are so many rumors about the story there."

This felt like a trap to get me into revealing information about the Gatsbys. I hesitated around my responses, but Myrtle looked at me like I'd committed a crime when I was silent.

"I . . . I don't know," I answered.

Buchanan took a sip of his water and then placed it on the table, biting his lip like he was upset. "Clarence, why's my water so lemony? I said one lemon."

Clarence had been lingering around the table. He arrived at Buchanan's side and said, "Apologies, sir."

Buchanan jumped up from the chair and smacked Clarence

with the back of his hand, as if cracking a whip, allowing his chair to fall indelicately behind him.

Clarence held his face, and the air fell into a thorny silence. Charlie and Myrtle both watched the table. Buchanan continued to watch Clarence, as if expecting another apology. His eyes were like the devil's. Breath rose and fell like his anger had hijacked his lungs.

Clarence turned around again. I made painful eye contact with him. I felt as though I'd slapped him myself by even sitting at this table, and he looked embarrassed to have gone through that in front of me.

Clarence swallowed and walked toward the house in silence.

Keep it together, Nick. But I couldn't. I just couldn't. The farther Clarence strayed from the table, the more I felt a kick from within to follow him.

Buchanan picked up his chair, cleared his throat, and smiled at everyone but me. "Where were we?"

I didn't ask to be excused. I got up from the table and trekked awkwardly toward the house—my stomach uneasy. Uneasy with the sound of his hand smacking Clarence.

The rich prized manners, but I had to recover in private. The image sat wrong in my system and was polluting my body like tobacco smoke.

I made it to the bathroom and sat on top of the toilet for a few minutes. Then I looked at the mirror, at my big lips. My hair had become kinkier in the daylight. I could slather straightening paint on it all day, but I'd still be disrespected by people like that man. There was no end in sight for his hate. All because some people were born browner? I hated Tom Buchanan! *I hated him!*

Once I'd cooled off, I opened the door and found Clarence standing on the other side.

He stared at me. "You don't have to walk all the way across the house and upstairs for this bathroom. There's two others by the drawing room."

"Oh . . . I didn't realize. Are you okay, sir?"

"Just fine," Clarence said, shrugging it off. "He don't do that a lot, you know. He did it because you here. I seen you being respectful toward them, but I hope you know Mr. Tom ain't a good man. His pop owned a cotton plantation, had slaves, all that—years after it was illegal. Then they freed 'em, paid 'em to stay silent."

"If I can ask, why do you continue to work for him?"

"Same reason you dine with them. Make some money. Get in where you fit in. You seem like a smart young man. Raised right. Just like Daisy. I seen her snooping around the place, trying to play it off. You have some relation, don't you? She's spoken fondly of a Nick before."

My heart sank a bit. How much did he know? Was he loyal to Buchanan?

"Yeah, Daisy is wonderful," I said.

"What's the real reason you're here?" he asked, suspicion in his eye as he leaned in further. "Because if it's for private information?" Clarence went on and gave a nod toward the set of French doors at the end of the hallway. "That's your destination.

Stay quiet." With that, he walked off.

The doors were closed, the curtains inside pulled over the glass windows. I had to make use of this time alone in Buchanan's house. Now was my chance to learn something, anything valuable, but my stomach rocked with nausea at the thought of getting caught.

I made my way to his study at the end of the hallway anyway and opened the door. Inside was a big reddish-brown desk. It was so clean that its owner might notice any tiny switch in how the pens leaned, or where the plaque sat.

I opened the drawers and found nothing interesting. And then I moved to a file cabinet in the corner, sorting through delicately. A tab was labeled *Records*.

I sorted through a few of them—real estate deeds, construction developments—boring! I finally pulled out a sheet of paper that caught my attention because Gatsby's name was on it. It read:

Dear Mr. Buchanan and Mr. Gatsby,

This letter is a confirmation that your insurance claim on the institution of West Egg Academy has been processed and accepted. In recognition of the damage of the building structure, colloquially called the Blue House, we have approved a payout of $30,000 to be issued on November 1, 1921.

I couldn't keep reading. November 1 was months ago and not one repair had been made to the Blue House. What was the $30,000 being saved for? Had it already been used for something else entirely? This much money could renovate West Egg, with some left over. So why wouldn't they do that?

Jay had said that his father wanted to make more money through real estate. Perhaps Gatsby was adopting Buchanan's business strategies for money. Jay had made it known they weren't flush with cash. That's why they got into bootlegging in the first place.

Could Gatsby be more intertwined with Buchanan than I'd ever thought? Using his share of the insurance money to fund his business ventures? Did Jay know about this?

As my questions began to leave me even more sick, I left the study, closing the door gently behind me. That was enough searching for one day. I was so tired of the rich acting like they didn't have money for things when they did. They just wanted to spend it on themselves, and I couldn't smile in their faces anymore. I had to leave this place so I could feel well again.

I'd seen more of the house than I ever had before and that'd have to be enough for now. I'll have Daisy's map memorized like the back of my hand to make up the rest.

I tiptoed down the staircase and back to lunch. Buchanan and Charlie were talking at the table and didn't see me as I walked to the door. I creeped up to the closed door just before the patio and stood off to the side, pressing my ear to the wall to listen in.

"I wonder if the *Chronicle* has become too invested," Buchanan said. "Are we showing respect to our neighbors or encouraging a revolution?"

"I think if we keep it politically neutral it will be fine. My new point of interest has been the Harlem nightlife scene ever since . . . *the purge*. It's fascinating to observe them let loose. And they play music well—it's how they've given such value to the city."

"So, you've taken a liking to them," Buchanan said snidely. After a pause, he added, "That's the son I raised! I have no issue with Negroes when they know their place. My maidservant is a fine girl—on time and efficient." It was like he added this because he knew I was somewhere listening.

My first thought was to jump out and interrupt—they were talking about my cousin! But I had to keep calm.

"You reward her nicely for a maidservant, father. Mother has begun to notice it."

"Well, I keep her close to keep a rapport," Buchanan said. "As you've done with the writer."

Which writer? Artie? Or someone else entirely?

"I think he's made good on our deal," said Charlie. "He'll do anything for a little money."

Artie. It had to be—

Someone stirred behind me. "Listening in?" said a feminine voice.

I jerked around to find Charlie's mother standing behind me like a statue. Her eyes were more vigilant than any police dog's, and the wrinkles around her mouth tensed with disdain.

"You are quite the snooper." She attempted a smile, but her eyes were daggers.

"I was just lost," I said.

"Young man, the private matters of our family should be of no concern to the people we deal with professionally," Myrtle said expressionlessly. "We don't go around looking through your things, now do we?"

Did she see me upstairs? How did I miss her?

"I should be going," I said, taking a few clumsy steps toward the front door. I wanted to be as far from this place as possible, and Myrtle didn't try to stop me.

I opened the door and heard Charlie's voice behind me. "Off so soon?" He was coming from outside, smiling big. "You hardly touched your food."

"I don't feel so well. I think I'll have to take myself to the doctor."

"Ah. Good luck with that." He gave me a wave, his grin insincere as if he knew what was making me feel ill.

And then I left. This place was not as beautiful as it was when I arrived. I was beginning to think all the fancy architecture of this estate was designed to hide the ugliness of its residents.

I walked past the stone lions—exquisite on my way in, which now seemed to forebode the ending of a horrible novel. A novel that had tricked its reader into thinking it was something it was not.

I shouldn't have taken this invitation, not even to spy. The more I learned about Buchanan, the more I wanted to hide in my corner of Harlem and never come out. I couldn't handle much more stress.

Why did I come here for a meal?

How could I have been so stupid?

19.

I TOSSED AND TURNED THROUGH THE NIGHT, my mind cycling through disturbing questions. *What if Jay was everything I'd hoped he wouldn't be? What if he and his father were just like the Buchanans?*

Morning came with the wail of a harmonica outside the window—someone was playing the Livery Stable Blues. As I walked into the kitchen, I realized from the calendar tacked on the refrigerator that today was March 15, which meant I was officially eighteen.

Did I feel any different? Not really.

The phone rang in the late morning, and I almost didn't bother picking it up. I figured it was one of Auntie's friends calling, but when I answered, Jay's voice came through.

"Nick? That you?"

I straightened, surprised. "Hey, Jay. Everything okay?"

"Everything's great. Still free today?"

I hesitated. "Uh . . . I guess. Why?"

"To spend the day together. Just you and me. Sorry I ditched you at the gala, just . . . needed some air."

I frowned, feeling queasy about where this invitation was coming from, feeling like I was being set up.

"Did something happen?" I asked.

Jay laughed, like he found my suspicion amusing. "Nothing but your birthday. I'm not letting you sit around like it's just any other day."

I froze, the words catching me off guard. How did he know? I hadn't told him, not that I could remember—or anyone, for that matter.

"You know my birthday?" I asked, my voice softer than I intended.

"Of course—they're all in the West Egg directory," he said, like it was obvious.

I laughed a bit through a pause.

When Jay spoke again, his voice was steady, serious. "Be ready in an hour? Wear something light—it's going to be a warm one."

Was I crazy to hold my chaotic thoughts in for one day? To allow my worries to fall away, for our last day of the weekend, for one drive to Coney Island?

Instead of talking, I hung my head out the window and let my hair catch the breeze.

Jay reached over and placed a hand on my thigh. I couldn't see his eyes because of the sunglasses, so he had the upper hand, and he caught me off guard.

When we arrived, the wind from the beach had bite to it, with the clouds trying to outdo the sunshine. I carried the basket and blanket from the car and laid them on the sand. I crossed my ankles in my red shoes and admired how they looked, like a vibrant Christmas bow.

I was close enough to the water to feel a sense of danger but far enough to avoid getting wet. I felt so in my element with this much sun on my arms. It confirmed my want for a farm and a simple, quiet life, and for nobody but Jay to know where I was. I wanted to ignore the things that kept me wound so tight and enjoy my day without distraction.

But Jay did not stop to chat with me, so I couldn't bring up what I'd found in Buchanan's study, even if I wanted to. Jay had this American flag kite that he had to fly down the beach. He started running across the mostly empty beach with it, looking up and back down as he tried to get it to fly. Each time the kite fell, he ran faster to keep it flying, and he shrank away from me, his slip-ons slipping off.

The ocean lurched closer to my blanket, its tongue stretching out for my toes. The endless water made me want to board a ship, travel across the ocean to the Kingdom of Benin.

That's where my great-grandpa Sumner was from—a place full of shining palaces and busy merchant squares. The people used to trade with Europeans, selling slaves for guns and other weapons. Slavers wanted to be rich, so they would kidnap kids from their homes while their parents were at work. My great-grandpa was eight when he was kidnapped and sold to an English slaver. The slaver threw him into a ship cargo with two hundred others before his parents noticed he was gone. They were headed for the United States. Some people knew what was in store, so they jumped overboard, but Great-Grandpa Sumner did not know where they were going.

Above me, birds soared upwind like flying ashes.

I thought of Great-Grandpa Sumner randomly sometimes and wondered what he did on that ship. If he had to use a chain for a pillow or eat wood to feel full. If he could manage to make it, pushing for years through his sadness to build a free life, I could too, right?

Jay was coming back now and laughing with joy because the kite was flying high. Would he turn out exactly like his father, wasting money on things that were unjust?

A lonely feeling banged my heart between its cymbals as I took stock of how long I'd been by myself on our beach date. I must've been a boring conversation partner.

He rejoined me finally at the blanket, picked an apple from our basket, and sank his teeth into it, so viciously the juice ran down his chin stubble. "This is really ripe," Jay said. "What else do you want for your birthday?"

He looked so good with his loose shirt blowing against his frame, I wanted to devour him like the meat of a coconut. There was no easy way to say that, no easy way to say that despite my suspicions of him, one look at him made my thoughts fall away. This was one time I did not want him to hear my thoughts. But windblown and talking about a ripe apple was one of my favorite versions of him.

And there was the ocean, planning our eventual demise, surging with the blood of my people. I wanted a mind like the sea that went on and on and on, until it forgot about civilization. One day I'd be one with the sea. Before then, I'd have Jay in every way he'd have me back.

"I don't know," I said. "Just hanging out is fine."

He reached out to run his fingers through my hair and then twitched as if he wanted to check for witnesses. But, in the next moment, he decided he didn't care. He'd feel me regardless.

I always thought love was something I'd have to change myself to find. That I wasn't enough for it. Love would find me fine! When I was with Jay, I was realized without changing a thing.

Jay cleared his throat and looked over at me, his voice low and serious. "I've been thinking about what you said," he began, keeping his gaze on the water. "About leaving it all behind. Running away together."

I felt a rush of adrenaline. "And?"

"I can say I don't hate the idea." He glanced at me, his eyes bright. "To be somewhere with just you, away from all of them, sounds nice."

My heart beat harder with the thought of escape. This was the opening I needed, but what if, at the mention of his father, I scared Jay away?

Surely, I could test where Jay's morals truly lay, without asking him to betray his father. Before I could hesitate, I said, "Jay, there's something else I need to talk to you about."

He raised an eyebrow as he watched me. "All right. What is it?"

"That night I went to Pierre's place . . . I found something that makes me think Buchanan is paying to drive Negroes out of Harlem and covering it up. Do you know about any of this?"

"It's like I said—I never trusted Buchanan. He's hateful and would do anything to convince people he isn't, just so he can get away with it." Jay nodded. "All the more reason for us to do this, right? Now you mentioned wanting me to throw a party at the beginning of all this."

"Your father likes throwing parties," I said, my worries only mildly soothed by Jay's answer. "Isn't that, right?"

"He used to do so." Jay considered that, running a hand through his hair as he processed. "Not so much anymore."

I nodded. "He'll need an incentive then, one that will have everyone wanting to come as well. Daisy already foresaw this problem."

"Of course." He laughed. "And did she come up with a solution?"

"An engagement party for you."

Jay weighed my words, mentally. "And who am I marrying?"

"Daisy."

Jay laughed. "That would be very nice, yes. I'll talk to him about it."

"Will you?" I said with a laugh.

"No!" Jay answered, brushing it off. "Of course not! Why would I marry your cousin?"

Perhaps this didn't matter in the moment. There were more pressing things at hand.

"Have we decided where we move when we're done with all this?" I asked.

"Paris?" he said.

"Too far."

"Egypt."

"Too far. We gotta go back to Oklahoma."

The sound of the waves was soothing and relentless in the following silence.

Jay chuckled and drew a line in the sand with his finger. "I'm not living in Oklahoma, Nick."

"Why not?"

"Is that rhetorical?" he said, laughing.

"Um, no?"

"It's not for me," he said. "But at the end of it all, I'm with you. Whatever you want."

I wanted to believe it, but *whatever* was a very strong word, and he wasn't looking at me.

The tide whispered to us as it crept closer to our feet. I watched Jay, and he watched the waves. Somewhere between us, the full truth lingered, distant as the horizon itself.

20.

AFTER THE BEACH, I DECREED WE GO FOR A drink at The Green Light. I knew Jay was thinking about it but didn't want to mention it so as not to sound like too much of a boozehound.

He only kept saying, "What do you want to do next?" until our car found its way to the seedy side of Harlem.

An hour after we left the beach, he was at the counter slurping down a Tom Collins, joy coursing through his body as he bounced on the stool like a restless boy. A white girl in a shiny dress and headband kept eyeing him from down the counter, until finally she caught his gaze, and Jay smiled at her, soaking up the attention.

I watched the pianist onstage play with his eyes closed, the keys so intrinsic to him he did not need to see them. I closed my eyes too, to see if being blind through the music might free me from my jealousy.

At some point as I sat with my eyes closed, I began to hear their conversation.

"This place makes everywhere else feel so tame in comparison!" the girl said. "Don't you think?"

"Wonderful, isn't it?" Jay returned, forming a natural chemistry with her.

But she couldn't see how Jay doubted himself, that he was afraid to be discovered as a fake in these meaningless exchanges.

There was a pause. I could feel the girl's eyes falling on me, even as I sat there in blackness.

"He a . . . *special* friend or just a friend?"

"Oh, he's . . . yeah, he's a friend."

You dirty dog! Low-down, no good, second of his name . . .

I jumped angrily off the stool and moved to the end of the counter. When I looked back, I caught him watching my every move, the soft light framing his focus as the girl continued to chat.

I waved the server down and said, "I'll have a straight shot please."

I hoped Jay would see me in a rage, but he put his focus back on the girl!

Break my heart wide open in public, leave it spilling like wine from a busted glass, but I'll never give you the power to see my pain. No matter how long it lasts.

He only glanced up briefly as I downed my shot. I ordered two more and drank them, and he barely even paid attention. There was my answer—he didn't care.

I wandered around the joint, a desperate thought chirping around in my mind. *Why not only me? Why?*

It seemed in each dim corner of the place, people were kissing and touching. Everyone had a person but me. I was unlovable! And therefore, I was unsafe in this world. Another year had gone by, and I was still a lone wolf, at least on the inside—a runt wolf, the smallest of the pack.

I went out to the walkway by the entrance, which burned under red light. I closed my eyes again. Tears were bubbling up like a volcano in me, but I'd give them no permission to fall.

"Why are you crying?" came Jay's voice. But when I opened my eyes, he didn't look very empathic toward me. Instead, he looked done with my mess. "If you want me to pay attention to you, you could just ask."

"Oh, you were very focused on the young lady, so no need," I hissed back.

Jay rolled his eyes. "Yes, there is a need. Every time you don't get your way you go throwing a tantrum. And for what? It will always be you I return to. Clearly."

I found myself pinching my fingers together, to test if I still had my shot glass at hand. "This could all be so much easier if there weren't other stops on your destination to me," I murmured.

Who are these girls that distract you, and what do they have that I lack?

"Other stops?" Jay lost even more patience with that, and yet it seemed to make him get closer to me, even as he folded his arms. "What are you talking about now?"

"You know what I'm talking about. All the time you spend proving you don't need me, and that you could have anyone and then trying to watch how I react! It's a game to you."

He let out an ironic laugh and looked around, as if to see if there were witnesses to get a load of me. But it was just us.

"It's not a game, Nick," he said. "People just come up to me. I would never play you on purpose."

"I don't believe it. You make a fool of me on a regular basis."

"I misguided you when I introduced you to liquor," he said, still laughing some. "Your overthinking becomes worse."

"I don't like you," I said, my voice hoarse.

Jay's expression became serious, as if hearing the words, even in jest, brought him pain. His charm disappeared. "Fine," he said, in a low voice. "I fold. The real reason I drift is because you matter *too much*."

I blinked, thrown off. "What?"

"You matter too much." He held my gaze, and I could see he'd lost interest in patching up his weaknesses. "You see the real me. Not the version of me I'm forced to be when I pal around with kind strangers, but the me inside. The exposed version. And that's scary! Say I get closer, and I lose you? Who's gonna see me then? Who else?"

It was my turn to say something, but I had no words. Nothing quite so earnest, anyway. It was hard to see Jay in such a fragile state, but it also made me feel more alive knowing how much I meant to him. To finally be sure.

"You're the one who keeps me at a distance!" he continued, his voice gaining volume and anger, through the pain. "You hold back too! *You're* inconsistent too! Every time I've tried to pull you closer—I mean, I asked you to the dance for crying out loud!" He covered his eyes with his hands and fell back against the bricks as if the memory took the life out of him. "You ran off when we were just getting started," he said, voice quieter, tinged with disappointment. "That was *you*."

And now, an accusation left me standing like a slain pig hanging in the window of a butcher's shop. My breathing was not flowing normally, though I'd only just noticed that. How could emotions make me feel this way? Was he right? Of course not—never.

We stood there, the music and noise of the juice joint fading into the background of our pregnant silence.

"Well, I am a coward," I said finally, my voice barely audible over the music. "What can I say? More reason to leave me alone."

I stormed down the alley. That would show him what it felt like to be abandoned. To be falling and wishing someone could catch you, but to never be caught how you needed to be.

"You can't be serious, Nick?" he called, following me out.

I didn't need Jay Gatsby! I only needed me!

"Nick!" he called.

To hell with his Nicking!

Whatever was just over the bridge of admitting our truest feelings frightened me to no end.

I continued to stumble toward the end of the alleyway until I lost him and met a street pole. I banged my forehead lightly on it just to feel the sensation. *What sense did it make to let someone else control you? To let emotions rule?*

A white woman was staring when I pulled my head back for

the third smash. She alerted her husband, and then they both stared.

"Yes! Drunken Negro boy!" I called out, but I barely recognized my manic voice. "Ever heard of one?"

They scurried off after that, not even caring to mask their fear. I fled the other way down the sidewalk and lost myself in another alley between two tenements. I stumbled a few steps and then I fell. I pushed myself up again and fell again.

"Never find me again, Jay," I growled, the rawness of the sun in my chest. "Just *stay away.*"

The pavement had me. My head was pounding, and the world was spinning. I couldn't separate up from down—cobblestones, bricks, and sky were everywhere I looked.

"Hey! Faggot!"

Was that for me? There were two belligerent men rushing toward me, and their tone was a promise for a beating. I fell right into a puddle, biting the street for a third time. In the reflection of the water was a boy with bloodshot eyes and saliva pooling in his mouth.

I spun around, sat in the water, and started to splash. The two guys rolled up their sleeves as they advanced on me.

"You kill Tony? It was you, wasn't it?" one of them screamed.

I got up to run the other way and then collapsed again. A pair of shoes became level with my eyes.

"Back up!" I screamed, turning around and scooting backward on my butt. "Back up or I'll alert the sheriff, and he will shoot you."

"The sheriff doesn't shoot, dummy," one of the men said.

He picked me up and slammed me down against the alley. I could not sense a thing but his foul breath when he growled in my face, "You the one who killed Tony?"

"Tony? I don't know a Tony!" I yelled back.

I didn't have a clue who that man could be. An Italian at the casino? Some enemy of Jordan's who had nothing to do with me?

A foot kicked my stomach, and it stole my breath.

Did I kill Tony? If so, I was sorry to Tony, whoever that was.

The Italian spat on me, and his saliva smelled of plaque. "We find out you're responsible, we will kill you. Understood. For now? A warning."

One boy punched my stomach so hard vomit surged in my mouth. He picked me up and threw me down again. All I could do was mutter, "Sorry . . . sorry . . ."

Then I was all dizzy, like those slaves who took alcohol and became so tired they couldn't think of escape. Free people didn't mess with wines, beers, liquors—free people were too focused. Why did I let Jay introduce me to that poison?

"Nick?" someone called from the end of the alley.

It was Jay . . . He was running to me.

"Jay, no . . ." I lifted up a weak hand to stop him, but he kept coming.

"What's going on here?" he asked, the lights dimming some in his eyes.

The other boy ran to him and gave him a good hard punch to the mouth, sending him down. Jay and I crawled to each other and grabbed hold of each other—me with a sore stomach and Jay with a busted lip bleeding in a silk line to the pavement.

"Remember this next time your folks think to mess with my family," one of the boys said.

And they both fled.

Jay and I sat up against the bricks, all covered in spit and blood and catching our breath.

"You know why things like this happen, right?" he asked.

"Because we're faggots," I said, and spit to remove the sour taste from my mouth.

"No. It's because we ought not involve ourselves in missions with Italian gangsters. I can't believe I allowed that to happen."

"You talk like you're my father." I nearly laughed through my shallow breaths.

"Sometimes you do need supervision," he said, with depth.

"Probably so. I'm a sack of trash. Not pretty and rich like you."

"You're plenty pretty, Nick." He rubbed a thumb against my cheek. "You're just down on yourself."

I turned to face him. "Am I not a social experiment? Like West Egg? You really like me?" I was a slurring mess, swaying left to right.

"You're falling over, Nick . . ." Jay reached over and caught me, pulling my shoulders so my posture was straight. "I wouldn't lie to you about liking you."

I was obsessed with him. His beauty, his aura, and our banter, which did something for me even after being beaten alongside him. I was hopeless to stop our magnetism, hopeless to stop hinging my zest for life on the destructive attraction that bloomed so quickly between me and Jay. But any friendship must bloom slowly with care so that it would be stable and make sense. Otherwise, it wasn't a friendship. It was something else entirely.

Jay unbuttoned his shirt and pulled it off his arms. It snagged a bit at the biceps, but he tugged it off and used it to wipe my mouth. The chain glinting around his neck, catching some of the light in this alleyway . . . I remembered that it was his mother's. I understood why he'd want to wear her around everywhere—I missed my mother too.

I played with the chain. He straddled my thighs, lifted a flask to my face, tipped my head back, and siphoned icy water down my throat.

I gulped. "Thank you . . ." And I gulped some more.

"Don't leave my sight in the juice joint again." It came as an order I was willing to obey.

One of Jay's hands tucked the flask back in his back pocket, and the other stayed near my chin.

"Why are you bossing me around all of a sudden?" I asked.

"Because you're mine," he said.

I felt one step away from breaking down. Or my longing had completed its circle with mutual desire. Or both. I felt undeserving when he cupped a hand behind my neck, and then deeply important when he kissed me.

The kiss commanded us to lean in, and then we started speaking to each other that way—with our lips. I told him silently that I understood his pain.

He told me that he knew how grief marked my bones like spit stains in the sidewalk, like fingerprints on door handles. My grief built more grief like construction workers built buildings to put this city's nature into an early grave. He didn't get it, not quite, but he'd support me through it.

When I kissed Jay back, all my sorrow had somewhere to go.

And when he pulled away, he said, "You're mine." Once more for emphasis. He leaned into my face, so my head was cupped between his shoulder and chest. "Okay?"

"Okay." His chest swallowed my words so they landed in his aorta, right where they should be—right where I aimed them.

Okay. I would give into his little kisses and orders. Because with him, Clumsy Nick was more than just a weakling, more than just a mistress, and more than just a friend! Nick Carrington, edition three, was not another cog in the machine. Because Jay saw something extra in me. Something in my personality that dazzled like elegant jewelry, and it was so rare, so untouched that even I couldn't see it!

But I had this pretty boy's attention! The boy whose beauty was as vibrant as the alleyway's gaslights. That meant that I was enough, with all my fractures and hitches, all the ways that I tripped, and all my confusion too.

We went back to Jay's place when we finally got off our butts. We had to tiptoe into his ensuite bathroom because his father was home, and this was the second time we'd been beaten up this year, so now we'd really be in trouble, even worse than last time.

Jay turned on the bathwater to let it run, undressed, and left his clothes in the shape of a Christmas tree skirt at his feet. "I have a lovely house, don't I?" he said. "I'll miss it when we take off."

Jay opened the balcony doors and angled his golden telescope at the house across the way, watching Buchanan's. The boat lights from the lake outlined the tower of his backside as he rolled a marijuana cigarette on the railing.

I joined him, standing slightly behind him, and we watched the lake. The room felt like an oasis on the Mediterranean Sea or the most important room in a palace. So far away from everything I'd started with. If we lived together, I'd want a little wooden swing hanging from the tree out front to remember the countryside I came from.

I swayed some in the breeze and asked, "Are you a homosexual?"

He laughed, as if amused. "What? I don't like that."

"What don't you like?"

"The word."

"Why?"

He took a drag from the cigarette. "Because . . . what's the point? It's supposed to be describing an identity, but it's got the word *sexual* in it."

I truly hated the smell of smoke. I wished he wouldn't do it anymore.

"The way you held me tonight . . ." I began.

"You had just been beat up and you were in pain."

"You kissed me."

Jay turned around harshly, as if I'd struck him. "So? I held you as anyone who'd just been beaten in the streets ought to be held." His voice was strong and defensive. "Is that bad? Did it make you uncomfortable?"

"No. I'm just thinking about it."

He took a breath and softened his expression. "Keep thinking. I like that about you." Jay looked like his father when he closed the balcony doors. More like a man.

He sauntered to the bathtub, naked body waving loose in the wind, arms like taut Roman marble. He needed a laurel crown. He needed a sword.

"When you picture yourself in the future do you see a wife?" I asked. "Kids?"

"I don't picture myself in the future," he said. "Mostly, I picture myself now."

The tub was filled, so he turned off the knob and sank into the hot water. Then he beckoned to me, bubbles and water dripping from one slick arm.

Arms folded in my robe, I drew toward the tub. "I . . . I'm worried." *Remember to breathe.* "The heat of the water will hurt my wounds." Everywhere was hurting, from my temples to my knees.

Jay found a quick solution by turning the cold knob. Then he lounged back, arms gracing the candlelight, waiting for my next excuse.

"Shall I join you?" I asked.

"You must."

Every step across the tile was like one into the ocean, with the waves rising higher to slap me in the mouth. I may as well not have had a mouth, the way I was skipping breaths.

I was very cold when I dropped the robe. I hurried into the tub as Jay turned the water off, and I sat across from him on the other side. His toe grazed the bottom of my leg and, with this sadness in his eyes, traced its way up my calf. I still felt breathy, like an iron puffing steam.

"Would you have me as you've had one of your girls?" I asked.

"As I have had one of my girls?" he said, as if the question was ridiculous. "In what way have I had anyone?"

"Haven't you?"

"Haven't I what?"

"Like . . . done it."

"Nick, what does this have to do with us? You're different from any girl I've been with in every way. I'd have you in the way I can have you without comparing you to anyone else."

But Jay and someone else made more sense—even Daisy. She was perfect, like him. I understood why his father wanted her for him.

"I just feel like I am invading," I said.

"You're not invading," Jay said.

"And it's probably because lots of people have tried to destroy me in the past. I can't bear another second of being destroyed so I want to push it away. If you regret today, don't pretend—better to tell me on the spot so I can just leave. I'm too sensitive for that."

"As am I," Jay said. "We have the same perspective, but you're endlessly stuck in the future or the past while I choose the present moment."

"We don't have the same perspective. Not by a long shot."

"Fine," he said, instantly resigning. "I won't fool with yours if you don't fool with mine."

If my heart was an apple falling from a tree, Jay Gatsby was quicksand or padded leaves. I didn't trust him all the way. Somehow, I still couldn't trust him, however much I told myself to do just that.

But before I met him, I was used to starting sentences and being interrupted. I was used to waiting for things to happen rather than making them happen myself. At least he let my words leave my mouth. And he encouraged me to do more. If Jay was going to betray me—be it for our current scheme or for some reason in the future—I was willing to take the risk. It was better than letting the possibility of Jay, and our freedom together, die.

"Thank you for not saying mean things," Jay said, in a soft voice. He moved closer to me in the water, and I followed. For every inch, I went a centimeter, until our fingers were grazing, and he was exploring them like the twigs of some twisted shrub.

He washed me, cleaning the open wounds the fiends left on my head, the bruises they left on my neck. I took deep breaths to remind myself it was okay for it to hurt, until my head was on his shoulder, arm resting on his leg, and we were facing the same way.

His water was soft, a water you didn't want to step out of. I once had nowhere to bathe—after hopping off that train I thought I might die. The finer things felt so nice when you'd known struggle and poverty. I never wanted to go back to the basic way.

The minutes stretched closer to an hour, and Jay broke apart from me and got out of the tub. He dressed us each in silk robes, one white and one blue, but then he asked, "Can I draw you?" He went to the bookshelf in the next room and pulled down a sketchpad and pencil.

"Draw me doing what?"

"Just existing. In your underwear, of course. Just so that I have you—a version of you—in case you ever slip through my fingers."

I followed his lead, enticed by how far this could go. I dropped my robe on the way to the cushy red velvet sofa in his bedroom. It had to be a two-hundred-pound piece of furniture that formed caverns of light and shadow in its cushion pattern.

I lay down and stretched my wings like a pterodactyl under the floor lamp.

I could see his work as he drew. Jay sketched my face with no mouth, eyes, or nose, but made my nipples so very pointy. He had the vein in my shoulder streaking like watermelon skin, and he put a wrinkle in the underwear. But he left out the bruises and scars.

All I could do as I posed was think of how I wanted to live with him in a secluded home with a field that went on forever, its beauty folding over the earth, us folding with it.

I couldn't go back to Harlem that night. So, after the drawing was done, we lay down in his bed together.

I was worried I'd do something wrong because every moment felt so right—too right. "How sad would you be if I died?" I asked in the end.

"Please, Nick."

"Answer?"

"Very, very sad. And this is morbid." He wrapped his arms around me.

I tucked my hands under the pillow as he grabbed my body and pulled me into him. "I'm glad you stopped hiding yourself," he whispered into my neck.

I didn't have eloquent compliments to give him in return. Only desperate, unreasonable requests, like *Hold me forever.*

It was only dreaming. This would only be real for a fleeting time, as Jay still pulled away from his truth. Jay thought the word *homosexual* was too sexual. I didn't think it was. It was simply a label, like saying someone was human—there could be dignity in it, if you gave it dignity.

I am a homosexual. That says nothing, by itself. The meaning of words was up to us; how we felt about them was also up to us.

"Thank you," Jay muttered, into my neck.

I didn't know what for, but he fell asleep waiting for a response. I stayed up for hours in turn, pondering my past and wishing I could make it leave me alone.

21.

ISAIAH WAS MY FIRST LOVE, BUT HE DIDN'T love me back. I was just his corny friend. His shadow.

He was athletic, with a sinewy, strong build. At pull-ups, he was perfect. When we ran track, he was perfect. I always fell behind as soon as the guns fired and we started to run. Many people were spurred on by the bystanders who were cheering from the stadium, but my father was never there, so what was the point?

Everyone else was bigger than me, backs more bricked up, legs longer. My competitors charged over the hurdles, brows clenched, mouths relaxed, red clouds kicking up when they landed. They took this very seriously.

But one day Isaiah tripped, and he and his hurdle skidded across the track. I was already behind, so I stopped for him as the rest of the runners ran.

"You losing the race," he said as I knelt by his side.

But I wasn't losing anything. I was helping my friend.

"Nick, this is stupid of you," he said. "I'm fine. Go."

If I could, I would stop all over again. The race could not ride bikes with me and shoot bottle rockets over the drugstore and lie in the meadow and talk about dreams—only Isaiah could. But once he realized I had that losing sprit, he tried to toughen me up.

The day after the race, he took me to the gym to do push-ups and then we went out behind the gym to cool off. Girls sat on benches, skirts riding above their knees for the summer, their brown legs gleaming under white sun, sun hats shielding their eyes, so that lips were all that showed.

They looked up when Isaiah walked by. He waved, and they giggled, turning away. He had his eyes on Pam Harris, who sat with her legs crossed, elbows back on the table as he passed. Those two understood the confidence thing before the rest of us.

Isaiah took a fighting stance across from me. "Throw a punch," he said, glancing over to Pam.

And I refused. We both knew he could make origami of my bones—no point in pretending I stood a chance. But when he swung at me, I was quick enough to duck and stumble like a deer from the encounter. He gripped my neck as I tried to escape and swiped my leg from under me.

He caught my shirt, before I fell, holding me dangling off the ground, like I was a puppet. He laughed at my resignation. "You not gonna fight me back at all?"

"Nope," I said. "Not at all." I had no shame. I didn't need to prove how strong I was. And most importantly—I didn't like to fight.

A cloud came to block the sun, and Isaiah looked up to the sky. I climbed his arm and regained balance.

Behind us, the girls got up from the bench and bunched under an umbrella together.

The first raindrops splashed our faces, and we ran to retrieve our bikes from their racks. Isaiah threw his leg over his seat and then noticed my teeth chattering. He took off his coat and offered it to me.

I slid into the padded coating beneath the wool, its protection like a blanket. "Thank you."

"No problem," he said, rubbing his hands together before strapping them to the bars.

We pedaled down the winding roads, which were quickly turning muddy from the rain. We had to go fast so we wouldn't drown.

Once we reached my house, we were soaking wet. We left our bikes leaning out front and covered ourselves under the porch roof.

Isaiah was still pushing me around, saying, "Fight me."

Unrelentingly, I said, "I'm not in the mood."

And the wood creaked under our feet.

I was sopping wet, and was I ever in the mood, in grade nine, for anything but to stare at nature, or to stare at the wall?

Isaiah jiggled my skinny arm. "You gotta put some meat on these bones," he said. "So you can wake 'em up if you need to."

"I think they're already awake," I said. "They don't need me to wake up."

Oh, I felt so powerless in those years.

I reached for the door to my house, but Isaiah stopped my movement, with a hand around my wrist. And he wrestled me down to the wood of the porch. And then he had me lying underneath him, with one leg on either side of my torso, and he was dripping rainwater off the side of his jaw onto my forehead, his shirt clinging to his body.

He pulled me up fast, when he was done, and I crashed into him, feeling a rush, a buzz from the universe as it moved me, called me to touch his face and lean in to a kiss. It felt natural. It relieved me of all violence, all tension.

But it did not do the same for him. Isaiah pushed me away, eyebrows furrowing like I had caused him great discomfort. "Nick, no." He was very serious as he took his jacket off me like I was a coatrack and not a person. "I don't do that."

There was no room to call it an accident. Isaiah knew already, somewhere deep down. It took so long for him to come around after I did that. He went on his track, making the connections that would get him a job at the Vanderbilt estate. I floundered desperately, looking for one business that would take me, ending up in the back of Mr. Wallace's shop.

Yes, that was where I belonged. For years, I knocked on my friend's door, and no one was home. He ignored me in school. I left him letters and got nothing back. I lost my friend.

Three years passed and Isaiah started to reach out again. It was as if the changing of seasons had wiped the memory of my mistake from his mind. We'd just gotten started again when the mob brought hellfire to Greenwood—otherwise his house would've been the first place I went when that was happening.

Where are you, Isaiah? Are you alive? Did you make it? I was wrong to think that if I did nothing wrong, no one would want to hurt me. People want to hurt people for no reason at all. So, all that fighting he taught me was worth it.

Now I know to hold fast to the friends I have because there is the risk I could lose them. I vow to hold them even when I have no arms around me and remember them when I'm held in someone's arms.

Everyone who's held me is still holding me, and I'm still holding them too.

Are you alive? I had a mental connection with him too, but only sometimes. *I have some stuff to do in New York, but I'll come back with enough money to surprise you. And leave you jewels, and money, and concert tickets to the Apollo if when I knock, you open the door. I'm so sorry, Isaiah. I'm sorry.*

Dreams of Isaiah still ran through my head when I heard the sound of Jay's door creaking. In the morning light, I saw his father walk into the room and stop mid-journey on his way to the bed when he saw us. He stood over us, clothes in his hand, and stared, stunned at the sight.

I couldn't move as I opened my eyes fully and looked at Mr. Gatsby. His expression didn't change. And then, he turned and hurried out, as if he'd forgotten something in the other room.

I got out of bed and threw on my pants and socks. "I'm not supposed to be here."

Jay was hiding under the pillow, still half asleep. What he mumbled in response was muffled. I prodded him with my arm, and he came up for air, squinting at the light from outside.

"Your father just saw us," I said.

"What?"

"He saw us." My heart was jumping out of my chest. What would Gatsby do now that he knew I was sleeping in the same bed as his son?

I couldn't trust a white man from a crocodile on the hunt. I imagined him returning with a golf club and swinging at my head, screaming, "Darky!" until I turned black and blue. Instead of defending myself, I'd say, *I love your son, sir, I love your son,* and let the damage be done.

"I don't care what he saw," Jay whispered, reaching out to me, his fingers like crane clamps.

I spun a circle about the room, feeling like a princess in a beam of twirling dust, the silk robe he draped me in falling off my shoulders. "Jay, it's morning."

I could smell tobacco. His father was in his room, puffing his pipe. Was he cooling off from his reaction? Would we have to fight?

I didn't want to fight him. I'd be sad to hurt the man who helped create Jay.

Pinwheels rolled around in my stomach as I checked the room for my jewelry. I was wearing a filigree ring with a green gemstone, and it was so pretty but so tiny and easy to lose.

Jay leaned up in bed, wiped his eyes, and yawned. "He knows already."

"Knows what?"

"That I like boys," Jay said. "He's asked me about it."

"Oh." Something about even that small reveal was satisfying.

Jay's eyes opened wider, and I almost gave him a kiss, but I could feel Mr. Gatsby watching this too, as if he had a ghost eye in the room. The moment broke and part of me curled inward as I sat back on the bed. It was sickening to think that I'd found no way, in all eighteen years, to do away with the impulse to be with a man.

So I just left. Jay called, "Nick?" but I kept going into the hallway, into the splash of front-of-house window sunshine over the upstairs balcony. On the wall above the side table was a giant mosaic portrait of Alexander Hamilton made of glittering diamond. *Why?*

What will Mr. Gatsby do with the knowledge of us?

I wandered aimlessly through the morning, letting the city guide me, its streets offering a subdued entry into the day: shopkeepers sweeping, delivery trucks rolling in and out. I stopped by the park and watched children kick a ball while an older man played a mournful tune on his trumpet. His melody pressed on my heartbeat, which was skipping through an endless rhythm of survival and the hope for triumph ahead. But more so lately, survival.

Down the busier avenues, life bustled with urgency that made my turmoil seem invisible. The day stretched into afternoon, my feet carrying me deeper past the brownstones and businesses and toward the places I felt most at home, but I still felt Gatsby's eyes following me.

I almost went down those streets darkened by alleyways, with the bootblacks and gamblers and gangsters, the drunks who emptied their pockets in the juice joints, to escape.

Instead, I chose to take another path.

Zihan's family's restaurant was still open, faint clinks of dishes and the simmer of steam drifting through the alley. And as the sun set, I climbed up their building's fire escape slowly.

Jazz poured from open windows beneath me, couples laughing on the street, the glow of streetlamps casting warm halos on the sidewalk.

Zihan was sitting on the narrow ledge outside his window, legs dangling over the fire escape railing, his head tipped back as he stared up at the pinkening sky. His gaze was distant, almost lost, like he was dreaming. He noticed me when I was a few steps away.

"Nick?" he said, his voice low and playful. "Did you change your mind about working here?" He gave a small laugh.

I settled beside him, taking a breath. "I don't know if I'll ever work a normal job again. At least not here."

He leaned forward, hands gripping the railing as he looked at me, dark eyes catching the sun. "All right? So what brings you here?"

"I never told you," I began. "But Jay and I . . . we have a plan to flee New York."

Zihan looked surprised. "To go where?"

"We don't know yet. Anywhere but here. But first, my cousin and I think we'll need more money to get this escape going. We think . . . we think it's best to take it from Tom Buchanan. To make him pay for his crimes against migrants in the city. He's been working with the guys who want to force families out. It would be like leaving justice behind us."

"Okay." Zihan nodded with interest, though his eyes widened with surprise. "How?"

"A party," I went on, voice steady but quiet. "A huge one at Jay's place—a fake engagement for him and Daisy. All of Gatsby's connections will show up, including Buchanan. While everyone's distracted . . . I'm going to slip into Buchanan's place and take what's stashed in his safes."

Zihan's eyes widened. For a moment, he looked like he wanted to laugh again—perhaps to brush it off as a wild idea. But he didn't. "And Jay agreed?"

"Getting there."

"And you need me to help," he said.

"More that I don't want to leave you behind." Zihan was one of the few people who ever accepted both Jay and me. He was a rare true friend in a world full of judgment. "But I wouldn't turn down the help either. Jay and Daisy will be busy entertaining guests, so I'll need someone to cover for me, to run interference if Buchanan notices I'm missing or watch my back in case anything goes wrong."

He looked at me, like he was pleased to hear the words, but perhaps not in this context. Then he looked down, tapping his fingers against the iron railing. "Nick, you're talking about breaking into Buchanan's place. That's very dangerous. Are you sure this is worth it?"

The question hung in the air, heavy as the Harlem night, whose sounds echoed through the narrow alleys around us. Buchanan existed to step on people. Who else was going to do something?

"I can't look the other way," I said. "People like him make the world unfair because they can. Because there are no consequences. He'll keep doing it as long as he thinks no one will stand up to him."

Zihan nodded. "Okay," he said. "I understand. All West Egg ever did was keep me in one spot. I owe the man nothing. If you and Jay really need to do this, I will help."

Relief flooded through me—Zihan was so brave! I let out a breath—did I know how heavily that one was sitting in my chest?

"Thank you," I murmured. "I'm glad you're with us. You've made much of my time here in Harlem better."

"I would say the same about you," Zihan said, smiling. "But make a promise to me," he said, his voice softer now. "That this is about justice, and not revenge. We are not stooping to his level but making the ground equal."

I met his gaze, absorbing his words. There was peace in them, and I knew he was right. Justice equaled the playing field. It brought things from negative peace to true peace. It made life fair for innocent people who'd been wronged.

But oh, how I wanted to hurt them back. To see the evil men pay. To burn all their houses down so they knew what it felt like. My pain had become something so dark and angry I had to hide it from Zihan to assure him this was all in the spirit of good.

"Justice," I said, with a level voice. "Of course. That's all I want."

Zihan nodded with assurance. And then, we sat in silence, listening to the city below, the faint music, the chatter, the heartbeat of Harlem. Even if it all went south, I would be happy. I'd be happy as long as I had friends beside me who understood my point of view. Deep down, even with the magic around me, an anger still writhed, something bigger planted by the cruelty of the world, which showed me the worst version of myself—the one who'd never be able to leave this city without getting some kind of payback.

I found the stoop outside Daisy's house illuminated by the single bulb, which was on its way out, buzzing in the night air. Jay was standing at the top of the stairs like a ghost, his presence dimmed, his energy drained. Something was wrong.

I climbed the steps quickly. "What happened?" I asked, while opening the door to let us in.

Jay didn't answer. He walked past me with hollow determination, eyes scanning the interior of the house. "Where is your room?" he asked.

I pointed him to my door, and he walked inside and sat down on the edge of my bed. The streetlight came in from the windows, casting dramatic lines on his features, making him look older.

"I spoke to my father," he said, rubbing the back of his neck, watching the floor. "He would barely look at me. Just sat by the fireplace the whole time, staring into it like I didn't exist. He told me I'm old enough to make my own choices but if I want to live a life with you, I'd have to do it somewhere else."

I froze at the words. "He threw you out?"

Jay nodded, finally looking at me. "I think so. I live by his rules or I don't live under his roof. So I told him what he wanted. I asked him if he'd throw a party. I told him I'd bring Daisy and said I'd marry her."

In that moment, I could see that Jay's final act in New York became all the more clear to him. All the things we had said to each other, the future we dreamed of, felt *real* for the first time. There were no other paths forward now that Gatsby had drawn this line in the sand. All Gatsby wanted Jay to do was have a perfect wife, who could help ensure their place in high society, and Jay would give it to him.

I sat down on the bed and took his hand in mine. "Okay, so that means that you're pushing your father to orchestrate a party."

He looked up and gave me a somber nod. "So that you and Daisy can orchestrate a robbery."

I felt this rush of exhilaration as the dream found its way to reality. "I spoke to Zihan about it too. He said he'd be up to join us, so I have backup at Buchanan's place."

"That's good," Jay said, still sounding a bit unsure. "I was sick at the thought of you going in alone. In fact, it was the main thing that put me off of it. The thought of you getting hurt."

This close to his face, I couldn't help myself, so I kissed him, wrapping one hand around his neck, and he kissed me back, his hands forming a desperate, strong grip on my arms as if I were a kite that would drift away if he didn't hold me hard enough. The world seemed to both quiet and buzz around us in perfect time with the rhythm of our lips.

22.

WE COORDINATED THE SCHEME FOR WEEKS, each of us stepping firmly into roles as final details fell into place. Daisy, with her ability to charm her way past doors in Buchanan's house, had been scouting out any more potential safes, taking note of where he stashed his ledgers and cash. Her findings shaped our plan, pinpointing the exact places I would hit while the party kept everyone distracted.

Zihan had been working out escape routes, sketching and resketching maps of Buchanan's estate and the surrounding waterways. Meanwhile, I kept us organized, pulling everyone together when nerves threatened to tear us apart.

Jay threw himself into the invitations, spending hours in the *Chronicle* office late at night, perfecting the gold geometric borders and ensuring every name in Gatsby's network—from business partners to students still lingering in the city—received a gilded invite.

JOIN US TO CELEBRATE THE
ENGAGEMENT OF JAY GATSBY JR. AND DAISY WHITLEY
THE GATSBY RESIDENCE
135 W GATE DR., HUNTINGTON, NY 11743
APRIL 14. 9–12 P.M.
ALL ARE INVITED!

When Uncle Beet and Auntie Lorraine saw the invitation, they pulled Daisy aside, shaking their heads over the news.

"You're not serious, Daisy," Uncle Beet said, his face all wound up with worry. "Getting married so young? To a man . . . like this?"

Auntie Lorraine surprisingly wasn't much softer. "We thought you'd take your time, look around, find the right person. But he seems like he's got a bright future. I suppose that's worth something." She gave a small sigh, trying to mask her disapproval.

Daisy only smiled, smooth and unaffected. "Trust me—he's everything I need, Mom. He'll give me the life I've always wanted! And maybe a little more."

They exchanged a look, but they knew better than to push further. Even if they didn't understand her choice, they couldn't argue with the security that a rich boy provided!

Some tension in the air lifted with Auntie and Uncle's blessing. It allowed us to get down to the real work, which happened in my room, where we went over blueprints and scrawled notes like battle plans.

Jay's hesitancy never truly left despite everything he knew

about the havoc Buchanan brought to Harlem. When I shared the implications of his ties to the Blue House burning, it wasn't enough to steel Jay completely either.

After the invitations were delivered, all Jay wanted to do was hide in my room and talk and play board games. So we sat on the floor the day after his arrival, playing Uncle Wiggily.

Jay was overthinking as the game went on, and I worried that nothing would induce him to speak until out of nowhere he said, "I still have my doubts."

"Please don't abandon this now," I said. "It's too late."

"I just feel nervous."

"I know. Me too. When we leave here, it'll all be over."

He played with a little green piece in the shape of a rabbit. "But it won't," he said. "They'll be after us. Would you kill the people after us? We never even got that far."

"I wouldn't kill anybody," I said. "What are you talking about?"

"They'd kill us," he said, in a deadpan way. "We're tempting death—don't you feel that?"

"Just think brightly. Please."

Jay was just whining. I knew he didn't mean it. We'd already gone to the trouble of duping his father into the party. It couldn't be for nothing.

"Don't you think we could elope and find jobs—wouldn't that be far more romantic?" Jay said. "We don't have to do it this way."

I wanted words to melt from his mouth more like a rockslide come to kill me and less like a fudge sundae. Because I wanted to do everything he said, against my best interests.

Daisy and I had planned this. We all had agreed to it. Why plan it if we weren't gonna follow through?

"Buchanan's done too much harm," I said, and that was my final answer.

The game was ruined now that we were bickering back and forth, so I went off to Daisy's room. I knocked and then listened at the door and heard the shower running from the bathroom.

I opened the door lightly and was greeted by her floral scent. And then I just stood in the middle of the room, not truly knowing why I came.

"Well?" Jay said. I turned around and found him standing behind me. "If we are going to do it, you'll have to find something to wear to the party then."

I smiled and went to Daisy's closet and pulled down a flapper dress. I took off my pants and shirt, careful to catch Jay's eyes trailing my body and his small smirk, which instantly made our bickering disappear.

I slipped into her dress and checked myself out in her mirrors. "What do you think of this?" I asked Jay as I spun around.

Jay fell on her bed and rested up on the pillows. Arm leaning over his stomach, he gave me this hungry smile. "Ravishing. Simply ravishing! Wear it to the party and Father won't even be able to tell the difference between you and Daisy!"

"I'll need eyeliner! Bracelets and anklets!"

I tried on another dress, and then another. I was on dress number three when Daisy came out of the bathroom in a towel, hair dripping and slicked back.

"I thought I heard voices!" she said. "Why are there boys in my r—?" She stopped when she saw me and tilted her head like she'd spied a curious animal in the woods. She was now in on my private universe as a glamorous woman! "The bust is far too big for you," she continued, calmly. "I know you're girly on the inside, Nick, but you can't quite fill that out. Mama can alter you a dress if you really want one, and in a color that matches your skin tone, because that's not it!"

I laughed and fell over. Somehow, Daisy calling me girly took all offense out of the term. I attempted to take off the dress, and Daisy helped me to pull it off my ankles.

I looked up at the light of her closet, all the fancy clothes. "Girls have it so easy. All you need is this one piece and some shoes, and you're set to attend any swanky event."

"You try being a girl one day—in public—and see what you say then." Daisy hung her garment and pushed Jay and me out her door so she could dress.

But she was free from her dread or had found a way to carry it. She didn't find the crust of all her fears in the corner of her eyes in the morning. She was still bubbly, despite the plan! What I'd give to be like Daisy.

Our ease with each other found once more, Jay and I spent the rest of the day together at the park, in the courts, on the empty lots, just talking. I stayed totally connected to him until the night, but when I expected him to go back home, he asked to spend another night.

We snuck inside and I locked the door of my bedroom, so I

didn't have to worry about anyone barging in on us. Then I got under the covers of my bed with him.

I held him this time, and we pressed our faces into two pillows. I whispered, "Will you tell anyone about how close we've gotten?"

"I won't," he promised.

Daisy could easily talk about her engagement to a man without a second thought. She could announce her love to her parents without fear. I couldn't even entertain the thought of telling Auntie and Uncle I shared something romantic with Jay.

Would anyone be left in our lives who cared, in the end? We'd be leaving soon—forever.

"I'm glad he saw us in bed," Jay confessed in a whisper. "I don't want you to think I regret choosing you. I just worry, because being with you has made me realize what life can be, when I truly connect to myself. I never knew anything before."

I rested my arm on top of his. "No one knows anything. Everyone's messed up and trying their best."

"You get it," he said, with a quiet laugh. "Of course you do. There are not enough words to express how much you mean to me, Nick."

Such beautiful words only scared me. I knew I was worthy of them, but I also didn't. There was a giant crack in the window to my heart. I was fixing it, slowly but surely.

I said nothing and just silently worried about losing him. I needed him now, more than anything, and I'd need him forever.

I almost believed Jay had fallen asleep after his confession, but then he shuffled in my arms and went down to fetch something from out of his pants, which he'd left lying at the edge of the bed. It was a folded letter.

"Read it," he said, handing it to me.

I turned around and sat up.

Dear Tom Buchanan,

If you are reading this, know that your crimes have caught up to you. We have the evidence that you plan to destroy Colored communities of Harlem and replace them with a new white gentry. Your wealth depends on it, but your reputation depends on keeping the peace with the integrationists whose missions work against yours. Therefore, you are a fraud.

Your time in this city is ending. We will come for your positive press and reveal what you did to the West Egg Academy—a school you helped set up and then helped to destroy. We will expose this information to every news outlet with cited sources unless you appear at the party of Mr. Jay Gatsby's on April 14, 1922, and meet us face-to-face.

Sincerely,
X

I didn't know what it said about Jay that this letter had been tucked away all day, before we'd even argued about actually doing this.

"It's the missing piece to our plan." He watched my eyes move across the lines of his letter. "Buchanan's always unpredictable. And it looks like he's about to have another falling out with my father. We mail this and he'll still come to the party in spite of their squabble. We'll have the house all to ourselves. You and Zihan take the boat I built across the water, slip in while they're busy, and by the time they realize what's happening, it'll be too late. No turning back."

Jay nodded with a silent pledge to continue forward. And his readiness made me even more eager to give the corrupt man everything that had been coming to him.

23.

DAISY STOOD IN THE MIRROR, GALACTICALLY lengthy in a shimmering purple undergarment set, a Buccellati diamond bracelet, and a Tiffany anklet.

It was the night of Jay's fake proposal to Daisy and everything had to be just right.

Jay stood next to her and practiced lines. "I'm so excited to be marrying—" He paused to change his inflections. "I'm *so* excited to be marrying beautiful Daisy Whitley!"

"Ugh," Daisy scoffed. "That sounded so *fake*, Jay! You can do much better."

Jay pulled a little ring box from his pocket and got on one knee. He popped it open to reveal a diamond ring. "And to be presenting her with a ring courtesy of Buchanan's Jewelers! See, father, I can be friendly with our neighbors too!"

"Pretty soon we'll be able to buy dozens of diamond rings!" I sang to the ceiling.

Daisy looked off dreamily about that. "We will, won't we?"

I thought back to Jay's words, in his moment of uncertainty, and then asked Daisy, "Do you ever feel a quiver of doubt about this?"

Daisy went into the closet. She was finishing her outfit, so all I could hear was her voice. "Oh, I don't think I've had a doubt in years. I've sat through Tom's endless stories about his *boring* life, and honestly, I couldn't tell you what half of them even meant. He's awful, really! He'd put everyone back where they started if he could, but somehow, he's still got everything."

Daisy emerged in a champagne-colored gown. She sat on the bench in front of her vanity mirror to put on two earrings, which were shaped like tassels, effortlessly dressing as she spoke. "Buchanan doesn't want harmony—he wants control. And so, there will always be a difference of vision between us. Nothing could make me work in that house forever."

"Shall we burn the mansion down when all is said and done too?" I asked gleefully.

"Oh, Nick, I've corrupted you!" Daisy turned to me with a mischievous expression as she took pins out of her hair, causing it to fall around her head in shimmering finger waves. "I should've never let you have that first conversation with Jordan. Now you're wrapped up in violence."

Daisy applied pink lipstick to her bow-shaped lips, then grabbed a white purse from her rack and posed in the mirror. "Anyone else excited for the party?" she chirped.

"Overjoyed," Jay said monotonously. He was sitting on the bed now, all dressed and slumped over, in a pair of gold-framed octagonal glasses, just for show.

The rest of his outfit consisted of a white shirt and a pinstriped blue vest. He was the color of the ocean and the clouds. And I, the grass, dressed in the green Norfolk tux of my Uncle Beet.

"Can't wait to betray the person I am for a *performance* of the person my father wants me to be," Jay said.

"The American dream!" Daisy exclaimed, with a laugh. She slipped into a pair of gold Spanish heels with diamond-studded buckles that completed the look. For the finishing touch, she sprayed perfume and spun through it, her shawl forming a parachute. I reached like a salivating lion for a hit of the soft scent, the rosy vapor she spun in.

She pulled a bottle from under her vanity, poured a glass of gin, and handed it to Jay. "You'll need this before the event."

He took a sip and his face soured. "This is more potent than I've ever tasted."

"Tom gets it imported! Calms me right down. Bottom line? I've had enough of Buchanan and his lot, and it's time to get lost."

Remember when I could not stand to be in the same room with them because I was so jealous? My cousin and friend were happy together and leaving me out of it. I wanted to be in on their lightness. Joy and tragedy were a moon cycle for them, my friends—their heartbeats were far more rapid than my quiet, dull thumping. I guess that was why I needed to love them.

They were there for me, and some of the only ones who'd never turned their back on me. They'd never let me down in this world so full of betrayal, and that counted for everything!

Gatsby's place was lit with an array of lights, which outlined every hedge, pillar, and fountain on his property. Upon our arrival, a carriage was waiting to bring us to the front doors.

We rode up to the entryway, and before we got out, Daisy subtly slipped me a key to Buchanan's mansion.

I stepped out first, into the noise—a Negro quartet played a song in the driveway. Music spilled out of the windows of Gatsby's mansion too—jazz.

I helped Daisy down from the carriage and then looked around. Rows of polished motorcars glinted under the glow of the property's lamps. Chauffeurs stood in neat uniforms. There was a large turnout of people who must have taken hours to get ready. Guests arrived in twos and threes. They were brushed with the finest skin creams and glowed like aliens dipped in otherworldly sparkle, their shimmering gowns catching light like tiny stars.

The inside was packed with servants who collected coats from the professionals, who were decades older than me. I had no idea who they were, but Gatsby's connections had come out in droves to witness the arrangement between Daisy and Jay and likely to see what Gatsby's mansion looked like on the inside.

People of all ages and races were brought here by the openness of this man. Some artists in colorful clothes with untamed hair studied the art on Gatsby's walls. Poor folks made reasonable efforts to blend in among the elites and had pulled out their best suits for the night. Gatsby had even employed some of the boys of Blue House to work the event. I spotted Zihan pouring champagne in a guest's glass alongside a servant.

I wandered around and landed at one of the refreshment tables. I admired the tiered trays of cakes and inhaled the freshly shaved cheese for the crackers. Rich ladies stood fanning themselves and looking around like they had somewhere better to be.

There was an undercurrent of quiet competition, as they peeped around at the other ladies' outfits, eyes murky with barely concealed judgments. They watched a white man take a Colored woman upstairs where there was privacy and whispered about it to each other.

I realized a moment too late that Jay had appeared at my side, checking his watch for the time. "Almost there," he whispered to me.

"Almost where?"

"Confetti explosion, of course."

Seemingly at his command, a big explosion of confetti burst from blasters around the ceiling. Jay laughed and the people looked up at it, surprised by the twisting pieces of color that filled the air. Some covered their glasses with their hands; others raised them.

Daisy scurried out of a side room, laughing at the confetti as if the biggest robbery in the history of this peninsula was not going to happen tonight.

Once the confetti settled, Jay whispered, "Incoming," and faded into the crowd of people.

I saw what he meant a moment later. Straight ahead, Charlie Buchanan was stuffing his face with a pastry and walking in my direction. "I'm sorry about what you saw at lunch," Charlie said, his mouth full. "My father is not usually like that. I believe it's because he was stressed on that day."

"He lost his temper," I said. "Let's let it blow over."

"Thank you, Nick," Charlie said, looking a little surprised. "My father only wants to make this city better. I hope you'll accept that."

"Of course." It was so easy to be nice when you had tricks up your sleeve.

"And I'm sorry about the fire too." At first, I didn't know if I heard what I *knew* I heard. And before I could even process it, Charlie kept going. "I thought it was a dramatic step. Others did not."

"Others? What others?"

"A lot of people didn't like the idea of a fully integrated New York. I say this because . . . if it was you who sent us that threatening letter, know that my father will stop at nothing to kill his enemies. You might think he has more empathy than he does! I don't want that to happen to you. Don't try anything. If you must think of exposing my father, talk to me instead."

"I have no idea what letter you're talking about," I lied. I couldn't help adding, "But you know who did it? The fire?" None of this made any sense. Everything I knew pointed to the Buchanans ordering the fire, but here Charlie was, ready to admit his father was not above murder to keep his reputation yet shoving the blame for the arson aside.

"Of course, everyone in the White House dorm knew it would

happen, including someone very close to you." Charlie raised his eyebrows like he knew something I didn't.

"How is this possible? Who else from White House would have reason to do so?"

"Shmoozing gives you privileges you couldn't even imagine."

Shmoozing? Who was shmoozing?

Mr. Gatsby's amplified voice reverbed through the house, announcing, "I would like to propose a toast. To my son and his new fiancée, Daisy Whitley . . . soon to be Daisy Gatsby!"

I walked out to the living room and found him standing on the makeshift stage installed for the party.

Charlie followed me and whispered, "I hope you'll understand it's for the best that whites and Coloreds stay separate." He pulled away from me and smiled, patting me on the back in a fake show of support. "Be well, Nick!"

I was so horribly nauseous from the stress. All this running around looking for the arsonist, thinking I had pieced together the story of this crime, and Charlie claimed he had information on the culprit the whole time that he was willing to give. Were the Buchanans even involved?

I walked around the party, mind filling with doubt, zeroing in on every white person under the age of twenty, examining their face for some sort of guilt.

I found Artie Botts with Stu Miller—an engineer from the White House who graduated to be a fitness model. Artie was twirling a lock of hair around his finger as he talked to the boy.

"Artie! How are you?" I shouted.

Artie turned to face me and frowned. "Oh, *you* again. I'm doing wonderfully! I just got back from Zora Neale Hurston's house. We're working on a new magazine, so I'll have to make time in my schedule for it alongside my other rigorous demands. What have you been up to lately?"

"Can I talk to you for a moment?" I pulled him behind a curtain where no one could see us. "Charlie told me every boy in White House knew about the fire long before it happened. I can't imagine that gossip would have escaped you, seeing as you work in the newsroom and know everything that happens on campus."

"They never said it was a fire," Artie said levelly. "They mentioned a *prank*. Like the midnight games. They were saying it would be the biggest prank on Blue House ever made—how would I have known the truth?" He looked uncomfortable but unwilling to take any share of the blame. "Charlie said if I stayed out of what they were planning, his father would give me a staff job at his new paper once all was said. A real, stable writing job. Bigger than the little *Chronicle* rag. The gossip was all just a stepping stool, you know—a way in."

Artie looked at the floor, his usual shallowness slipping into something more thoughtful. "What I really wanted was to write about stuff that actually matters. Human rights, poverty—the real issues." Then he looked at me, covering up his emotions with a smug sneer. "No one knew the building would *actually* burn down."

"But you knew it would happen in advance. You could've done something when you saw the fire starting."

"Or *not*! Do you know how fast fire spreads?" Artie scoffed and flipped his hair. "Why are you so eager to blame me? You might want to ask Jay what *he* knew of the fire. Ever think of that?"

It dawned on me that this was the second insinuation in one night that Jay had something to do with it, but at the very least, it stood to reason that he must have heard the rumors.

I refused to believe it. Jay would have told me. Jay loved me.

Artie was jealous and Charlie was a nut who'd been jealous of Jay his entire life. They could have each other.

"He may have fallen for your innocent act," Artie said. "But I know who you *really* are. You are a destroyer of property, and my lawyers *will* be in touch."

"People could have *died*! Maybe you didn't know what the prank was about then, but you do now—and you seem not to care at all about people who were hurt by it."

"Because *I* didn't do anything," Artie retorted. "Why should I suffer getting blackballed by every family with a white boy at West Egg? Everyone found their way out, didn't they?"

"Artie . . . I mean this with the utmost disrespect. You are one of the messiest little girls I have ever met in my life."

"And you? You're a street rat on the path to ruin. Good luck in prison!" He threw his head back and cackled.

I put one hand firmly on his shoulder, and he froze. "You know why the Buchanans are so comfortable with you? Because you have no real ethics. All you do is bring people down to prop yourself up."

His face was a cracked pot of anger—all his insecurity melted from his eyes and spilled through the corners of his mouth. "And you? You will *never* be good enough for Jay Gatsby."

"But he still likes me, so shove it up your ass." I pushed past the curtain, leaving him alone, and smiled graciously at the party guests, as if nothing had even happened.

"It was a bunch of people," Artie said behind me, his voice small. "But Cannon started the one in your room, specifically."

I turned around, thinking at first that I heard wrong. "What did you say?"

"Hmm." Artie turned his nose up. "That's why you should know the facts before you start *cornering people*! Gee whiz!" With that, he trotted away to continue his conversation with Stu.

He'd never lie about that, would he? Artie was one step away from being cut from the same cloth as that guy. Why would he say that if it weren't true?

I was careful to hide my reaction to this revelation. I kept my face neutral, like a well-behaved, nice young man. I would show that I was good at dinner parties and good for civilized society and that I could speak like the queen.

I smiled at someone. *Ignore me! Nothing to see!*

And then, I found Jay again in the crowd standing at the table of pastries, stress eating lemon squares and licking the powdered sugar off his fingers. He looked so beautiful with his hair laid like that.

I knew now how I wanted him. I didn't want to parade around in the open air for people to gawk at us. I'd rather sit in the intimate quiet of a room and share bits of knowledge with my lover.

Was that so wrong? To not want my life commented on by the public?

I grabbed Jay by the strong arm. When he looked at me, I had to resist the urge to kiss him in front of everyone.

I trust him, I reminded myself. I leaned in and whispered, "I think it's time."

When I pulled away, Jay nodded, still with some uncertainty in his eyes. "You're sure this is what you want?"

"Yes, of course." *Please don't do this. Not after Charlie's words. Not after Artie's confession. Please don't make me doubt you.*

He had fallen so far from the hopeful rich kid he was, his sheltered balloon popped by the needle that is me. "Okay," he said, with reluctance. "I'm ready then."

Jay was letting his mind torture him. Were his insecurities because I'd rubbed off on him? My confidence because he'd rubbed off on me? We were no longer on a tightrope. We were together, through everything!

I saw Daisy up on the staircase with Mr. Gatsby, trying to catch my eye, and I nodded at her in confirmation. Mr. Gatsby was standing still, a suspicious look on his face, but he didn't do anything. He couldn't, now that I was one step ahead.

24.

THE PLAN WAS IN MOTION. ALL THERE WAS TO do was follow through.

I slipped into the washroom when everyone was suitably distracted. No one noticed me, and it was all for the better now.

From there, I escaped through the window to the backyard. Past the lawn, I found Jay's boat tied to a post on the little lake. This was where Zihan and I agreed to meet. We'd take the boat across the lake together, but he wasn't here. I waited a few minutes and he still didn't show up.

The show must go on.

I stepped onto the boat and turned off the lights. Then, I began rowing. Fireworks burst from behind Gatsby's house and lit up the sky, distracting me. They were in the opposite direction from Buchanan's property, so they distracted everyone else too.

I rowed, placid like the lake I was floating on, away from the people. The shores of Tom Buchanan's mansion sloped up like some gothic, ancient island. The lawn looked designed to welcome me.

I anchored the canoe, ran aground, and walked up like a king, the waves sweeping dramatically around the bottom of the island. It felt too perfect.

I unlocked the side door with Daisy's key and stepped into the house. The open floor plan stretched out before me, vast and empty, like a hotel with no guests. I traced the polished silver crest on the bronze vases perched on the entryway pillars. Art deco wallpaper covered the walls, showcasing paintings of futuristic buildings that reached for the clouds. I couldn't help but think—if I could, I'd take this whole house with me.

There were so many drawing rooms designed to let the light pour in, so much space. Floral patterns on the lamps and couches screamed Myrtle—her taste was everywhere. Above the fireplace, a deer's head jutted out from the wall, its hooves pointed at opposite angles.

I took the staircase down to the cellar in between the main floor and basement, realizing again I was not a pampered prince like Jay, but for just these moments, I could pretend.

I could pretend it was all mine!

I passed by a mirror on the wall, on my way down the rest of the steps. Who would've thought a limp-wristed hoodlum would look so pretty robbing a house full of stolen fortune?

The first safe I found was up against a wall in the crawl space of the basement, just where Daisy had placed it on the map. I climbed inside, with the insulation and dust, and pulled out my tin of grease to melt the door off.

I crawled away from the smoke and melting metal, watching the door break down little by little. Then I saw it—gold. Solid bars, stacked neatly, each one gleaming like a small fortune. And, nestled beneath the bars, were beautiful necklaces of gold, emerald-studded bracelets, rings of bright ruby, and deep cobalt—precious stones that sparkled with their own light.

I dug deeper, pulling out handfuls of cash, crisp bills in stacks and bands, enough to fill my bag and then some. There were stacks of bonds wrapped in silk—old enough to be priceless. An overflow of pearls, diamonds, and jade, each one more exquisite than the last! It felt like I had opened the vault of a hidden empire—buried treasure from somewhere beneath the equator, far beyond what we needed, and enough to set us up for a lifetime.

Once my bag was full, I was eager to move on to the next safe. Heart racing, I went back upstairs, and on my way up, I heard a sound. Buchanan? Charlie? Clarence?

I tiptoed around the corner and up the stairs. In the kitchen, I found Cannon Cleary, dressed in his police uniform, pulling a wine bottle down from its rack. He glanced at me, smiled, and then returned to his business as if I were his brother coming down for a midnight snack.

I placed the heavy bag on the bright, big counter. "Um . . . Cannon? If I may . . . what the hell are you doing here?"

Cannon shrugged, a little. "Pass me that corkscrew, would you?"

There was a wooden appliance holder just by my elbow that hosted a myriad of cooking contraptions. I pulled out the corkscrew—half metal, half mahogany, sprouting two wings in the shape of throwing stars and a curly stabber in the middle.

I tossed it to Cannon, and he screwed the bottle open while sighing. "I had a long day. You ever have a long day?"

"Most of my days are quite long." I examined his uniform. "I take it Charlie hired you to do mansion security?"

"Lots of undesirables on the peninsula tonight." Cannon chugged the wine, pulled the bottle down and belched, and then tapped his fist into his chest. "Wow. I didn't think you had it in you to break and enter, Clumsy Nick. And trying to blackmail Tom Buchanan? Not the smartest move,"

"How did you find out?"

"They showed me the letter! Men like Buchanan always thinks money buys them loyalty. I used a lot of goodwill to make them doubt it was you—they were *so* sure—just to save *your* sorry ass from another arrest!" He took another swing from the bottle. "It *was* you, wasn't it?"

"That's sort of touching that you'd protect me, Cannon, but you also tried to burn me alive, so it doesn't quite land."

Cannon paused to look at me and then resigned himself to my knowledge of his crime. "You really are a better journalist than I thought."

"Why'd you do it?"

"You survived, didn't you? If I wanted to kill you, I'd have targeted the bed." He looked guilty, for a moment, and then straightened his face. "They said they'd promote me. And if I get promoted, it gives me a chance to change it from the inside. There are *battles*, and then *wars*."

"I'll deal with you later," I said, rolling my eyes. I wasn't going to allow my attempted murderer to preach to me. "If you don't mind, I have a safe to break. And if you know what's good for you, you'll stay out of my way."

This was not West Egg anymore. In Buchanan's house, absent its owners, I could say anything I wanted.

Cannon put down the bottle and slow clapped, pretending to be impressed. "If you're determined to do this, I wish you good luck, Nicholas. We'll see how Buchanan reacts when he hears you've broken into his house in an effort to rob him."

He walked toward a phone, where it was sitting on its base on a table by the couch. I ran toward it, ripping its curly stem out of the wall before he could get to it.

Cannon froze, mouth twitching a bit. Then he grabbed a camera from a utility stand I didn't even notice was there and snapped a photo of me. "All those theatrics," he said. "And you still lost! The absurdity writes itself."

"Are you not ashamed to be turning me in like this?"

"Oh, brother. Now the radical's going to preach to me." He stormed over to the counter and took another sip of wine, pulled it down, and grunted like a lawn mower. "Don't act like you don't walk around like you're better than us now that Gatsby's made you his lapdog. Your problem is you have no idea how arrogant you really are."

"I'm not the one trying to sell out my own people for a quick buck."

"Lovely story," he said with a hand wave. "My choice to take the evidence back to the precinct is so that all of Harlem doesn't have to bear the consequences of your actions if you were to succeed. Do you really think you could do this and *no one* else would have to pay for your hubris?" Cannon skipped from the room with the camera.

I chased him and he sped up, looking quickly over his shoulder with alarm. I tackled him down the three steps and into the den. We rolled through a brass table and an urn collapsed over us.

Cannon scratched my face as we rolled across the fur rugs. "I tried to help you, Nick!"

The soaring ceilings rolled into the upholstered furniture into oak banister as we grappled with each other. And then, Cannon slammed my head into the table and stood up.

"Sorry," he said, with a little chuckle. "That last one was kind of rough."

As a spot of blood trickled over my eye, I blinked and found my bearings. Someone else in the mansion, who must have heard the commotion, ran into the room. The moment Cannon spun around, Zihan jumped like a frog over the couch and landed wrapped around Cannon's body, a rag clapped over his face.

Cannon passed out in seconds, and I stood up, brushing dirt off my clothes.

"Sorry I am late—I was helping Jay," Zihan said. "Gatsby's party will be over soon! People have already started to leave."

"There's two more safes," I said, while I relieved Cannon of the revolver strapped to his body.

Now that a Buchanan accomplice knew I was in here, there was a witness, and I needed to make this worth it. I had to get everything I could, and I didn't want to leave behind the safes in the vents before I went. It was there that I might find evidence of Buchanan's wrongdoing secreted away. The first safe may have secured our fortune, but this could be the thing to undo Buchanan.

"Wait," Zihan said, stopping me as I turned to head up the stairs. "If you're going for the other safes, you'll need me to cover you again. Cannon won't stay down for long."

He glanced at the unconscious Cannon sprawled on the floor, his breathing shallow beneath the rag Zihan had used. Zihan used a length of rope to bind Cannon's hands.

Together, we hurried upstairs to Buchanan's library, our steps light on the plush carpet. I led Zihan to the vented wall panel. Behind it, I knew, was the second safe—one that could hold his most damning secrets.

"Here," I said, kneeling. "Help me unscrew this."

Zihan knelt beside me, producing a pocketknife from his jacket. He pried at the screws while I kept an ear out for any signs of Cannon regaining consciousness.

The vent came free, revealing a small but sturdy safe embedded in the wall, its surface gleaming. My heart pounded as I fumbled with the grease. Zihan kept watch, his eyes darting between the hallway and the vent, as I rubbed a pipe cleaner through the little tub.

"What's in this one?" Zihan asked.

The safe door burned off and inside was a stack of thick envelopes.

"Documents," I replied, not looking up from my work. "Everything Buchanan's used to ruin lives."

I rifled through them quickly, scanning the contents. Contracts, deeds, and a letter signed by Buchanan detailing a payout to that rich politician trying to kick migrants out of the city.

Dear Mr. Buchanan,

I'm grateful for your soon-to-be-deposited donation of $15,000 into my campaign fund in exchange for my continued efforts to restrict migration to New York and hasten the rezoning of Harlem properties. This money will ensure the swift removal of Negroes and other undesirables from our schools and neighborhoods and pave the way for white-only redevelopment.

Thank you for your donation, critical to the success of our shared vision for the city! Rest assured, all business will be handled discreetly.

Sincerely,
A. Mitchell Palmer

"This is it," I whispered. Here, on paper, was what Buchanan's half of the Blue House payout was funding. "This is the proof we need. It'll ruin his reputation in the city."

Zihan leaned in, reading over my shoulder.

"Take this. There's sure to be more inside the rest of the papers." I handed Zihan the letter and the other documents, along with the loot from the first safe. "Head back to Gatsby's now and make sure it gets to Daisy or Jay. I'll finish clearing the last safe."

"And leave you here?" Zihan asked, frowning. "What if Cannon—"

"I'll be right behind you. Go, Zihan. We can't risk both of us getting caught."

He hesitated but nodded, clutching the papers tightly before slipping out of the room. I turned back to the safe, taking a steadying breath. There was still work to do.

The final safe had to hold the promised $15,000 donation. That was the payoff, the jackpot. Taking it would make sure that Buchanan couldn't use it to cause any more trouble.

I went to Buchanan's bedroom, and I found the main vent just under a leg of his king-size bed. I opened the vent and climbed inside, sliding myself along the ice-cold metal.

I moved down the tunnel, and turned, and turned again. I found myself in the same place. I passed the same room three separate times, but I couldn't find anything. I started to feel claustrophobic, with all this changing direction horizontally in a tight space.

So, finally, I gave up, and when I came out, it was to Buchanan's study. There was a large red carpet, a big wooden desk, and three walls that opened to a larger drawing room.

A person appeared from around the corner, and I almost had a heart attack before I noticed it was Jay.

"Jay? What are you doing here? You were supposed to be watching Buchanan," I said, surprised.

Jay watched me as I gathered my bearings. I was waiting for my vision to readjust itself from being sequestered in the vents, but he was growing impatient. "You were taking so long I got worried. But never mind that, are you ready to go?" he said, grabbing my arm and pulling me toward the doors. "We have to stop now."

"I couldn't find the third safe. There wasn't one in the bedroom, where Daisy had said to look. I turned four different directions in that vent and I saw no safe!"

"We don't need it. We just need to go." He seemed all fidgety, like he had to make sure the timing was right for some other reason than to save ourselves.

And the nervousness was not lost on me.

I had to get a question off my chest before we left. "Why did Artie say you had something to do with the fire?"

"Now, Nick? Not now."

"Well, did you?" What if it was all true? What if I had to fight my lover, at the end of all of this? What if he was setting me up and his agreement to all of this was a trap?

"I did not start it myself," he said, and the ambiguous answer sucked all noise from the air.

"But . . . you knew about it?"

"Of course he knew about it," a voice said.

Jay and I turned to find Charlie and Tom Buchanan standing in the drawing room just outside the study. They were still as statues and seemed completely unsurprised to see us.

"Oh, Lying Nick, the letter *was* from you," Charlie said, laughing.

"Bravo," Buchanan said with a chuckle. "I laud your bravery. But you're a lot stupider than I thought, getting caught like this." He looked at Jay. "And you. You are a traitor to your father's good name."

"Why don't you finish telling him about what happened at West Egg?" Charlie said.

Jay looked at me, and his expression was embarrassed and out of place. You'd think he was in an entirely different room from the rest of us—a room all on his own. "I should've warned you it would be dangerous for you, with your writings," he said softly.

"Oh, stop bulling him!" Charlie screamed. "Tell him the truth!"

"You let them try to kill me?" I asked.

"I watched closely to make sure you'd escape—that *everyone* escaped," he explained frantically. "I would never let them do that."

"All those boys that had to go back home after losing their place at the academy . . ."

"West Egg was never a good home for them anyway," Jay said, his voice still meek. "You saw what they did to the Colored boys there. And it was inevitable—my father was new money. He didn't have enough for what we set out to achieve, setting everybody up for society and giving them a place to live. We were going to lose everything!"

"So, you and your father hired Cannon and the others to burn it down?" I could feel myself starting to shake. "To cut the student body in half, collect the insurance money, and use your half of it to rebuild the Gatsby name and fortune while Buchanan used his share to destroy Harlem? That's what you did?"

"That isn't the whole—"

"Don't lie to me!" I shouted, the words tearing from my throat. I barely recognized my own voice. "You were the missing link? All this time . . . I blamed the Buchanans. They were the bad guys. The Gatsbys were good. I made excuses for you, your father. I told myself you were different, you cared . . . and oh my goodness, I did it to myself, for what? For you?"

All those doubts and questions—I had been a fool not to listen to them! Now my heart was a deflating balloon.

"I didn't want them to do it," Jay said softly, eyes welling with tears. "I tried to stop it, but he never listens to me. He said we'd lose everything! I . . . I should've done more. I regretted it right away after it happened."

"You're gonna regret a lot more than just that," Buchanan said.

Before I could even process his reentry into the conversation, he pulled a gun from his jacket pocket and aimed it at me. He pulled down the hammer. I couldn't prepare for what was coming next before Jay jumped in front of me. And Buchanan pulled the trigger.

Jay hit the floor, and all I could hear was a ringing, blurring everything around me. But I couldn't yet look down because Buchanan was preparing for another shot.

I pulled out Cannon's gun. Buchanan ducked behind a corner while Charlie stood still.

For a moment Charlie and I stared at each other. *What's it gonna be?* Both of us were stranded in indecision. And then Charlie ran off to be with his father.

And I fell like a dying rose petal to the side of the boy I loved.

"Sorry," Jay choked out, with a laugh. "You have no reason to believe me, but I really wanted to stop them. I didn't . . . mean to get shot." He was bleeding from his beautiful stomach and laughing about it.

I held his face in my hands, my heart opening like a crater. "It's not your fault . . . I . . ."

I didn't care what he'd done anymore. To hell with it. Couldn't we just start over? Like we always did?

His wound was deep, bringing thick, dark stains to his shirt, and every moment I hesitated felt like watching as the life was drained out of him, but the life was being drained out of me, just from looking at his face, pale and strained, its color contrasting the dark red blood against his beautiful stomach, now crumpled beneath the weight of a deadly bullet.

I tried to force myself to think—make a decision—do something. But all I could do was hold him, trying to keep him tethered to this world, trying to keep him here with me, even as his pulse slowed beneath my fingertips and my chest caved in.

There had to be something to save him here. I stood up to call after Charlie and ask him for help—forgetting for a moment we were in the middle of a shoot-out.

Buchanan was sneaking up again. He shot at me once more and missed. The man really wanted to kill me, even if I didn't want to kill him.

I pulled the trigger of Cannon's revolver, shooting back. The smell of wildfire filled the space in front of me, a cloud of smoke blocking my view of the Buchanans.

I waved away the smoke and saw them fleeing the room like the cowardly rats they were. I took the chance to open Buchanan's drawer and loaded more bullets into the revolver.

Jay's words rang in my mind. *Would you kill the people after us?*

The question was simple but heavy. And it needed no answer when rage consumed you.

All I could feel was rage as I stormed into the other room, my footsteps loud in the silence. Buchanan and Charlie were deliberating in the shadows. I raised my gun at them again, but this time, instead of shooting, they fled, branching off in separate directions.

I almost chased Charlie and then I stopped myself. He was like a dummy for Buchanan, raised to be part of a legacy he barely cared about, out of duty. The true enemy had always been his father.

So I thrashed after Buchanan.

I turned the corner out of the sitting room and nearly slid on the rug, as the house opened up to me. Buchanan ducked around the corner and returned with a shotgun. I took cover as he fired, his bullet shattering a mirror behind me.

A ringing in my ears, like a church bell dinging.

I ran back into Buchanan's study, almost falling over, and knelt to Jay's side again. He was bleeding but still awake. "I'm sorry," I whined, cradling his face in my hands.

"You didn't do anything," he sputtered. "But you have to go—fast. Before the cops come."

"You have to come too."

"I'm dying, Nick."

I lost. It was over.

Pa was dead.

Jay was dying. And I was crying, once again, as life turned its darkness on me.

What would I do now? Who would I depend on? Buchanan could take me out. I was vulnerable, an open target, but he didn't come. He abandoned the fight.

The house fell silent. I had this feeling that someone else was still inside, but they were hiding now. They were probably waiting for backup.

I stood up and picked up the phone to dial the telephone operator. I told them I needed an ambulance. They said someone would be on the way.

Eons went by and I sat stranded on my knees with my lover in my arms. There was so much to say, but I couldn't say anything at all, so I just rocked with him. I'd spend as long as I could with him, at the very least. I wouldn't let him have his final moments alone.

"Change your name," Jay whispered.

"To what, Jay?"

"Nick Gatsby," he said, laughing.

And then he laughed his way to sleep.

And I closed my eyes with him and rested on his chest, until the men came through the room, screaming, "Freeze!" They ripped me away from his body.

25.

Dear Jay,

There is no reason why I should have to lose everyone close to me. I'm going to pretend it didn't happen, just for now.

Yours,

Nick

Dear Jay,

They're feeding me garbage. I'd kill for some fresh fruit. We don't always get what we want though and that's the challenge—putting one foot in front of the other even when there's no one else to walk alongside you.

I used to think I was too smart for jail, but jail is, in fact, a great place to do some reading and figure out who you are. I've decided here that I have no specific idea in mind for how I want to be seen in society. I don't believe that being seen is the point for me. That feels too outward, with so little light to shed on the soul. I only want what makes my soul feel good, moment to moment. You spoke to that want, in our private moments, and that's why I feel so broken without you.

Jail is not bad, but it would be a lot better if you were here. I want to make another friend like you, but the people here are very gruff. It's dawned on me you're not coming back, but it must dawn on me again and again and again before I can stop writing to you.

I regret convincing you to get involved and I hope you will forgive me. I see your shadow dancing across the wall, getting yanked off the sidewalk by Zihan. How clumsy! And yet, they called me Clumsy? You were always Clumsy Jay! That's why we fit so well together!

Yours,
Nick

Dear Jay,

Day three and these cops have gotten out of control. I had a conversation with a guard today and he kept calling me "boy" and I don't like that.

It makes me want to cling to you even harder because if I'm being honest this is all getting scary! If you'd like to come back as a ghost, I'd be willing to accept that.

It hurts to think the soul stops existing when the body dies, so I will not accept that.

We should have kept it at friendship. I wouldn't feel this pain so hard if we did! But I also think that would've been less fun. I've never wanted to be so close to someone that I stopped existing anymore, at least half of the way. I guess that means I love you.

You're still seeing my every word and reading this over my shoulder and stretched out on the bed telling me to come nearer. You are all of this matter around me, and I see you all the time.

Death is no ending! I can still hear your thoughts. You're saying you love me.

I love you too, in a way that death cannot stop.

Yours,
Nick

I only just finished signing my name when the guard arrived to take me into a room for questioning. I sat at the other side of a silver table, under an intense spotlight.

Cannon walked into the room, in his new uniform, and sat across the table. "I was sorry to hear about Jay."

I stared at him. "Okay."

It was as if Jay's death was a stunt—a joke.

I couldn't accept he was gone. He could come through the doors at any moment, cracking jokes with the cops. I would be angry at that, and he'd grasp at justification for his light-skinned behavior, but it would all sound very privileged.

"The charges that Buchanan intends to press are for robbery and attempted murder," Cannon said. "But there's a way you can get out of it. And that's by telling us the name of your boss. Who put you up to this, Nick?"

"Nobody."

Cannon raised an eyebrow. "Do you not care that you may be in prison forever?"

"Why would I? I'll have every meal I need to sustain me. I'll have a gym too. It will be nicer than West Egg."

Cannon seemed to shiver at the words. Then he started fidgeting. The room picked up every noise and made it echo tenfold—so I could hear the tapping of his fingers on his pants.

Cannon had to be some kind of plant. A spy sent by that new government bureau to shut down movements for Colored people. Only problem was he was Colored himself. Was this the point of the white man's violence? To make us just like them? This would never do.

"Wasn't starting the fire enough for you?" I asked.

Cannon took a deep breath and looked at me, poker-faced, but said nothing.

I leaned in closer, just in case they were listening. "Why are you destroying UNIA rallies? Burning down our housing?"

"The UNIA's ideas are nonsensical," Cannon said, rolling his eyes. "And dangerous. It's much more sensible to just get a job and fix it from the inside than boycotting the entire system."

"People who try to change the system from the inside end up turning into agents of the system themselves."

"We're fourth generation removed from Africa—you really think they'd want you frolicking around their countries dressed up like a lady? You're an American."

"I know I'm an American. I can make no claim to anything else."

"Then start appreciating it." Cannon looked at me with pity. "I wanted to help you. Maybe even right my wrong." He sighed. "But you won't take it. Keep seeing how all this protesting works out for you." He gave me an ugly look and left the room.

I watched him go, and it made me happy for a moment, but then a white cop with a square head came in to take his place and he instantly punched me in the face. "Who do you work for?" he grunted.

Stars swam through my eyes. My jaw felt like it had been broken into three.

The cop said, in a calmer voice, "Just tell us and we'll let you go."

But I still couldn't answer that. The hit made me too dizzy to even remember things.

"You don't want to be free?" he asked.

"I am free," I mumbled, drool coming out my mouth.

That's what they didn't see. I was free in a mansion. I was free in a cell. I would be free in Hell, if there really was a Hell. The only way I'd not be free is if I couldn't see beyond the walls of their silly prisons, but my spirit itself could not be captured or chained. So, anywhere I went, I would be free.

The cop gave up on questioning me, eventually. He let me out of the interrogation room and shut me back in my cell.

I fell to my knees at my bedside and closed my eyes. *God*, I whispered. *If I have to starve in jail, please let this be worth something to keep going, even with grief rearing through my throat. Show me how to stand up from a puddle of tears and keep going.*

The next morning, I woke to a guard banging on the bars of my cell, screaming, "You have a visitor."

I took another dreary walk through the hallway to the phone, which was on the wall inside a little booth. There was a glass panel, and on the other side was my visitor with another phone already pressed to her ear—Daisy.

I sat down and picked up the phone.

"How are you holding up?" she asked.

"I'm okay," I answered. "I don't know if they'll lynch me, but for now, I am okay."

"Don't say that." Daisy's face, for a moment, looked fragile with emotion.

"I'm joking," I said. "Dark, I know, but it helps sometimes."

"I'm sorry, Nick. I should've never gotten you into this. I should be in there with you."

"No," I said. "You have to hand over the evidence we have for some journalist to publish an exposé about Buchanan and Gatsby," I told her. "We have to expose him, and them, and only you can do that."

"Nick, I don't care about that anymore," she said. "I care about getting you out of here right away." She whispered the next bit into the phone, so her voice came in muffled. "There was a showdown between Jordan and another crew—they blame her for what happened with Pierre—and it attracted police attention. They found her hideout, took some of the money she had stashed, and now, she's on the run. If they connect you to that,

I don't know what will happen."

"I'll get out of here," I said, but the words felt more like hope than sureness. "But we have to finish the mission. The public has to know exactly what Buchanan has been doing so that all of the tension in the city can be put to rest. And when the day comes for my freedom, I'll meet you and we'll leave the city together."

"We'll get you out of here." Daisy held the phone tight. "Whatever we have to do."

The guard screamed, "Time's up!" as he came to hang up my phone and escort me away.

26.

EACH DAY, I DID PUSH-UPS AND SIT-UPS ON THE floor of my cell until my body screamed for mercy. I kept going anyway, stopping only when my muscles gave out.

I was midway through my evening sets when the guard appeared again, his boots heavy against the cement floor. "You've got another visitor."

I wiped the sweat from my forehead, stomach churning. I wasn't sure I could endure another lecture or thinly veiled threat. But when I stepped into the visiting area, I froze.

Jay Gatsby Sr. sat on the other side of the glass, his face exhausted, his features crumbling under the weight of grief. I didn't expect any sympathy—I braced myself for the most verbally abusive encounter of my life. Yet when I picked up the receiver, he said nothing cruel.

"How you holding up in there?" he asked softly, his voice devoid of its usual bravado.

"I'm fine," I said, though it wasn't true. "As fine as I can be."

Was he here to bail me out? To adopt me, even? My heart rebelled at the thought, but I couldn't deny it—I wanted a father. Even a flawed one.

"Jay really loved you," Gatsby said after a long pause. He winced, like saying it aloud brought him pain.

The feeling was mutual. "Jay is . . . Jay was an amazing person. I'm happy I knew him."

"I wish I could have been there more," Gatsby murmured, his voice heavy with regret. "I wish I could have made him feel safer."

I didn't know what to say. How to comfort the man who'd helped orchestrate a fire that destroyed so many lives? He was guilty. A monster. I would not comfort him.

But I brought Jay into it all myself. Jay was gone because of the choices we made together—because I'd convinced him to take that final risk.

"I just hope he comes back," Gatsby said, his tone distant, almost wistful.

"Comes back?" I asked, confused. "From the dead?"

"They haven't told you." Gatsby's eyes met mine, startled. "Jay disappeared from his hospital bed."

My chest rose with hope. "He's alive?"

"It's my hope that he is." Gatsby sighed. "The doctor said his wounds were severe. It's dangerous for him to have left. But this is all we have." He slid an envelope under the glass. "It was hidden in his vest pocket. Says it's for your eyes only."

I stared at the envelope, my name scrawled in Jay's handwriting across the front. My hands trembled as I reached for it.

"Wait to open it," Gatsby said quickly, his eyes darting toward the guards behind him. "Out of respect for your relationship, I left it sealed. And Nick . . . thank you for being there for him. He was happier after meeting you."

He focused intently on the table between us, refusing to meet my eyes. "You know, when I was young, my father taught me the only thing a man needed was the will to succeed." His voice cracked slightly before he forced it back under control. "Said if you looked the part, and spoke the part, you *were* the part. People would believe in you . . . even if *you* didn't believe in you. All that mattered was what people saw." His mouth twisted into a wince, his eyes reddening. "But I see now, that wearing the mask isn't enough.

"I wore it too tightly and forgot to uncover what was underneath." He shook his head, his hands gripping the counter as he took a breath. "Jay saw through me better than anyone ever could. He tried to better me, to *be* better than me, and I am so proud. I thought I could build something lasting. Something my son could be proud of me for. But all I did in the end was destroy it." He met my gaze then, intensely, suddenly. "Do me a favor, when you see him again? Don't hold *me* against him."

Gatsby hung up the phone before I could respond, his stately facade crumbling the moment he broke my gaze.

But I didn't know what I'd possibly say to this version of him.

Gatsby? The Great Gatsby? Vulnerable and laid bare?

He stood abruptly, his chair scraping against the floor. As he turned to leave, I watched Gatsby, observing him as if he were some animal that had escaped his enclosure and didn't know how to weather the civilized world.

He stood stiff and straight-backed, stilling the emotions on his face, being sure to carry himself with the posture of a man who believed he should look strong, even if inside, he was dying.

He walked off, his composure still intact, nodding at the guard as if sadness could never bend him entirely—as if nothing could.

So, that's where Jay got it from.

I returned to my cell, my fingers clenching the envelope as if it might vanish from my hand. Sitting on the thin mattress, heart climbing up my windpipe, I slid my thumb under the flap and opened the letter.

Dear Nick,

I'm sorry I couldn't stop it. I instantly regretted it. I was too afraid to tell you the truth of what I had known and for you to never forgive me. It would have destroyed me—it still may.

Please know I made sure that everyone in the Blue House was safe when I knew it was happening. I've been determined to find a way to make amends ever since and so I made a plan of my own when I agreed to yours. While you were absent from the party, I was clearing my father's safes and sending Z off with the loot. I told Z the truth, and it's very likely he didn't turn on me because of the trust you had placed in me. He believed I would do the right thing, thanks to you.

Father, if you're snooping through my things and seeing this, well—I do love you and Nick at the same time. I can no longer deny that. It was not fair of you to get in bed with Buchanan for the sake of our vision—the deal polluted our mission with West Egg the second it was struck, and your willingness to sacrifice the Blue House boys to the streets proves it. I was not brave enough to stop you then, but I'm brave enough to walk away from you now.

Nick: We will see each other again. Know that no plan is complete without a backup, but I will withhold my cards from this letter in the event unauthorized eyes might come across it.

Just know that I would never leave you behind.

Yours,
Jay

So, Jay was alive? Out there somewhere, waiting? Or did he pen this letter, knowing he'd be risking his life for me? Was he a ghost?

I lay in bed with the paper pressed close to my chest. This was all I had of him.

If Jay was not really dead, that opened numerous possibilities. Someone would be bailing me out of here, in a way that may or may not be cryptic. It may or may not be illegal. In any case, I had to prepare for our biggest stunt yet.

I was wandering around my cell, finding small ways to occupy myself. I had nothing here, so I mostly relied on remembering good times I'd had in Mr. Wallace's shop. Had I known I'd end up here one day, I may not have complained so much about being there.

I'd just begun to laugh at one of his old jokes when the earth shook, throwing me off balance.

BOOM! An explosion rocked the foundation of the precinct.

I froze as I sat up in bed and a burning smell filled the precinct. There was a ringing in my ears, followed by a commotion. I heard grunts and whacks, like people were fighting. Smoke flooded the hallway outside of my cell.

The fighting noises continued as a masked man came and unlocked my cell, with the keys they'd stolen from the guard. I could tell who it was by his skin and eyes through the mask.

"Zihan?" I said.

"Come quickly before they call for backup," Zihan responded.

I followed him out to the front room of the precinct. It was a mess of wood, brick, and smoke, one wall completely blown off to open it to the street. The bricks around the big opening formed stepping stairs, crumbling with flames on their tips. Two cops lay unconscious on the floor—one of them Cannon Cleary—and another guard was tied up and blindfolded, wiggling around in his restraints.

Across the street outside, a horse reared its legs up between a police car and streetlamp, and Daisy was pulling the reins to bring her back down. She must have gotten it from one of the stables near the precinct. I knew this must be what Jay arranged, and I wanted to run out and hug her.

But I had to make one stop before leaving. I lifted the key ring off Cannon's waist and went to the evidence lockers, located at the back of the precinct.

They were big silver compartments built in the wall, and each key on the ring matched a letter in the locker. This was where they kept evidence, which meant it was where they'd store money related to crime.

I unlocked the doors one by one until finally I found six bags filled with bands of dollar bills. I removed the bags from the lockers.

There were sirens in the distance. More cops would be here soon for backup. If ever there was a time to flee, it would be now.

I ran out with the bags to the main room where I met Zihan. "We have to leave New York," I said. "It's time!"

Zihan looked at me, his face set in a careful, unreadable expression.

The sirens were getting louder, closing in. The pressure was building.

Zihan stepped closer, and calmly, he said, "I won't be joining you."

"What? You have to. What about everything that's happened?" I said, gesturing around us. "How will you get away with this?"

Zihan smiled wistfully. "New York doesn't care. It is too big. Too busy. People come, people go. People forget who you were and what you did, as long as you keep moving." He grabbed my shoulders in support. "You don't get that in places like Oklahoma. But you go. Quickly—before they get here."

I stood there, struck silent for a moment, feeling the weight of possibly never seeing Zihan again. It was hard to bear, but this place was right for him, even if I didn't belong. Maybe the city still had space for him to reinvent himself even if I didn't feel the same.

I dropped the bags and pulled him into a hug. Our bodies became like two logs on fire in contrast to the chilly night air.

"I will be okay," Zihan whispered into my neck. "And so will you! I hope you and Jay get married."

I pulled away from him and we both laughed. "Thank you, my friend," I said as the sirens were getting louder, closing in. "You always remind me there is hope beneath the messes I make."

A whistle blew through the night. I turned to find Daisy beckoning me across the street. I gave Zihan one last glance goodbye, and we ran our separate ways—he to flee the scene at the precinct and me to meet Daisy and the horse.

They were waiting by a blue mailbox and a shop. I attached half the bags to the stirrup on the horse's saddle, and then I strapped the rest over my arms. I stuck my foot through the foothold and then threw my leg over the horse.

"Ready?" Daisy asked.

"Ready," I returned.

Daisy kicked the horse off, and the urgent clatter of hooves on cobblestone beat in time with the faint echoes of the night's music. The cool night air brushed against our faces, and with it, the smell of chimney smoke and street vendor food.

Bags of money weighed down my wrists and arms as we rode through the streets. It was the last time I'd see these streets. The last time the lights would frame me and then escape me, as if I were a dark apparition.

These six bags of bootlegging money would need somewhere to go! Some of it chose its own destiny, blowing from the bags where the zippers weren't tight enough. Blowing like bark stripped by a sawmill and landing on the sidewalks of Harlem's streets. Some people caught it in their hands as if it were a miracle from God, jumping up and down and cheering, sharing it with the friends they'd come out with. I laughed alongside them.

There'd be a bag for Kirby's Diner—Mr. Kirby couldn't be bought! He'd keep cooking those meals, hiring those wayward cooks, and running business until he couldn't stand up anymore!

A bag for Vivian's salon! May the signage grow brighter and the clients come from farther when she wakes to find five hundred dollars at her front door!

Three bags for the park! One for the basketball court, one for the clock tower, one for the crossing guard who manned that crosswalk and kept the kids safe!

It was easy to know what to do with this money, which otherwise might have sat in the police station forever.

We'd give it to Harlem. That way, no matter who came to take it away, Central would be here to stay.

Daisy pulled on the horses' reins outside of her house, and we dismounted. I had a bag of money saved for the Wash 'N' Fold, which I left just inside the house. Auntie Lorraine deserved a vacation, but after what we attempted to do, we couldn't stop to talk to the grown-ups. Daisy and I had to leave before someone found us.

I pulled my suitcases out of my room and as we walked down the stoop I told Daisy, "You're crazy for that . . . but thank you."

She winked at me. "It's the only way I know how to be. But don't thank me before our ride gets here."

"Our ride?"

An Austin Twenty zoomed down the street, its engine loud, before stopping just in front of us. Driving the car was someone who looked suspiciously like Jay. "Who . . . who is that?"

Daisy smirked knowingly as the car stopped rumbling. The person who looked like Jay limped out of the car, holding his side as if he'd been shot.

"I could've sworn I watched you die," I said in disbelief, looking from Daisy to Jay. "Am I crazy?"

"You are crazy, but I'm not dead," he said, taking my suitcase, throwing it into the back of the car. "But I will be if we don't get out of here quick. Step on it!"

"I cried over you!" I told Jay, and for emphasis, I slapped him in the shoulder. "All to find out you were fine?"

He laughed. "I'm glad you're finally comfortable hitting me! You got my letter, didn't you?"

I hadn't yet wrapped my head around the fact that he was still here and not a ghost. I could feel his flesh. I could see his hair blowing in the wind. And behind him, the stoops and the dim streetlamps gave his beauty a perfect backdrop. His heart always craved surroundings like these.

"Thank you, Nick," Jay said. "I thought I was a goner too, but I'm afraid it's gonna take more than one little bullet to kill me."

I was only half upset. There was peace in my soul as we got into the car and started to cruise down this open road, headed for the state limits. Rarely did I get back the things I lost in so satisfying a way.

We were made to be hooligans on the run! That's what we'd become, refusing to sink to the bottom of the fountain with the other pennies. We'd be rejected from society. But we'd land where we landed.

Life was one big caper, wasn't it? I was still so young, with so much to take from it. I still wanted a seat in the nice train car! I wanted the full car, the full train, the railroads, all the land that the railroads touched. This land was my land too! I would set justice upon it even if people didn't recognize it as justice. That was a promise I could make to myself.

EPILOGUE

DAISY EXPLAINED THAT JORDAN WAS SMART enough not to keep all her assets in one place. Before the cops busted her, she gave all her girls their cut of the business: two thousand dollars in cash and, only for Daisy, thirty quarter sticks of dynamite to use to save her favorite cousin.

By then Jay had made his way to Daisy, and together, they made plans to stage a breakout at the precinct and make our exit. But there was one last task to do beforehand, and Daisy accepted—Buchanan's invitation to dinner. He wanted to chat about everything that happened and see if she knew about my criminal activity.

Buchanan had taken a liking to her. He felt that having her work for him would serve as some sort of penance in the fight he felt he'd lost against me. Even though I was in jail and Jay Gatsby Jr.'s life seemed to hang in the balance, it wasn't enough for him. He still felt that he had lost and he had a problem.

There were three people in the room that night and he needed

Daisy to make it seem like it was me who shot Jay in a fit of murderous rage after finding out he enabled the fire. She was on his staff, seen nearby at her engagement party next door. She weaved a story. In return, he offered her a permanent place in his home.

Daisy nodded, agreeing to slander my name, which made him comfortable. He asked Daisy to refill the pitcher and make a few drinks since his butler had quit, and it made things far less efficient around the house. She went to the kitchen and mixed a drink with liquor, sedatives, and lemonade. And once he started slurring his words and passed out on the table, Daisy searched the house.

Daisy removed the final safe and set off for her freedom, taking after our grandma. Inside just like I'd hoped was the $15,000 we so sorely needed.

With the money Jay had taken from his father's safe, Daisy and Jay reassembled the $30,000 Gatsby and Buchanan had conspired to obtain and redistributed it among the Blue House boys. Jay sent a mass of letters to every prominent paper in New York, including the *Manhattan Quarterly* and *The Saturday Evening Post*, outlining Tom Buchanan's crimes. He tipped off local authorities on where to find more proof of Buchanan's true intentions at Pierre's tenement. That way, his prejudiced aims would be clear. There would be no more pretending to be a charitable man, and everyone would know who he was.

And so, our road to Greenwood was long and full of stops but paved in victory, nonetheless. We returned to rebuild, with all the money we earned from our time in Harlem. And we found that because of the work of its remaining residents, half the place had already sprouted anew!

I took a horse to Isaiah's home in the morning, down the old road I knew so well. I stepped down just beneath a tree, brushed dust from my jacket, and saw him as he emerged from his home and went to slide into the back of a black Model T. I watched through the window as he laughed softly at something the driver said. His smile hadn't changed, though time had added weariness to his eyes. He glanced around, not seeing me, then the car took off.

I froze where I stood, gripping the reins and watching him go. I thought of calling his name, jumping out, making a big scene for the rearview mirror, but something stopped me.

He didn't look like someone carrying the weight of old memory. He didn't look like someone waiting on his friend to come back. He moved easy and sure, like someone going to work, keeping track of the niceties, moving on with life.

The departing car left an ache in my chest. It spread to my fingers and toes and rooted me in place for a while. And with it came a dull acceptance. Life would keep moving. Our story would take up space in a corner of history's library.

I took in the crisp morning air, my breath shaky in my ears, and looked to the sky, feeling thankful for my present.

We'd outgrown each other separately. But at least now I had someone who wouldn't push me away when I kissed them.

I left Isaiah's and made my way over to my old house. The

living room had remained largely untouched. Things were kicked over, some glass was broken, but after the invasion, the house remained.

Standing there between the kitchen table and the living room, I realized I could sit in the ashes and feel sad about my past or help light a new fire, and I had the freedom to decide which.

I looked around at the remnants, the shadows of what had been. And I realized starting over was about more than just rebuilding a house. It was about rebuilding a life—and maybe this time, I wouldn't have to do it alone.

Jay had been with me through it all. No matter how much we'd pushed each other away, Jay was there, unwavering. Even when we were worlds apart, I could feel him in my bones. There was a new kind of stability in that. He wasn't a piece of the past I needed to walk away from. He was someone I could count on.

Some days, I wanted no more memories, only static where my memory should be. Some days, my memories were all that soothed me.

Pa told me once you couldn't cry no more after twelve, that you had to be a man. But at eighteen I made my own decisions about what it means to be a man!

I cried laughing when I thought about Jordan's off-the-cuff jokes! And with joyful remembrance when I thought of Zihan's loyalty. I cried happily when I heard my mother's singing voice faintly down a tunnel in my memory. It would always be there.

I cried for the place I'd left, for the ones I meant to say goodbye to, and the ones meant to be revisited. Auntie's cooking,

Uncle's sure-footed calm, Mr. Wallace's wise smile, Mr. Kirby's endurance—they all lingered in my chest. New York was temporary, but I was at peace with my memories. The smell of the Wash 'N' Fold flew through my nostrils like a lavender-scented wind. The music of The Green Light rattled the walls of my brain. I held those moments like sand escaping through my fingers, their minerals sticking to my skin like crystalline glitter.

Now, when I hear a mail train whistle in the distance, it reminds me life goes on. And when I stand in the sun, I love the way that heat beats on me and browns my skin. I am proud of where I came from! Proud to be back, and making my own decisions, and proud of the life I have with Jay. A life that consists of giving whatever I earn back to the cities that shape me, and, in turn, shaping cities entirely new.

Daisy, alongside Jay and me, gets her hands dirty in the rubble. She isn't the kind of woman to fade into the background, nor to leave a pile of dust where there was hope of rebuilding something beautiful. She'd help map out stronger foundations for our homes, design new businesses to fill the streets. And on the days when Jay and I feel the weight of what we'd lost, the possibility we'd lose more, Daisy would keep us focused on the future.

"Just keep building," she'd say, her eyes bright with determination. "Build it better!" she'd croon, as she lay down the new bricks of our world.

The new Greenwood would be even more prepared for an attack! We'd build our houses stronger, our businesses bigger, our hospitals with more rooms. We'd build hotels for tourists and parks for neighborhoods of kids! How many foreigners could we gather here in one hundred years? How much color and noise could fill our streets?

Perhaps a mob would come for us again and kill me for real next time. And so be it! I do not fear death. It would stretch the bounds of my body so far that I could live in every country at once. There'd be much to look forward to, even after the ending! Like saying hello to the folks I lost!

We'll be the stars that salt the night with light, the dogwood shedding petals in a brutal hurricane. Our tears will wet the earth like rain in the fall, when it's time for a season to start anew.

ACKNOWLEDGMENTS

This story came to me in many forms—through poetry, prose, music, film, and nonfiction. I'm grateful to the artists and writers whose work paved the way for me to write this book, from the 1920s to the present day.

To my editor, Carolina Mancheno Ortiz, thank you for helping shape a version of this story that feels honest, lived-in, genre-defying, and sharp in all the ways I hoped it could be.

To the team at Harper, thank you for the care you brought to this book's design and release, and for making it so beautiful.

To Jerry Thompson, thank you for giving me my starting rec list in the early stages of development, and for making me feel like I could pull this off.

To my friends, support system, and loved ones, thank you for being there for me as I plug away at this unstable career. I couldn't have done this without you.

And lastly, thank you to those who've taught me what it means to be loved, and to live with an open heart, even when it leaves me exposed.

—Ryan